DIRTY HEADLINES

L.J. SHEN

ISBN: 978-1-7326247-0-2

Dirty Headlines
Edited by: Angela Marshall Smith, Jessica Royer Ocken
Cover Model: Lucas Loyola
Cover Designer: Letitia Hasser, RBA Designs
Interior Formatting: Stacey Blake, Champagne Book Design

"Love looks not with the eyes, but with the mind,
And therefore is winged Cupid painted blind."

—*William Shakespeare, A Midsummer Night's Dream*

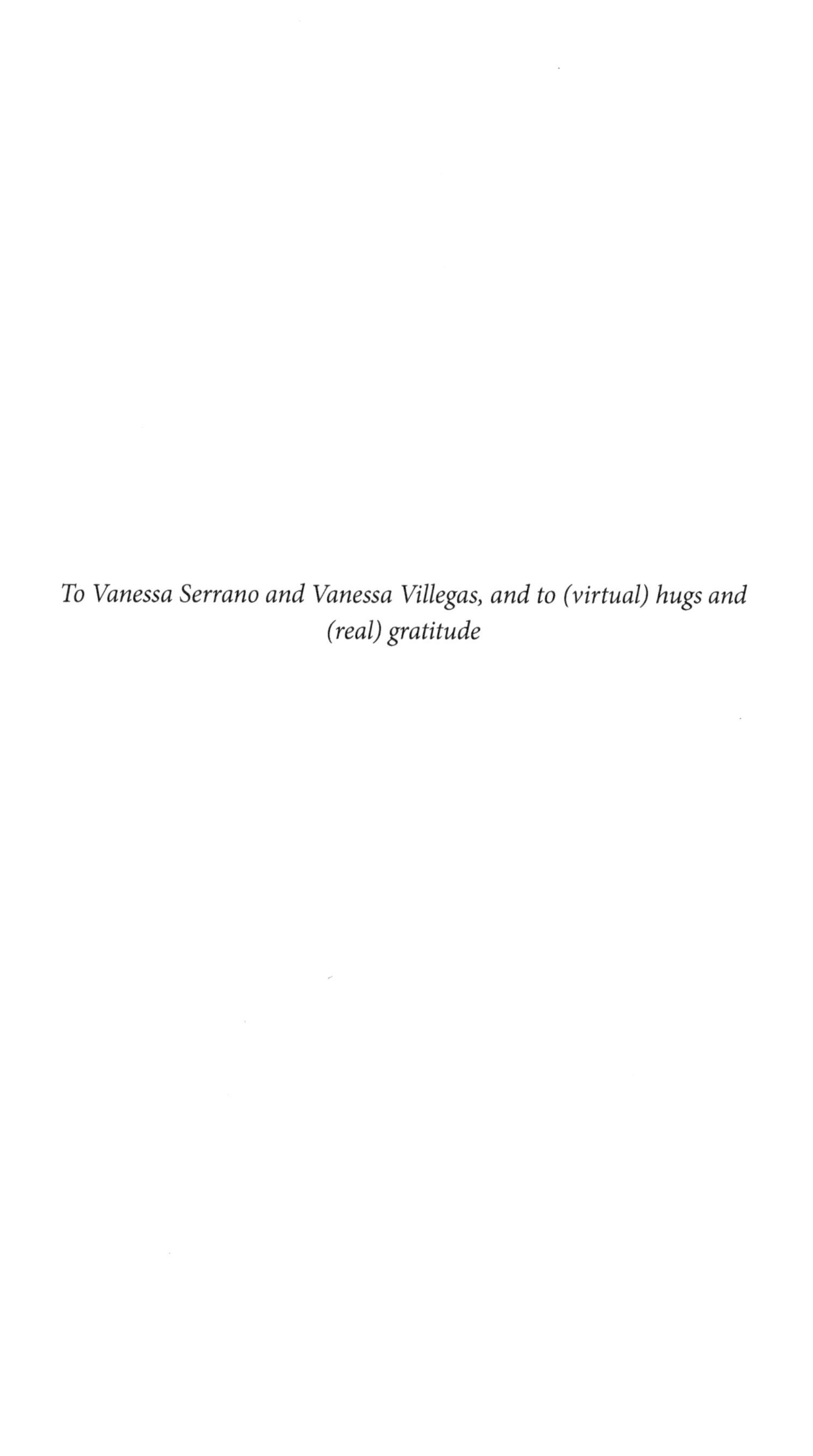

To Vanessa Serrano and Vanessa Villegas, and to (virtual) hugs and (real) gratitude

"Promiscuous"—Nelly Furtado and Timbaland.

"How Soon is Now?"—The Smiths

"Le Chemin"—Kyo feat. Sita

"Makes Me Wonder"—Maroon 5

"Anybody Seen My Baby"—The Rolling Stones

"Bloodstream"—Stateless

"Hey Jude"—The Beatles

"Down"—Jason Walker

"Moi Lolita"—Alizée

Célian Laurent.

Manhattan royalty.

Notorious playboy.

Heir to a media empire.

...And my new boss.

I could have impressed him, if not for last month's unforgettable one-night stand.

I left it with more than orgasms and a pleasant memory—namely, his wallet.

Now he's staring me down like I'm the dirt under his Italian loafers, and I'm supposed to take it.

But the thing about being Judith "Jude" Humphry is I have nothing to lose.

Brooklyn girl.

Infamously quirky.

Heir to a stack of medical bills and a tattered couch.

When he looks at me from across the room, I see the glint in his eyes, and that makes us rivals.

He knows it.

So do I.

Every day in the newsroom is a battle.

Every night in his bed, war.

But it's my heart at stake, and I fear I'll be raising the white flag.

Prologue

Jude

On her deathbed, my mother said the heart is a lonely hunter.

"Organs, Jude, are like people. They need company, a backup to rely on. That's why we have lungs, tonsils, hands, legs, fingers, toes, eyes, nostrils, teeth, and lips. Only the heart works alone. Like Atlas, it carries the weight of our existence on its shoulders quietly, only rebelling when disturbed by love."

She said a lonely heart—such as *my* lonely heart—would never fall in love, and so far, she wasn't wrong.

Maybe that's why tonight happened.

Maybe that's why I'd stopped trying.

Creamy sheets tangled around my legs like roots as I slipped out of the king-sized bed in the swanky hotel room I'd been occupying for the last several hours. I rose from the plush mattress, my back to the stranger I'd met this afternoon.

If I stole a glance at him, my conscience would kick in and I'd never go through with it.

I was choosing his cash over my integrity.

Cash I very much needed.

Cash that was going to pay my electricity bill and fill prescriptions for Dad this month.

I tiptoed across the room to his dress pants on the floor, feeling hollow in all the places he'd filled in the previous hours. This was the first time I'd stolen anything, and the finality of the situation made me want to throw up. I wasn't a thief. Yet I was about to wrong this perfect stranger. And I wasn't even going to touch the one-night-stand issue for fear my head would explode all over the lush carpet. I didn't normally do one-night stands.

But I wasn't myself tonight.

I'd woken this morning to the sound of my mailbox collapsing from the weight of the letters and bills crammed into it. Then I'd failed a job interview so miserably, they'd cut the meeting short to watch a Yankees game. (When I'd pointed out there was no game—because, yes, I was *that* desperate—they'd explained it was a rerun.)

Defeated, I'd stumbled my way through the cruel streets of Manhattan, the early-spring rain loud and punishing. I'd figured the best course of action would be to slip into my boyfriend Milton's condo to dry off. I had the key, and he was probably at work, polishing his piece about immigration healthcare. He worked for *The Thinking Man*, one of the most prestigious magazines in New York. To say I was proud would be the understatement of the century.

The rest of the afternoon played out like a bad movie piled with clichés and reeking of bad luck. I'd pushed Milton's door open, shaking the raindrops from my jacket and hair. First, low, guttural moans seeped into my ears. The unmistakable visual followed immediately after:

Milton's editor, Elise, whom I'd met once before for drinks, bent over one side of the couch we'd picked out together at my favorite flea market, as he relentlessly pounded into her.

Thrust.

Thrust.

Thrust.

Thrust!

"The heart is a lonely, cruel hunter."

I'd felt mine shooting an arrow of poison straight to Milton's glistening chest, then heard it crack, threatening to split in two.

We'd been together for five years. Met at Columbia University. He was the son of a retired NBC anchor. I was on full scholarship. The only reason we hadn't lived together was because Dad was sick and I didn't want to leave his side. But that didn't stop Milton and me from crocheting our plans into the same colors and patterns, entwining our lives one dream at a time.

Visit Africa.

Get assigned to the Middle East.

Watch the sunset in Key West.

Eat one perfect macaron in Paris.

Our bucket list was etched in a notebook I'd keenly named Kipling, and it was burning a hole through my bag right now.

I hadn't meant to throw up on Milton's doorstep, but it was not a big surprise, considering what I'd just walked into. The bastard had skidded on my breakfast as he chased me down the hall, but I'd pushed the emergency stairway door open and taken the stairs two at a time. Milton had been very much naked, with a condom still dangling from his half-mast dick, and at some point he'd decided bursting into the street in his birthday suit was not a good plan.

I'd run until my lungs burned and my Chucks were wet and muddy.

Bumping into shoulders, and umbrellas, and street vendors in the pounding rain.

I was angry, desperate and shocked—but I wasn't devastated. My heart was cracked, but not broken.

"The heart is a lonely hunter, Jude."

I'd needed to forget—forget about Milton, the stacks of bills, and my unfortunate lack of employment the past few months. I'd needed to drown in alcohol and hot skin.

The stranger in the suite had given me exactly that, and now he was about to give me something we had never agreed on.

Judging by this place, though, he won't have trouble paying for the cab to the airport.

A curved, wrought-iron staircase that cost more than my entire apartment stared back at me, leading to a Jacuzzi the size of my room. Plush, red-tufted velvet couches taunted me. Floor-to-ceiling windows dared me to drink in the view of well-heeled Manhattan with my poor eyes. And the teardrop chandelier looked eerily similar to little sperm.

And to make it through next week, Judith Penelope Humphry, you will stop thinking about jizz and move on with your plan.

I reached for the back pocket of his Tom Ford dress pants, where he'd tucked his wallet shortly after sliding out a chain of condoms, and examined it in my shaking hands. A Bottega Veneta leather creation, black and unwrinkled. My throat bobbed, but I still couldn't swallow my nerves.

I flipped the wallet open and slipped out the stack of cash. Turned out Stranger Junior wasn't the only thing thick about this one. I counted hurriedly, my eyes flaring as they took in all the cash.

Hundred…two…three…six…eight…Fifteen hundred. *Thank you, Jesus.*

I could practically hear Jesus scolding me. "*Don't thank me. Pretty sure* thou shalt not steal *was way up there on my not-to-do list.*"

Yanking my phone out of my shoulder bag, I searched the brand of the wallet in my hand. Turns out it cost a little less than seven hundred bucks. My dysfunctional, albeit heavy heart pounded as I began to toss out plastic cards without giving them a second glance. The wallet was sellable, and as it turned out, so were my morals.

My gut knotted in shame, and I felt my face growing hot. He was going to wake up and hate me, regret the minute he'd approached me at the bar. I wasn't supposed to care. He was going to leave New York come morning, and I would never see him again.

Once his wallet was empty, and all his cards and IDs neatly arranged on his nightstand, I slipped back into my dress and electric pink—although crusted in mud—Chucks and chanced one last look at him.

He was completely naked, his groin haphazardly covered by the sheet. With every breath he took, his six pack tightened. Even in sleep, he didn't look vulnerable. Like a Greek god, he rose above susceptibility. Men like him were too conceited to be played. I was glad there was going to be an ocean between us soon.

I opened the door and hugged its frame.

"I'm so sorry," I whispered, kissing the tips of my fingers and brushing them over the air between us.

I waited until I was out of the hotel before I let the first tear fall.

Five hours earlier.

I stumbled into a bar, hiccupping a whiskey order to the bartender between sniffs and shaking the rain out of my long, dirty-blond hair.

I tugged at the collar of my black dress and groaned into the drink he slid across the bar for me. My Chucks—I'd opted for low-top pinks this morning as I'd still been foolishly optimistic when I left the house—dangled in the air while my 5-foot-2 frame sat on the stool. My earbuds were firmly tucked into my ears, but I didn't want to taint my playlist of perfect songs with today's shitty mood. If I listened to a song I liked now, I'd forever associate it with the day I found out Milton liked it doggy-style after all, just not with me.

I tried to give myself an internal pep talk as I gulped whiskey I couldn't afford like it was water.

My job interview had gone horrifically bad, but my heart had never been set on working for a Christian gluten-free-diet magazine anyway.

Milton had cheated on me. But I'd always had my doubts about him. His smile always dropped too soon after we'd hung out with my dad or met someone on the street. His right eyebrow always arched when someone wasn't in agreement with him.

As for the growing medical bills—I would find a way to tackle them. Dad and I owned our apartment in Brooklyn. Worse came to worst, we'd sell and rent. Besides, I didn't need both my kidneys.

I was sniveling into my drink when the scent of cedarwood, sage, and an impending sin skulked into my nostrils. I didn't bother to raise my head, even when he said, "Semi-drunk and conventionally beautiful: a predator's wet dream."

He had a strong French accent. Smooth and raspy. But my eyes were locked on the amber fluid swirling in my glass. I wasn't in the mood for small talk. Usually I was the person who could make friends with a brick. But right now, I could stab anyone with balls simply for breathing in my direction. Or any other direction, really.

"Or a horny man's worst nightmare," I responded. "Consequently, I'm not interested."

"That's a lie, and I don't do liars." He rolled a cocktail stirrer between his teeth in my periphery, shooting me a wolfish smirk. "But for you, I'll make an exception."

"Cocky *and* full of yourself?" I inwardly slapped myself across the face for even answering him. I had my earbuds in. Why had he talked to me in the first place? That was the international signal for leave-me-the-heck-alone. Never mind the fact that I wasn't actually listening to anything, just wanted to push away potential conversationalists. "Good thing you didn't say you put the STD in *stud* and now all you need is U."

"I take it you've been hit on by extremely unsophisticated men. How rough was this day of yours, exactly?" He erased the rest of the distance between us, and I could now feel the heat of his body radiating from beneath his tailored suit.

I had a feeling if I turned around and looked at him—really looked at him—he would steal the breath from my lungs. My heart, angry and wounded from earlier today, thudded dully in my chest. *We don't want any intruders, Jude.*

Tall, French, and Handsome slipped a one-hundred dollar bill to the bartender in front of me. His eyes caressed the side of my face as he asked him, "How many drinks did she have?"

"This is her second one, sir." The bartender offered a curt nod, wiping the wooden surface in front of him with a damp cloth.

"Get her a sandwich."

"I don't want a sandwich." I yanked my earbuds out of my ears and slammed them on the bar, finally looking up and spinning on my barstool to stare back at him.

A colossal mistake if I'd ever made one. For the first few seconds, I couldn't even decipher what I was seeing. He was a level of gorgeous most people were not programmed to process. I'm talking Chris Pine perfect, Chris Hemsworth mammoth, and Chris Pratt charming. He was a triple-C threat, and I was S.C.R.E.W.E.D.

"You'll have to eat one." He didn't bother sparing me a look, tossing his phone on the bar. It was lighting up like crazy, with dozens of emails pouring in every minute.

"Why?"

"Because I'm above fucking a drunk girl, and I would very much like to fuck you tonight," he said calmly, peppering his casual statement with a dimpled, bewitching smile that turned my guts into warm goo.

I tried to blink away my shock, still staring, cataloging his face. Deep blue eyes—tiger-slanted and dark, dark, dark like the bottom of the ocean; mud-brown hair tousled to a fault; a jawline that could give you a papercut if you touched it; and lips made for saying filthy things in a sexy language. He was a specimen I had yet to encounter. I'd lived in New York my entire life. Foreign men were *not* a foreign concept to me. Yet he looked like an improbable cross between a male model and a CEO.

His navy suit made him look severe. The curves and edges of his face were ruthless. Filling in between those cutthroat cheekbones and square chin were a pouty mouth and straight nose.

I averted my gaze to his fingers to check for a wedding band. The coast looked clear.

"Excuse me?" I straightened my spine. Just because he looked like a god didn't mean he had the right to act like one. The bartender slid a hot plate with a roast beef, mayo, tomato, and cheddar cheese sandwich on a brioche bun in front of me. I wanted so badly to remain defiant and tough, but unfortunately, I also wanted to not puke up pure whiskey in about an hour.

Hot Stranger Guy leaned against the bar, still standing—*six one? six two?*—and cocked his head to the side. "Eat."

"It's a free country," I quipped.

"Yet you seem chained to the idea that fucking a stranger is somehow wrong."

"I'm sorry, I didn't catch your name, Mr. Not Getting The Hint." I yawned.

"Will Power. Nice to meet you. Look, you're obviously having a bad day. I have a night to burn. I'm flying back home tomorrow morning, but until then..." He jerked his arm, allowing the sleeve of his blazer slide up as he glanced at his vintage Rolex. "I'm going to make sure whatever's on your mind is forgotten for the night. Miss...?"

Screw it. And him. He was the kind of hot I very much doubted I'd even get to *meet* again in my lifetime.

I could put the blame on Milton.

And the medical bills.

And the whiskey.

Hell, I could blame the entire state of New York after the day I'd had.

"Spears." I narrowed my eyes and took a bite of the sandwich. *Darn.* I flipped the napkin that came with the sandwich to check the name of the bar. *Le Coq Tail.* I made a mental note to return in about twenty years, after I'd finally paid my dad's medical bills and stopped living off ramen noodles.

"Like Britney Spears?" He arched an incredulous eyebrow.

"Correct. And you are?"

"Mr. Timberlake."

I took another bite of the sandwich, nearly moaning. When was the last time I'd eaten? Probably this morning, before I left the house for my job interview.

"You're getting on my nerves, Mr. Timberlake. And I thought it was 'Will Power'?"

"Cry me a river, baby. I'm Célian." He offered me his hand.

His poise unnerved and fascinated me at the same time. He was carved like a god but looked vital and warm to the touch like a mortal. It clouded my judgment, messed with my senses, and made my stomach feel like hot tongues of lust licked it from within.

"Judith, but everyone calls me Jude."

"I take it you're a Beatles fan."

"Presumptuous. Your list of negative traits is never-ending."

"Not the only long thing about me. Eat, *Judith*."

"Jude."

"I'm not everyone." He threw an impatient smile my way, looking like he was over our conversation.

Bossy bastard. I took another bite. "This doesn't mean anything."

I was pretty sure I was lying, but I was too emotionally exhausted to deny myself things tonight.

He leaned toward me, entering my personal space the way Napoleon blazed into Moscow, with the pride and discretion of a pagan warrior. He brushed his thumb along the column of my throat. A simple touch, and my entire body broke out in violent goosebumps. It was the combination of his feral, male ruggedness, his accent, and his sharp everything else—suit, scent, and features.

I was helpless.

I wanted to be helpless.

"The heart is a lonely hunter." But my body needed company tonight.

He leaned forward, his lips close to my ear, and whispered, "Oh, but *this* does."

"You're not my type." I grinned into the rest of the whiskey I downed.

"I'm everyone's type," he said matter-of-factly. "And I'll make it good for you."

"You don't know what I like," I shot back. Ping-ponging with him was fun. He was curt, sharp, and unaffected, but oddly, I didn't find him rude.

"Bet you all the cash I have on me that I do."

This is interesting.

"What if I fake it every time I have an orgasm and act like I don't?" I tucked my iPod and earbuds into my bag. This conversation couldn't possibly be weirder. He smiled a smile I'd never seen on a human face before—so predatory my insides clenched on nothing, my panties dampening between my thighs.

"Clearly you've never had a real orgasm. When I make you come, you'll be lucky to keep your fucking kneecaps from snapping."

"Self-endorsem—"

"Save me the sass, Spears."

Ten minutes later, we were crossing the street on the way to his hotel. I tried hard not to lose my cool when we entered the glitzy lobby. The Laurent Towers Hotel stood across from the LBC skyscraper, home to one of the largest news channels in the world. The place was buzzing with people, but we were the only ones waiting for the elevator. We both stared at it silently while my heart screamed, nearly bursting from my chest. My knees shook under my cheap black dress. I was doing this. I was really having a one-night stand. Granted, I was twenty-three, newly single, and freshly vindictive. I knew there was nothing immoral about sleeping with him. But I also knew this was a one-off I would likely laugh about years from now.

"I don't normally do this," I said when the doors to the elevator slid open and we stepped inside.

Célian didn't answer. When the doors glided shut, he stalked toward me, his eyes cool and detached, his mouth pursed. He cornered me against the wall, every step more voracious than the last. My pulse wrestled inside my throat. He considered me with those cocksure eyes, and I lifted my chin, feeling my nostrils flaring.

Célian cupped me through my skirt, and I whimpered, my body arching against the wall behind me. His thumb found my clit and dug its way through the fabric, pressing hard and massaging it in lazy circles.

"Don't try to convince me you're a good girl," he hissed, his breath—mint and fresh coffee beans—skating along my throat. "I don't give a fuck."

"Your English is very good for a tourist," I noted. His accent was thick, but he used words like a weapon. Strategic, sparse. Each syllable a vicious strike.

He took a step back, watching me through a curtain of indifference. "I'm quite good at a lot of things, as you're about to find out."

The elevator dinged, and he disconnected from me.

The doors opened and an elderly couple smiled at us, waiting for us to leave the elevator. Célian looped his arm in mine like we were a couple, and dropped it casually the minute they were out of sight.

The walk to his suite was silent, but I nearly drowned from the noise inside my head. I convinced myself this was the right thing. A no-strings-attached night of pleasure with an inhumanly beautiful tourist would take the pain away. I trailed behind him, watching his broad back and lean figure. He looked like he worked out for a living, but dressed like he had no time to hit the gym. His profession, however, would remain an unsolved mystery. He was flying back to France tomorrow, and whether he was a hot-shot lawyer or an assassin made no difference to me.

Once we were in his suite, he handed me a bottle of water.

"Drink."

"Stop ordering me around."

"Then stop staring at me, doe-eyed, waiting for instructions."

He removed his blazer and kicked off his shoes. The suite was plush and tidy—too much so for an occupied room. It was huge, but I couldn't detect any suitcases, phone chargers, a desolate shirt lying on the ground, or any other telltale objects.

On one hand, it looked suspicious. On the other, he looked exactly like the kind of psycho to not leave a trace behind. And I was in his room. Fantastic.

Note to self: After your actions today, try to base all your future decisions on fortune cookie advice. You'll do better.

I drank the water he'd handed me without realizing I did so, then dropped the bottle in the trash like it was on fire, my rebellious soul dying a little.

It's not too late to bail. Tell him you're not feeling well and leave.

"I think I should—" I started, but I never got to complete the sentence.

He slammed me against the wall, his lips fusing to mine, shutting me up. My eyes rolled from the sudden pleasure and stars exploded behind my eyelids. I clutched the collar of his shirt as he hoisted me up in his arms and dug his fingers into my butt. My legs wrapped around his waist in no time. He gyrated against me, igniting lust in my lower belly, and when I moaned, he pinched the side of my thigh so hard I tried to fight him off, only to find sinking my claws into his skin felt a lot like drowning in an eternal kiss. His lips were crushed, hot velvet. His body stony marble, and hard everywhere.

Célian slid his tongue into my mouth, and I let him.

He rolled his hips, his hard—*very* hard—cock pressing against my slit, and again, I let him.

He bit my lower lip harder and growled, then sucked the pain away. I cried for more.

He slipped his hand between us, nudged my panties aside, and dipped two fingers into me.

I was embarrassingly soaked.

The sexy stranger tore his mouth from mine, staring me down. "Time to finish your sentence, Miss Spears."

"I… I…" I blinked, flustered.

He began to thrust his fingers in and out of me—slow, so tauntingly slow—his face still dead serious.

Who was this guy? He looked so unaffected, even when an involuntary groan escaped my lips every time he dug deeper and deeper into me, his fingers curling and hitting my G-spot. His other hand traveled up to my breasts, twisting one nipple roughly.

"You said you should do something." His hand left my sex momentarily to paint my lips with my desire for him, before returning to its new favorite place between my legs. He tasted me on my lips. "What was it, Judith?"

Judith. The way he rolled the J between his teeth made me want to die in his arms. His hot tongue was on my neck, chin, lips, and then between them again. We were tangled together like we needed each other to survive. I knew it was just one night, but it felt like so much more.

"I…eh…nothing," I said, fumbling for his zipper between us. He pressed one of his hands over mine, pushing my palm against his huge hard-on. Now I had a whole different reason for panic. That thing could maybe fit in my gym bag. Not my vagina.

"I set the pace," he said.

I shook my head. He wasn't the boss of me. He slipped two more fingers into me—most of his hand—and I was so full I thought I was going to smolder. A growl escaped my mouth. He swallowed it into our filthy kiss, and I came on his fingers in an instant.

The pleasure was so intense I turned to mush against the wall, sliding along it like spaghetti. Célian elevated me back up, digging his fingers into my cheeks, holding my jaw in place and tapering his eyes at me. "You better taste as good as you look."

He slid to his knees in one swift movement, flipped my dress up and threw one of my legs over his shoulder. His tongue drove into me with my panties still nudged to the side, and rather than licking and sucking, he started fucking me with his tongue. I threaded my fingers through his hair, noting that it was softer than mine, and rolled my head against the wall as he awarded me with the kind of oral sex I'd never thought was possible.

Milton was a generous, albeit robotic lover. This man was a walking, talking orgasm. I was pretty sure I would come if he sneezed in my direction. An intense desire to clamp my thighs around his face and keep him there forever slammed into me. My second climax soared from my toes to my head like an electric shock, sending me to heaven, and when he closed his lips over my swollen clit and sucked it with force, I was pretty sure every angel in my vicinity got their wings. By the time he stood up, rid himself of his dress pants and shirt, and ripped a condom wrapper with his teeth, I knew that whether I could accommodate him or not, I was willing to end up in the ER trying.

Célian drove into me all at once, crashing me against the closet behind us, lacing our fingers together and essentially handcuffing me to the surface. The pleasure was so penetrating I writhed between his arms, fighting his hands so I could claw and touch and rip to match him, thrust for thrust.

"Fuck," he hissed. "Judith."

"Célian." It was the last thing I said to him for a while, before we both drowned in hot sex.

On the floor, like two savages.

Doggy-style on the bed while he was facing the TV—watching CNN.

Then when I told him he was about as gentlemanly as a sack of rocks (he let out a soft curse when Anderson Cooper presented an exclusive item about voter fraud that even I was half-tempted to listen to), we got into the shower and he ate me out again, this time paying extra attention to my clit.

Then we went at it again against the sink.

Finally, when I collapsed into the bed, he handed me another bottle of water and said, "I'm leaving at six. Checkout is at ten, and they don't appreciate tardiness at the Laurent Towers."

I wanted to tell him to: A, take a hike, and B, that it was a brilliantly bad idea for me to stay the night. But I wasn't entirely sure I could face my ill dad after all the sex I'd been having, and *not* with my newly ex-boyfriend. I didn't have to stare at the mirror to know I looked thoroughly screwed, with cracked, engorged lips, stubble marks covering every inch of my red skin, and three bite marks on my neck—not to mention my eyes were deliriously drunk, and not from the whiskey I'd consumed hours ago.

Reluctantly, I texted Dad that I was crashing at Milton's and scooted up Célian's bed, closing my eyes. I felt orphaned in the world. No one knew where I was, and the only person who cared—Dad—couldn't particularly help me, as he barely left the house anymore.

That's when I decided I wasn't even going to tell Robert Humphry about my breakup with Milton Hayes. Dad had put all his Hope chips on my boyfriend, counting on him to take care of me once he was gone. Everybody needed someone, and other than Dad, I had no one.

Célian slid into bed behind me, his swelling cock pressing between the backs of my thighs.

He traced a rough-padded finger over the side of my ribcage, along the tattoo I'd gotten the day I turned eighteen.

If I seem a little strange, that's because I am.

"So you don't like The Beatles, but you do like The Smiths." His breath caressed my shoulder blade.

I grew up with a single dad who was a construction worker in New York. Money was tight, and sitting on the floor listening to his vinyl records had been our favorite pastime. We read books about Johnny Rotten and invented deliberately misleading music trivia games to pass the time.

"Careful, you might get attached if you get to know me," I said quietly, staring out the floor-to-ceiling window overlooking New York.

He began to drive into me from behind, silent. "I'll take my fucking chances."

The position reminded me of the front-row seat I'd had for Milton and Elise's adulterous performance. My feelings tangled and knotted. My body was elated, but tears gathered in the corner of my eyes. I was glad my one-night stand couldn't see them, though they were definitely a mixture of happy from all the orgasms and sad at the prospect of going back home tomorrow morning to face reality.

No boyfriend.

No job.

A dying father and a pile of bills I didn't know how to pay.

After we both finished, he kissed the back of my neck, turned over, and went to sleep. And me? I had a direct view to his dress pants and the outline of his fat wallet, which seemed to glare back at me.

My heart was a lonely hunter.

Tonight, I'd let it feast.

Jude

Three Weeks Later.

"How do I look?"

"Nervous. Anxious. Sweet. Pretty. One of those ought to be the right answer, right?" Dad chuckled, rubbing my arms.

I had put on a white pencil dress and my black Chucks. Classy. Understated. Plus, I was going for serious and professional today. My dark blond hair was styled in a loose chignon, and I'd streaked my hazel eyes with a dramatic eyeliner. This wasn't my usual attire of flannel shirts, skinny jeans, and faux leather jackets. Then again, it was my first day at my new job, so not looking like a Tokio Hotel dropout was a priority.

I stroked Dad's bald head—forsaken patches of white hair scattered around it like sad dandelions—and kissed his cheek, where his veins stood out through pale, bluish skin.

"You can call me any time," I reminded him.

"Oh, yes. My favorite Blondie song." He grinned.

I rolled my eyes at his dorkiness.

"I'm feeling fine, Jude. Are you coming home after this or staying at Milton's?" He ruffled my hair like I was a kid, and I guess to him I was.

He launched into another coughing fit mid-sentence. Which is why I felt slightly guilty for the lie. He thought Milton and I were still together. My dad had stage three cancer in his lymph nodes. He'd officially stopped attending his chemo sessions two weeks ago. Time was slipping through our fingers like sand.

His doctors had begged him to continue treatments, but he'd said he was too tired. Read: *we were broke*. It was either refinance our house or give up treatment, and Dad didn't want to leave me with nothing—no matter how hard I fought against that decision. Now I was guilt-stricken, walking around with my lonely, worry-soaked heart, carrying it like a chest full of gold—so many precious, heavy, useless things inside.

My voice was gruff from yelling at him to just sell the damn apartment. I'd finally stopped when I realized I was just putting him through more unnecessary agony and stress.

"Back here." I kissed his temple and waltzed to the kitchen, pulling out the meals I'd made him for the day.

"You don't spend much time with him lately. Everything okay?"

I nodded, pointing at the Tupperware in front of me. "Breakfast, lunch, dinner, and snacks. There are fresh blankets on your bed in case it gets cold. Did I mention that you can always call me? Yes. Yes, I did."

"Stop worrying about your old man." He mussed my carefully done hair again as I exited the kitchen, walking to the door. "And break a leg."

"With my luck, I don't doubt it." I grabbed my shoulder bag, watching as he groaned when he settled in his armchair in front of the TV.

He was wearing the same PJs I knew I was going to see him in when I got back from work God-knows-when. Most people wouldn't have invested in Netflix when they were neck-deep in debt, but my dad barely left the house. Up until very recently, he'd always been suffering from nausea and felt extremely weak. Chemotherapy killed not only his cancerous cells, but also his appetite. The only thing he did have were shows like *Black Mirror, House of Cards,* and *Luke Cage.* No way was I going to deprive him of his only entertainment, even if I had to pick up another job on top of this one.

And this is the part they don't tell you about losing a loved one to cancer: They're not the only people being eaten alive. When they get it, you get it. The cancer nibbles away at your time with them, feasts on the happy moments, feeds off every second of bliss. It devours your paycheck and savings. It nourishes itself on your misery and multiplies in your chest, even if you don't have it.

I lost my mom to breast cancer ten years ago.

Now my dad was next, and there was nothing I could do to stop it.

The ride from Brooklyn to Manhattan was long, and I didn't have my iPod with me. That's what you get for being a shithead and stealing from a stranger. I'd left it, my earbuds, and my morals back in the hotel suite. No matter. The money had paid two red electricity bills and covered our weekly grocery shopping. And now I had time to read through all the material I'd printed out in advance about the Laurent Broadcasting Company. LBC was headquartered in a gigantic high-rise building on Madison Avenue. They were one of the top four news channels in the world, alongside MSNBC, CNN, and FOX. I'd accepted a job as a junior reporter in their beauty and lifestyle online blog division, which wasn't exactly my lifegoal. Then again, not drowning under past-due bills *was* pretty high on my to-do list.

I was grateful for the opportunity, and had almost toppled over when I'd gotten the acceptance phone call. My chance at the newsroom would come. I just needed to work my way up.

For now, I had to make sure I kept this 75k-a-year job. It wasn't only a great way to get my foot in the door; it could also help me convince Dad to give chemo another shot.

The lifestyle blog—aptly named *Couture*—was located on the fifth floor of the building, the same floor as accounting.

"They don't treat us as real journalists," I'd been warned by Grayson, AKA Gray, the chatty guy who had hired me. "The toilet seats in this place get more respect than the beauty and entertainment blog. They also get better ass, I'm sure. There're literally no hot people here in accounting."

I'd come in the day before to get my tag and electronic card and to fill out the paperwork. The job offered kickass health insurance and free gym facilities. In short: if I could marry this job, I would make sure it was happy and give it a foot massage every evening.

I was over a half-hour early, so I made a donut stop and bought enough sugary goodness for the entire floor. The receptionist, an auburn-haired girl around my age named Kyla, was already behind her desk, typing away when I came in. I offered her a donut, and her timid eyes scanned me as if I was trying to sell her an unregistered gun.

"They're good. I promise. My mom and I used to come all the way from Brooklyn to Manhattan every Saturday just to have them." I smiled.

"People are not nice here at LBC, though." She tapped her desk nervously.

"Well, I am. So…" I shrugged.

She plucked a chocolate-glazed donut and showed me to my office. It wasn't an actual office, but a cubicle on an open-space floor: beige on white and clinically depressing with its uniform plastic dividers and creaking office chairs. Each cubicle had four desks. I'd share mine with Couture's staff. We'd be three people in total.

"Gray should be here any minute," Kyla said between moans of pleasure.

I dumped my mismatched backpack under a chair that faced one of the desks without photos and knickknacks, and looked out the window. I had a direct view of the Laurent Towers Hotel, where I'd spent the night with Célian. Three weeks later and it still felt surreal that a man I didn't know had been inside of me multiple times. Even stranger was the sharp pang of regret that pierced my chest every time I thought about the money I'd stolen from him. I vowed to never do it again, and tried to tell myself that entire night had been out of character for me.

Grayson arrived twenty minutes later. He looked like the lovechild of Kurt Hummel from *Glee* and your best friend's hot brother, and he dressed like Willy Wonka. The deep maroon velvet blazer he had on today would've looked like a crime scene on anyone else. He waved his hand theatrically as he entered, his eyes still curtained by his huge Prada shades. He sipped his Starbucks as he showed me around the floor, which was beginning to fill with personnel. The accountants and secretaries nodded at me grimly as we passed them by.

"Feel free to erase every single person and face I've introduced you to from your memory and use that space to remember Dua Lipa's beauty ritual, because none of them talk to us or acknowledge our existence. We were illegally and brutally deported from the sixth floor—AKA the newsroom—after the incident-that-shall-not-be-named last year."

He fell into his executive chair and ran his fingers through his raven hair. "This made *Couture* extremely difficult to work on, but we still manage."

"What happened?" I propped my elbows on my knees.

"The big bosses lost someone important."

"What did it have to do with you?"

"That someone was our boss, and every time they look at us, they see her. Which is why they never look at us."

I reached out and squeezed Gray's hand, just as my second and only colleague in *Couture* strutted in.

"Ah, my fellow lepers and partners in being-pretty crime." She offered me her hand, her fingernails brushed in blue and green. "I'm Ava."

I shook her hand. She looked to be in her late twenties like Gray, and dripping chic from head to toe. With tan skin, big curls, and catlike eyes—plus a red leather mini dress and vintage yellow boots—she could give any pop princess a run for her money.

"Is this dress up as a bipolar nurse day?" She scowled at my white dress. I opened my mouth to explain I was about as fashionable as her keyboard, when she broke into a grin and Grayson laughed from his desk, shaking his head.

"A wrap dress and Chucks? For real?" She wiped tears from the corner of her eyes.

"Which part is more disturbing to you, the thrift-shop dress or the Chucks?" I poked at my lower lip.

"Pretty sure the part where you look like a kid high on Jamba Juice who raided Mrs. Clinton's closet. Do you have a name?" Ava swiped her gaze along my body.

"Judith. But people call me Jude."

"*Hey, Jude.*" She winked.

"Sure she hasn't heard that one before, Av." Grayson swiveled his chair to his Apple screen, double-clicking the envelope icon.

The kids in my neighborhood had decided I was too much of a tomboy to have such a feminine name when I was about seven, and that's how Jude was born. Judith died a slow death, coughing signs of vitality every time I needed to fill out an official document.

"Jude can touch the tip of her nose with her tongue and make fart noises with her armpits."

"Jude can teach us how to skateboard."

"Jude knows how to make water bombs."

"Speaking of disturbing things, Mr. Laurent will be making an announcement today at three, so maybe it's a good thing little Miss Reese Witherspoon is covered up in a dress so ugly it should be illegal."

I shot Ava a look, and she snapped her gum in my face. "He likes the ladies, but worry not. His son puts him on a leash."

Hours ticked by, hoovering the minutes and sucking them into an entire sun-deprived day. I spent them researching the many disturbing ways you can freeze, melt, and scrub cellulite to death. When the clock hit three, the elevator *dinged* chirpily. But that was the only chipper thing about the occasion. Time stopped. So did the clicking of keyboards, and the radio stations blasting over the floor along with the general chitchat. By the way the air hung and dangled like a sword above my neck, I guessed that Mr. Laurent, the owner of *Couture* and LBC, had arrived.

Grayson pushed off his desk and motioned for Ava and me to get out of our cubicle. I wiped the cold sweat on my palms over my dress.

"Main attraction's here. Let's hope Laurent Senior doesn't grope anyone and Laurent Junior doesn't fire us all because he's on his period." He catwalked to the main lobby of the floor, hips swaying.

I chuckled. So the infamous New York royals, the Laurents, were a pain in the butt. Hardly made any difference to me. I very much doubted they worked on this floor or that I'd see much of them. I knew of Mathias Laurent, the French mogul. He sounded too important to hang with us mortals on the fifth floor, crunching numbers or trying samples of new, gluten-free perfumes.

The minute we stepped into the already-full reception area, my jaw slacked. It fell to the floor, and my tongue rolled out like a red carpet, cartoon-style.

Jesus Christ.

I could practically hear Jesus in my head, waving his fist. "*Stop using my name in vain every time you remember a sin you've committed.*" He had a valid point. At this rate, I needed to say so many Hail Marys, I wasn't going to be done until my thirtieth birthday.

Standing in front of me was the hot French tourist who'd done unholy things to my body three weeks ago, looking no less god-like than he had that night, with one exception—now he looked a whole lot scarier.

Célian wore pale gray slacks that seemed like they'd been sewn directly onto his body, a white tailored shirt, and a formidable scowl. He looked ready to behead Kyla and feed her limbs to the crowd of people who'd gathered around him. Beside him was a white-haired man an inch shorter than he was.

Mathias Laurent had small, black, vacant eyes—the opposite of his son's deep indigos. But they had the same disapproving frown that made you feel like the dirt under their Bolvaint shoes.

And probably the same amount of authority to fire yours truly.

"Let's cut to the chase. Technically, this is an issue for accounting, but we've decided to throw *Couture* into the mix since you guys are a money pit deeper than Kidd Mine," Célian began, the icicles he called irises still focused on his phone screen.

My eyes rolled inside their sockets as my knees threatened to buckle.

He had an American accent. Not French. *American.* Smooth. Familiar. Ordinary. He fired out sentences at the speed of light. I heard him, but I couldn't listen. Shock gripped my body as the pieces of the puzzle fell into place. My dirty one-night stand was my boss. My lying, American boss. And now I had to deal with that—hopefully for a very long time, because I desperately needed this job.

Someone snapped their fingers, and my gaze shot from Célian's face to Grayson.

His forehead had crumpled into a frown. "You look like you're trying hard not to cry or having a really intense orgasm. I'm hoping for you that it's the latter and some kind of a weird-slash-awesome condition. You okay?"

I nodded, scraping up a smile. "Sorry. Zero orgasms happening under this dress. I just zoned out for a second." *Lies.* I was about to orgasm just remembering how good Célian had felt parting my thighs with his big, callused hands and dipping his tongue into my slit.

Then words stopped streaming down on everyone's heads like a scalding shower, and I realized that indeed there was something worse than hearing Célian speak in his perfect American English. And that was *not* hearing him speak at all. Because now the icicles were pointed at me like a cocked gun.

I glanced up to meet his gaze. He stared at me for exactly one second before his focus snapped to Grayson. "Am I understood, Gregory?" he asked.

Gregory?

"Crystal clear, sir," Grayson bowed, his voice trembling at the edges.

Célian jerked his chin toward me. "Your cover girl material is going downhill."

God. Damn. Bastard.

He recognized me, and I knew it. His eyes had kindled, melting the ice and growing darker the minute our gazes mingled. He remembered, and maybe it killed him that I was here in the same way it buried me.

I want my iPod back, my gaze told him. I had over three thousand songs on that thing, and they were all too good to be wasted on that jerk.

"Jude Humphry. Junior reporter. It's her *first day*," Grayson highlighted, almost pleadingly. He shifted in my direction, as if he might need to physically protect me from the sharp-tongued, suited monster.

I suppressed a smile when I realized I'd told Célian my last name was Spears. Well, he certainly wasn't a Timberlake. He was a Laurent. An American monarch through and through. A billionaire, a powerful force, and judging by our one and only encounter—a raging playboy.

This man was inside you, I internally shrieked. *And not just once. His cock was buried so deep in you, you screamed. You can still taste the salty, earthy flavor of his cum. You know he has a freckle on his lower back. You know what sound he makes when he empties inside a woman.*

I internally thanked my mind for ruining my panties in public, and nodded. "Pleasure to meet you, sir." I offered him my hand, my face flushing with embarrassment at my choice of words.

Everyone was looking at us, and there were at least fifty people in the room. Célian—if that was even his name—ignored my outreached hand. Instead, he turned his face to the man beside him. "Mathias, any other words of wisdom?"

Mathias? Wasn't that his father? Just how cold was the man with the icy blue eyes?

"I think you *touched* everything," said the big boss—and he *did* have a heavy French accent, so at least the lie had a seed. Mathias stared at me placidly, like he could read the secret his son and I shared on my face.

Célian spun toward me, uncuffing his cufflinks and rolling his sleeves up his veiny forearms. "Accounting can go back to their unfortunate line of work. *Couture* is excused from this meeting—though not forgiven for their horrid blog. Miss Humphry?" He snapped his fingers impatiently.

He was already waltzing down the narrow hallway, knowing I'd chase him like a puppy, and no doubt taking pleasure in that fact.

"I have a bone to pick with you."

Bone, boner—same difference, right?

I shot Grayson a please-save-my-butt look. His eyes said, *I would but I still have a life to live.*

I followed Célian down the hall, my Chucks slapping the floor in a hurry. He sliced through the throng of accountants, then stopped at a corner office, opened the door, barked "Out!" to the man inside, and tilted his head for me to go in. I did. He closed the door, and it was just the two of us.

Two feet of empty space between us.

His eyes said war.

Which didn't bode well for me, since he had bombs, and I barely had sticks.

"Where'd your accent disappear to?" I asked through a painted smile.

"Where'd my fucking cash disappear to?" He answered in the same light tone, but the smirk on him was different. Sinful.

I felt my expression fall. I was so disoriented by seeing him here, I'd forgotten that had happened, too.

"I took it." I swallowed hard.

"Well, I faked it." He meant the accent.

"Coincidentally, so did I." I *didn't* mean the accent.

I just remembered the bet we'd had at Le Coq Tail. If he didn't make me come, I was allowed to take all his cash. Truthfully, I'd never come so hard in my life, but I wasn't going to admit that. Not after he'd made me feel like a fool for the second time that day, faking a stupid French accent to shake me off his back in case I wanted to exchange numbers.

"Miss Humphry." He *tsked* with pity, like I was adorable and exasperating at the same time—a puppy pissing on his two-grand loafers. "It'll be a long time before you stop thinking about my cock every time you masturbate at the end of a long workday under your cheap covers."

I was going to kill him.

I knew it right there and then.

Maybe not today and perhaps not tomorrow either, but it was going to happen.

I blew out air and folded my arms over my chest. "I'm sorry I took your money." It hurt to apologize to him, but I had to do it for my conscience, not to mention my employment status.

He stared through me, like I'd said nothing. "I expect you to keep your lips sealed about our little..." He ran his eyes over my body, but not like he wanted me. More like he wanted to get *rid* of me.

I batted my eyelashes. "Cat got your tongue, sir?"

"No, but close." He leaned his shoulder against the door, making shoulders and doors everywhere pale in comparison to how sexy he looked. "Your pussy got my tongue—several times, actually—but also my cock, fingers, and frankly everything else in that suite I could fit into you. I'll spare you the sordid details because A, you were there, and B, we're going to keep it strictly professional from here on out. Understood?"

Jesusjesusjesus. The mouth on this guy.

"Lady, if you don't stop using my name in vain, I'm taking my complaint to a higher level," Jesus grunted in my head.

"Aren't you going to apologize, too?" I parked my fists on my waist.

"What for?" He sounded genuinely interested.

How old was he? Thirty? Thirty-two? He didn't look so young

anymore, now that I was sober and watching him through a curtain of red anger and sheer embarrassment.

"For lying to me," I raised my voice, on the verge of stomping my foot. "For faking an accent and telling me you had a flight back home. For—"

"Not that it's any of your business." He lifted one hand, cutting into my stream of words. "And not that I will ever provide you with any more personal information, seeing as you're officially an employee, and a junior one at that," he reminded me coolly. "But I actually did fly out to see my mother in Florida. *Home* isn't here. But it's not in France, either."

"And the accent?" I wished I could club him over the head with a stapler and still keep my job. Unfortunately, I was pretty sure HR would frown on that.

He tugged at his collar, his smile wolfish. "I have a taste for simple, meaningless fucks."

"No. You made sure I wouldn't ask for your number or try to give you mine." I had zero control over my voice at this point, and I think he knew I was a step from punching him square in the face.

He looked at me flatly. "Crazy is not a good look on you, Spears."

"Well, consider yourself lucky, because I have no intention of exchanging anything with you, be it numbers, fluids, or pleasantries." I turned around, ready to storm out the door. I took the first few steps, but Célian grabbed my wrist and spun me in place. His touch sent a jolt of electricity straight to my groin, which only proved that my mind was savvy, and my heart was lonely, but my body was just a dumbass.

"Keep quiet," he warned.

I rolled my eyes. Like letting my boss screw the living hell out of me was something I wanted to send a press release about.

"Yes, *sir*." I shook his touch away. "Anything else, *sir*?"

"Watch your attitude."

"Or else?"

"I'll make your life very miserable. And enjoy it, too. Not

because we slept together, but because you stole my cash, wallet, and condoms."

To be fair, the condoms were inside his wallet, and I'd simply forgotten to discard them. Which gave the whole thing an extra layer of embarrassment. I knew I was skating on thin ice, and I didn't want to crash my way to the bottom of the unemployment ocean. I decided to change the subject.

"I forgot my iPod in the suite. Did you happen to find it?"

"No."

Damn. "Am I excused?"

He took a step back. "I hope to see very little of you, Miss Spears."

"Duly noted, Mr. Timberlake."

I slapped my forehead the entire way back to my cubicle, thinking things couldn't possibly get any worse. The future owner of LBC looked royally vindictive, regally pissed, and majestically explosive. Because of me. I knew he was going to avoid me at all costs. And it embarrassed me that I was saddened by that, because his scent, voice, and the insanely inappropriate things leaving his mouth fascinated me no less than they infuriated me.

When I got back to my cubicle, my first instinct was to drown myself in perfume samples. But as soon as I walked in, I realized I had some explaining to do. Grayson and Ava sat side-to-side, cross-legged, staring at me like I was a National Geographic special. All they needed was popcorn.

Grayson jerked his thumb in the elevator's direction. "Explain."

"There's nothing—"

Ava butted in. "Mr. Laurent Jr., AKA the news director slash executive producer of the prime-time news show and Lord Assholemort, never offers people eye contact, let alone talks to them."

He doesn't, now? Shocker.

"You better start singing like it's *American Idol* and I'm Simon Cowell, girl." Grayson snapped his fingers, wiggling his ass in his seat. "I want to know the how, when, where, and how long. Especially the long part. Inches and all."

I guess I deserved this. Célian had no business seeking me out and having a private conversation with me on my first day. Besides, these were shaping up to be the only friendly faces in all sixty floors.

I stared down, my toes squirming in my shoes. "You're making a big deal out of nothing. We've met before. Briefly. At a…social function." *What's more social than sucking each other's privates?* "I think we were just surprised to see each other is all."

The way the lie slid effortlessly from my lips scared me. First stealing his wallet, and now this. Célian Laurent sure brought the worst out of me.

"So you're saying you don't *know* each other." Ava tilted her chin down, inspecting me like I was a Russian spy.

"I'm not even sure what his first name is." This was actually true.

"It's *Célian*. Now, question—did you listen to anything he said in that meeting?" Grayson raised an eyebrow.

"I…" I searched for words.

Normally, I was far more eloquent. Debate had been my favorite subject at school. I'd gone head to head with my articulate, overtly opinionated, politician-wannabe classmates at Columbia—sons of lawyers and daughters of judges. But just like any woman determined to be taken seriously, I had an Achilles heel. Being caught getting freaky with the boss and salivating all over him was going to make my career freefall like a shooting star.

"Let me help you with that." Grayson waved his hand. "Mr. Laurent said they're slicing the budget of *Couture* by at least ten percent, which may not seem like much, but our blog is virtually running on fumes as it is. I thought this was the extent of it. I was wrong."

"I'm not sure I'm following." I frowned.

Grayson leaned forward, catching my gaze. "I'm going to ask again—how do you know the Laurents?"

"Why?" I felt my heart thudding against my chest. Now we were talking in plural?

"I just got this email." He turned his monitor around so the three of us could huddle in front of it and take a look.

From: Mathias Laurent, President, LBC
To: Grayson Covey, Editor, Couture Online Magazine

Dear Mr. Covey,

As per our earlier discussion and in line with the recent cuts made at Couture, we shall be needing further assistance in the news department.

We will be transferring one of your employees to the newsroom starting tomorrow at nine a.m. Seeing as you and Miss Jones have worked together closely for the past two years, the person reporting to the newsroom will be Miss Humphry.

Regards,
M. Laurent.
President, LBC

"What's going on?" I swiveled Grayson's chair, grabbing his shoulders.

I was mildly elated and a whole lot frightened. Working in a newsroom had been my dream for as long as I could remember, but working under Célian was sure to be a nightmare. My feelings were at war, fighting and tugging between joy and abject horror.

"I have no idea. Mr. Laurent Senior has never addressed me in person. I wasn't even sure he knew my name." Grayson rubbed his forehead, looking disoriented.

"You think it's got something to do with Célian?" Ava asked.

Célian was about as readable as a blank sheet. He was a mystery wrapped in an enigma. He'd seemed pissed at me, sure, and he'd been clear he didn't want to see me again.

"Doubt it. As I said before, we don't know each other," I parroted myself.

Grayson darted up to rub my back. "It's okay. You'll be fine. Célian made a name for himself as the cruelest man in the business, which is why we've actually been leaving CNN and Fox News to eat dust the last couple years. But at the end of the day, there will be people around. He can't maim you."

A ping sounded from Grayson's computer, and our eyes shot back to the screen.

From: Célian Laurent, News Director, LBC
To: Grayson Covey, Editor, Couture Online Magazine

Gary,

You were expected to send us the Swedish royal wedding piece two hours ago. Unless you're fond of long unemployment lines and downgrading to a Bronx apartment with unreliable electricity, I would advise against testing my limit when it comes to punctuality.

They're called deadlines for a reason. If you fail to deliver the piece on time…

Célian.

Grayson double-clicked the little X on the right-hand corner of his monitor, closing the email program.

"About the maiming thing…" He cleared his throat, looking skyward and shaking his head. "Wear a helmet tomorrow morning, just in case."

Célian

"Good morning, Mr. Laurent! Here is your grande Americano, daily schedule, and the news bulletins for today. You have a ten o'clock meeting with your father in his office, and a noon lunch with James Townley and his agent regarding renewing his contract. Your dry cleaner left a message that your navy blue Gucci pea coat is missing. They sent their apologies and offered a twenty-percent discount off your next visit. What would you like me to do with this information, sir?"

Bunch a lawsuit into a ball and shove it down their throats.

Overall my PA, Brianna Shaw, was an okay kid.

A law school grad who I was pretty sure still thought *pro bono* referred to being a U2 fan, she did make an effort—something that couldn't be said about the pile of self-entitled, snotty millennials who'd come in and out of this place trying (and failing) to assist me. Brianna wheezed like she was in the middle of an orgy when she talked to me, which made understanding her a struggle. Maybe it had something to do with the fact that she had to chase me up and down the hall. She was short and stocky, and I was tall and ran seven miles a day.

I bookmarked the idea of hiring a tall, athletic, *married* assistant the minute Brianna threw in the towel. Which, judging by my track record, should be any week now. My assistants usually quit at the two- to three-month mark. Right around the time either of these grave realizations hit them:

1. I was an insufferable asshole.
2. I was not going to fuck them.

Brianna now hovered near the four-month threshold—a trooper if I ever saw one, or one masochistic lunatic.

"Fire them," I snapped. "I don't work with thieves."

Unless they have an ass worthy of every rap song I've ever heard. Judith Humphry assaulted my mind. *Then I let them keep their job.*

Though that was bullshit, and I knew it. Miss Humphry didn't work for me. Chances were, I wouldn't see her for months on end. She worked on a different floor, in a different department. At any rate, I never screwed the same woman twice, and I would never touch an employee. She was officially as toxic as poison ivy, and after stealing from me, just about as tempting.

Brianna licked her lips, pushing her dull, brown curls behind her ears as she huddled beside me. I was dashing from the newsroom into my office. "Sir, that would be a challenge, seeing as, according to this spreadsheet—" She swiped the iPad screen in her hand. "You have officially blacklisted every single dry cleaner in Manhattan."

I pried the device from her fingers, my eyes skimming the lines of red-stricken shops. Un-fucking-believable. Human nature was designed to take what it wanted, consequences be damned.

Again, I thought of little Miss Humphry. She had no business barging into my thoughts. I usually forgot my one-night stands before the cum on my cock dried up. Then again, she had stolen from me.

And I took something of hers.

The Smiths? Bloc Party? The Kinks? Babyshambles? Dirty Pretty Things? The girl knew her way around a record shop.

"Fire them," I repeated.

"But, sir..." Brianna gasped, a rather dramatic response for the occasion.

I stopped in front of my office door. She did the same. Her face was so red I thought she was going to spontaneously combust. I hoped she wasn't. I had a new Brioni dress shirt and apparently no honest dry cleaners within the city limits.

"You have no other option, unless you want to go back to one of the dry cleaners you've previously blacklisted," she explained.

"False. There's a third option."

"There is?" She batted her eyelashes.

Not many of my female employees had the balls to do that. First, because I was the president's son. Second, because I was just a tad more intimidating than Lucifer himself. And third, because I was, as my associate producer Kate labeled me once, "Devastatingly unavailable." Which essentially meant I wasn't distracted by a perky set of tits.

"You can be there to monitor them while they work on my items."

"But..."

"You're right. *Can* is a casual word. It *is* what's going to happen."

"Sir..."

"Clock starts now. Better run—they get busy around noon." I tapped my Rolex, storming into my office and shutting the door with a thud.

An hour later, my lousy excuse for a father wandered into my office like a tourist in a gift store wondering what the fuck he'd like to break. Technically, I was supposed to meet him in his office. But if we were talking technicalities, he was supposed to act like a dad and not a skirt-chasing, social-climbing douchebag, so I called us even. He leaned his shoulder against the doorframe, his hands tucked inside his pockets.

"*Je n'aime pas que l'on me fasse attendre.*"

I don't like to be kept waiting. Hard to believe this asshole was the president of an American broadcasting news channel. He still insisted on speaking French to anyone who would listen. My mother had stopped being one of those people a year ago, when my sister died. She'd promptly divorced him, moved to Florida, and found a new boy toy to play with. I visited her every few weekends to get away from the bullshit and nagging loneliness. Bonus points: Floridian pussy was tanner and not half as uptight as the New York variety. And it was so much easier to pull the tourist thing without people realizing I was a Laurent. The Laurents, Maman's family—Mathias took her last name as a part of a draconian pre-nup—were royals in the upper-class crust of Manhattan. We kept our shit secretive and tight-lipped, and we were almost as scrutinized as the people we reported on.

"Chances are you'll live," I said in English, still typing on my laptop. *Unfortunately.*

"Look at me when I'm talking to you," he barked.

I did.

I could tell my compliance startled him, because the great Mathias Laurent cleared his throat, walked over to the seat in front of mine, and collapsed into it like he'd been holding his breath for the past year. Which was pretty much what we'd all done since Camille died.

"We're having an identity problem that causes ad space to tank." He slapped the chrome desk between us.

"Let's agree to disagree. I know exactly who I am: a newsman who's grossed the highest network ratings every night for the past two years and the son of a philandering idiot. If you suffer from memory loss, I'd suggest ginkgo biloba, B-12 vitamins, and fatty acids." I kept my eyes on the screen.

"Listen, son..."

He crossed his legs, and I did my best not to laugh. Really? *Son*? That was rich.

"Your work here is appreciated, but it's time to play nice with new advertisers and harvest fresh revenues."

"You mean now it's time to let parties' propaganda and every dick with an alcohol bottle or cigarette brand sell have air time?" I sat back and laced my fingers together. "Because we already have commercials coming out of our asses. We just don't run the spots that bring in the big bucks, because people tend to lose their trust in a news channel who tells them they should buy a pack of condoms and lubricants to go with their booze."

He rolled his eyes like a teenager. "*Il n'est pire sourd que celui qui ne veut pas entendre!*" *No one is as deaf as the one who refuses to listen.* "Perhaps a few simple endorsements on air will do. I'm meeting you halfway here, Célian."

"I'd rather meet you in court when I sue your ass for shitting over my soon-to-be network." I stopped him mid-speech. "This news channel will report the news. Nothing more. Nothing less. It is the sales department's job to find lucrative deals."

"*Précisément*. They simply can't. You've made this network the goodie two-shoes of TV. We're never biased, never wrong, and never profitable. And that's an issue."

"Don't give me the profitable bullshit. I watch the numbers closely. I'm about to inherit this place." We were making clean profits, just not major revenues like we could if we sold our soul to the devil. I preferred my soul intact. It was bad enough I didn't have a heart.

"Continue this line of behavior, and you will inherit nothing." My father reddened, his face swollen with blood and anger.

I smiled impatiently. "It's not up to you, and you know it. My mother gave you the keys to this ride, and you shall return them when you're no longer fit for the job. The difference between us is that *I* am a newsman, and *you* are a lucky bastard."

"Watch your tone with me." He punched his thigh, his face so red it was starting to look purple.

I knew I should back down before he suffered another heart attack. I hated my father with a fiery passion, but I didn't want his death on my conscience. I knotted my fingers together, leaning forward and meeting his gaze. Nature must've known what I'd found out when I wasn't even ten—we weren't going to be close. I'm certain that's why I looked so much like my mother. Light eyes, dark hair. Only things I'd inherited from Mathias were his height and ability to make people want to commit murder.

"I pride myself in bringing to the table impartial, factual, bulletproof information. In having a proven track record of clean kills every night. What our viewers do with this information is up to them. You will not inject any pro-Republican, pro-Democrat, or pro-bullshit propaganda into my news show. You will not air ads for casinos, alcohol, or condoms. You will not ruin this business for me."

"We need to stay profitable, Célian." My father adjusted his silky red tie. "And when it comes to thinking for yourself, at least have the decency to sound a little less adamant. *Your* track record hasn't exactly proven that you do as you preach."

I knew exactly what he was referring to, and I wanted to staple his face to my goddamn door for the hypocrisy. He'd dug the hole I was sitting in with his own dick, and now he was shoveling mud to bury me inside of it.

"If you don't want me to touch your show, I will have to cut back on your staff. I will make the necessary arrangements to let go of the interns and stand-by reporters."

Fucker. But it beat drowning in ads for casinos and experimental drugs.

"You do what you have to do," I hissed. "Any more words of wisdom from a man who doesn't know where our studio actually is?"

"We should rid ourselves of James Townley if he makes any further salary demands." My father flattened his hand over my desk.

For a reason beyond my grasp, my father fucking hated our anchor of the last thirty-five years. James Townley had come to this station when he was twenty-four years old, and over the years, he'd miraculously received everything he'd ever asked for—including, but not limited to, setting up his son, Phoenix, with a job here. Said son stirred up so much trouble on this floor, my father'd had to strategically remove him to the other side of the world. He was now on the Syrian-Israeli border, reporting on all things Middle East. It was my educated assumption that ISIS would sponsor the next pride parade in Damascus before trying to kidnap Phoenix Townley. Yet James was still pissy about Mathias putting his son's life in danger.

Townley was a lovable prick, and he was well-spoken, well-respected, and well-received. He also looked like Harrison Ford's fake-tanned, bleach-haired twin brother, which didn't exactly hurt our ratings. If he and my father could've killed each other without legal consequences, I'd have two less headaches to worry about.

"Are you done?" I sat back and rolled a pen between my fingers. I was going to have a double-serving of this nonsense in about two hours when I met James and his agent for lunch.

"Almost. I added a little something special to your team I believe you're going to appreciate." My father raised his hand to the glass wall, and my eyes followed the direction to the fishbowl newsroom.

Judith Humphry.

She stood there, statuesque and holding a cardboard box to her chest, refusing to look petrified. With her sun-kissed hair and a dusting of freckles covering her button-like nose, she was the type of beautiful that suddenly sneaks up on you. The more you looked at her, the more you realized how striking she was. She looked like she belonged on a beach, running barefoot. Even in her size-too-big potato sack dress, she looked like freedom and tasted like a piece of the sky. I wanted to grab her and slam her over the desk, fucking her three ways to Sunday in front of my entire news crew.

Problem was, Judith also had a mouth. And it talked back. Always. It annoyed and delighted me in equal measure. Part of me wanted to screw her, the other to spank her. Those two didn't necessarily contradict one another. But I wasn't the type of asshole to sleep with an employee.

My father, however, didn't seem to share my moral standards—or any morals, for that matter.

"We'll make do without her," I snapped. "Even after the intern cut."

"She'll make for pretty decoration in the newsroom." He ignored me, sitting back and eyeing her. My father had an office over fifty floors up, on the sixtieth floor. However, he was here a lot, and he couldn't exactly fire his own secretary and replace her with Judith. Mainly because he already had a reputation.

"She's not a vase." I refused to spare her another look.

My dad shrugged. "Both have holes."

My eyelid ticked. *Your face can have one, too, if you don't shut the hell up.*

I gathered the paperwork for the morning's rundown and stood up. "Out of curiosity, are you moving her here because you want to fuck her or because you think I will?"

He'd obviously filled in the gaps yesterday when we'd made the *Couture* announcement. Mathias threw his hands sideways with a smile. "Why not both? This could go in so many interesting directions."

"No. It won't. You won't touch her, and neither will I."

"Because...?"

My father still hadn't received the memo that he was well into his sixties, and that the only reason young women weren't slapping him into unconsciousness was because he had more money than he could spend in six lifetimes and a name that was synonymous with power.

"Because she's an employee."

He raised an eyebrow, silently reminding me that when he set his eyes on a woman, he liked her small, dependent, and very much unemployed. If it was up to him, he would saunter over to Judith right now and whisk her to the same suite we'd shared at the Laurent Towers Hotel next door. If she proved to be good in the sack—which she would, I knew that, because I'd been balls deep in her not even a month ago—he would lock her in a golden cage and provide her with a luxurious life of imprisonment: an apartment, a private driver, a credit card with an outrageous cap—all to keep her happy and available until he got bored with her.

I pointed the stack of documents in his face. "Move her ass back to the fifth floor before the end of the day."

He smirked. "May I remind you who is the boss around here?"

I pushed my door open, throwing him a glare soaked with repulsion. "The boss is the asshole who makes your show worth something, Father. You're just the fucking purse."

I ended up ignoring Judith for the rest of the day.

It wasn't intentional, but satisfactory all the same. I didn't even bother to show her to her desk. I wasn't entirely sure what my father wanted her to do here, but I knew after the faceoff this morning I'd better keep her, or he'd find another way to sabotage my show.

She was probably a wannabe fashionista who thought working at *Couture* was an honor akin to receiving the Nobel Prize. I needed to get creative with giving her a task she could perform well that would still put some distance between us.

After lunching with James and his agent, I had to do a final run-down before the show. James was having a meltdown two floors below because the makeup artist didn't have his shade of foundation and he was afraid he'd look like an Oompa Loompa, and an interviewee had been involved in a car accident on his way to the show.

Since Judith didn't have a desk, a computer, or anyone to talk to, she sat on a chair by the door and wrote furiously in a thick notebook. I imagined her diary to be filled with her latest thoughts about Shawn Mendes and anal bleaching.

By the time I had a minute to spare, it was seven-thirty. Everyone had already left for the day. I grabbed a chair and plopped down next to her, folding my arms over my chest. She looked up from her note-book, uncrossing her legs and tucking her Chucked feet under her chair. She looked like a newswoman like I looked like a fucking clown. The mere acknowledgement of her existence here was spit in my precious time's face.

"This wasn't my idea," I clarified, rubbing my face tiredly.

She broke into a smile—not fake, not calculated, and also not constructive to my twitching dick. "Good show."

"I know."

"But I thought your interview with Faceworld's CEO could have gone differently."

"Next time I'll make sure he wears Hermes when he talks about the Russian hacker threats."

"Or maybe next time make sure he's not blowing smoke up your anchor's ass, excuse my *French*." If nothing else, her dig was kind of funny. "Seeing as your main competition ran a story tonight about how said CEO is now accused of being an avid user of Cotton Way, a darknet website where you can buy heroin and guns for competitive prices." She handed me her phone.

It was the main item on their website now. *Fuck*.

"This place look like TMZ to you?" I motioned around the room with my finger.

"There's nothing sleazy about this item, and you know it. I came here to make the news. To keep the masses informed, and to serve my country."

She surprised me, her eyes shooting daggers at mine. Why did her words surprise me? Because she was gorgeous, and young, and fuckable to a fault. But didn't that make me the misogynistic, judgmental bastard my father was?

"Your station." I stood up and cleared my throat, sauntering to the middle of the room. I'd deliberately put her somewhere I couldn't see clearly from my office. I knew my dick better than to trust it around Miss Chucks. "See this?"

She slid into the chair in front of the monitor. "Reuters."

We have a genius on our hands.

"Your job is to stare at this screen all day and sort through the relevant news items on this site. Yellow items go to Steve, our junior reporter—well, slightly less junior than you. Orange items go to Jessica, our in-house reporter, and red items go straight to Kate, my associate producer."

I scribbled their emails on a Post-It note and slapped it on her monitor.

"And what happens when I see a yellow with the potential to become a red?"

Your yellow hair would look nice on my thighs as you suck me off and I make your ass red with the spanking you clearly deserve.

"Fat chance." I straightened up so I wouldn't have to smell her vanilla and warm ginger scent. My dick didn't need this kind of negativity in his life.

"It could, though."

I turned around, facing her again. "And what are your credentials to make such assumptions?"

She stared at me flippantly. "BA from Columbia Journalism School."

Fuck-hot.

Smiths enthusiast.

Well-educated.

And a lying thief.

I needed to stay away from her, send her ass packing and relocate her to our Chicago branch. For now, though, I was mainly interested in why a Columbia graduate had stolen my goddamn change and condoms.

"Before you ask, full scholarship. I have no money."

She was a mind reader, too.

I stroked my chin. "Didn't ask; don't care. You'll also be my assistant's assistant."

"Your assistant has an assistant?" She swiveled in her chair, eyes widening.

"She does now." I smirked.

"You disgust me," she said.

"You have a weird way of showing it."

"Weren't you the one who gave me a twenty-minute lecture about never mentioning that night again?" She darted up and stomped her foot, her hands balled into fists.

I would pity her if I didn't remember how I'd felt when I'd realized my wallet was missing. She actually thought we were playing by the same rules. We were toe-to-toe now, and even though the room was empty save for her and me, I could feel it burning up with our anger. I liked her hot and bothered, but that didn't mean I was going to dip my dick into her again. I didn't break my rules for anyone.

Let alone an employee.

That didn't interfere with the fact that my balls tightened, though.

My muscles tensed, too, with the frustration of not being able to remind her that she might hate me outside of bed, but inside it, she'd been purring like a kitten.

"Judith." I clasped her chin between my fingers, angling her face to meet my gaze.

"*Jude*," she corrected.

She wanted me to be like everyone else. That ship had fucking sailed the minute I'd spotted her in the bar, and all I could see were her pink-Chuck-clad feet wrapped around my shoulders as I drilled into her.

"Let me be clear about one thing: my title may be news director, but sometime in the next five years, I will be the president of this company. Better yet, I will be the *owner* of every single floor in this sixty-story building, top to bottom, staplers and coffee machines included. The rules do not apply to me. You have laws, but I operate in my own little dictatorship. As long as it's legal and does not cross the employer-employee relationship, I can say whatever I fucking want to you. Since I have a rich legal background—Harvard Law, in case you were wondering—I know where the line is drawn, and I intend to walk it like a tightrope if you cross me."

Her breath caught in her throat, a caged, helpless animal, and my eyes focused on her big, russet hazels, knowing that if they drifted downward, to her cleavage, I was liable to rip her clothes off and fuck her against the desk.

"Ambition," she whispered, running her hand along my dress shirt.

What?

"I wore the black Chucks because black represents ambition. Motivation. I want to work here. I want to prove myself. I have a lot to offer, in and out of the newsroom."

What the fuck was she doing? Touching me in the office? She wasn't exactly trying to seduce me, but she wasn't not-trying to, either. Turned out two could walk that tightrope.

"You're playing with fire," I warned.

Her hand crawled up, touching my mouth, her thumb hovering over my lower lip, tracing the seams, reminding me of three weeks ago. "Maybe I want to get burned."

I grabbed her wrist and lowered her hand, as gently as I possibly could without pressing it against my raging hard-on. "I don't shit where I eat."

"Give yourself some credit." She licked her rosebud lips. "You weren't that bad."

I chuckled, shaking my head. Say what you want about this girl, she had balls the size of watermelons.

"You can join my ship." I grabbed my new wallet and phone, tucking them in my back pocket. "As long as you realize I'm your captain, and that there will be no more fucking around, literally or figuratively."

Instead of giving her the pleasure of formulating a response, I turned around and walked away, muttering under my breath. "Just don't expect me to help you when you drown."

Jude

Things got progressively and methodically worse in the week following my move *(Grayson: "deportation!")* from *Couture* to the newsroom.

The place was a zoo made out of silver chrome desks glued together in a wave pattern, circling huge monitors that broadcast different news channels from all over the world.

The newsroom was round, with glass walls. Nearby was another conference room—made of glass as well—in which fresh pastries and fruit sat in fancy baskets and elegant glass water bottles were lined together neatly. There were hundreds of monitors, switchboard phones, keyboards, and cables running from side to side. There was a stairway to the seventh floor that led to a door with a plaque plastered on it: *Magic Happens Here*

This referred to the actual studio, where the prime-time news show was recorded.

But I couldn't feel the fairy dust on my skin, because I was too busy trying to survive my life as I knew it.

Milton was the first to kill my mojo.

My cheating ex had decided that the fact he'd been boning his editor was not, in fact, grounds for a breakup. First came the flowers and text messages. When those were ignored or given to the lonely, attractive neighbor upstairs (the flowers, of course. Forty-something-year-old widow Mrs. Hawthorne didn't need to read the douchecanoe's apologies for dipping his sausage into a different ketchup tub first thing after coming back from a grueling shift as a nurse), Milton started asking our mutual friends to be mediators. Said friends, who were neck deep in kissing his ass for landing a job at a prestigious magazine, explained that Milton was the one. *My* one. That we had something special going on, and it would be insane to throw it away because of one mistake.

"He was going to help you pay your debt," one of our friends, Joe, even added. "Consider that, too."

I told Joe and the others that if they were going to plead the case of a cheater who'd decided to throw our five years down the drain, they might as well delete my number. I was in an anxiety-filled headspace, consisting of a sick father, a new job, and a stack of bills that remained impressive even in my employed state. Acting diplomatically was not high on my list of priorities.

Then there was work.

Célian Laurent was the biggest jerk to ever walk on planet Earth, and he carried that title like a badge of honor. The only silver lining was that I now knew it wasn't personal. He was just a dick—a dick who did a phenomenal job making news and surpassed every single talented newsman I'd ever learned from, but a dick nonetheless. And speaking of penises, contrary to my impression from our last encounter, he'd kept his tucked firmly inside his slacks all throughout the week. Not that we had any chance of working one-on-one in a busy newsroom, but when he did acknowledge my existence (albeit reluctantly), he remained cold, aloof, and professional.

And me? I tried to forget the moment of weakness during which I'd touched him.

I didn't know why I was looking for a connection with him. Maybe

I recognized how similar we were. He was bitter, and I was angry. He wanted casual, and I… I didn't think I could afford anything else with everything that went on in my life. But I couldn't forget how it felt when he touched me.

When his mouth was on mine.

When his hands pinned me to the wall.

When he made me forget about my sick father, piling bills, and unemployment.

True to his word, Célian had put me in charge of Reuters. The only qualification I needed for the job was the ability to distinguish between yellow, orange, and red. Most reporters—even junior ones like me—had plenty of tasks. I had just the one, to rot in front of the monitor.

Oh, and help his assistant, Brianna Shaw.

Célian's PA was the definition of candy sweet. Unfortunately, she was also a ticking time bomb. Célian was such a tyrant, she spent the majority of the day running after him, taking orders, or sobbing softly in the restroom. Today was the third time I'd found her doing that—on a Friday, of all days, a second before everyone in New York poured into fancy bars and hole-in-the-wall pubs to celebrate the weekend freedom—and I silently slid a box of tissues and a mini-bottle of whiskey into her stall.

She'd been too scared to ask for my help, and I didn't know how to broach the subject without making her feel weak. But that third time in the restroom broke me. To hell with my boss and his deep blue eyes, his pouty lips, dirty mouth, and Zac Efron body.

"Hey." I squatted down, my butt hovering over the floor. My Chucks were gray today. *Moody and depressed.* "You need a break… and a drink. Let me help you. I have plenty of free time." And I did. My job was as challenging as tying one's shoes. Brianna hiccupped from the other side of the stall, unscrewing the bottle and taking a sip. "I…" she started. "He…" I strained my ears to listen. "He needs to have his suits cleaned."

"I'll drop them off in half an hour. Just give me their address," I said.

"N-no. He demands that you stay at the dry cleaners and watch them clean his clothes."

What?

"You mean make sure to take the receipt?" Maybe he had a favorite person cleaning his clothes. What a diva. Rich people had ridiculous whims. In Célian's case, he was picky about who cleaned his suits, but was perfectly content with eating a stranger's ass.

Brianna hiccupped again. "No, I mean he makes me sit there and look at them as they do it."

"Why?" I gasped.

"Because they sometimes steal his clothes."

"Why are you still working here?" I would have stabbed him in the face through the power of telepathy by now had he done that to me.

"Because he's smart, pays well, and…I mean…" She downed the entire drink. I heard her gulping it. "He's seriously handsome. But of course, I know he'd never look at me. He once said my legs are awfully short because I need to run to catch up with his pace. He probably thinks I look like the Pillsbury Doughboy."

I'd had enough.

Enough of him treating Brianna like a pest.

Enough of him allowing everyone else in the newsroom to overlook me. (I hadn't been introduced to *one* person. The associate producer, Kate, asked me once where my parents were.)

Enough of sneaking to the fifth floor every lunch break to spend time with Grayson and Ava, because Célian invited *everyone* in the newsroom to the conference room to eat lunch every day. Every. One. But. Me.

I darted out of the restroom. My eyes found him like that's what they'd been trained to do. He was in his office, the door thrown open, typing away and ignoring the hustle and bustle in the hallway. I knocked on his door loudly, my anger climbing up my throat and balling into a scream. I walked in without permission.

"Yes?" he said without looking up.

"I need to talk to you." I was surprised at how heated and cross my voice sounded, like liquid lava slithering between my lips.

"I beg to fucking differ. You're reporting to Steve, Jessica, and Kate. In that order. Think of this place as a church, Judith. When you make a confession, you go to a priest. You don't have a direct line to God."

Did he just…? Surely, he didn't…

"Did you just compare yourself to God?" I tried to wrap my head around this.

But of course he did. He had his PA monitoring his dry cleaners. The guy was obviously more bananas than a tropical island.

And he was *still* typing away and staring at the screen. I slammed the door behind me to get his attention. Finally, he looked up. I swallowed the saliva pooling in my mouth. His crisp white dress shirt rolled up his elbows, his tan and muscular forearms with the veins snaking down to his big hands, and the carved, severe expression on his face—so sharp it could nick and make me bleed to death with a glare alone.

"You're making Brianna sit at your dry cleaner's for hours on end and watch them clean your clothes?" I seethed.

A toxic grin spread over his face. "I'm guessing by your reaction that you inherited the vexing task."

"A task I will not do."

"A task you *will* do, unless you want to get fired, gray or not."

"Huh?" I seethed.

His eyes dropped to my Chucks. *He noticed.*

"Just because you're in a shitty mood doesn't mean you get to boss your boss around. Learn your place, *Chucks.*"

"*Chucks?*"

His eyes traveled down to my feet, and he raised one lonely eyebrow.

Whatever. I stomped my foot, seething. "You're being unreasonable! You need to stop walking so fast, too. Brianna is running after you, and her feet are all banged up."

"Miss Humphry, hell will freeze over before you dictate my movements, in or out of my newsroom."

I threw my hands up. "I give up. Please transfer me back to *Couture*. Making news was my life's ambition, but self-fulfillment is not worth working with you."

What was I saying? Why was I saying that? I didn't want to go back to *Couture*. I loved Ava and Gray, but I wanted to stay here and make news. I just wanted him not to treat me like I didn't exist and cut Brianna some slack.

"You like the news? Here's a newsflash for you: you don't always get what you want. Are we done here?"

No. We were definitely not done. But I couldn't jeopardize my job, so I turned around and was about to storm straight to Grayson's office when I crashed into something hard. I looked up. It was Mathias Laurent, and he was smiling back at me like a cunning cat who'd just eaten a canary, a few yellow feathers still sticking out of his mouth.

"Hello," he said in the same French accent Célian had faked the other day.

Unease slinked down my spine. "Sir." I nodded, making way for him to enter his son's office. In my periphery, I caught Célian perking up, drinking the two of us in.

"Mathias Laurent. Please, call me Matt."

He offered his hand. I shook it. Well, at least Laurent Senior wasn't a douchebag. I gave him my name, and he took a step toward me, still at the threshold.

"We didn't get to properly meet last week, Miss Humphry, but I always try my best to get to know everyone in the LBC family, no matter the position."

"Could have sworn horizontal is your favorite position," Célian snapped, standing up and grabbing his jacket from the back of his chair.

Mathias continued, ignoring him, "I would love to have you come to my office to discuss what you are seeing and experiencing in my newsroom. Monday at ten?"

I smiled, opening my mouth to accept the invitation, when Célian's hand locked around my wrist and dragged me out of his office and down the hallway. I stumbled over my own feet. What the hell was his problem? I must have uttered the question out loud, because he let out a frustrated growl more fitting for felines in the wild. He pushed open a door leading to a dim, empty room I'd never been in before and slammed it behind us.

The power room.

I grunted as my back hit rough buttons and cold metal. Célian was pressed so close, I could feel his hot, male presence squeezing the lust out of me, which made a very different groan escape my lips. He took a step back, as if my touch was lethal.

"Stay away from him." His voice was so low and menacing, I felt it in my stomach.

"Hmm..." I grinned, swiping my tongue across my bottom lip and staring at him through hooded eyes. "I think I just talked to the real God around here, and Jesus got pissed."

Inwardly, I could hear Jesus rumbling, "*Yup. She's throwing me under the bus again.*" I made a mental note to visit my local church on Sunday.

"I'm not in the business of repeating myself," he seethed, ignoring my jab, and if I knew one thing about Célian, it was that he never passed an opportunity to outwit you once you threw a jab at him. "And I don't want you near him. His intentions aren't pure."

"And yours are?" I huffed. "Look, I can't—and won't—ignore my boss. My *real* boss. The man who pays my salary."

He bent down to bite my ear. "I'm the man who fucked you senseless and you can't stop thinking about. I'm the asshole you masturbate to in order to get off. I'm the guy who will *destroy* my competition, especially when it comes to Mathias Laurent. So, do yourself a favor and keep your pussy—*my* pussy—as far away from him as possible. *Compris*?"

His tight chest and hard abs against my soft body. His tall, commanding figure enveloping my small one into submission. He was touching me without really touching me, and I wanted him to swallow me whole, like a Venus flytrap—clamp his jaw and absorb every inch of me.

Touch me.

Fill me.

Drown me in your poisonous kisses.

Let me die from your venom, buried under your sinful skin.

"I hate you."

"Would you like to test that theory?" He chuckled, forever standoffish, even when it felt like thunder cracked between us in the dark room.

I should have said no, but something else slid from my mouth breathlessly. "Yeah. Fact-checking is your craft, isn't it?"

Without looking back, he reached behind him, locking us in. My heart pitter-pattered into submission, no longer lonely and resentful. Célian grabbed my jaw and crashed our lips together in an animalistic kiss that somehow started from the middle, with tongues battling, fingers unbuttoning clothes, and hands roaming, searching, squeezing, and twisting every inch of flesh and fabric. I was out of breath before my dress hit the floor, and out of my mind the minute his cock pressed against my stomach.

"Haven't had the chance to read the employee manual of LBC yet. Is this an official part of our one-on-one meetings?" I laughed, my heart threatening to burst out of my skin and fall at his Italian-loafered feet.

"Am I doing anything you don't want me to do?"

"You're doing less than I want you to do," I admitted.

"Then no talking, Humphry. I like you better that way."

"Still hate you," I mumbled into his mouth, clawing at his shirt. He was dressed, so very dressed, and I'd never wanted anyone more naked in my life.

"Still don't care," he hissed and hoisted me up against the door, slamming his groin into mine.

"Condom," I ordered.

No matter how sexy Célian was, he still gave me the vibe of someone who'd been around the block, and this was Manhattan, so there were plenty of dubious blocks to choose from.

"*Fuck.*" He bit down on my lip punishingly, pulling away from me, plastering his forehead against mine, and rolling it from side to side. "I'm clean."

"I don't care."

"Surely you're on the pill." His cock dug between my legs, and it was hard to deny him anything, decapitating me included.

"We're not at a point in our relationship where we're having this conversation. I want you to get me off, not get me pregnant. I need to forget."

Forget that my life is a mess, that my dad is dying, that I'm drowning in bills.

But of course, he didn't ask. Didn't care.

He looked down at me. For a second, something passed between us. Despite his perpetually cold exterior, he seemed to understand loss and disappointment—in a fundamental way that tainted your entire perception of life.

He spun me around and slapped my bare knees like a scolding headmaster. It wasn't the burn, but the shock that made me fall down on all fours. I was blinking away the surprise when I felt him lower to his knees behind me.

His mouth found my hot center from behind, and he licked me slowly, making my thighs quiver with pleasure. The sweet, almost seductive licks became strokes. He parted my butt cheeks with his strong hands, plunging his tongue between my folds, thrashing against my walls. My moans were becoming increasingly loud, and he threw a piece of fabric at me.

"Bite."

I sunk my teeth into the cloth as his fingers dented my thighs red and blue.

The orgasm ripped through me was like a bucket of hot water. It washed over my body, sudden and violent. I bit so hard into the fabric I thought I was going to rip it apart. I collapsed to the floor, but Célian didn't give me time to recover. He flipped me over expertly and climbed atop me, naked from the waist down but still wearing his shirt. I didn't know when that happened, but I was starting to come to terms with the fact that I acted very drunk and very stupid every time he and his mouth entered my general vicinity.

I thought he was going to poke his engorged penis between my legs and was about to protest, but he surprised me by scooting farther up until his ass was aligned with my chest. He plucked the fabric from my mouth and threw it on the floor, guiding his cock into my mouth with his palm. "Still gonna fuck you today, just not the hole I was aiming for."

"Wait," I snaked my hand between us, squeezing his girth. Even though he was a control freak, his eyelids slid shut and he let me stroke him back and forth. "If you want me to suck you off, you need to drop the whole dry-cleaning thing. Be in charge of your own dry cleaning. Give them the clothes yourself, and while you're at it, make an official complaint. That way, they'll think twice before stealing, because the suit has a face. Agreed?"

He threw his head back and laughed. "*Disagreed*. Fuck that."

"Apparently so, because it's not me you'll be screwing."

That sobered him up quickly. I wiggled underneath him, pretending to move away, and he sank more weight against me, pressing a playful palm to the base of my neck.

"Are you blackmailing me, Miss Humphry?"

I clasped his penis harder, pressing my thumb against the pearl of pre-cum gathering at his tip, bringing it to my lips and tasting it with a sweet smile. If he was expecting an actual answer with words, he underestimated me. Actions spoke louder, and right now, I had him by the balls. Almost literally.

His nostrils flared, and his mouth pursed into a scowl. "This better be one hell of a BJ."

With that, he grabbed the back of my head and pushed himself all the way into my mouth, until I could feel his tip at the back of my throat. I wanted to gag, but that involved showing him vulnerability, and I had managed to go without it so far. So I took it all in and even let out a sigh of pleasure. His balls tightened against my chin, and I felt myself dripping on the floor, my thighs spreading involuntarily. He began to thrust into my mouth, and I sucked hungrily, loving his taste. My hand snaked behind him, and I began to play with myself as I sucked him off. He took ahold of my hair, elevated his ass for a better angle, and thrust harder, slapping my hand away.

"My turn."

But I couldn't help it. The need to get off prickled between my legs. Plus, I was certain I was going to regret every moment, so I might as well leave this room thoroughly orgasmed. I arched my back, trying to grind against the air and whimpering in frustration around his cock.

"Coming," he announced, not even asking if it was okay to do what he was about to. Warm, thick liquid swam in my mouth a second later. I swallowed it before it managed to hit my taste buds, holding my breath, as I used to do every time I was on the giving end of oral sex with Milton. Célian pushed off me onto his shins, still holding my hair in his fist. He looked as pissed as he had walking into this place, not even mildly affected by what we'd just done.

I cupped my mouth, realizing a thin river of cum was sliding from the corner of my lips.

"What have I done?" I whispered.

Reality came crashing in on me. I'd done it again. Only this time, it was a thousand times worse. Because now I knew he was my superior. He wasn't a confident and assertive tourist; he was actually a raging American asshole.

"Your boss, it seems," he said with his signature jaded tone, standing up and buckling his slacks. He balled my dress and threw it into my arms. It was wet and wrinkled to death. "Can't really fuck your boss *and* his father, can you? Guess I made the decision for you."

Why the hell did he think I'd sleep with Mathias?

"Also, I'd advise against walking out of here in the next hour. You really did a number on your dress," he smirked and excused himself, sauntering out and closing the door behind him.

I threw an arm over my face and groaned. *Bastard.*

That evening, Dad wasn't there when I got home from work.

Panic gripped my throat, squeezing hard. Dad never left the apartment without letting me know. His absence sobered up my Célian-induced haze quickly. I rummaged the house like he might be hiding in the cupboards, then grabbed my keys and roamed our street, shouting his name into the late-spring drizzle. He couldn't have gone far. We didn't have a car anymore, and he loathed the subway. The realization that I should call someone—anyone—had settled in, but with it came the recognition that I had no one to turn to.

Usually at this point, I called Milton.

But Milton and I were no longer together.

Our mutual friends were too busy telling me I was naïve and judgmental for not giving him a second chance. Grayson and Ava were great, but I didn't know them well enough to dump my personal problems on them. And Célian…a bitter chuckle escaped my lips. I would rather die before confiding in him that I needed help.

Forty minutes later, I decided to go back home to recalculate my moves. I went into our building and found Dad sleeping in the aged-wood-scented stairway. His bald head was perched against the banister, drool leaking from the corner of his mouth. He looked serene and fragile, like a piece of old art.

I shook him awake.

"Where have you been?" I was shouting and shaking, and I didn't even care that I scared him.

His eyes snapped open and he blinked, startled. Tears of relief began to flood down my cheeks and neck, and I knew there was no point in wiping them just to make room for more. I held onto him like an anchor—both of us sinking down to a lonely, stain-carpeted stair—and buried my head in his neck. The overwhelming notion that sometime in the near future I wouldn't be able to do this any more squeezed my throat, suffocating me, and I heaved.

My father was going to die.

I was going to be left all alone in this world.

"I'm okay, Jojo. I'm fine. See? Look." He wiggled his hairless eyebrows, tapping his chest like it was an old TV that coughed out bad signal. "I just went to visit Mrs. Hawthorne. She was under the impression that I'd sent her flowers. Can you believe that?"

I could. Because I was the one who'd left them at her door. Mrs. Hawthorne was fairly new to our building. She'd moved out of her huge Rochester place when her husband died, seeing as her kids were married and out of the house.

"Anyway," he chuckled. "Must've gotten tired on my way down and crashed. I'm sorry. I didn't mean to worry you."

I was torn between letting myself break down completely front of him and keeping myself together *for* him. I clutched his cold cheeks and angled his head so we looked at each other. My dad was a big guy. He'd worked as a roofer in Brooklyn his entire life before cancer came barging through our door. But somehow along his journey with the disease, he'd become scrawny. So frail, in fact, that whenever he accompanied me to the supermarket, I was the one supporting him—the man who'd carried me on his shoulders until I was in first grade.

"Excuse me, little girl, did you follow me?" he'd always said when he put me down.

I always laughed. *"You carried me, silly!"*

"Huh..." He'd stroked his chin. *"Whaddaya know? You're light as a feather."*

I helped Dad into our apartment. No matter the weather outside, it was still subzero, somehow. I was playing chicken with the thermostat, trying to walk the line between a sensible electricity bill and not freezing to death in this particularly chilly spring. It's like New York had decided to make life even more difficult on us. I wondered how it felt to be Célian, who probably had heated flooring in his bathroom and never had to experience any discomfort.

I pondered what my boss's apartment might look like as I made Dad chicken soup, sans the chicken. We ended up watching a rerun of SNL under blankets in the living room. Some might call it a sad state of affairs for a woman in her early twenties to be hanging out with her dad on a Friday night, but there was nothing I could think of that would be better. Even though we were both silent, I drank in his presence, so acutely aware of the elephant in the room.

"Milton has been looking for you," he said when I got up and stretched after the show was over.

My heart missed a beat. Countless times, I had wondered if I should give Milton a heads-up about my father not knowing about our breakup. But since he was seeking me out so actively, I figured talking to him, no matter the capacity, would just encourage his cheating ass.

"Oh?" I hoped it sounded like, *Oh, he has?* and not *Oh, I forgot to tell you. We broke up a month ago because he was screwing his boss while I was tending to my sick dad. But hey! Now I'm screwing mine, too. The circle of life, anyone?*

"Called me on my cell. Asked if I could tell you to get back to him. I'm sure you have by now, but I just thought you should know. Will we be seeing him this weekend?"

Dad fingered his empty bowl of soup and sucked on the leftovers. He liked Milton. Every time I asked him why, he said, "Because he is smart enough to love my daughter."

"Hard to say, Dad. We're both very busy with work."

This was tearing me apart. I hated not being honest with my father, but I hated the idea that the truth would hurt him even more.

The minute my head hit my pillow, I started sobbing. Not just crying, but full-blown, so-sorry-for-myself bawling with tears and snot. The whole shebang.

I was not a crier. I'd cried the day my mother died and on a few occasions after that, like the day I'd gotten my period without her there to calm me down and after I'd stolen that wallet. But tonight, it felt like the weight of the world rested squarely on my shoulders, and I wanted to throw it away or let it bury me in the ground.

The thing about crying for hours is, you always end up sleeping like the dead afterward. It happened to me the night after my mother died. (The night she did, I couldn't sleep a wink—was too afraid the world would collapse if I let my eyes drift shut.) Misery has a way of pulling you down and drowning you in it. It's sweet and suffocating, like a lullaby, soothing you to sleep.

That night, I slept like a baby.

Célian

Living alone was a choice I made rather happily.

The alternative was living a lie, and I didn't do lies, nor theft—not since both things had exploded in my face in spectacular fashion. Even though I had a car, I took the subway to work every morning. And since everyone in my family for the last three generations had personal drivers, I was seen as the black sheep of the tribe. Luckily, the tribe had dwindled and was nearly nonexistent, so it's not like I had anyone to impress.

Besides, I liked the smell of piss and the general misery of harsh city life. It reminded me that I was a lucky motherfucker, even on the days I felt like God—if he existed—had made a point of pissing all over my plans.

On my way to work, I thought about what had driven me to pull Judith into the power room on Friday and fuck her mouth into what could have been a mass power outage in one of the largest skyscrapers in New York. My jizz definitely shouldn't have been anywhere near all those electrical switches.

I was definitely trying to piss all over my territory, but in the process, I'd also pissed over my no-repeats rule, as well as my professional relationship with her. Currently, I was trying to decide if I should go back to normal and act like she didn't exist until she quit and the problem took care of itself, or figure the damage had already been done and make her a booty call for when I was too tired to go on the prowl.

Pros: the Manhattan singles scene was beginning to grate on my nerves. I was starting to see the same faces in the same clubs. Every hookup and Tinder profile blended together in my head. At least with Judith, I had sexual chemistry.

Cons: her pussy aside, she had an annoying, holier-than-thou attitude, not to mention, she was mouthy, and I really couldn't fucking stand her.

When I got to the office building, I had to take a phone call. Lily. I normally sent her straight to voicemail, but this was the third time she'd called since I'd gotten off the subway, so I wanted to make sure Madelyn, her grandmother, was okay.

"Anyone dead?" These were my exact words when I took the call.

I didn't go into the building, knowing things could get pretty crappy and fast when it came to Lily and me. I rarely raised my voice, but for her, I was always happy to make an exception.

"What?" Her default voice was whining. The kind that sounds like a fork scraping against a plate. "No. Grams is doing great. I was just wondering if—"

"No need to wonder. The answer is no."

"*Célian*, wait! I—"

But I'd already hung up. I turned around to walk through the double glass doors and spotted Judith sitting on the top stair reading, soaking in the first rays of sun like a thirsty flower. She wore one of her crumpled, wannabe-grownup black suits and hugged her backpack.

Her Chucks were red today. *Oh, boy.*

She wiped her eyes quickly, but I wasn't sure whether she was crying or about to. She was talking on the phone, and any other bastard would've turned around, walked away, and vowed to stop making her life more difficult.

But I was programmed differently, carved from stone like the very people who'd created me.

I rounded her tiny, blond figure, half-listening to her conversation.

"Okay, Milton. Just…please don't tell him."

Milton sounded very much male and very much like a douche-bag. The latter wasn't based solely on his affiliation with Judith, but also his name. Now I was fully invested in the conversation.

"I'm really not interested in hearing what you have to say."

Pause.

"Please don't make it any more difficult than it already is. Promise me you won't tell him. That's all I ask."

Pause.

"Yeah, well, I have a job to go to. Bye."

She stood up. I pretended I didn't see her, pushing the door open and waltzing to the open elevator. She was a few feet behind me, so when I turned around, our eyes met. She hurried to catch my elevator—of course I didn't push the hold button—and sneaked in at the last second. There were two more people inside. Two assholes who went to the second floor. HR.

"Hi," she breathed, turning around to give me her back and ass. Not a bad deal.

I nodded solemnly.

Silence. Silence. Silence. She didn't act shy or awkward. Something about this morning told me she had more pressing issues to deal with than sucking her boss's dick, and I decided on a whim that I needed to know what was on her mind.

Naturally, talking to her was out of the question. She sassed way too much and always nagged me about my behavior. No. I fired a quick text message to one of my reporters, Dan, with her name and address while the elevator made its way to the sixth floor in record negative time.

Célian: Judith Humphry. Her file is with HR. I want to know everything there is to know about her, from her education to her favorite color. Who she fucks, who she lives with, who she talks to.

I fingered my chin, watching my message and firing off another one immediately.

Célian: And how many pairs of Chucks she has.

Strictly speaking, it wasn't any of my business. But Judith was shaping up to be such a trainwreck—stealing from her boss, then fucking him, then avoiding him, then sucking him off, then having public fights with people on the phone outside her work building—I wanted to make sure she was on the sanity spectrum.

When we got to our floor, we walked straight into the newsroom. The first rundown meeting was in ten minutes. She walked over to her desk with that damn notebook clutched to her chest.

"Humphry, join us in the conference room," I heard myself say.

She perked, bit down a smile, then opened the notebook and scribbled something into it. Fast. *Lord.* She was so fucking thirsty for the job. I let Brianna dispose of the iPad in my palm and shooed her away.

"You'll be taking notes, Judith, not making suggestions," I said.

I was careful to treat her exactly as I would any other reporter in her position. I was already an insufferable prick, so I wasn't particularly awful to her. But I was also fair, and after a week, she'd earned the right to sit, listen, and absorb.

She kept her eyes on her notebook. "A girl can dream."

"Happy to fulfill your other fantasies." Good thing Brianna had started working on her cardio and was already on the other side of the floor. We were almost alone, early, eager fuckers that we were.

"I actually have one you could help me with."

"Unless it involves me tying you to a bed, I'm not really interested in hearing about it," I said, setting fire to the entire conversation we'd had last week about my dancing on a red line. I sprinted through that fucker all the way to the finish line of sexual harassment. Not that I was harassing Jude, as evidenced by the enthusiasm with which she sucked my dick, but if she wanted ammo on me, I'd stupidly given her that.

"It actually involved *me* tying *you* to a bed." She batted her lashes, and for an unknown reason, didn't look annoying doing so.

Normally, I liked being the one doing the tying, but for Humphry, I could make an exception. She stepped toward me, her tongue sweeping over her lower lip.

"Then I'll strap a ball gag to your mouth..."

I curved a brow, raking my eyes slowly over her body and undressing her item by item. She was high if she thought I'd put anything in my mouth that wasn't a part of her body. By the time she was in front of me, she was stark naked in my head, her voice dripping honey and sex all over my fucking loafers.

"Then," she whispered, her pillowy lips moving against my ear. "I'll set the whole damn thing on fire, with you in it."

I smiled. Judith Humphry was a massive pain in the ass. Not only was she a natural blond, shit-hot, and the owner of the best pair of lips in the tristate area (both pairs, if we're perfectly honest), but she was also sharp as a razor—the opposite of my usual pushover flavor of the night.

"If you ever had the pleasure of getting in bed with me again..." I narrowed my cold eyes on hers. "You would be the one to catch fire, and we both know it."

With that, I curled my finger, motioning her into the conference room. People had begun to trickle straight into it with their coffee cups and sleepy eyes. Judith obeyed, her catlike, limber walk telling me she knew I was looking.

James Townley opened the door for us before he walked in.

"Son." He clapped my back.

"Call me that again if you want a one-way ticket to early

retirement," I muttered.

"Junior." He winked at Judith.

"Mr. Numbers." She saluted.

They shared a knowing smile. I punched him in the face. Internally, of course. My limits were few and far between, but they were there. Besides, James had just married the morning show's latest weather girl—who was thirty, both in age and IQ points—in a Hamptons ceremony that made Harry and Meghan's royal wedding look like a karaoke evening for a low-budget Jersey Shore bachelorette party. That thing got more news coverage than the North Korea threat. I shot James a don't-fuck-with-me frown—just to make sure *he* knew that *I* knew he'd checked out Judith's ass when she walked in—and he pretended not to notice me.

From that point forward, it was same old, same old. My staff presented me with their ideas for tonight's show starting with Kate beside me—my right hand—then moving to the person next to her and so forth.

Kate (forty-something, happily married, and openly gay) suggested we start with the volcanic disaster in Maui. Jessica (twenty-something, single, and clingy as saggy balls) came up with new details about the EU crisis, and Steve, the newbie who was shaping up to be a little less useful than a bag of unwashed anuses, suggested we talk about the cheese crisis in Belgium. I braced my hands on the back of the chair I stood behind so I didn't accidentally punch him from across the table.

"*Junior*?" Frankly, I did it because I didn't want James and her to have something uniquely theirs—a pet name, a connection.

"Me?" She pointed at herself, looking up from her abused notebook.

I shot her a condescending glare and punctuated it with a raised eyebrow.

She tucked her hair behind her ears and cleared her throat. "Yes. Okay. Good thing I have Kipling."

Kipling? Who the fuck is Kipling?

"So, there's a YouTube blogger..."

"Next," I barked.

This wasn't *Couture*. I doubted our viewers wanted to hear about some chick showing people how to apply eyeliner for twenty minutes, unless she was dead and chopped into tiny pieces, spread across the five oceans.

"*Wait*," she bit out, her teeth grinding together. "There's a YouTube blogger with over two million viewers. He just posted a video telling people he hid a body part of someone close to him who passed away in the woods near his house. Whoever finds it will get ten grand in cash."

"What?" Kate nearly spat her coffee all over the desk. "How did we not hear about this until now?"

"First of all, we *are* the news." Judith smiled apologetically, and my jaw ticked, fighting a smirk. "And it happened literally ten minutes ago." She swiveled to Kate, her chest rising and falling. "Honestly, I doubt it will warrant much reaction at first. Most of his viewers are minors following his journey as a pro skateboarder. But this is definitely something we should be alarmed about. Can I?"

She pointed at Steve's iPad. Steve dragged his eyes to me, a question mark and boredom shining through them.

"Give her the iPad, doofus." I shook my head.

Five seconds later we were looking at Cody McHotson—not his real name was my wild guess—wearing a Viking helmet, sleeveless Billabong tank top, and a smug smile that flashed bleached teeth. He looked like the reason they invented guns, but he was actually doing this—sending minors out to look for a body part.

"It's not gross or anything." He tucked a lock of his blond side-bang back into his hat. *"Like, don't expect to find something super weird. But it's there, and hey, if you feel like making a buck, you should go for it."* The stoner laughed into the camera, sending a plume of smoke toward the lens.

"Is he a minor?" I turned to Judith.

She shook her head. "Twenty-one."

It was official. This generation was too dumb to repopulate. Hard to believe I would be dependent on his likes fifty years from now.

"Good lead, Humphry. Jessica, follow it."

"I'm on it." Jessica saluted, typing away on her phone.

"Hey, what about me?" Steve flung his arms in the air.

"You gave me a lead about Belgian cheese. Be happy my shoe is not in your ass."

"Ugh," he wailed, picking a pastry from the basket and stuffing it into his mouth.

He was of the Phoenix Townley brand—a rich boy who'd wormed his way into my newsroom through connections. My father had paved the way for people who were incapable of consuming a latte without burning themselves in the process, let alone making one, yet simply had the right last name. Of course, same could be said about me. With two differences: I hadn't asked for this job, and I'd goddamn well earned it.

People were leaving the conference room when I jerked my chin toward Judith. "A word in private."

"Here?"

"Yes, Einstein."

The room had floor-to-ceiling glass walls, exactly what I needed to keep my hands off her. Once we were alone, I shut the door and sat down in my seat, linking my fingers together. She straightened, her chin high, watching me closely.

"This can't happen anymore." I motioned between us.

I wanted to make sure she wasn't going to blow our dirty fucks out of proportion. The last thing I needed was for her to think we were in a relationship of sorts. I needed to keep my work area efficient and professional.

She clicked her pen, nodding. "Agreed."

"Anything you need help with?" I gestured downstairs with my finger, but I could see by her flaring hazels that this was not the way she interpreted it. "I saw you crying outside this morning." My lips flattened. "This was not an invitation for a cock-ride."

Her cheeks pinked. "I fail to see how that is any of your business."

"My employees are my business," I shot back drily.

"Their performance is, yes. You don't have to worry about that. I assure you."

Judith didn't have the tools and means to fight me. But other than that, she did a damn good job of standing up to me.

I was getting tired of beating around the bush, so I just gave it to her straight.

"Was the phone call about us?"

She tilted her head back, laughing. "No. There is no us."

"Quite right. Good job on the YouTuber." I stood up, ironing my shirt with my palm. This was good. I could go back to ignoring her from now on. I was about to do just that, marching over to the door, when I saw the face behind it and froze.

Lily Davis stood on the other side, her glossed lips grinning at me.

Lily Davis, as in the woman I *should've* been fucking.

Lily Davis, as in the woman Humphry knew nothing about.

Lily Davis, as in my fiancée.

Jude

Some girls looked like they had the world at their Louboutin-clad feet, and the leggy brunette who burst through the glass door with a megawatt smile was one of them. Her flowery perfume made my eyes water, but maybe I was just on the verge of crying because of my exchange with my boss. She gripped Célian's collar—flashing an engagement rock the size of an entire Tiffany's store—and planted a wet kiss over his scowling lips. He held her shoulders and took a step back, giving her a frosty onceover, as if assessing the damage on a recently purchased wrecked car.

"Lily."

"Fiancé."

What?

It shouldn't have surprised me. Célian was gorgeous, successful, and a billionaire in his early thirties. Why wouldn't he have a fiancée who looked like sex on heels? But the irony wasn't lost on me. He had managed to put me firmly in Elise-the-editor's shoes. The other woman. The homewrecker. The moral-less girl. Only difference was, Elise had known for a fact that Milton had a girlfriend. I, on the other hand, had had no clue.

I stood on shaky legs, waiting for Célian to introduce us. He did no such thing.

Throwing Lily a cold glare, he ground out, "This is a surprise."

And not a good one, his eyes said.

"I had a fitting just around the block, and Mom wanted to buy macarons for Grams, so I thought I'd drop in and say hi. You know how I get stabby when there are carbs around since I started keto." Her thick eyelashes fanned against her cheeks as she clung to him, as if worried he could slip out of her hands like butter. On top of being a brunette version of Blake Lively, with a summer dress and bright yellow sandals, she looked wildly in love. Undeniably so.

But I wasn't going to do that to myself—be jealous of her. The poor thing had a cheating scumbag for a fiancé, and even now, he looked about as remorseful as a used tissue.

"And you are...?" She circled her manicured finger around my face.

The idiot your partner cheated on you with.

I wanted to fall down on my knees and come clean. Tell her I'd had no clue he was taken, that he was lying, that he was a *jerk*. Of course, I didn't have a death wish.

So I settled for a faint smile. "Jude Humphry."

"*Jude*. Oh my God. Love your name. So chic. I'm Lily Davis. But, you know, not for long." She ran a possessive hand over Célian's muscular arm.

A needle of guilt pierced my heart, my agony pouring out.

"Wow. Congratulations."

Célian stared at her like she was an alien, a perfect stranger who'd walked into his life unannounced. Sweat coated my upper lip.

"Oh, this little thing?" She wiggled her fingers, flashing a rock that made Dwayne Johnson look miniature. "We've been engaged for as long as I can remember. I finally got around to planning the wedding." She rolled her eyes, laughing. "It is *so* exhausting."

Coincidently, so was holding my smile intact while she told me about her relationship with my boss. I decided to excuse myself before I did something that would secure me a night in jail—like slap Célian across the face several times.

"I'm sure you'll rise to the seemingly impossible challenge." I reddened, watching the cheater smirk in my periphery. "Well, I have a lot of work to get to. So…" I tilted my head to the door and found my way out. Célian stood next to Lily—they were a united front, after all—staring at me with quiet interest.

Engaged. He is engaged. I was so flustered, so blind with fury, I didn't even know how I would proceed with my day without doing something stupid and irrational, like trash his entire office.

I stumbled toward my station, keeping my eyes on my Chucks. A hand snaked behind me, clasping my elbow and spinning me in place. I slapped it away instinctively, thinking it was Célian.

It was Steve, sitting at his desk, his dull eyes zeroing in on mine.

"Happy with yourself, *Junior*?"

What in the fresh hell did he want from me, and did he realize how extremely poorly timed his question was? I couldn't be less happy with myself right now.

"Define happy, and please don't touch me again." I jerked my arm back.

He stood up. Steve was a little pudgy, and not very tall, but he was handsome in the way men who had all the money and time in the world could be. Groomed to a T.

"You made me look like an idiot back there, and we both know it," he pointed at the conference room, whisper-shouting.

Puzzled, I cocked my head, thinking he must be giving me some kind of backhanded compliment. When his face remained thunderous, mine followed suit.

"I'm not following."

"You came with that stupid YouTube idea no one knew about. Why did you even talk at all? You're the lowest goddamn person on the totem pole. Guess that's all it takes these days. Know how to give a good BJ, get your foot in the door."

My eyes flared. Not that the accusation was far off the mark. But while Célian Laurent could be blamed for a lot of things—all of them scoring him brownie points in the Asshole of the Year contest—giving me perks for whatever we did or didn't do wasn't one of them. When it came to integrity, we both had it.

Besides, there was no way Steve knew about the *power room incident*. He wanted to rile me up.

Mission accomplished.

"Steve, you're making a pretty serious accusation here, so unless you're going to back it up with facts, I would kindly ask you to never speak to me again in a non-professional capacity." I crossed my arms across my chest.

I didn't know why the universe had decided to rain calamities on me today. I just knew the day needed to end before I stabbed someone with my mechanical pen.

"I've got my eye on you." Steve pointed at his eyes with two fingers and poked my arm. *Again.* I did the only thing I could without actually putting that mechanical pen to use. I bumped my fists against each other twice, giving him the finger *Friends*-style.

"Did you just…?" Kate pushed off her desk, her chair wheeling backward. She held her Sharpie like a cigarette in her mouth.

"I did." I cleared my throat. "Please don't judge me. Living with the fact I did it in public is punishment enough."

She shook her head, her chest vibrating with laughter. "That was totally epic, in a weird, nerdy way. Good work on the YouTube piece, by the way. I'm Kate." She offered me her hand.

"Jude." My tight expression finally melted into a smile.

"Steve, let's go into Célian's office." Kate jerked her head toward the hallway, and the bastard actually had the audacity to stomp under his desk. How old was this guy?

I got back to my desk and stared at the Reuters reports, chewing on my lower lip and trying not to think about Célian's fiancée. I knew I was being irrational, but I still logged into the LBC software's messenger app and group-messaged Grayson and Ava. For the past week, I'd been spending my lunch breaks exclusively with them. Not surprisingly, they had their noses in everyone's business.

Judith: Did you know Célian Laurent is engaged?

Grayson: What's it to you, Miss I-don't-know-him-hey-look-a -squirrel?

Judith: It was a surprise, is all.

Ava: They're childhood sweethearts.

Grayson: Sans the sweet part. I've seen them together enough to know the man loves her as much as I love getting my crotch waxed. (The results are far more aesthetically pleasing than shaving, if you're wondering.)

Ava: We weren't, but thanks for the mental image.

Judith: Célian doesn't look like the kind of guy to do something he doesn't want to do.

Grayson: Let's just say it's an arranged marriage of sorts. Célian is doing it for the same reason he does everything—to get ahead in the game.

Ava: Her father owns Newsflash Corp. They distribute eighty percent of the magazines in the US market, plus her family has ten-percent equity in LBC. Don't worry about Célian. No chance of him ever lifting a finger without calculating the consequences and risks.

"She's right," a husky voice boomed above my head, and I snapped my gaze up, my blood freezing in my veins.

My knee-jerk reaction was to apologize profoundly, but then I remembered what had brought this conversation on. My browns met his blues. I tilted my chin up.

"I do whatever—and whoever—I want, and my favorite finger is the middle one. Makes for very unhappy critics. *And* one-night stands."

How had this guy not been assassinated yet? He was a walking, talking personal offense.

I kept my mouth shut. We were in a room full of colleagues. No way I could tell him what I thought of him and end the day still gainfully employed.

"Let's take this conversation somewhere soundproof," he ordered.

"Pass." I gathered some reports I'd printed out earlier and began to highlight the headlines I thought would be of interest to Jessica. Hadn't we agreed our fling was over? It was none of my business that he was a cheater. Even if it made me want to staple my fist to his face for falling under his charm. *Twice.*

"The sooner you realize I don't use question marks, the easier you'll adapt here. Up." He turned around, storming toward his office. I followed him because I had to. We went in just as Kate and Steve were coming out. He closed the door behind them and leaned against it, hands in his pockets.

"You're engaged." I narrowed my eyes into slits, giving his hard pecs a shove. He didn't move from his position against the door. Just stared at me with his bone-chilling indifference. "Freaking engaged, *Célian*!"

"I'm sorry, were you expecting a ring after our one night together?"

I hate you. I hate you. I hate you.

"No, but I was not expecting you to be engaged to another woman. Had I known, I never would have touched you. Just because you don't have any morals doesn't mean I don't, either."

"Please tell me more about your morals, Miss Still-Owes-Me-A-Grand," his eyes traveled along my body with boredom.

Fifteen hundred, actually, but that wasn't something I was eager to correct him on.

I waved a hand at him. "Just say what you want to say and let me get on with my day."

I turned around, staring at the wall and refused to show him my pain, which he seemed to thrive on.

His posture unstiffened, and he stuck a hand into his unruly, tousled curls. "That being said, it is *not* what it looks like."

"Hmm… My favorite cheater line—right after, 'I can explain.'" I clucked my tongue, still staring at the wall behind him.

"Are you going to listen?" His lips thinned in annoyance.

"Not if I can help it." I shrugged.

"Then I guess you can't. Lily is well aware of the fact that I'm seeing other women. We do not share a bed, a house, or even a joint gym membership. As your friends pointed out rather bluntly, my engagement is one of convenience." He dragged his long fingers over his jaw.

I chose my next words carefully.

"You said your life is none of my business. I tend to agree with that sentiment, especially now that we're officially done with each other. So while I appreciate you explaining yourself," I spat sarcastically, "I really think this conversation is over."

I made a move toward the door he was blocking. He stopped me, resting a hand on my wrist. Our eyes met, and I found his bleeding with pain. But his set jaw, high cheekbones, and smooth, regal forehead all told a story of a formidable man. My lonely heart believed his eyes. The rest of my body knew it made no difference.

"Chucks."

Stop calling me that. Stop giving me nicknames and orgasms and hope, I internally screamed.

"You said you were legal-savvy. Now's a good time to withdraw that hand of yours," I whispered.

He did. I thought he was going to send me on my way angrily, but he didn't.

"Was Steve giving you trouble?" His voice didn't sound like steel anymore, though it was nowhere near soft.

"Don't." I shook my head. "Don't pretend you care. Don't even try to be the good guy. You're as bad as they come, and now that you *came...*"

His mouth twitched with a smile.

"...it is time to move on. Congratulations on your engagement. She'll make a beautiful bride."

Grayson: Jude? Are you still there?
Ava: Maybe he fired her :/
Grayson: Maybe he kidnapped her :O
Ava: Stockholm fantasies much?
Grayson: The guy does look like Theo James's beefed/baller/ macho brother. Him not knowing my name aside, I would let him show me a good time even if I ended up in his trunk at the end of the night.
Ava: You need professional help, Gray. I'm not equipped to deal with your type of crazy.
Grayson: It would be a spacious trunk, too, I bet.
Célian: If you two were to read anything more substantial than the *National Enquirer*, such as our company's newsletter from three months ago, you would know that messenger chats on our web software are now publicly available to view by any user in the company.
<Grayson left the chatroom>
<Ava left the chatroom>
<Judith sent a gif of Ross from *Friends* bumping his fists together>

Célian

If there was one thing I'd learned from producing news for over a decade, it was that wars are not measured in words, or declarations, or assumptions. They are defined by results, the number of casualties, and land conquered. The colder they are, the longer they last.

I made my way back from picking up my own dry-cleaning *once again* on a spring afternoon because Miss Humphry, my assistant's assistant—who'd blackmailed me into the task with a blow job more than a week ago—was adamant I didn't deserve her help. She had won the first battle.

Currently, Judith was avoiding me. I was avoiding Lily, and my father was loitering around my newsroom, sending Jude looks that made my skin crawl so violently, I was tempted to shed it completely and dump it on my office floor. I thought things could not get any worse, but I'd obviously underestimated the clusterfuck called my life, because sure enough, Dan—the reporter I'd tasked with getting info about Jude—stood at my office threshold when I returned.

"Are you ready for this?"

I was somewhat surprised to learn he'd spent the last week actually working on this and not drinking his body-weight with the advance I transferred into his account.

I waved for him to close the door and take a seat. "Drop the game show mannerism. I'm not a '60s housewife."

"So, Judith Humphry is neck deep in shit and currently trying to swim her way out against the stream. Mother died when she was thirteen; Dad diagnosed with cancer about a year ago." He rubbed his fingers across his lips, delivering the news dryly while settling into the chair opposite to mine. "When your girl found out about her pops, she quit her prestigious-yet-underpaid internship and took two temp jobs to help with the bills. But obviously, her income still couldn't cover a mortgage in New fucking York, not to mention the everyday life of a property owner in Brooklyn. Her dad recently stopped going to chemotherapy because they can't afford it. Their bills are unpaid, their fridge is mostly empty, and they live in Bed Stuy."

If I'd had a heart, it would've slowed, almost to a halt. But as it happened, I didn't, so all I could manage was despising her a little less for the wallet stunt. My face remained placid, so Dan took it as a cue to continue.

"She had a boyfriend, but he seems to be out of the picture. The day you two disappeared into the Laurent Towers Hotel together—and don't give me any details, because I sure as hell don't wanna know—was the last time she was seen at his apartment building, according to the CCTV footage. Your girl is unaware of the fact that said boyfriend, Milton, purchased an engagement ring that he is still keeping in his nightstand drawer. But based on the active ghosting she's doing every time he calls, it's safe to say a comeback is not in their cards. By the way, did I use the term *ghosting* correctly?"

I felt my nostrils flaring, and I wasn't entirely sure what pissed me off more—the fact that Dan was trying to younger than eighty-five, or that Jude could've fucked her boyfriend on the same evening I'd had my dick inside her.

"Continue."

"As far as her hobbies go, Judith likes reading thrillers while sitting on her porch on Saturday mornings, and she prefers Costa over Starbucks and bagels over tacos. On Sundays, she goes to the New York Public Library and reads everything from *Newsweek* to *The New York Times*. She skips the *Post* every single time, never touches the gossip columns, and munches on Sour Patch Kids when no one is watching.

"She shudders when people dog-ear books, and always stops to listen to buskers. Sometimes she throws money into their instrument cases. She prepares an extra sandwich every morning and gives it to the homeless guy living outside the train station near her house." He paused, letting out a belch. "Put simply, Jude Humphry is barely existing at this point, moneywise. Even so, she seems to be in good spirits, so if you're worried about her stealing from her workplace or becoming a double-agent for another broadcasting company, I would say it's pretty unlikely."

I was hardly concerned about Jude's loyalty, but I couldn't tell Dan I'd had him check on her because my dick and I shared an unhealthy obsession with the girl.

"How much is my father paying you here, Dan?" I stroked my chin, changing the subject.

His gaze shot up from his phone. "A hundred and twenty K. Why?"

"I'll pay you one-fifty to work for me exclusively."

"Okay." The leathery-skinned, fifty-something man smiled at that.

Dan hit the bottle three times a week, and we couldn't rely on him to chase news around New York without making a pit stop at every bar. But he sure was good enough for digging up dirt.

"I want you to keep an eye on this Milton kid—the boyfriend."

"Got it." He wrote something in his notepad. Dan was severely old school, with his tattered courier bag, tape recorder, thinning amber hair, and hate for everything with a flat screen.

"Also, find out who Kipling is. But most importantly, I need you to follow my father."

I didn't miss a beat, watching said creeper through the glass wall as he approached Judith. She looked up and pushed off her desk, standing. Her puzzled eyes studied him intently, but otherwise her mouth was curved in a polite smile. My father motioned upstairs, probably to his office. My fist clenched and my jaw tensed so hard I thought my teeth were going to turn to dust.

Dan's head shot up. "What are we looking to find?"

"Everything and anything that could take him down."

Before Dan could nod, I smoothed my tie and pressed the switchboard button connecting me to Brianna. "Get me a discreet meeting with Mr. Humphry."

"Sir, as in Judith Humphry's father?"

"No, as in Humphrey Bogart. He died sometime in the fifties. I'm sure he's not a hard man to track."

Silence from the other end.

"Yes, Brianna, Judith Humphry's father. And make sure this doesn't get back to her in any way."

"Yes, sir."

More silence. Then, "Sir?"

"What?"

"Thank you for doing your own dry cleaning. I really appreciate it."

She needed to thank Judith, but of course, I would never admit that. It felt like waving a white flag, and all I could see was red, all I could feel was history repeating itself—with my father trying to seduce Judith and her dress ending up in a puddle, like water on the floor of the electrical closet—Catastrophic.

I put the receiver down, waving Dan away like he was a waiter who'd messed up my order. His chin jiggled, along with his stomach on a chuckle.

"When you least expect it, eh?"

I would've asked what he meant, had I cared. "Out," I said instead.

"Sixteen, by the way." He pushed himself up, groaning.

"Huh?"

"You asked me how many pairs of Chucks she has. I counted. At least sixteen."

That's a lot of fucking moods for one tiny thing.

Shortly after sending Dan on his way, I waltzed out of my office and into the newsroom. Grilling Jude about my Dad was tempting, but I wasn't a hypocrite, and she didn't owe me shit.

Besides, it was likely she already felt extra salty after what had happened with Lily, and she had enough on her plate without having my dirty laundry to sort through. I was going to talk to Kate about an item I wanted to scrap from the show tonight when Steve blocked my way to her desk, throwing his body between us like a hysterical mother in front of a speeding car.

Big. Fucking. Mistake, Dudebro.

"Can I help you?" I raised an eyebrow.

"I have something you really wanna see, Célian."

"Please, call me Mr. Laurent. Only my friends call me Célian. Chances are I'll stab myself in the eye with a fork before initiating a conversation with you about non-professional issues. Start talking."

I followed him to his desk, and he pointed at his screen, his smile oozing stupidity in a way I didn't know was physically possible.

"Look."

To me, it looked like a picture of a random, middle-aged chick trying to sit on a cucumber.

"Are you sharing your porn stash with me, Steve? Because A, my taste is a little more conservative, and B, it is strictly forbidden to access erotic websites in this building."

"She's the vice president of Together Forever, a non-profit organization for people with ADHD. Got caught doing this salacious act at her bachelorette party." Steve cackled, his smug smile screaming *jackpot.*

"Here's the part where you tell me why I should care." I began to sort through emails on my phone, losing patience.

"Because…because…look what she's doing!" He cried out, pointing at his screen. "She's legit trying to fit a cucumber into her vag."

I turned around and walked away. This wasn't an item. It wouldn't even be an item if she was a legitimate celebrity. That was Gary and Ava's jurisdiction. But it highlighted the fact that right now, Steve was using a lot of space, resources, and oxygen that should have been offered to someone more capable than him. Kate was already standing up when I approached, her flame-red bob appearing sharper than usual.

"He's impossible." She pretended to puff on her pen. Ever since she'd stopped smoking, she did that with everything from Sharpies to asparagus stalks.

"My dog can do a better job than him." I braced my hands over her desk. "And I don't even have one. A word?"

"Oh, no. Smells like a canned item in the making." Kate and I walked to the conference room, and I shot a look at Judith to see if she'd followed us with her eyes the way I followed her everywhere she went in the office. She was typing away, looking at her monitor. Kate caught my ogling and smirked. I rarely spared my employees a look. Her eyes joined mine on Jude.

Did I fuck up by not giving Jude a heads-up about my situation? Yes. But did I think my one-night stand was going to end up being my employee? Hell no.

"She is pretty." Kate leaned her head over my shoulder. I shrugged.

"Arguing with that would imply that I'm blind, which I'm not."

"She's also kind, smart, and funny. A natural in the newsroom."

"Get to the point sometime this calendar year, please."

"You've got it hard for her, Célian."

Kate ran a hand over my shirt, and I had to clear my throat, because this was wrong on so many levels I couldn't even begin to count them. My job was to expose unethical behavior and bring factual news to the table. I wasn't going to piss all over it for a girl with feline eyes and hair like yellow autumn leaves. Not to mention, to most people in the world, I was an engaged man. But not to Kate. She knew my story, *all of it*. Which was why she refused to speak to my father under any circumstances.

"Can't do anything about it." I tapped away on the table I leaned against.

"You can if it's consensual. People fall in love at their workplace all the time. It's not against the law."

"I'm her boss. Also the devil spawn of the owner."

"An owner who is actively trying to get into her pants." Kate raised a finger, pointing it out.

"Precisely. Besides…" I rubbed my face. "Lily."

"Break up with her. Call off the engagement. And don't give me the Newsflash Corp bullshit. It's about time."

"Like hell I will. My father would have a fucking field day if I give up the only leverage I have on him."

Ever since my baby sister died, I'd become even more career driven. My eyes were on the prize and had never shifted—until Judith walked into this building. Lily Davis had an influential father and her siblings had both given up on their family business. Lily was going to inherit Newsflash Corp, and her family was a shareholder at LBC, with as much as ten percent. So joining their family meant I could overthrow every decision my father had made, if I combined their shares with my mother's. The merger between LBC and Newsflash Corp was going to make me one of the biggest tycoons in the world once my father stepped down.

Which was why he'd done what he did and ruined what little promise I had left going on in my life.

"Irrelevant. Your father is a douche and his feelings toward what you do, or lack thereof, should not determine your choices."

I hated that Kate was the voice of reason. I also hated that she was pretty much the only friend I had who I was certain wouldn't stab me in the back the minute I turned around. I was short on friends, seeing as I trusted no one, including my fucking coffee machine.

"As for your world-domination aspirations..." She raised her hand to pat my cheek, clucking her tongue. "Grow up, Célian. What's the point of being powerful if you're miserable?"

I changed the subject, because none of it mattered. I wasn't throwing away my plans, nor my idiotic fiancée. Judith was...*Judith.* Undoubtedly beautiful, not in the way women in magazines were, but in a way that makes you want to mark her with your teeth, tongue, and piss if need be. Hardworking and smart. There was a chance—albeit a small one—that if I broke things off with Lily and told Judith the entire story, she would still be willing to give the enemies-with-benefits thing a chance. And Kate was right. A consensual affair in the workplace wasn't unheard of.

But we weren't going to be lovers.

We were going to be two people fucking each other into submission, and a fuck—no matter how good—wasn't worth my entire future.

I fell to my seat, noticing that Steve was throwing a fit and yelling at Jessica in the middle of the newsroom. Jude hurried over to them, took Jessica's hand, and led her away.

"We're canning the flammable cellphone item," I told Kate distractedly. She punched the desk between us, then noiselessly yelled at the pain. "I knew you'd do that."

"Get everyone in the conference room. Now."

Five minutes later, everyone was inside, including a solemn Jessica and a defiant Judith. Kate was outside, on a quick phone call.

"We need a new item to close up the show. At this point I'll take anything. A feature. A kicker. A piece about anything that's not completely stupid. Brainstorm away." I tapped my finger over the chrome conference table.

Everybody looked at their digital devices, typing text messages to their sources and generally being productive. Steve, however, sat with his arms crossed and sulked like a toddler in the midst of a tantrum.

"Got it! A pop star with an American passport was just murdered in a strip club in Korea." Kate swung the door open and walked into the fishbowl meeting room, still staring at her phone.

"Steve, I know you like a good gossip. Can you follow that up?" Kate was already texting her source.

"Sure. North or South?" He scratched his head with the tip of his pen.

The silence that followed his question almost made my ears bleed. He thought there were strip clubs in North Korea?

That was it.

I was done.

"Out of my newsroom. Now."

"But—"

"Another word, and you won't be working anywhere on this street for the rest of your life."

"I just—"

"Manhattan."

"Mr. Laurent! I—"

"You've just been blacklisted in the entire city of New York."

"Please!"

"Correction: state."

"I didn't…" Steve darted up from his chair with his arms stretched wide, looking left and right for support. Unfortunately for him, he'd managed to piss off my entire staff in the two months he'd been here.

"Steve, you are on the verge of metaphorical deportation. What's not to understand? Get the hell out. Humphry, you're replacing him as a slightly less junior reporter starting two minutes ago. And since Jessica is hard on the Wall Street item, you're taking over the pop star coverage."

The only thing I had in mind was to get someone with a functioning brain to write me the report, and fast, because all my reporters were drowning in work, and Steve obviously couldn't scratch his own head without cutting it off. I didn't favor her in any way because I wanted into her pants. I also knew she would die before getting ahead in the game by *giving* head.

Steve growled, throwing his hands in the air and stalking out of the conference room. He collected his crap from his station and dumped his employee card in the trash can by the door, which was technically against the company rules, but didn't put a damper on the fact I'd finally gotten rid of him.

"Me?" Jude looked up, her green-brown-golden irises dilating. It was excitement, I think, and it made me so fucking hard I was surprised I didn't tilt up my side of the table.

"Jessica will help you with whatever you need."

Jessica nodded, squeezing Judith's hand. "Of course. I'm here for you, JoJo."

JoJo shot up from her seat. "I will not let you down, sir."

I know, and hell if that doesn't make me harder than an oak tree.

I was so used to people fucking up that having someone constantly step up their game was a disappointment in itself. She was the kind of good I'd only seen one person exhibit proudly. And that was Camille.

Fuck. Where did *that* come from?

"Back to work, everyone." I collected my things and opened the glass door, motioning for people to leave. I expected Judith to do what they all did when I promoted them. Stop. Thank me. Melt into a puddle at my feet. Alas, Miss Humphry merely passed me on her way back to her station, not sparing me so much as a glance.

In a moment of madness, I decided to go the stupid route and touched her back ever-so-briefly. She turned around, cocking an eyebrow.

"Tomorrow. Lunch." The room was empty, so why did it feel like I was suggesting I ravage her on James Townley's desk during primetime, tinting her ass red with my open palm?

"I'll be busy," she said flatly.

"This will be a professional meeting regarding your new position." Probably should have started with that. *Idiot.*

"And I will *still* be busy. Whatever you need from me, I am happy to talk about it right here, in the office. Now, I have an assignment to do. Will that be all, *sir*?"

I let her walk away, briefly wondering when the tables had turned. She'd started as a nameless dirty fuck, and had somehow dug her way out of that compromising position. The girl who'd stolen from me was now getting a promotion, getting me to do my own dry cleaning, and sassing back.

Yeah, I don't think so.

Jude grabbed her phone and started dialing, already flipping her recorder on and connecting it to her cell.

"Hello, my name is Jude Humphry, and I'm a reporter at LBC's Daily Newsnight. I'm calling about the unfortunate and untimely death of Sung Min Chae..."

I looked down, and I was still hard.

I think I'd changed my mind about Chucks after all.

She deserved a few more fucks before I stopped giving any about her.

Jude

"G*o shorty, it's your item.*
We gonna party like it's your item,
And you know we don't give a fuck it's actually Kate's item..."

Grayson was twerking on his stool by the bar, sipping his Bacardi and generally acting like a cheerleader in a horror flick mere seconds before she gets chopped into lamb kabobs. Ava knocked back her third martini, fluffing her thick black curls and staring at me from behind the rim of her empty glass. They were both celebrating my first real journalistic accomplishment. Even when I'd pointed out that someone had *died* and maybe we should hold off the celebrations, they weren't convinced.

"That pop star tried to rape a chick," Gray pointed out. "We *are* allowed to celebrate."

"Sure you don't want anything to eat?" Ava quirked a brow. "You look a little pale."

We were at Le Coq Tail across the street from the office. I was dying for that roast beef sandwich. In reality, I was drinking a glass of tap water and faking a headache, because I couldn't afford anything more, and maybe it was my poor girl's pride, but I couldn't stomach anything Ava and Gray were going to pay for, even though I knew they'd be delighted to treat me after I'd successfully fulfilled my first assignment.

Seeing as I'd kept mum about my situation with my dad and my debt, they both bought into my migraines excuse. Watching them get drunk and talk about their weekend plans—all of them involving spending money—sent jealousy nibbling at the corners of my gut.

"I want Grayson to stop singing 50 Cent. Can you make that happen?" I took a small drink of my water.

"Unfortunately, no." Ava shook her head. "But I can tell you he's one drink away from passing out, so the singing will be over soon. Are you coming with us to The Met tomorrow? We're going to check out the Indonesian restaurant they wrote about in *Timeout* afterwards."

I wish I could, but I'm probably going to help my father crawl into the shower, then argue with service providers on the phone to try to get them to give me more time to pay.

"Got plans with my dad. Maybe next time."

Jesus had probably kept good on his word to keep God updated about all of my sins, because, of all the songs in the world, "Promiscuous" by Nelly Furtado and Timbaland blasted through the room. The place was bustling, and the scent of stale tap beer, deep-fried everything, and urban stench clung to our clothes.

Grayson was hiccupping and talking at the same time, and I tuned him out to people-watch, until he said, "Oops, Jude, *yorbassazarr.*"

"What?" I shouted over the music.

"Your. Boss. Is. Here!" He yelled into my ear. "And he is looking fifty shades of great."

Grayson, I'd discovered, had the tendency to be cheesier than a Taco Bell enchilada when he was drunk.

"Where?" Ava looked around.

"Three stools down."

I craned my neck, my face heating before I'd even spotted his broad back, still clad in the ink black textured wool YSL jacket he'd had on in the office. There was nothing saint-like about what *this* Laurent was doing, though. Even with his back to me, I could see the woman he was talking to clearly. She ran a pale-pink clawed finger down her neck, giggling like a schoolgirl, and purred at something he had said. Célian must have been in top form, because whatever came out of his mouth next caused her to have to right herself by clinging to his shoulders, she laughed so hard. They shared a quick, intimate hug, and I was a witch, burning at the stake from the inside, wanting to break free from whatever spell he'd put over me that made me feel so completely and unbelievably miserable.

Beautiful. She was beautiful, with hair a shade darker than his, sapphire-blue eyes, and a sunkissed tan. Célian obviously had a type, and it wasn't a dirty blond, hazel-eyed woman who dressed like a headmistress in a British movie from the fifties, except with Chucks. Purple today, by the way. *Dignity and pride.* But I had a feeling I was about to lose both.

"Earth to Jude?" Grayson slurred, elbowing me in the chest.

Ouch. I shot him a dirty look. "Yeah?"

"Is it just me, or does it look like he's flirting with another woman?"

"I don't care." I jutted my chin out.

"Yeah, we didn't think *you* would. But his fiancée might." Ava blinked, staring at me like I was a weirdo.

Which I was. Of course they'd meant Lily and not me. Suddenly, I felt very tired and very hungry—like the air was dense with misery, soaked with toxins. Every breath was lethal. I grabbed Gray's Bacardi and tossed it back in one gulp, then slammed it against the bar. "My headache is getting out of control. I'm going to the restroom to wash my face and pop some Advils. Be right back."

I wobbled my way on a path to the ladies room, which took me by Célian and the mystery brunette. Once I was close enough to them, I slowed my pace, hearing them speak in French. The words rolled off of their tongues, and my vindictive heart nearly burst into flames.

Here he was, pulling the same old trick he'd used on me while his fiancée was sitting at home, making plans, dreaming about their future. Fake or not, he was still in a relationship. Parading with women in bars was in bad taste.

Since I didn't actually need to pee, I settled for pacing in the bathroom, stewing in my own anger.

Did I need my job?

Yes.

Was I excited to be working in a newsroom?

More than anything else in the world.

I still hadn't told my college friends, but I knew they were going to go crazy when they heard the job I'd snagged at LBC. None of that mattered right now, though, and maybe it was the Bacardi I'd gulped on an empty stomach, but confronting him seemed like a terribly good idea.

Emphasis on the word terribly.

I darted out of the bathroom and pushed through the crowd. Once I got to Célian, I tapped his shoulder. He turned around in slow motion, his smug smile undeterred, even when he saw my face, charred with agony. The woman next to him shot me an interested look, but didn't say a word, cradling her glass of white wine.

"Humphry," he said.

"Laurent," I quipped, feeling bold. "Does she know?"

"Know what?" His lips broadened into an even wider grin, but that meant nothing. Célian was always nonchalant. A meteor could be speeding toward Earth at the speed of light, crashing and killing all of us in exactly two hours, and he still wouldn't skip the foreplay when he took this girl to his presidential suite for their sexcapade.

"Any of the following things, really. One—" I jerked my thumb up. "That it's your thing. You pretend to be a French tourist and take women to a hotel suite for the night, even though you're American, born and bred. Two—" I pointed my forefinger at him. "That you have a fiancée waiting back home, and three—"

I gave him the middle finger, narrowing my eyes as I tried to come up with something… There *was* a three. I was certain of it. Unfortunately, I'd forgotten what it was.

He stared at me expectedly, his smile threatening to slice his face in half. I never realized he was so devastatingly dashing and boyish. His smile felt like a deep, lazy kiss under a perfect sunset.

"Three doesn't matter right now," I amended. "Does she know those other things?"

He turned to his companion and stroked his chin, looking thoughtful. "Do you know all those things, cuz?"

Cuz?

She offered me her hand, and I shook it, my mouth agape. "Hi. I'm Emilie, Célian's cousin. I study fashion here in New York. First year. Célian is helping me… ah, what's the word?" she said in her ridiculously enchanting accent. "Settle in."

She squeezed his forearm, and I saw it in the way they looked at each other. *Family*. I began to look for a rock under which I could hide for the next decade.

I pretended to gravely consider this new information while stroking my chin. "Hmm, yes. Célian is definitely good at settling." *Someone shut me up. Anyone. Please. Bartender?*

I was ripping into his relationship, and playing Russian roulette with my job.

"You're too kind." He ran a seemingly friendly hand along the back of my arm, his rough palm sending waves of lust to my lower belly, dampening my panties. "Humphry, in contrast, excels at looting." His tongue moved across his upper teeth, like the bad wolf he was. "Practically stealing all the dirty headlines from our competitors."

I took a cautious step back. Why did I have to be so impulsive? Why had I assumed the role of his fiancée's keeper? I had a sick father to take care of at home. Luckily, Célian didn't look even half offended by my antics. I wondered if it was because I'd slayed the South Korean pop star assignment. His attitude toward people did seem to stem directly from their performance in his newsroom.

"I think I'm going to go." I swallowed.

"Good *thinking*. You should do it more often." He reached for his whiskey casually. "Enjoy your night, Chucks."

"You too, Mr.… Laurent. Boss. Sir."

I wish I hadn't been standing on my feet. Shoving one of them into my mouth seemed like a great way to put a lid on this conversation. I made my way back to Ava and Grayson. Luckily, they hadn't noticed the Célian debacle. They were too busy arguing about the merits of saffron lollipops as a weight-loss method. They were so engrossed in the subject, they didn't even notice when the bartender slid me a plate with a roast beef sandwich, a bottle of whiskey, and three glasses.

He leaned down. "From the gentleman three seats to your left. He said to tell you that you should *eat your meat*."

My heart cartwheeled, finishing its flip with an Olympic bow.

It's okay. I can't fall in love. Mom said so herself. What I'm feeling right now is a mixture of nausea, heartbreak from Milton, and guilt over what happened with an engaged man. The Bacardi certainly didn't help, either.

I didn't know if I should be mad, flattered, or crushed by his gesture. But I was starving, desperate for a drink, and dizzy from low blood sugar. I was also oddly relieved to know Célian was going home alone tonight. I didn't want to be a charity case. But Célian wasn't privy to how bad things were at my home. He had no way of knowing how dire the situation in my bank account was. My decision was made when the smell of pan-seared roast beef crept into my nostrils. I tore into it like a wild animal. Ava and Grayson stopped the chatter and stared at me.

"Did you just order a bottle of whiskey that's worth two hundred bucks?" Grayson slurred, launching into a fit of hysterical laughter. Ava was busy cracking it open and pouring each of us a generous glass.

"I…ah, I'm celebrating getting over my migraine," I mumbled around a hot piece of roast beef and the lettuce in my mouth. "Not the untimely death of a pop star."

"God bless Advil, right? And handsome bosses." Ava swiped her eyes along my chest, like she could see the thing inside of it stumbling all over the place, drunk as she was. The way her lips curved knowingly made me wonder if she *had* caught some of my exchange with Célian.

"I'm just glad the headache is gone." I filled my mouth with more food. Talking wasn't doing me much good at this point.

"Your boss is about to be gone next." She drank in my reaction, and I gave it to her, my curiosity getting the better of me. I tilted my head to the side, catching Célian helping Emilie into her jacket as they made their way to the door.

"Seems so." I picked a cherry tomato from my plate and popped it into my mouth. I sneaked one last glance at him, even though it was wrong. Even though he wasn't mine to look at.

Célian ushered his cousin into an Uber, kissed her forehead, and tapped the roof in goodbye. Then, as if my gaze was an invitation, as if he could feel it on his back, he turned around and stared directly at me from the bar's window. Our eyes locked, and everything stopped.

I'm not for the taking, my eyes said.

That's for me to decide, his hissed.

"You still want to tell us there's nothing going on between you and Bossman?" Grayson taunted from the periphery, his voice crawling into me, rattling something I was trying hard to keep dormant.

I opened my mouth, ready to defend myself, but the lie wouldn't come out.

Sundays were library days.

Days of echoed silence and old ink and yellow paper. Of munching on sweets and stealing glances at eager, young students, reading and writing away their future, one word at a time.

Today, Dad had practically pushed me out the door. He'd made some excuse about me getting some Vitamin D, but it wasn't even that sunny. Nonetheless, I figured he wanted time alone. The apartment *was* small. Besides, getting some me-time to think wasn't the worst idea I'd had. I also needed to read more about the Sudanese crisis. I'd felt a little unequipped and uninformed this week when we'd discussed it in one of our rundown meetings. Célian shot facts from his sleeve at a speed I could barely register. Not only did he have the general knowledge of Google, but he delivered it with the charisma and finesse of Winston Churchill. I'd wanted to curl up like a kitten under his desk at that moment and listen to him talk all day.

That sounded degrading, even in my head, but it didn't make it any less true. Hell, at night, when I turned off the light and looked out my window, I imagined myself sucking him off as he wrote the latest newscast. The man's mind was even sexier than his looks. He was an amazing sight to behold, in and out of the newsroom.

"It'll be a long time before you stop thinking about my cock every time you masturbate at the end of a long workday under your cheap covers."

God, I hated him.

And he was three-carat engaged.

I settled into a chair and chewed into a retro foam mix of sunny side ups and banana-shaped candy, flipping pages. Two hours passed before my head finally lifted from the magazine I was reading. I could have stayed like that forever, but a shadow had darkened the glossy pages. I snapped the magazine shut and stared back at a stranger's face.

"Hello." His smile was lopsided. Lazy, but kind.

"Uh…hello."

He looked familiar, yet somehow I knew I'd never met him before. If I had, I would remember. Tall. Attractive. With blond curls, deep-set blue eyes, and a tan that could only be the result of endless days in the sun. He looked to be a little older than me, maybe late twenties, and a whole lot sweet, with life-earned creases around his mouth and eyes. When he smiled, he did so with his entire face, and I found myself smiling, too.

"Sorry to interrupt, but…you snagged the last copy of *The Times*." His grin was dimpled, like I knew it would be.

I stuttered an apology and handed him the paper, which I'd already read. "Sorry."

"Never apologize unless it's warranted. Besides, we seem to be sharing the same interests." He glanced at my desk.

"Mine's work." I felt the need to explain, as if my usual hobbies consisted of being suspended in the air by nothing but nipple clamps and swimming with sharks.

"Mine too," he beamed. "Where is work?"

"LBC."

"The coincidences continue." He wiggled his brows.

Hey, Jesus? Did you send me someone to get over my obsession with Célian Laurent?

"Girl, I'm not even talking to you after the last few weeks."

"Really?" I cleared my throat, straightening in my seat.

I mean, he could be working for the website three floors up. But he seemed like the kind of guy who didn't have an office job. He took the seat in front of mine, leaning forward and thumbing through the magazine I'd just dropped. "Yup. Just got back from a stint in Syria yesterday. I'm catching up on things now. And, of course, eating my body weight in Katz's cheesesteak."

I laughed. "That good?"

"You never had it before?" His eyebrows shot to his forehead. "We'll need to rectify that as soon as possible, before you get your New Yorker card suspended."

"I'm Jude." I offered him my hand. He took it and kissed the inside of my palm—which was ten times more intimate than doing it the right way—and the butterflies I thought could only flutter for my boss stirred in my chest, stretching their wings, albeit lazily.

"Phoenix Townley."

"Just like James Townl—" I started, before pulling my head back to examine him thoroughly. So *that's* why he looked so familiar. His father was the anchor, or *Mr. Numbers* for the high ratings he scored every night. Now I was the one beaming, and it felt strange, but good. Like someone had unlocked a new setting for my face.

"I can see the resemblance. I like your dad a lot."

"Ditto. Well, most of the time." He reached for my candy bag without asking and bit a foam banana in half. "Another hour of fine reading and then a trip across town for that cheesesteak?"

It was scary, the way I accepted the invitation with little to no additional thought. Jude Humphry was a calculated girl. She'd been shaped and molded through the heartache of knowing how unpredictable life could be. I wasn't planning on dating anyone anytime soon, especially after the entire Milton fiasco. Part of me didn't even know if I should. If I wasn't going to fall in love, was there really a point in trying?

But Phoenix was nice, and he seemed to be easygoing and fun. He would make a good friend. And, not only was I single, but the man I pined after was engaged—full-blown about to marry someone else. Not to mention, he was into an open, uncommitted relationship, and I wanted more. I *needed* more. Maybe Phoenix Townley was exactly what the doctor ordered. Maybe he would rise from the ashes of my love life and defy my mother's curse.

We read together, then left the library with arms swinging. And even though it didn't feel like he could reach into my chest, grab my heart, and pull it from my body like a certain news director could, I still enjoyed my time with Phoenix.

"Can I ask you one question?" I stopped when we got to the deli.

He pretended to weigh that for a second. "Okay, go ahead."

"Why did you come back?"

He looked down and pulled up the long sleeve of his shirt, and a tattoo of a girl I didn't recognize smiled back at me from his inner forearm. "Time is too precious not to be spent with the people you love most. I learned that the hard way. Because of her."

Célian

Going into Chucks's apartment wasn't the most constructive thing to do, considering the little fixation I was developing.

I could smell her skin, the undertone of her vanilla scent, and her ginger-and-jasmine shampoo on every piece of furniture in her tiny apartment. The place screamed Judith. Her personality jumped out of every corner of the rooms.

I saw her in the cider-scented candles lined up neatly on the mantel like soldiers and in the framed pictures from her graduation—her hugging her father with a huge smile on her face and kissing someone I assumed was Milton, the brainless dick. She was in the curtains that were drawn open, inviting the sun to pour into the room, and in the small, organized stack of newspapers and books on the coffee table, as well as the ring stain of a mug beside them that told me her favorite pastime. And in the unlikely picture hanging above the TV, of a girl reaching up to a heart-shaped balloon, watching it drift skyward and away from her.

Snap out of it. She's a hot piece of ass. The world is not running out of pussies. You have a plan. Stick to it.

"Her mother bought that picture," her father told me. "It doesn't go with anything around the house, but neither of us has the guts to take it down."

He stopped by the picture, staring at it. I grimaced, knowing how it felt to keep everything while you waited for your dead loved one to miraculously reappear. Grief was pathetic. That's why I didn't let myself dwell on it.

"Don't know if your daughter is not brave enough to do anything," I said with disdain.

Her father considered that for a moment. "Perhaps *guts* was not the right word. Jude is just very good at remembering. And loving."

Robert Humphry was an impressive man.

Strong, silent, and polite—the no-bullshit type. I would be jealous of Judith if it wasn't totally fucked up. Her father was a standup guy, and I wondered what kind of person I would be if I'd had someone to look up to.

Rob knew his daughter better than I did, so he agreed that keeping our arrangement a secret was in everyone's best interest. Lying to her wasn't ideal, but we both knew that if Judith found out I was helping them by paying her father's way into an experimental treatment program for people with advanced cancer, she would throw a fit, accept the offer nonetheless, then let it eat at her conscience.

I'd had Dan find the experimental program, because I didn't want Brianna to know anything about Jude she hadn't volunteered herself. Since Robert wasn't doing incredibly bad for someone with stage three cancer, he was easily accepted into the trial—after a large donation to the clinic.

Getting help from me was going to mess with Jude's sense of integrity. She was fiercely independent, and I didn't want this gesture to have the aftertaste of quick fucks and sardonic office whips. Besides, it wasn't solely about Judith. I wasn't a heartless prick. Helping Robert was my way to atone for what had happened to Camille.

I'd taken a life, what was the harm in trying to save one?

Robert didn't ask me many things that weren't related to the treatment he would be provided. He didn't ask me, for instance, my motivations for helping his daughter in the first place. And so I spared him the story of our first meeting, in which an hour after I'd bought her drinks, my tongue was already rimming her crack while my fingers plunged into her pink, soaking wet pussy. I didn't normally eat ass, but hers was too sweet to pass. At any rate, I did not consider it a compliment worth mentioning to her ill father.

We arranged that a cab would pick him up twice a week for the treatment, all expenses paid by me. As far as Jude was concerned, this was an experiment he'd been offered by the insurance company they were now a client of through her employment at LBC, free of charge. It wasn't farfetched, and this way she wouldn't have to worry about paying me back or think I was expecting something in return.

This was not about getting my cock sucked, although, truth be told, based on the way she'd looked at me the evening I hung out with Emilie last week, it hardly seemed she'd mind paying in that dubious currency.

After we talked shop, Rob and I ended up chatting for another hour. It wasn't like I had a ton of things to do on a Sunday when I wasn't in Florida visiting Maman. It turned out we had a lot in common. We both thought Shake Shack was overrated, that the Rockefeller Christmas Tree should be illegal (or alternatively, that tourists should be illegal. But one or the other had to go for the sake of the city's citizens' sanity), and that the Yankees were the best thing to ever happen to our NYC.

On the subway, making my way back to Manhattan, I sorted through my inbox on my phone. An email popped in from my father, and everybody in the office was CCed.

It was a reminder for an invitation to a gala in the Laurent Towers Hotel next weekend. The original invitations had been sent weeks ago. Of all things, we were celebrating the #MeToo movement, raising money to be donated to several women's shelters across the country. LBC had put the spotlight on #MeToo, relentlessly chasing stories about sexual assault and gender discrimination since the movement had exploded. My father prided himself on taking a stand, while at the same time taking advantage of his position to coax women into his bed. The list of former and current employees he'd slept with was longer than *War and Peace*, and just as disturbing. His moving Judith to our floor was a blunt way of trying to get both into her dress and under my skin.

I'd blow his cover in a second if it wasn't for the fact that at this point, he was recovering from his fourth heart attack, newly divorced, and too tired to fight back. I liked my wars fair and didn't need another death on my conscience. I was waiting for him to quietly step down from his position so I could assume it and cut my ties with him permanently.

I RSVPed to the stupid event and bounced my foot, looking up for a distraction. The woman in front of me—late twenties, good looking in a corporate-wallflower, champagne-blond kind of way—smiled at me from behind her hardcover Oprah's Book Club novel. I didn't smile back. I wasn't looking for a hookup for hookup's sake. I wasn't a player—whatever the fuck that meant—and, unlike some, I didn't treat fucking as a national sport.

My one-night stand with Judith had been one of a handful. I usually spaced them out to every other month or so—just enough to keep my sexual appetite and libido sated without having to worry about my dick falling off from an unknown disease. At any rate, I'd fucked Jude not too long ago, and would be going for round two soon, if it was up to me.

The woman tucked her book into her bag, got up from her seat, and walked toward the doors, waiting for them to open. She shot me another look, this time wistful.

"Taken?" she mouthed.

I nodded.

"All the good ones are." She stepped outside.

I should have thought about Lily when I confirmed my status. She did, after all, walk around with a ring that cost considerably more than Judith's apartment—a family heirloom that should have been given to Camille.

But all I could think of was the girl who'd yelled at me last week at the bar, then sought me out with her green-brown eyes and wouldn't let go of my goddamn thoughts, long after I got back to my apartment.

And into my shower, where I'd fisted my cock and imagined her smart mouth wrapped around it as I came all over my dirty blond tiles.

The hashtags #CharityGala and #MeToo stared back at me from the cream banner as I entered the event, celebrated on the massive rooftop terrace of the Laurent Towers Hotel. Sleek pink and peach carpets, roses spilling from sculptures like rivers, and long tables covered in velvet black tablecloths—no matter how much money my father was going to raise here, it wouldn't cover half of what this evening had cost.

I wore a tux and a scowl, Lily trailing alongside me in her gold chiffon dress that managed to have too much fabric yet still expose the better half of her tits. Not that I cared. I knew Lily was screwing around, too. I wasn't a hypocrite, and I was about as possessive of her as I was of the piece of human turd I'd nearly stepped on as I walked into work yesterday morning, exiting the train. I didn't want to bring her, but even I recognized that we needed to show some kind of united front. Plus, it was a good opportunity for me to check in on her family, most of whom I actually liked quite a bit.

"Your parents okay?" Our arms were locked together, but I stared straight ahead.

"They miss you." She couldn't even answer a simple yes-or-no question.

"Your sisters?" I ignored her pleading tone. I missed them, too. But spending time with them like nothing had happened was impossible.

"Yes, Scarlett and Grace are doing all right."

"And Madelyn?" There was a lot of estrogen in her family. Her father was surrounded by three daughters, a mother, and a wife.

"My grandmother is peachy. She really wants you to visit her. Said she'll even make your favorite pie."

"I might," I rasped, meaning it. Madelyn Davis was a fucking rock star.

The minute Lily and I entered the room, I began to search for Judith with my eyes like a thirteen year old who's just discovered his cock. It wasn't intentional, but primal nonetheless. I wanted to see what she was wearing, how she'd done her makeup, and who she was with. My educated guess was Gary and Ava. She seemed to be spending a lot of time with them, even though she'd formed strong relationships with Kate, Jessica, and Brianna, too.

Lily did the annoying thing she tended to do on the rare occasions we were out in public, and tugged at my sleeve to make sure I was no more than three inches away from her. We were exchanging pleasantries with a bunch of regular guests on the show—a prosecutor, two judges, and a former producer of a competing network. My father ambled toward us, armed with a date who looked fresh out of high school, his laughter sending uncomfortable chills down my spine. She wore an Oscar De La Renta number and beamed like he'd just picked the stars from the skies and rested them in her palm.

"Célian, Lily, such a handsome *couple*." He tapped my back in a fatherly way and proceeded to hug Lily and kiss both her cheeks. She winced in his arms, struggling for a steady breath, and took a step back.

"Mr. Laurent."

"Please, call me Matt," he chuckled, spraying his fake-ass smile around everyone like a skunk's fart.

"Yes. After all, you do know him rather well." I glanced at my Rolex, then resumed my efforts searching for Jude. I was sure Lily noticed, but couldn't find it in me to care. Her throat bobbed, and she turned crimson next to me.

"This is Chardonnay." Dad introduced us to his date.

I smiled coldly. "Hello. How's spring break treating you, Chardonnay?"

"Célian!" Lily and Mathias scowled in unison.

"I'm sorry, that was impolite of me. Spring break is over, right? Finals are probably killing you. Let me guess, you're in cheer? Love Harry Styles? Think *13 Reasons Why* is an adaptation of the bible?"

There was more sulking and complaining, but everything muted into the background the minute I spotted her among the sea of puffy black and white dresses and big hairdos. Wearing a knee-length, powder blue dress and that inconspicuous expression that seemed to speak the secret language of my dick, she looked like Cinderella after a good fuck, her butterscotch hair twisted up with stray locks ribboning down her neck and cheeks.

My mouth had curved with a satisfied smirk at how beautiful and elegant she looked, yet so unassuming, her beauty humble and clean, when my eyes traveled to the person she was talking to.

Phoenix Townley.

I knew he was back in the States. His time in Syria and Israel had made him tanner, seemingly taller, and more lean and muscular. He carried himself with even more confidence than before. He said he'd come back to spend some time with his family, but as far as I was concerned, it was a great excuse for him to take a part-time job at LBC and spend the rest of the time reminding me I had a hole in my heart the size of his fist. Phoenix wore a blue tux (douchebag), and whatever he said to Judith, she found funny, because she shoved his chest playfully, as if he was misbehaving.

Lily was telling me something in the background, but unless it was warning me that the place was on fire, I couldn't have cared less. I knew I had no right to barge into Jude and Phoenix's conversation and make a scene. To show up with my fiancée in tow and claim someone else's time would be an especially douchey move, even by my very low standards.

"Champagne?" One of the servers slid a tray in our direction. Lily took two and handed me one, gluing her side-tit to my arm.

"I think they make a good couple." She followed my line of vision.

I ignored her, throwing back the champagne like a shot, and walked over to Kate, disposing of the glass on a table on my way. Lily followed me, like a hot-piss stench at Times Square station. Kate, who had her back to me, turned around with a smile. I hugged her and her wife, Delilah. Kate's rubicund hair was spiky, and her dress seemed extra black, somehow. She offered Lily a frosty look, which the latter didn't even bother to return.

"Me Too, huh?" She rolled her eyes.

Kate was by far one of the most outspoken feminists I knew. This entire evening was a big fuck-you from my father to everyone around him.

I crooked an eyebrow. "I don't make the rules. I just follow them. For now."

We'd spent ten minutes talking about work, with Lily clinging to my arm like the floor would otherwise swallow her whole, when Kate puffed on a celery stick and said, "And where's Mathias, Célian?"

"Why would I care where my fa—" I started, my eyes already darting to the spot where they'd last seen Jude, and found him talking to her, his hand on her lower back.

On.

Her.

Fucking.

Back.

You've been warned, Papa. And you have failed.

A heavy rock churned inside my stomach. My fists curled beside my body while I sliced through the crowd, galloping toward them without even distinguishing what was going on around me. I wasn't thinking straight, and I was about to yank him away from her by the back of his collar and plant a fist in his face.

The only thing that stopped me as I got there was realizing that was exactly what he wanted—me losing control over a woman who wasn't Lily in order to create a scene. So I joined them, my smile oh-so-polite as I grabbed the cigar my father was puffing all over her face and nonchalantly dropped it into a half-full glass of champagne.

"Mind if I butt in?"

"I do, actually," Mathias said, his eyes raking over Lily, who finally stood a few feet away, knowing better than to join us. She stayed the hell away from my father whenever possible after what happened. She knew acknowledging his existence was playing with the kind of fire that could burn down forests and incinerate our prestigious engagement.

"Well, life's tough. Better get used to it. How are you doing tonight, Humphry?"

"Great." She gave me a panicky, what-the-hell-are-you-doing look, cradling her champagne.

Mathias stared at me like he was about to do something he was going to regret, so I entered his personal space with two fluid steps, whispering in his ear, "I could blow up your entire party by telling them you shoved your cock in my fiancée's mouth while she was in a very compromising position, filling in as your temporary secretary because you had to fire your old one, who'd fucked you long enough to expect more than the average New York salary. But I won't have to do that tonight, will I, Father? You will step back and get the hell away from Judith Humphry like I asked you to. Because the next time I have to remind you to stay away, I won't be nice, and *she* won't be annoyed. She'll be scared. For *your* life."

I took a step back and watched the color drain from his face. For a second, I thought he was going to have another heart attack. Then he tipped his head goodbye to Judith and scurried away, looking like a ghost of himself. We both watched him join his date. I knew that if I took my time, Lily would approach us, now that Mathias was gone.

"He's trying to hit on you," I told Jude, too pissed to look her in the eye without snapping further.

"That's his business, not yours," she said evenly, placing her delicate glass of champagne on a table behind her. The spring air was crisp and chilly, and her whole body blossomed into goosebumps under that dress.

"Stop playing nice with him."

"No, *you* stop butting into my relationships with other people, Célian. You have no right."

I suppose it wasn't a good time to tell her that Phoenix Townley—who'd wandered out on the terrace mere minutes ago, probably to snort a line—was a douchebag who got sent away to the Middle East after he was caught shooting heroin with a crackwhore in his Chelsea apartment.

The last and only other time we'd been in this hotel together, Chucks and I were on much friendlier terms. Frankly, I was fed up with this entire bullshit situation where all we did was fight. We were on the same page. Both our lives were hot messes. And we could make each other forget. I brushed my arm against her shoulder while we people-watched the fancy guests, our colleagues laughing, dancing, and drinking away their long working week.

"Inappropriate physical contact? *Me too*," she taunted, but the smile on her lips was pure mischief.

"Miss Humphry, please utter the entire sentence—*I do not want you to touch me*, so I'll really have an incentive not to do the things I want to do to you."

She said nothing, fingering the thin gold necklace resting against her clavicles.

Then she whispered, "Touch me how?"

Can't stop this, huh? Neither can I.

I smirked. "You're not very good at following directions, are you? I refuse to land my ass in hot water, even for a good lay."

"Hot water with your company or with your date?" she snapped.

"My date is fake, but my commitment to my network is real."

She considered it, chewing on her lip. "It won't get you in trouble."

"That won't hold up in court. Say it explicitly. Use your words. I. Want. It."

"I don't know what *it* means."

I shook my head, taking a side-step away from her.

She weighed the situation, still playing with her necklace. I caught a glimpse of Kate talking to Lily, and knew she would never initiate a conversation with Lily in a million years. She'd done it for me.

A forty-six-year-old lesbian who thought white, upper-class men were Satan was my wingman. I think I wanted that on my fucking tombstone.

Jude swallowed. "I want you to do *it* to me…no matter what it means. So, what do you want to do to me?"

"Well, Humphry, I really want to finger your ass," I said conversationally, smiling to a colleague when he saluted my way and nodding at him courteously as I smoothed my ironed dress shirt. "While eating your pussy until every drop of your cum is on my tongue."

I could see her throat bobbing in my peripheral vision, and damn if it didn't make my cock twitch. I needed to get out of here before it became very apparent that I was talking dirty to my employee, while sporting a hard-on that could very well tear through my briefs and tux, and at this rate, perhaps even bend solid steel.

"You have a fiancée," she murmured.

"A *fake* fiancée. Don't pretend you don't know that. Our relationship is a joke, and we only half-bother to hide it."

Jude and I were still pretending to talk shop casually when I slipped my hand back to touch hers on the table she had braced herself against. The tip of my little finger curled against hers. I'd forgotten how good she felt, and that infuriated me, because not many things felt good these days.

"I don't know," she said.

"What do you want me to do? Kiss you in front of all these people? I will. Granted, we'll both get in trouble, but I will."

"You wouldn't…"

I spun around toward her and pressed a hand against the small of her back, drawing her close. She nearly jumped out of her skin.

"Don't," she said, her voice pitching high.

I shoved my hand into my pocket, producing one of two cards I always had on me when I was in the Laurent Towers Hotel.

"Fifteenth floor," I said. "Swipe it on the elevator screen or the door won't open. Ten minutes. We don't need to be here when my father talks about workplace fraternization."

I slipped into the crowd and disappeared before Lily could find me.

And before I lost my mind.

Jude

For all the disdain I tried to muster toward Célian, I couldn't stop my legs from carrying me down to the fifteenth floor.

Overeager, reckless, and in serious need of intervention. That's what I was.

Besides, he said ten minutes. I'd darted straight to the elevator, not even giving it a second thought. Phoenix—who'd given me a ride to the gala but cut his stay short because he was a recovering alcoholic and didn't like to be around booze—was nice, but he didn't make my heart clench and stutter like a lovesick puppy. He was funny and charming, but everything about us felt casual and overfamiliar. His voice felt like feathers on my skin. When Célian talked, it was like he squeezed the back of my neck, like a predator. And as much as I hated that Célian was staking his claim on me, Mathias was, indeed, a level of creepy more fitting behind bars than behind a network president's desk.

He'd commented about how pretty I looked tonight, which was fine, but then proceeded to tell me about the champagne suite of the hotel, which was not fine. Of course I'd refrained from letting him know his son had already shown me around it, managing to defile me in six different spots inside said suite.

The fifteenth level was a private floor. In the elevator index, it was described as the Art Room. When I got to the floor, I swiped the card against the digital screen and watched a green light blink back at me. The door slid open. I stepped out into the room, my heels hitting the marble floor. The breath knocked out of my chest.

The vast, open room was full of replicas of famous sculptures—life-sized models of *The Thinker* by Auguste Rodin, *The Discus Thrower* and *Venus De Milo* by Alexander Antioch, and the Elgin Marbles. Then, in the center, Michelangelo's *David* stood staring at me, imperial and almost patronizing, a towering more than six feet of sheer maleness—much smaller than the original, but just as striking.

My legs shook at the mesmerizing beauty and violence dripping from the sculptures. One thing they all had in common—they were stark naked, unapologetically erotic. The room had no chairs. No couches. Nowhere to do anything other than stand and admire the beauty in front of you. I briefly wondered whose idea this room was, but I didn't have to think about it. Not really. I already knew.

The man who was as beautiful as a painting, as ruthless as art, as hard as marble.

I sauntered across the room, my hand brushing over the broad, carved chests and mouths slacking open in pleasure. The room smelled clean, cold, and of chipped stone. It was dimly lit, and mostly dark blue.

I thought about Dad, about the experimental treatment our new insurance company had offered him this week, about the hope in his eyes when he'd broken the news to me and the faith in my heart, its seed blooming into something I was afraid was going to grow beyond my control. Everything was moving too fast and yet not fast enough since I'd joined LBC.

"I'm scared." I crouched down and stared at a marble woman sitting in a bath, fingering herself. She wouldn't spill my secret in anyone's ears. She would listen. Maybe she would even understand. Her face was defiant. Fearless. She wasn't ashamed of what she was doing.

"My life is in shambles, and my father is dying. All the things I want seem unachievable, so far away. Is your heart lonely too?" I whispered, caressing her cheek.

I can't fall in love. This is lust and confusion. This is what happens when you're about to lose a parent and gain a dubious lover.

I'd come to this room to be with Célian, but Célian wasn't mine to be with. If I told the Jude of three months ago what I was about to do, she would punch me in the tit, because an engagement was an engagement. The word's definition meant he was committed to someone else.

Then I remembered the way he'd looked at her up at the gala, like she'd killed his dreams.

And the way she'd clung to him, like she knew and didn't care.

"Yes," a dark, masculine voice whispered behind me, and I twisted around to take him in. Célian stood at the elevator's door, a shoulder leaning against the frame, playing with the electronic card between his fingers. "That's why we do what we do. Why we can't stop this."

He took confident steps into the room, each of them making my heart swell a little more, until there was a monster in my chest, hungry for his touch. The look on his face alone engorged my clit. I squeezed my thighs together, my underwear damp between them.

"Whose idea was this room?"

"Mine."

"Why?"

"Because I like beautiful, lifeless things." His finger hovered over my face, making minimal contact with a lock of my hair and moving it behind my ear. "They can't talk back. They can't screw you over. They can't fuck your future."

"Is this where you take all your one-night stands?"

His slight smirk made my chest hurt.

"If you were a *one*-night stand, you wouldn't be *standing* here. And no, I don't make a habit of fucking women against these replicas.

They're worth over 300k apiece, and hard to come by. Pick a favorite," he ordered—not asked—gesturing to the vast room.

I resumed my stroll among the marble statues, feeling his eyes burning a hole in my back, seeing through my dress and skin and bones, devouring me from the inside. I studied every sculpture carefully, like there was a wrong and right answer, before finally gesturing at *David*.

I turned around to face Célian.

He *tsked*, running his callused fingers over his jawline. "You can do better."

"What's more beautiful than Michelangelo's *David*?" I challenged.

"Not many things. Which makes it very cliché. The first nude statue made in the Renaissance and the one sculpture every eejit knows. The Beatles aren't your favorite band, right, *Jude*?"

"No," I scoffed. "Too mainstream. Actually…" I licked my lips, snorting out a laugh. It was a ridiculous thing to say, but I didn't mind showing Célian my weirdness. For all the bad things he was, he never judged me. "I always thought David's penis was disproportionately small. And, um…soft."

Yep. That just came out of my mouth.

"The original one is attached to a seventeen-foot-tall sculpture. Pretty sure you still couldn't fit it in your smart mouth. Think harder, Humphry."

I resumed my walk around the room. He was right. I needed to push myself harder, to pay attention and not just go with the flow. Wasn't that what a good newsperson did? I stopped at a statue of a man sitting on a throne made of a beast standing on all fours. He was naked, sheathed by a toga over his privates, staring up to the sky. He looked like a gladiator, wounded and taut and muscled. I didn't know this piece, but it spoke to me.

He was obviously in pain, yet his face was fierce with defiance.

He was completely unknown to me, yet his battle so familiar.

"*The Warrior*." Célian spoke into my ear, and I shuddered with pleasure. I felt his body close to mine, yet he didn't touch me. "By an anonymous artist. Special shipment from Italy. A spur of the moment purchase, but I liked the pain in his eyes. So very intimate, don't you think?"

Of course I did. Happiness was something you were eager to share. It was pain you wanted to keep private.

"Why did I have to choose?" I asked, still staring at the statue.

"There's a camera in the right-hand corner of this room, just behind my back. I could take you to the presidential suite and fuck you to oblivion and back, but I'd much rather do it somewhere I can send the message home to Mathias."

"And the message is?" I turned around to face him.

"That you're *mine*."

"Yours I am not." That was a lie I wished I could believe, about a man I wished I could forget. My body responded to him in a way I'd never experienced before.

I belonged to him, and he belonged to someone else. What did that make me?

The circumstances were pure semantics. Sins wrapped in sugar so I could swallow them more easily.

Célian cupped my cheek. "Yes," he whispered. "You are. You're so far gone you can't even see me sharing a drink with my cousin without losing your shit."

"You're someone else's," I said.

He shook his head. "No one's."

"And Lily…?"

"Haven't touched her in over a year."

His words cut the rope of anxiety wrapped around my throat, and I felt like I could breathe again.

"Not going to, either. I have no plans of fucking anyone but you, but I would stay away from Lily even if she was the last proud owner of a pussy on planet Earth. I don't do cheaters, and she is one."

"Oh?"

"With my father." He paused, studying my reaction, and I tried hard not to throw up in my mouth. "Shortly after…" His jaw snapped shut as if he was swallowing down nausea himself. "Never mind. Point is, this is not for you to worry about. She knows it, too," he explained, his calm and poise returning.

I licked my lips, staring at his. A few months ago, the girl who'd been with Milton would have told him she wanted everything. That she *deserved* it, too, and screw the empire he was trying to build on lies and revenge. But right now, standing in front of him, trying to make it in this cruel, real world, chase debt, and look after my father, something was better than nothing—especially something that came from him.

We were both drowning, and when we were together, and it felt like I was coming up for air.

"And she knows you're not faithful?" I stressed.

"There's nothing to be faithful to. It's not a relationship. We live apart. We sleep apart. We live our lives—apart."

"I'm not an exhibitionist." My eyes traveled to the red-dotted camera above our heads.

He advanced toward me, cupping my cheek and brushing his lips against mine erotically. My stomach twisted and dropped, like I was falling.

"Neither am I." He pulled my lower lip between his straight teeth, tugging hard before releasing it slowly, prolonging the sweet, delicious pain. "But I'm willing to make an exception to make sure the message hits home. Wrap your arms around *The Warrior*'s neck."

I blinked at him, disoriented, but did as I was told, first lowering myself to sit on *The Warrior*'s lap. I felt the statue's stone chest behind me as I carefully clasped my arms around his neck. From this position, it looked like he was gazing down at my rack.

Célian lowered himself to his knees and drank my little moan of excitement hungrily with another kiss, this time tonguing my mouth, fighting his way through the walls of it, and claiming every growl and moan that sat there dormant, waiting for him to unleash it.

"I'm going to wreck you," he hissed, shoving his palm into my sweetheart neckline and cupping one of my tits. He took the nipple out and sucked it savagely before moving away and blowing cold air on it. I arched against *The Warrior*, feeling his cold marble toga digging into my butt. It was hotter than sin, but Jesus, it was weird.

Jesus:...

Célian's hand found the zipper behind my back and began to roll it down, his eyes hard on mine. I whimpered at how commanding he looked when he did that. Because my dress was strapless, the minute I arched my back it slid down and pooled at my feet like a pale winter lake, with little to no effort from him.

I was completely naked, save for my soaked white cotton panties and my Chucks. He lowered himself to my nipples and began kissing and biting them, keeping me sandwiched between him and the statue and drinking his attention thirstily. Every time I tried to touch him, he plastered my hands back to the statue. I was put on a pedestal, to be seen and admired by his father.

To be devoured by Célian.

Only him.

Only ever him.

I tried to rub myself against him, but that resulted in him moving away. He continued to tongue me, all the way down to my stomach, screwing his tongue into my navel and groaning, his nose paving its way down to my panties. He used his teeth to lower my underwear to my knees and stared at me for a few seconds, burying his nose in my slit and taking a lungful of air, breathing it in.

I nearly burst out of my skin, every nerve in my body dancing to the rhythm of his heartbeat.

"This pussy is mine no less than it is yours." He kissed the slit, flicking his tongue over it and teasing my clit. "Spread them wide, Chucks."

Chucks.

I didn't have to be asked twice. I threw one leg over each of the statue's thighs, spreading myself so wide my inner thighs burned. Célian licked me crack to slit before plunging deeper. Every once in a while, he brushed his thumb or forefinger against my leaking center and pressed it between my butt cheeks, wetting the area. I'd never done so with anyone else, but there was something about Célian that made me want to be a little submissive. In the newsroom, we were at war, but in private, our main battle was trying to keep our clothes on.

He teased my backside with his fingers, playing, poking, *flirting* while eating me out, and I exploded from within like fireworks, moaning his name so loud my ears rang. I let go of *The Warrior*'s neck, sliding down to the floor, my thighs still shaking from the climax ripping through me. Célian straddled me at the sculpture's feet, still fully clothed, and unzipped his dress pants.

"I'll ask again," he growled. "Are you on the pill?"

"I am," I whimpered, clawing at his suit as an excuse to touch him and opening my legs as far as I could with him pinning me to the floor.

"Good, because I want to fuck your pussy and then come inside your mouth. And this time, you won't be swallowing it. You'll be tasting and enjoying every second of it until I've had enough. Understood?"

I nodded. His first bareback thrust into me made my eyes roll in their sockets. He was so hard, his cock so velvety and hot, I thought I was going to die from the intense pleasure. I dripped against his cock and on the granite floor, and the more I moaned, the more intense his movements became. Rougher. Deeper. Faster. Like he was punishing me for wanting to screw me so badly.

I think we were both alarmed by the strength of our attraction to one another. I wanted to keep my job at all costs, and he didn't need the complication of anyone finding out, not to mention tying himself to an affair while he was engaged.

Was that what we had now? An affair? I knew if I started labeling it, I would fall off the orgasmic cloud I was riding.

He throbbed inside me, hitting my G-spot again and again and again, his hand snaking toward my ass and now fully toying with it. In. Out. In. Out.

"Breaking you in slowly for next time." He kissed the side of my face, almost romantically, and I nearly laughed.

"How do you know I haven't done that before?"

He somehow managed to throw me a patronizing look, even mid-sex, thrusting into me so punishingly now that I grazed his butt with my fingernails, tears of pleasure pooling in the corners of my eyes.

A few more plunges, and the orgasm climbed up from my toes to the rest of my body like an earthquake. I screamed, this time enjoying a slow, sensational feeling of warm honey coating my entire body as the climax washed through me.

"Close," he panted, picking up his speed. A minute later, he pulled out of me and shoved his dick into my mouth, making me taste myself in a way I never had before. I was sweet and musky—not bad...but too familiar. His warm, thick cum came in spurts inside my mouth, and my eyes fluttered shut with pleasure again.

"Taste me this time," he ordered. I did. I let his cum sit on my tongue, tasting its earthy, salty tang. I smiled, my mouth full of him. He smiled back, and he was so heartbreakingly beautiful, for a short moment, it occurred to me I might never recover from this guy, no matter what my mom had told me.

"Now swallow."

I did.

"Open your mouth," he ordered.

I did that, too, feeling oddly comfortable with being bossed around.

"Atta girl."

We put our clothes on silently. A part of me was still delirious at what we'd done together, and another part wanted to throttle myself for letting him do this to me when he had a fiancée upstairs. And... *the tape*. God. Had I actually allowed him to record everything? How stupid was I?

Very stupid when it came to his penis, apparently.

"Célian?" I asked as I retied my Chucks. Swan white this time.

He turned around and pinned me with his gaze.

"No one can know about this." I pointed at the camera.

He nodded. "We'll go down to the second floor and destroy it so you can sleep tonight."

Confusion must have colored my face, because he pressed his knuckles to his lips, stifling one of the dazzling smiles he refused to share with the world.

"You're not usually agreeable," I noted as we walked toward the elevator, our steps and voices echoing around the mostly empty room.

"Neither are you. That's why I wanted to see how far you'd go for this. Turns out…" He grabbed my waist and yanked me under the crook of his arm. "You'd go pretty far to be fucked by me. I *will* tell my father that if he messes with you again, he is in for hell on Earth. But I would never let anyone see your tits and cunt."

"This is going to end badly," I murmured, not even sure if he could hear me.

We slid into the elevator, and he pushed the second floor button, smirking. "But we will have one hell of a ride."

Célian

I'd never believed in miracles.

My experience with life had been that it was pragmatic, uncontrollable, and unpredictable—with a royal introduction to all three when I'd caught my father with our maid's mouth wrapped around his dick when I was only five years old.

He'd told me they were playing, and I'd believed him. Moreover, it looked like a pretty fun game, too—I *loved* touching my penis, loved being tickled, and combining the two seemed like the kind of idea to land you a Nobel Prize—so of course I ran it by Maman. Needless to say, Maman was not impressed with the way my father conducted his spontaneous playdates with the help.

The maid was fired, my parents had a huge fight, and from that point forward, I can't remember a time when we were a happy family.

Or just happy.

Or just a family.

For all the shit both of them had been through together, for all the affairs and infidelities and fighting through lawyers and stooping so low they made me wonder just how bad, exactly, humans could be, they hadn't gotten a divorce until last year.

My father, however, had never loved me. His disdain was fundamentally present in the way he looked at me, the way he sneered, and the way he deliberately avoided anything I liked or that mattered to me. He thought, in some fucked-up way, that I was responsible for the slow and unstoppable breakdown of his marriage. Which only went to show how little responsibility he took when it came to his problems.

That's why I had very little faith in this thing called life. If something went right, it was probably because it was taking a turn on its way to go seriously wrong. Give it time, and it would happen. Life was about putting out fires, or, if you worked in a newsroom, about starting them.

Which worked well for me. My personal experience with people was lackluster. So I didn't mind screwing them over if they did something bad that deserved to be publicly discussed.

Anyway, like I said, I'd never believed in miracles, and that's why I knew there was a reason Lily had left the gala before Jude and I got back to the terrace. Unfortunately for all parties involved, I didn't have it in me to care enough to check. Lily was part of my plan, sure, but my plan was already in motion. I would deal with her little tantrum later, remind her about my parents' chateau in Nice—the one she wanted to renovate and live in during the summers so badly. I'd buy her another ticket to the Maldives to vacation with her friends, soothe her the way she was used to being soothed—with pretty shiny things and negative attention.

"Oh my God! Célian!"

After all, not long ago I'd caught my fiancée on all fours, taking my father's cock in her mouth in his office while he caressed her bare, fake-tanned ass—much like the maid had all those years ago.

It hadn't been coincidental, and I knew it. My father was a sick prick, and he'd figured I remembered the day he'd buried his family six feet under—not only by cheating on my mother, but also by deciding it was my fault for ratting him out. He made me feel like I was fundamentally defective. So I became what he treated me as: a world-class jerk.

"*Why would I not be here? I work here.*" I'd clucked my tongue, ignoring the entire scene playing before me with pure nonchalance, like my father had been sitting at his desk and Lily was typing away on her desktop as a part of that bullshit internship she'd wanted to take for half a second to impress me and prove she was worthy of inheriting Newsflash Corp.

I'd walked into his office with purpose—he'd invited me there, so he knew I'd catch him—and of course, I couldn't give him the pleasure of seeing me hurt, so I poured myself a glass of scotch. I took a seat across the room on a brown leather settee and sipped quietly, watching the view from his window.

Lily had finally had the audacity to tuck her shirt into her skirt, roll the latter down her bare thighs and wipe her lips, running like a headless chicken across the room. She'd reached out, about to throw herself at me.

"*Get anywhere near me and your life, reputation, and social circle, as you know them, will cease to exist.*" I'd sipped my drink, crossing my legs.

She'd halted in place, collapsing onto the carpeted floor. My father had chuckled, taking his time to zip himself up. I remembered thinking no son should see his father's penis at that age, unless it was because he needed to give him a bath because he was too sick to do it himself.

"*Son,*" he'd finally greeted.

I'd smiled, thinking, *Not anymore. And maybe not ever.*

"*Cela aurait dû être toi sous ce bus et non ta soeur*" he'd said. *It should have been you under that bus, not your sister.* But his tone had been kind, apologetic—like he'd been pleading Lily's case. Bastard.

I'd answered him in French. "*You know, Papa, I wish that too, every single day. And I know why you do. Because the minute I get the chance, I'll ruin you. Completely.*"

After Jude and I reached the second floor and destroyed the video, we went back to the terrace shared another drink with our colleagues, blissfully ignoring each other—another thing about her that made my dick happy. She wasn't clingy or needy or even particularly interested in claiming me or my attention. She did her own thing. Like me, she simply had needs that needed to be met. Call me a saint, but I was happy to take one (or six) for the team.

When it was time to go home, most people shared an Uber, others opted to walk, and many just cabbed it and saved the receipts for expense purposes. I didn't want Jude to take the subway back home this late, but I didn't want to offer her a ride, either. It wasn't worth the aftermath of endless gossip and possible false assumptions on her end. I barely looked my staff in the face, let alone offered them a ride. This led me to resort to asking a rather pathetic favor of Kate, who, for an unknown reason, had decided to get here in a car.

"First things first, thanks for the pussy breath." She took a pull of her beer and a step away from me.

"Figured you'd appreciate it," I deadpanned, unblinking. "You need to give Judith a ride."

"We live in NoHo. She lives in Brooklyn," she stated matter-of-factly, as if logic had any place in my decision.

I couldn't care less if she lived on the moon, and the way I unclasped her fingers from her drink, downed it, and discarded it in the trash communicated that perfectly to her. Kate shook her head, poking my chest. "Fine. But you should really dump the lollipop in a wig."

"The lollipop in a wig has a pedigree and a ten-percent share of my company."

Besides, Lily was hardly a factor. Even if I were officially single, I still wouldn't openly court an employee. Not that I wanted to court Judith.

"Funny, I didn't peg you for a man who'd allow someone to have him by the balls."

"I wouldn't allow Lily to suck them, let alone hold them," I quipped. "My tolerating her is strictly business."

"Then you're a very bad businessman, because she has leverage over you."

Shooing Kate away with a wave, I got back to entertaining my investors and colleagues, but not before ordering her to never mention her favor for me to Jude. The feisty little *fou* didn't do weakness or vulnerability, which made breaking her in bed so much more fun.

A few minutes later I watched them make their way to the exit and tossed my head back, knocking down another drink. I realized I hadn't thought of Camille the entire evening.

A sharp pain sliced through my gut, and I let it bleed agony, because I deserved it.

Because I was a bastard, and everyone knew it.

Camille.

Maman.

Mathias.

Lily.

Jude.

Kate.

And anyone who'd ever worked with me.

The Warrior knew that, our juices still smeared on his gladiator boot.

Even the silent walls of the art room knew, and the security tape we'd stomped on and hidden in the bottom of the security room's trash.

Chapter Nine

Jude

I was bouncing on the balls of my feet, staring at Célian's locked office door.

Happiness tasted weird in my mouth—not unpleasant, but surprising all the same. I was so used to worrying, I'd forgotten how it felt to simply *be*. But this morning had started off with Dad dashing out to his experimental treatment, grabbing the bag with the lunch and snacks I'd made for him ("Forever the worrier, just like your mom," he'd said as he kissed the crown of my head.) on his way to the cab waiting for him downstairs. I'd asked him a thousand times if he was sure they paid for the transportation, and he'd said yes.

It made no sense, but I let it slide. It had filled my heart with hope, even before I got the text message from Phoenix.

My new straight, male BFF said he couldn't follow up on the lead he'd mentioned to me because he was having a father-son retreat with his dad. I thought it must be weird to have James Townley as your dad, but that was all Phoenix knew. He left me the details he'd received and asked me to go for it and let him know how it went.

Célian arrived at his office at nine o'clock sharp, wearing a navy two-piece wool suit and the usual get-the-fuck-out-of-my-face expression. I had started to get used to his air. Dare I say, it made my lady parts tingle and fist-bump one another.

I squeaked internally when he arrived. He pushed a hand into his pocket and produced his key, unlocking his door.

"Can I help you?" he asked dryly.

"I've been waiting for you." I clapped my hands together.

The first rundown meeting for the show was usually at ten o'clock. I couldn't wait an entire hour to tell him about the lead I'd just confirmed on the phone, and Kate and Jessica were still out of the office.

He pushed his door open, his face blank. I followed him in, plopping on the seat in front of him. I opened Kipling, my notebook.

"I can't fuck you here," he said, tossing his phone on his desk and taking off his blazer.

My head snapped up and my mouth slacked.

He threw two mint gums into his mouth and took a sip of his coffee, going through his morning routine. "But if you want to get dicked tonight, you can come over after work. *Separately*, of course."

I nodded, pretending to consider it. I did want to have sex with Célian again. We were as good in the bedroom as we were bad for each other out of it. But for him to assume that's the reason I was there was downright ridiculous.

"Tell you what—I'll tell you why I'm really here, you'll apologize for being an ass, and we can both move on with our lives. Deal?"

He sat down. "Okay, little grasshopper, let's see what you've got."

I rolled my eyes and pushed my notepad his way, speaking fast. "Phoenix texted me early this morning. He has a huge lead but doesn't have time to chase it. It's about—"

"Stop hanging out with Phoenix." He cut into my words.

I clamped my mouth shut, frowning. *What?* "Excuse me?"

"You're excused, because you didn't know what kind of a douchebag he is. But now that you're fully informed, drop him. He's bad news."

"And you're good news?" I huffed.

"I'm the best fucking news, have been for two consecutive years, and I have the numbers to back it up."

Okay. Well. I did kind of step into that one.

I shook my head. "You can't tell me what to do, and you're wasting time right now talking about Phoenix when we have a huge headline to chase," I seethed, snapping my fingers in front of his rather amused face.

He pursed his lips into a ruthless smirk. "Go on."

"The president of Trust State, Arnie Hammond, is going to announce that he's stepping down from his position this evening." I snatched Kipling back from him, flipping through it urgently as I spoke. Trust State was one of the biggest insurance companies in the country. "Not many people know about it yet, and it's only a speculation. However, it *is* happening, and the reason is rather scandalous. Remember how Trust State filed a huge lawsuit against Germany thirty years ago?"

"They represented holocaust survivors who weren't eligible for compensation. And their families." Célian nodded, *finally* focusing on what mattered. "It was a huge deal. Gained a lot of publicity and new clients after that."

"Well, apparently, Hammond pocketed a lot of that money, and an internal investigation just blew that case to the sky." I licked my lips, feeling every cell in my body dancing in excitement. "I contacted the source Phoenix gave me. He's high up in the Trust State food chain. I'm going to meet him this afternoon."

"Is he going on the record?" Célian's eyebrows jumped to his hairline.

"Uh, yeah, but he wants to remain anonymous."

Célian frowned. "Fuck that. A faceless source is like a cuntless whore."

"Thanks for the analogy. And that's not going to happen. He'll lose his job."

"Not necessarily. I'm coming with you," Célian said.

"No, thank you."

"It wasn't an offer, Judith. You're good, but still learning. I'm a veteran. And this is not about stroking your precious little ego. This is about scoring the best story we can get and giving it to our viewers before everyone else. There's no I in team."

"There is in Tim," I grumbled, though I knew he was right.

He smirked. "Annoyingly adorable. Almost tempted to let you suck my cock right here in the office."

I rolled my eyes, stood up, gathered my things, and exited.

"And delicious," he called to my back.

I didn't turn around, but I did stop at the door and smile to myself, thinking rather sadly, *and screwed.*

My source, Finn Samson, was late.

We were sitting at a kosher deli on a side road slicing Canal Street. The scent of moth balls and stale bread floated around the room. Célian had ordered a coffee and a bullet, because he couldn't stand the stench. He'd only gotten one of his two requests. The good thing about the place was it was dead, but still a friendly territory. This meeting was too delicate for a Starbucks.

I tapped my fingers over the table, chewing on my lower lip and looking around. Célian stared at me, bluntly, and instead of feeling awkward, I soaked it up, drinking his attention like fine wine.

A part of me was embarrassed that Samson hadn't arrived yet. I knew Célian was impatient. This made me want to distract him. I tapped my side of the table a thousand times.

He looked under our table at my Chucks. Orange. "Stimulation, sensation, and heat," he commented. "Even you know I'm going to fuck you tonight."

I rolled my eyes. "Can I ask you something?"

"You clearly just did. If this was twenty questions, you'd already have a disadvantage."

I pretended to examine my nails while giving him the finger. It made him chuckle, and his voice danced in the pit of my stomach.

Are you sure about the love thing, Mom? Because if we miscalculated this, I'm in deep, deep trouble.

"Go ahead, Humphry."

"What happened a year ago? Grayson said something happened that made you guys exile *Couture* to a different floor. I know it's around the same time you and your fiancée..."

He stiffened in his seat for a second, then relaxed, throwing an arm over the back of his chair. "My sister died."

My eyes met his across the table. I wanted to take his hand and comfort him, but he didn't look like he needed any comforting. He'd said it methodically, like he was reciting someone else's story.

"She was *Couture*'s editor in chief. Was in charge of Gary and Ava."

"Grayson," I corrected.

"Whatever. After what happened, Mathias and I couldn't really look at them without remembering..."

"Her," I finished for him.

He nodded, taking a sip of his coffee and looking outside to the quiet side street. An older Asian woman crouched down to pet an even older dog. Its owner smiled at her petulantly, but kept texting with the hand that wasn't holding the leash. The world seemed so cold all of a sudden, and hugging Célian became a physical need—a necessity, rather than an act of affection.

"It was my fault." He cleared his throat, flipping his wrist to check his Rolex. I'd never seen him like this before—opening up while completely shutting down. His eyes were anywhere but on me, but the rest of his face was tense and strong.

He didn't want to break.

But something told me the version of him I knew was already beyond cracked.

"How?" I whispered, trying to coax him with my eyes, which he couldn't even meet.

"That's why everything is a complete clusterfuck, Judith. It was my fault. Suffice it to say I killed her—much like I killed my parents' relationship. And then it's come to all this because my father finally decided he'd had enough and retaliated—stuck his cock in my fiancée's mouth three days after the funeral. Apparently all it took to bed my fiancée was a Parisian weekend and a broken fiancé who didn't want to fuck her because he was too depressed to scrape himself off of the bed that weekend."

I bit down on the curse that threatened to slip out of my mouth.

"I broke off the engagement at first. Up until then, Lily and I had been a real couple. But then I figured, part of why Mathias did that was because he was getting weaker. He'd had several heart attacks, and he knew he was going to pass the president's seat to me. He couldn't stomach the idea of me doing a better job than him, making more money. At the same time, my father has never been a newsman. He's just a businessman who got very lucky. He knew the merger between LBC and Newsflash Corp would make me an unstoppable force, so killing my engagement and shitting all over my career plans was the perfect two-birds-one-stone scenario for him.

"For that reason alone, I agreed to take Lily back, but in a very different capacity. Come August, we will get married, and I will inherit most of her family's business. First technically, and then when her father steps down from his official duties, also officially. She will have nothing but a personal trainer to fuck and an empty existence to maintain, with one miserable thing going for her—she will be married to the asshole all her preppy Manhattan friends had wanted when we were growing up."

Tears shimmered in my eyes, and I didn't want to blink, knowing they would freefall the minute I let them. So this was why he was marrying Lily. To spite his dad. To spite *himself*. To take what he thought he deserved from a horrible situation.

My crucial teenage years had come and gone without a mother. I'd almost resented her, in a selfish, weird way—like she'd had a hand in not being alive anymore, like she could have fought a little harder against her disease. But I'd never known how it would feel not to be wanted by my parents. They'd always loved me, and hard. They weren't rich or powerful or even mystifying in the way the Laurents were. But they'd made me feel so important. It always felt like it was us against the world. Even now, with Dad being sick, we had a bond that defied death—the type in which I felt treasured, even by those who weren't alive.

I grabbed Célian's hand and brought it to my face, kissing his palm like Phoenix had done to me. Intimately. Devastatingly. Warmly. We were out in the open, and it was downright outrageous, but he didn't pull away. He stared at me, a little confused, his mouth parting. Some of the menace left his face, and that was worth the embarrassment of doing something I shouldn't have.

"What happened to your sister? How did she…?"

"Judith Humphry?" A pudgy man in a wrinkly, mud-colored suit appeared in front of our table. Célian withdrew his hand from mine and straightened, standing to introduce both of us.

We all sat down, and I wiped my eyes quickly. For the next forty-five minutes, I watched Célian as he grilled the guy like he wasn't the one doing us a huge favor, but vice versa. I asked a lot of questions, too, but in the end, it was Célian who coaxed him to come speak on air. He was relentless, charming, and extremely convincing. Finn Samson was worried for his job—and rightly so—but Célian spoke to his heart, reminding him of his morals and all the holocaust-surviving pensioners who had lost so much money.

"Speaking up will not get you fired. If anything, it will get you a fat promotion. Anyone touches your position, we're going to make it such a shit show, the whole nation will back you up. Every network in New York will rally for you, and that's a fact—and a promise." Célian handed him his business card.

That was the scariest thing about my boss. He could talk you into donating your organs to science while you were still very much alive. He had the uncanny ability to make you want to please him, even though he didn't do anything to earn such devotion.

When we left the deli, I was still disoriented from Célian's dazzling show of authority. And I kept my mouth shut, not wanting to rock the boat. I hadn't expected him to open up the way he had before Samson showed up, and I didn't want to push him for more. Célian Laurent was like a flower. To enjoy his full bloom, I needed to bide my time. I was also embarrassed for taking his hand and crying a second before we'd met an interviewee. So much for keeping it cool and professional.

The cab ride was completely silent, and when we were about two blocks from LBC, the traffic got so bad Célian ordered the driver to pull to the curb and let us walk the rest of the way.

"Are you sure?"

"Do I look like a person who is unsure of anything he does?"

"Okay, man, okay."

Guess we'd be walking the rest of the way. Célian's eyes were set dead on the street ahead of us, and his face was murderous when he said, "She was upset and ran straight into traffic. Got hit by a bus in front of my own eyes."

I coughed on a bitter lump of agony, choking back a sob I dared not release. Oh my God. His sister. Camille. He stopped. So did I. People brushed past us, muttering profanity, the lights and faces blurring into nothing. All I could see was him.

"We'd had a fight."

"What were you fighting about?" Every single word I uttered was cocked and ready to create an explosion. I wasn't normally like this with Célian, but I wasn't scared of him. I was terrified *for* him. I hadn't known he harbored so much pain.

We resumed our walk to the next traffic light. He stared at his huge hands. "Camille was my baby sister, talented as hell and seriously fucking beautiful, inside and out. You remind me of her in the way you're passionate about a story. Only she had the same feeling for fashion."

That curved my mouth in a smile. I believed him. Célian looked like a god among men. There was no reason to think Camille would be anything less than striking, not to mention ambitious and highly intelligent.

"Camille only had one problem, and that was her boyfriend."

"What? Why?" I asked.

The light turned green, and he seemed in a hurry to get to the office. I had to practically jog to keep up with his pace.

"Because the bastard's name was Phoenix Townley."

I sucked in a breath. Phoenix represented a tragedy bigger than he could shoulder.

"Camille and Phoenix had a bit of an illicit affair at work. I didn't particularly like it. Then again, I hardly gave a fuck about who she was fucking as long as she was safe. My father, on the other hand, lost his shit. Cam and Phoenix were young and volatile, not to mention they once did very unprofessional things against her office door that I will never be able to erase from my memory—and trust me, I've tried to forget those sounds." He cringed visibly. "If there's one thing my father and I were in agreement about—and it's not a stretch when I say it was literally *just* one thing—it was that Camille and Phoenix weren't a good match. Phoenix was reckless as hell, and she was a good apple he wanted to take a bite from and throw in the trash. He was a damn good reporter, despite the fact that his daddy got him the position, but he also liked crack and whores, two things that didn't mix well with the fact that he was dating my baby sister."

Jesus Christ. Phoenix had done a lot of growing up during the time he was away. I knew that, because there was no way the man I knew today was a drug addict.

"I'm not even sure why the fuck I'm telling you this." Célian ran his hand through his hair, shaking his head, exasperated. "But I'm halfway through, so I better finish. My father decided to send Phoenix off to the Middle East. You can never run out of action there. I tried to convince him not to play God, because that shit is dangerous—doesn't matter what the cause is. Camille was livid, even after Phoenix was gone and my father told her about the crack and the whores, trying to convince her to forget him. As he put it, Phoenix had clearly chosen his work over her, so there was nothing to lament. But she was lovesick. Or maybe she was just sick, but she loved Phoenix, and Mathias didn't respect that."

We now stood in front of LBC's building, neither of us making a move to go inside. There was a finality about stepping back into the realm of the office, where we'd have to remain professional, that we didn't seem to want to face.

My lower lip trembled, and I felt my nostrils moisten. I wanted to cry so badly, but I kept myself strong for him.

"What did you tell her?" I asked. "What made her run into the street?"

"After he'd been gone a few months, she decided to go visit him. They'd been secretly talking and were going to meet in Istanbul. She sold it to Mathias as a business trip. She'd write a piece about the thriving fashion industry in Turkey. She told *me* she wanted to marry Phoenix, that she couldn't sleep or eat or shit without thinking about him. She'd lost so much weight. She said he'd been clean for a while, that they were going to give it another shot, that Mathias and I didn't know the whole story. In that moment I felt so filthy about what my father had done that I decided to tell the truth. I told her Phoenix had never had any doubts about her, but that Mathias had kicked him out of her life, shipped him away, and I hadn't tried hard enough to stop him—probably none of us could stop him."

"But you didn't have a hand in doing it," I said softly.

He shrugged one shoulder. "I couldn't stop Mathias. His hatred for the Townleys knows no bound. If you think I'm a hateful fucker, you've seen nothing yet."

"Why is that?"

"Because Townley is actually loved and respected? Because his son didn't ruin his marriage? The fuck should I know? To me, they're just another champagne-and caviar-eating family LBC needs to feed."

Célian bowed his head. His face was stoic, but his eyes bled pain. He looked like *The Warrior*, shredded into ribbons and tough as steel.

"The moment I confessed, she bolted. The hurt and rage I saw in her eyes… I ran after her when I saw her under the bus's wheels. Dragged her out. At first I thought she was okay. There was no blood or anything. She died eight hours later of internal bleeding. My father can't look me in the face anymore because I told her the truth, and I don't exactly blame him. If it wasn't for the other shit between us, I would actually understand."

Silence hung in the air. I wanted to hug him, but knew better than to try. So I did the next best thing, the thing my mom used to do whenever I cried, which wasn't that often. She'd kiss the tips of her fingers and press them against my heart.

He scowled. "The fuck you doing, Brooklyn girl?"

"Kissing your pain away," I whispered, not wondering, even for a second, how he knew where I lived, "Manhattan prince."

He turned around and headed for the building silently, and I followed suit. The entire elevator ride upstairs, I thought about Phoenix. About what it must be like for Célian to see him around after what happened. About the tattoo on Phoenix's forearm, of the smiling girl. Of *Camille*. And how he, too, was still dealing with the aftermath of her death. About how it must feel for Célian to spend time with his father here every day, or even look at his fiancée's face. *August*. My mind reeled. He said they were getting married in August. Less than three months away.

The elevator dinged, and we both rushed out. I didn't dare look at his face after all he'd shared, after how he'd opened up to me. Then it occurred to me that my boss didn't know anything about my personal life—not about Dad, not about Mom, and certainly not about Milton. I arrived at my desk, sat back, and stared at nothing for half an hour.

A message from Grayson in our company's chatroom snapped me out of my reverie.

Grayson: Reminding you to call your insurance like you asked me to.

Grayson: Another friendly reminder: I'm not your PA.

Grayson: Mr. Laurent, I know you're probably reading this, so let me just say I admire the suit you're in today. Not that I'm checking you out. And not that you don't normally deliver in the fashion sense. How do you undo a message? God, if you can't send me an Abercrombie and Fitch model as a boyfriend, at least send me filters.

Oh, yes. I'd told Grayson I had an insurance issue so I wouldn't forget. I'd *lied.*

I took my phone out and dialed the collection agency to talk about different payment plans. Now that I had a real job, I needed to start working through our debt.

I gave the representative on the other end of the line my name and details, then asked if she needed my credit card number. It was going to suck to see the money finally coming into my bank account just evaporating right back out.

She snapped her gum in my ear, her voice lethargic. "No need, ma'am. Says here the account's been settled."

I blinked, staring at all the yellows and oranges and reds on my screen, not really deciphering her words. "Excuse me?"

She sighed. "Says here a payment has been made. You no longer owe us anything, ma'am. Anything else you need help with today?"

I raised my head and looked into the conference room, where Célian sat with Mathias and a bunch of guys in suits he referred to as *bigwigs*. They were probably discussing money issues and ratings. Those were the meetings the staff wasn't invited to. I'd once heard Mathias shouting at Célian that he was sheltering us from the bad stuff, and Célian had laughed and retorted, "*As your son, let me assure you, you have a lot to learn about protecting what's yours. Take a fucking seat, old man.*" Célian was talking to one of the suits animatedly, then he smiled his patronizing smile and patted the back of his hand like he was the most adorable idiot he'd ever had the displeasure of meeting.

Could he?

Did he…?

Mathias stared at him with a disdain that chilled my bones. All the other men and women in the room stared at him intently, listening to every word he said.

No.

Célian was too brutal, too callous to do something like this.

Besides, how would he even know?

Then, as if sensing my gaze, his face angled toward mine and he shot me a look I couldn't decode. Anger? Annoyance? Desire? All three?

"Ma'am? Ma'am, is there anything else I can do for you today?"

I shook my head and got back to the woman on the phone. "No, everything is perfectly clear. Thank you very much."

Célian

Jude never got a follow-up on that sex-a-thon invitation from this morning.

After spilling my guts all over her orange Chucks earlier in the afternoon, watching her eyes swim with emotions that had threatened to drown me into despair, I had decided it was in everyone's best interest if we took the night to reevaluate the clusterfuck known as our office fling.

To say I wasn't the oversharing type would be the understatement of the millennium. Yet somehow, in that kosher deli that smelled like death and looked like clinical depression, I'd talked about Camille in a way I never had before—not with Maman and not with Kate, and certainly not with my sorry excuse for a fiancée or deadbeat father.

I grabbed my coat and made my way out of my office after we finished the show. Judith was still typing away on her computer, paying her dues as a junior reporter. She actually had the audacity to look pissed again, for a reason beyond my grasp or care. Most women were content to simply spend time with me, in any capacity. Yet Jude got to get fucked, have lunch dates, *and* have me pay for her fucking life—granted, unbeknownst to her—and she still acted like I was public enemy number one.

After a grueling ratings meeting with the bigwigs earlier today, I'd taken my father aside and explained to him, again, that if he ever touched Jude, I was going to unleash his dirty laundry, one stained panty at a time, and kill the pristine Laurent name he'd been riding all the way to the bank.

Anyway, seeing as pussy wasn't in the cards for me tonight, I decided to settle for going face to face with a dick.

I'd pay Phoenix fucking Townley a visit.

Phoenix lived in SoHo, which hardly surprised me. It was a great place to find any of your vices, from crack and dope to dead prostitutes. I located his new address in his HR file and took an Uber straight to his house.

He opened the door on the third knock, wearing nothing but white briefs. His blond curls fell on his forehead, his face flush with the humidity that knocked New York on its pale ass on the verge of every summer. He no longer looked like a kid, and it bothered me that he'd continued aging, while Camille stayed frozen, and that Judith might see him in that light—as a man, and not a bad-looking one at that.

"Cel." He greeted me with no particular tone to his voice, like my presence on his doorstep was ordinary.

He left the door open, turning around and ambling back to his couch in a silent invitation. The apartment was small, new, and hip. And yes, I died a little using the word *hip*, even if just in my mind. I strolled directly to the red-bricked, trendy kitchen with intentions of fixing myself a drink. But the cupboards were full of bullshit ramen noodles. I opened the fridge and found nothing but root beer, pink lemonade, and nyloned wet cat food. Not a drop of alcohol in sight.

"Just because you're a pussy doesn't mean you need to eat like one." I slammed his fridge shut, groaning.

"There's a stray under my building that I feed. Lost souls connect to one another in a quiet way. If you're looking for booze, hate to break it to you, but I quit." He freefell to his couch with a thud, slouching and flipping channels on his TV. Was he expecting a medal? A bright sticker? Or maybe just for me to not punch him in the face.

Phoenix settled on BBC America. I hated that he wasn't stupid. It made hating him more difficult.

"Mouthwash?" I asked.

"Nope."

"Pot?" Everyone had fucking pot, even my fifty-seven-year-old Eastern European housekeeper, who also had a crucifix the size of my bathroom dangling on her meaty neck.

"Quit everything," he said. "The alcohol, the drugs—"

"The whores?" I cut in, swiveling around and cracking open a can of root beer. I took a sip, decided it tasted like rotten anus, and dumped it in his sink.

Last time we'd had an actual conversation was when he'd tried to convince me to talk to my father about sending him packing to the Middle East. I'd said I'd try, and I sort of had, but in all honesty, I wasn't convinced he deserved my sister. Also, I had no power over my father, especially when it came to Cam. He'd barely let me hang out with my own sister when we were kids, deeming me the troublemaker and her his princess.

The time we'd seen each other before that, Phoenix and I hadn't really done much talking. I saw Camille upset after the entire doped-whore incident and had decided to rearrange the attributes of his face. A broken nose and three cuts in his eyebrows later, Phoenix had a pretty clear idea of my feelings toward him.

Consequently, he knew this was not a social call.

He shook his head, staring at the ceiling, his hands tucked under his head. "I never touched the prostitute. We scored some drugs together, yeah, but she was half-naked because she was an idiot and tried to seduce me. I never cheated on your sister. I was a fucked-up boyfriend, sure, but I never wronged her."

"I'm sensing I should somehow be impressed by this revelation." I yanked his fridge open again, this time trying the sugar-free, organic pink lemonade.

Spat it out.

Maybe sober life is punishment enough for Townley Jr.

"Not everything is a battle of words and power, Cel."

He was the only person to call me that, and I'd never understood why. We weren't close, before or after he'd dated Camille.

"You know, I tried to call you several times after she died," he told me. "I couldn't stop going over the last thing I said to her, the last thing she said to me, when we were about to meet in Turkey."

I rubbed my jaw, moving it from side to side. I'd come here to warn him that my stay-the-fuck-away-from-Judith warning for Mathias extended to him. But somehow, we were now talking about Camille. It was the second time today I'd had to share her memory with someone else.

Not to be a sappy shit, but I really did miss my sister every single minute. She was the only thing that had resembled normal in my family. With Cam, things had been simple.

I loved her, and she'd loved me.

I'd had her back, and she'd had mine.

Mathias had fucked up, and I'd failed her, and then I'd chosen to tell her the truth when she was standing on the edge of the fucking street, like an idiot.

"Say it," I spat.

I wanted to have that piece of Cam, too—a new piece that would make her feel alive, even if just for a second.

Phoenix sat forward on the couch, his elbows propped on his knees. He clutched his head, staring down at the floor.

"I told her I was clean, that I'd changed, and that I was crazy about her ass. She believed me. We talked about Istanbul, and she said she was going to wait for me until I came back from the Middle East, no matter when it was. Do you know what I said to her after that?"

He looked up to me, his eyes shimmering. I shook my head. I understood love as a concept, but every time people started talking like Phoenix, I automatically assumed they were reciting a Sarah Jessica Parker movie. It didn't seem real.

"I told her I'd never wanted to give her up, that what we had wasn't simple, but it was real. That I needed her. That I didn't know if we could work it out, but I would damn well try my best." He looked up at me. "I knew your dad had a bounty on my head, but I didn't care."

I filled in the rest in my head. And then Camille had talked to me and found out why Phoenix really left—that they were Romeo and Juliet. That they stood no chance, because their families—*my* family—would never let them be together.

He reached out to me, and I froze. If hugging it out was his way of getting over his feud, he was obviously still doing drugs. Then I looked down and noticed the tattoo: Camille laughing back at me—a familiar smile with too much teeth and the eye wrinkles that upset her every time she looked into a magnifying mirror but I thought only made her prettier.

"Why did you come here, Cel? I can't bring her back, and you don't want to patch things up between us." He wiped his nose on his bare bicep.

"I didn't come here for Camille. I came here because if I find you going anywhere near Judith Humphry, I will bash your head against the first available surface and get rid of the evidence in a way that would make it impossible to find you."

I knew what I'd just had said could bite me so hard in the ass, I would have nowhere left to shit from. Still, I couldn't help myself.

Phoenix stood, walked over to his open-plan kitchen, and poured himself some of the nasty lemonade. "That's for Jude to decide."

Had she told him about her father? About her debt? About her *life*? I inspected him with a frown as he swiveled to face me and continued.

"Jude is building a network of friends at work. I'm glad to be one of them. You, the Laurents, hold so much power that you sometimes forget you're not real monarchs. People—your employees—are not your servants. Look at what happened to your father. He's done everything he could to try to control me, and his staff, and even *you*. Where is he now? After multiple heart attacks, he's professionally irrelevant. You're the one calling the shots at LBC, and your mother—his divorcée—is the one controlling the board. He has nothing left. To maintain power, you have to distribute it, too.

"I won't let the Laurents dictate my relationships with people anymore," he added after a moment. "Just look at the state of your family. You hardly know what you're doing."

He wasn't wrong. Regardless of Lily, I knew very well that I had nothing to offer Jude. I didn't do love. I sucked hard at relationships, and harder at feelings. She deserved a lot more than me—something I would never admit out loud, but knew very well deep down. A decent man would take a step back and give her a chance to meet someone who could be there for her.

I wasn't a decent man, though.

Not to Judith, and definitely not to Phoenix.

In one move I cornered him against his fridge, clamping my hand over his neck and squeezing until my knuckles whitened. My face was relaxed, my pulse steady, but the way Phoenix's eyes bulged told me I looked the way I felt: lethal and beyond repair. I never used physical violence to get places. In fact, the last time I'd had my hands on someone, it was him, because of Cam. But Phoenix *really* needed to know Jude was off-limits.

"I will say this again, Townley, and this time, pay careful attention, because I wouldn't mind throwing both you and your father's ass out on the street. You messed things up with my sister, and you do not get a second chance with my employee. You want to sit in Judith's friend zone? You're welcome to rot there. But if you so much as touch one of her blond locks, brush your hand over her skin, it's game over for you. And I'm not the king."

I let go of his neck, and he gasped, crouching down and gripping his throat.

"I'm the goddamn God in this place. Fair warning: you've already proven to be a sinner, and no amount of Hail Marys is going to wipe clean the debt you have with me."

I dashed out of his apartment, thinking tonight couldn't possibly get much worse.

But of course, I was wrong.

Because Lily was waiting for me at my apartment building, ready to prove it.

Lily had lost her key privileges the day I caught her with my father's dick in her mouth. Not an overreaction on my part, I think everyone would agree.

That was also the day I'd broken off our engagement, and even when she came crawling back, dangling Newsflash Corp in my face, I'd never bothered to return the spare key. Since my building employed enough security and receptionists to open a mall, Lily couldn't waltz in and wait at my door. The staff knew people who came to visit regularly: Maman, Kate, and Elijah, a producer and fellow Yankees fan from work. For Lily, my instructions were clear and simple: if I wasn't around, she was to wait in the lobby.

Which was why I found her coiled around a glass of champagne, wrapped in a black satin mini dress, and flipping through a magazine at the golden marble bar in my building's lounge.

The minute I walked through the skyscraper's revolving door, she shot to her feet and flung herself at me. Seeing as we hadn't spoken since she'd left the gala without me last weekend, I was mildly surprised to see we were still on friendly terms. My surprise was not warranted, I discovered, when Lily stopped a few inches from me and raised her hand to slap me across the face. I stopped her, grabbing her wrist and lowering her arm.

"Lily," I said through gritted teeth.

"*Fiancé.*" She spat out the word. "We need to talk."

"Talking doesn't require you to touch me. I'm surprised you haven't figured that out. You spend most of your days gossiping with your friends like it's an Olympic sport."

She pouted in defeat, then wiped strands of her hair from her face. I headed to the elevator, not really giving a shit if she followed. She did. In the elevator, she turned around and tried to rub her crotch against my thigh. I took a step back, *tsking*.

"You lost your cock rights long ago."

"Fuck you, Célian."

"In your dreams. And even there, only from behind so I don't have to look at your face." I smiled politely, checking my Rolex. There was nowhere in particular I needed to be, but I decided to give her exactly ten minutes to tell me what the fuck she was doing here. What can I say? I was feeling generous.

When we got to my apartment, I finally fixed myself that long-awaited drink while Lily paced back and forth in my living room. Everything was made out of sleek black granite and oak paneling, with sterile-looking, minimal white furniture. The Japanese interior designer who'd come here had asked what I wanted to convey when I moved in. I'd told her "nothing." She thought I was being literal.

Now my apartment looks exactly like my heart. Hollow.

I'd been living here for the past three years and had only fucked one woman in this place. It was Lily, and it'd been over a year since that happened. Other than that, I mostly used my place for sleep.

"Talk," I ordered, and the minute I did, Lily's mouth opened and the words flew from it like she'd been waiting for my permission for years.

"Look, I get it, okay? I screwed up, Célian. Do you think I don't know that? Do you think I don't understand the gravity of my mistake? Of messing with your dad while you were grieving your sister?"

Camille and Lily were the same age—three years my junior, which made her twenty-nine—and had attended the same private schools in Manhattan. They weren't friends. Barely acquaintances. My sister wrote journals, went to poetry nights, and was obsessed with autobiographies about high-end fashion designers, while Lily was focused on partying, boys, and diets. They had nothing in common, and even though Camille had never said it in so many words, I knew that before I came into the picture, Lily had been harassing her to set us up when she wasn't mini-bullying her in the high school halls for her goodie two-shoes ways.

So, Lily mentioning my sister dampened my already pissy mood.

"But trust me when I say it didn't come out of left field, Célian. Even when we were a functioning couple, you looked at me, but never really saw me. You merely let me crawl into your bed and attended my family functions so you could get ahead with your merger plan. I wanted to get your attention at any cost. It was stupid, I know, and I regret it, but this has gone too far now. I want you back. I want *us* back."

"I want a Ferrari and a month-long vacation in the Caribbean." *And Judith's mouth around my cock.*

Lily flung her arms in the air. "You could get all of those things! So why can't I get you? I will be good. Faithful. We've been together for so many years, Célian. Don't let this ruin us."

"No."

"I'll let you keep your side pieces. I know they're nothing but sex. I don't mind. I'm willing to share..."

"Still a no."

I placed my glass on the metallic mini bar, and when I turned around, I found her undressing like her satin number was on fire. The heap of fabric fell to the floor, and she tried to wrap her leg around my waist, losing her balance when I took a step back. She reached to grab my hand for balance and fell flat on her ass. I looked down at her, noticing that she hadn't worn a bra or panties under her dress. I picked up her clothing and threw it at her.

"Get out."

"I want to get pregnant."

"There are plenty of men who will be willing to fuck you. I can call you an Uber to the nearest bar. Try not to catch an STD while you're at it. It's touch-and-go when you don't use protection."

"You're my future husband. I want *you* to get me pregnant."

She was still sitting on the floor, her thighs spread, her pussy staring at me, and I was morbidly bored by this act. Lily had done this every few months since we'd announced our engagement was back on. Normally I ignored her. But tonight, after a disastrous meeting with the bigwigs, a weird encounter with Jude, and talking to Phoenix fucking Townley, I wanted to minimize my contact with her crazy ass.

"Put your clothes on," I repeated verbally, swiveling to get another drink. My back was to her as I poured scotch into a crystal glass and stared down at the liquid.

Thin arms wrapped around my torso, and Lily's body made a second appearance, draping around me like an octopus. How many limbs did this woman have? I shook her off again.

"Have you lost your mind?" I turned around, pushing her away. I'd been candid with her from the beginning when I'd agreed to take her back. The chances of us being intimate again weren't much better than me spontaneously joining the circus.

If she wanted kids, she was welcome to have them with someone else.

If she wanted sex, she was welcome to fuck around.

If she wanted both, she could move one of her one-night stands into the three-story refurbished house her father had purchased for us ahead of the wedding. Because I sure as hell wasn't going to be found anywhere near it.

"Don't pretend like you're immune to sex, Célian. That's what we do. We're a mess, but we're a hot mess." She slid down to her knees and started fumbling with my zipper. I stared at her in disbelief, swatting her hand away like she was a nagging fly. Someone here was a hot mess, but it sure as hell wasn't me.

"Are you drunk?" I asked, point blank.

"Drunk enough that you can't kick me out of here," she sneered, licking her red-glossed lips.

She underestimated my dislike for her. Because twenty minutes later, she was already tucked inside a cab, me sitting beside her and staring out the window.

"You can't take me to my apartment. There's no way to tell what I'll do to myself. I'm depressed. My fiancé doesn't want to touch me!" she wailed, sniffling and puffing her hair in the rearview mirror. Our driver, a young Indian man in a Manchester United shirt, rubbed his face with his hand, shaking his head. He had a picture of a woman—his wife, I assumed—and two small boys dangling from a keychain on the rearview mirror. They were all smiling, wearing cricket gear.

I wondered if he wanted my Rolex and three-grand suit like I wanted his normalcy and family life, and if that shit mattered. At all.

"I'm not taking you to your apartment. I'm taking you to your parents'."

I didn't believe for one second that Lily would hurt herself—this chick would cold-bloodedly kill a puppy before letting someone who wasn't a professional cut her bangs—but I wasn't one to take chances, either. If she was feeling suicidal, her parents could take care of it. I'd been a very doting boyfriend while she went through her dramatic phases, prior to the moment she'd decided to give head to the man who'd created me.

Lily kicked her feet against the driver's seat. He winced.

"Ugh! I don't want to go there," she hiccupped. So fucking drunk. "It's depressing. My mother cries all the time, and my grandmother looks like a mess. Besides, my sisters are bitches."

Her sisters, Scarlett and Grace, were a nurse and a physical therapist—both decent women who'd opted out of the media life. Unfortunately for Lily, they frowned upon the lifestyle she led, in which her only contribution to society was having a fine ass and tipping service providers well. She was the only person in her family who didn't hold a job. Lily claimed there was no need. She was busy planning a wedding, a bachelorette party, and a honeymoon. I wasn't entirely sure who she was going to take the honeymoon with, but we both knew I'd board a spaceship with a one-way ticket to the sun before getting on a plane with her. At least I hoped we did.

"Your sisters don't live at home, and what do you mean your mother is crying? Is Madelyn okay?"

Lily tucked her chin and fiddled with her fingers. She looked guilty, and that worried me, because this girl had the moral compass of a human-trafficking pimp.

"Lily?"

My fiancée shot the driver a dirty look through the rearview mirror, asking him not to judge her without realizing she was ten minutes too late. "Scar and Gracie moved in two weeks ago because Grams is not feeling very well."

I dropped my arm to my side. "What do you fucking mean, not feeling well?"

The one thing I always loved about Lily was her family. Hell, I'd started dating her solely for the fact that her grandmother was always there, with a homemade pie and crazy stories about the guys-and-dolls era of New York. My entire senior year had been spent stuffing my face with Madelyn's cherry pie and listening to Broadway gossip from the fifties, then stuffing my face with Lily's pussy and hearing her moan my name like a prayer.

Up until a year ago, I'd taken Madelyn out to Broadway every other month. We'd watch a show, go to a small Italian place, and talk about the news. Her late husband had incorporated Newsflash Corp. It made me a first-class asshole that I'd cut the tradition short when Lily and I broke up. Even after we were back together with our new arrangement, I couldn't face Madelyn, knowing I lived a lie—one in which I fucked over her family and what her husband had worked for to get ahead in the game. I didn't offer her granddaughter love. I merely offered her a semi-tolerable relationship.

Lily averted her gaze to the window, blinking away tears.

"She's...been drifting in and out of consciousness. She's really old, baby. Ninety-something, or whatever. She had a good life. She lived with us the entire time after my granddad died."

"Any particular reason I'm just finding out about this now?" I always asked Lily about Madelyn and her parents. *Always*. Six months ago, when Madelyn was admitted to the hospital with chest pain, I'd rushed in and stayed by her side all night because Lily's parents were abroad and her sisters lived on the outskirts and couldn't make it. Of course Lily had been too busy partying.

"I thought if you knew the only thing to keep you with me other than Newsflash Corp was gone, you'd…" Lily wiped her tears quickly, before they ruined her mascara. "She was your favorite. I didn't know how you'd react, and I didn't want to know, either."

"*Is*. She's still alive."

"Not for long, baby. I'm sorry, but there's no way she'll make it to our wedding."

The cab came to a stop in front of her parents' Park Avenue building. I shoved my hand into my pocket, producing my wallet and plucking out a chunk of notes. I slapped the cash in the driver's hand and told him to wait under the building. Lily stared at me, a slow grin spreading on her face.

"If I'd known that's what it takes to get you into my place…"

"Shut up, Lily. I need to say goodbye to Madelyn. This is not about you."

Half an hour later, I was back in the cab, my mood hitting an all-time low. Madelyn wasn't awake. Lily's parents—while happy to see me—were also wondering where the fuck I'd been for the past few months. Things were tense and awkward. They no longer felt like the family I never had, and why would they? I hadn't bothered to pick up their calls in months.

By marrying Lily, sticking it to my father, and finalizing the merger, I was not only ruining my own life, I was ruining theirs, too. And that was something I'd yet to consider.

I gave the driver a Brooklyn address I had no business visiting, and asked him to roll the windows down so I could breathe in unrecycled air.

A little while later we stopped in front of Judith's building. Her living room window was wide open, like I'd known it would be. Jude's entire personality was inviting. Her generosity and kindness said *come in*, and I wanted to stomp into her territory and conquer every inch of her life. I sat in the cab and stared into her window, realizing I was acting like a creep, and not giving half a shit. The cheap yellow lightbulb of her foyer flickered, and because she was living on the ground floor, I could see that there was a small table set for dinner, with a salad bowl, pasta, and garlic bread. Basic, but I knew it would taste better than the bluefin tuna sushi I was going to have for dinner.

"Sir?" The driver cleared his throat.

I slapped some more money into his hand without taking note of how much it was.

"A few more minutes."

I'm way past creeper and treading into restraining-order territory.

"Of course."

You should probably pick up the phone and fucking report it, man. I would. In a heartbeat.

Five minutes later, Robert walked into the dining room, easing slowly into his chair. He still looked fragile and older than his years, but he had a smile on his face. Less than a minute later, Judith appeared wearing a blue and white Yankees hoodie and tiny high-waist shorts. Her legs were tan, muscular, and glorious. She was laughing and mounding pasta onto her dad's plate. He coughed and she stopped laughing, walked over to his seat, and rubbed his back.

He caught her hand in his, looked up. They shared a smile.

His lips moved. "*I'm okay, JoJo. Really. I'm fine.*"

She cracked two beers and poured them into tall glasses, her lips moving, smiling. She was singing.

I looked away, because I didn't expect to feel the way I did—like I wanted her and envied her and pitied her.

Wanted her because she was tailor-made for me.

Envied her because she had a real family, or whatever was left of it.

And pitied her because I couldn't quite let go, and I didn't do love. Only hate and anger and revenge.

One thing was for sure, Judith Humphry and Lily Davis weren't cut from the same cloth, and I wanted to wear only one of them.

One girl disarmed me, the other fucked me up, and over.

One girl was loyal, the other shallow and empty.

One claimed she was mine, but it was the other I wanted to own.

Jude

"We need to talk." I stormed into Célian's office when the clock hit nine am.

Brianna, who had been waiting in an invisible line by his door to see him, had clutched her iPad to her chest and stared at me with sheer alarm when she saw me advance toward his office and walk in without knocking. Célian was already behind his desk, sipping his one of three morning coffees, chewing his mint gum, and flipping through the daily newspapers, not sparing me a look. He wore his indifference like chipped armor, a white knight with a very dark soul.

"Disagree, but you're already here, so you might as well spit it out."

"First of all, did you know Brianna is waiting for you outside?" I threw a thumb behind my shoulder, cocking an eyebrow.

"I did, and she can knock."

"She's scared of you."

"You'd be wise to be the same," he whiplashed, still not looking up to meet my gaze. "Are you here to talk about Brianna, Miss Humphry?"

Damn him. He sounded like Harvey Specter on speed. Only crueler. And ten times handsomer. If Célian met chivalry in a dark alley, he would beat it to death, then find its sister, generosity, and kill her too.

"I came here to tell you I found out, and I'm pissed."

"Explain, and save me the ambiguity."

"Are you too precious for eye contact anymore? Is that now saved for the moments I'm writhing under you and you want to see me vulnerable?"

I couldn't believe the words had left my mouth. Shakily, too. I glanced back. Brianna wasn't in the hallway anymore. *Phew.*

Célian dragged his gaze up slowly, his cobalt blue eyes extra frosty on this warm day.

"Do. What?" He highlighted every word.

"I know you paid my father's medical bill. All of it. You're not my sugar daddy, Célian. I appreciate your good intentions, but I don't need help. I'm not a damsel in distress. I don't need anyone to save me."

I don't want you to pity me. I don't want you to look at me as anything less than an equal. And I don't want you to be engaged. In fact, I especially don't want you to be engaged and pay for my things. It makes me feel like the other woman.

Those were all the things I wanted to say but knew I never would. It wasn't anyone's fault but mine that I'd agreed to be put in this position, or that I still craved him like a junkie, even though he was a drug that could kill me.

He leaned back in his seat, his index fingers tapping.

"Do you have any way to prove it was me?" he asked.

Was he kidding me? There were no other suspects. The money hadn't simply fallen from a tree straight into the wide, black hole called my debt.

"Are you really going to play that card?" I folded my arms over my chest.

He shrugged. "Not many cards I can play. I'll take what I can get."

I laughed, despite still being furious. He was goofy and charming when he wanted to be. Unfortunately, most times he was content with being a jerk.

"Now I feel like I owe you, and I hate it."

"Don't. I didn't pay your medical and student debt because I'm fucking you. I paid them to unfuck you."

"You paid my student loan, too?" My eyes were ready to pop out of their sockets and roll on the floor. I still stood by his open door, trying hard not to have a mental breakdown. It was flattering, but also infuriating, this assuming I needed him to save the day, that he had the power to make my problems go away like some kinky fairy godfather.

He looked down, flipping another page of the newspaper in front of him. "You were riding a full scholarship and living at home. It was hardly a substantial amount."

"For you," I gritted. "Not a substantial amount for *you*."

"Tuck your pride back in, sweetheart. You're coming off as a little ungrateful, and it's unflattering."

"Screw you, Célian."

"Please tell me that's an invitation."

"I hate you!" I yelled in his face, stomping—actually stomping, me, a grown woman. He looked up and raked his eyes over my body quietly. Our gazes halted on my Chucks. Red. *Anger, passion, war.*

"Do you, now?"

He had no business butting into my life more than I had allowed him to, more than I had willingly shared with him. I didn't share this with anyone. There was a reason why I'd never told him about my debt or my family life. Not even about Dad.

Dad.

My blood froze in my veins. No. There was no way. Still, I needed to ask, just to make sure.

"Do you…do you know about my father's situation?"

He got up from his chair, grabbing his pea coat and sliding into it.

"I need another cup of coffee for this conversation. Walk with me, Chucks."

I followed behind him. His broad shoulders were big enough to carry the entire world. He gestured for me to get into the elevator before him, and the minute the doors closed behind us, I turned to him.

"You know about my dad, don't you?"

I didn't know why it upset me so much. Sure, Célian was rich, successful, and prevailing, but in my eyes, we were still on the same level, as crazy as it sounded.

He now offered me his sympathy, but I rejected it, wanting to toss it back in his face. I wasn't ashamed of my father's illness. I just wished it was for me to decide when and where I told people about it—*if* I told them about it.

"I do," he said tonelessly.

"Please don't tell me..." I cupped my mouth. Not that it would have made any difference. My father was going to proceed with the experimental treatment, even if I had to donate a functioning lung to make it happen. But I didn't want it to be true. Didn't want to know that that's what we were, Célian and I: a rookie Brooklyn reporter with a nice pair of tits and a sugar daddy boss who was about to get married to someone else and had guilt-bought his way to her affection.

I was officially the mistress, silenced by shiny, pretty things—by money and a healthcare program, and a good, steady job. A role I'd never agreed to take.

The power imbalance was now personal, and degrading, and *real.* I was indebted to a man I was sleeping with, no matter how we tried to spin it. A man who was taking more and more space in my life, conquering lands in my heart without claiming them. Without civilizing them. Without nurturing them.

The elevator slid open, and I walked out first. I was desperate to put some distance between us so he wouldn't see how flustered I was, how embarrassment colored my cheeks, how I felt my whole body turning pink.

I heard him groaning behind me. I looked down and realized I was wearing a conservative, pearl-colored sheath dress that was snug around my waistline, and probably highlighted my butt.

"Like what you see?" I gritted sarcastically.

"It would look better with my hand marks all over it. Are you going to stop running?"

"Are you going to explain yourself?" I pushed the door to the building open, and we were on the busy sidewalk, facing each other and blocking the downtown human traffic by standing there like two statues.

He ran his big palm over his face, and for the first time since I'd met him, looked somewhat affected. I shouldn't have felt so triumphant for being the one who'd put agitation there, but I was.

"It's not like that."

"Then tell me what's it like."

"I didn't pay it because I wanted you happy or content or on your fucking knees."

"Really? Did you know Jessica's mother has Alzheimer's? Did you help her out? And what about Brianna, your PA? Did you pay her student loan debt? Oh, let me guess—Elijah, who you actually talk to pretty often, also didn't get a fat bonus this year so he could help his parents with their remortgaged house."

"How do you know all these things?" He frowned.

"They're my colleagues, my new friends, and I talk to them." I flung my arms in the air. "Maybe you should do that sometime. Actually make an effort. Be nice."

His jaw tensed and locked in anger, and I figured I had two choices: either get out of there or slap him across the face, a treatment he'd earned fair and square. I chose the option that wouldn't land me in hot water with HR. I turned around and crossed the street toward the Duane Reade on the other side of the road. The light was green, but New York drivers were being…well, New York drivers. A purple taxi came to a halt, screeching three inches away from me and sputtering a cloud of black smoke. The scent of burned rubber filled my nostrils, and before I knew what was happening, I was on the ground.

Shielded by Célian's body.

All of him.

On top of me.

On the hot, stony crosswalk.

I squirmed against his hard body, balling my fists and hitting his chest on instinct. I was angry. So angry. Beyond reason, belief, and logic. Another girl might feel elated to be saved—both by a man's money and his own body. But it wasn't just my debt, or Dad and Célian lying to me. It was the fact that I had begun to truly care for him, knowing I could never have him. Not really.

"The heart is a lonely hunter, Jude."

No, no, it's not, Mom. It's the prey, and Célian is digging his claws deep into it.

"Get off of me," I seethed.

His nostrils flared, but he did as I said, offering me his hand after gliding back onto his feet. I took it, still disoriented from being thrown to the ground—by him. People gathered around us on the sidewalk, watching. Célian sent a punch to the taxi's hood, denting it in the shape of his fist.

I yelped. From this angle, it looked like he might have broken every bone in his hand, but if it hurt, he didn't let it show. His face was back to being scarily blank and emotionless.

"Hey, man! What the hell!" The taxi driver stuck his head out his window, waving an angry fist in our direction.

"Hell is what I'm about to unleash on your ass. You had a red light and almost ran over my employee, so I pimped your ride. If you have a problem with it, you're welcome to take it up with the team of fucking lawyers who occupy an entire floor in my building."

The driver said nothing, tucking his head back into his taxi and cursing under his breath.

Célian looked like he was about to explode, and I had to pull him into an alleyway between two buildings and plaster him against the wall, squeezing his shoulders. His breathing was hard and slow, like the mere act hurt him.

"Are you okay?" I asked.

He inhaled deeply through his nose, then shook his head. "Are *you*?"

"Yes. He didn't hit me, Célian."

The taxi wouldn't have run me over even without his help. I knew Célian had just had a knee-jerk reaction after what he'd been through with Camille, and I felt horrible for my lack of sensitivity. The light was green, so I'd just gone for it.

"Do yourself a favor and look left and right before you cross the fucking street," he hissed in annoyance, suddenly looking embarrassed and disturbed.

His armor clattered to the ground, and I saw him for what he was: raw and incredibly tormented over what had happened to his sister, broken by his relationships with his father and fiancée, lost in a sea of people who admired and looked up to him, but were always too scared to show him real love.

"You wanted to save my life." I cupped his cheek, not knowing if I should, but not caring much, either.

He put his hand over mine and scanned me from under his thick lashes, his throat bobbing with a swallow. His pulse slowed under his tailored suit, and we were now breathing in sync. It was reckless to touch him anywhere but behind closed doors, but I couldn't help it. His eyes were crushed ice—beautiful, blue, and tarnished.

He clasped my chin between his fingers and brought my mouth to his. "Don't flatter yourself, sweetheart."

He cupped my breast over the fabric of my dress and squeezed, tonguing me ruthlessly without warning. My mouth fell open and accepted the invasion. I wrapped my arms around his neck, grinding myself against him and knowing this was not enough, not even close to it. I wanted to get rid of our clothes, our underwear, our inhibitions. I wanted to strip down to the very last item on my body, then tell him all my secrets with every thrust and kiss and bite.

And I wanted to do those things not because he'd saved me—twice—but on the contrary, because for the first time since I'd met him, I recognized that he needed to be saved. From himself.

He disconnected from me, holding my jaw between his fingers and staring me down with his usual air of privilege, thick and heavy, clouded by lust.

"Eight o'clock. A cab will be waiting downstairs. You will wear the same dress, and no bra or panties. You will be mine for the evening. You will not talk back to me, just let me fuck you the way I want to—not because I paid for your shit, but because we both need a distraction. For every sass you give me, I will slap your pussy. For every *no* I hear, I will deny you an orgasm. Am I clear?"

I nodded, dropping my eyes to my shoes. I loved this part. Being his in a deprived, sick, and tortured way.

"Good. Now go get me a fucking lead."

Célian

She did.

She got me the mother of all leads.

"The Vice President, Brendan Creston, did *what*?" Kate sprayed her coffee all over her iPad in the conference room.

Judith Humphry was an ambitious little Chucks. She managed the workload of two people. Whenever anyone had a contact or a lead they didn't want to chase—whether they were too lazy, too busy, or simply unsure if it would result in a dead end—they threw it her way.

"Brendan Creston leaked these compromising emails." Jude nodded, typing away on her laptop. "Now people are saying the President knew, and they were meant to be leaked. If it's true, it's a game changer."

"How do we find out?" Elijah scratched his head.

"Grill the spokesperson." Jude's eyes shone.

I saw the way Elijah looked at her, and I didn't like it. It was the same way I did, like a jackpot he was eager to hit—hot, smart, ambitious, and compassionate.

"Jude, you're a natural." Kate drumrolled on the desk.

Jessica squealed next to Phoenix, and another male reporter next to Jude low-fived her. Everybody was rooting for the new kid.

And I was the one screwing her—both over and her pussy.

"All right, let's not cream our pants because Judith can read text messages and follow simple leads." I waved everyone back to work.

Four hours later, we wrapped up one of the most outrageous news shows we'd ever produced, with James Townley's name blowing up on Twitter like he had a sex tape featuring three NFL stars and a circus clown.

Everyone was talking about #LeakGate.

Coincidentally, the top floor of LBC had never been quieter.

I knew Mathias had brought Jude to my newsroom to stir shit, and in a sick twist of fate, not only had she turned out to be immune to his nouveau riche charm, but she also left mouthwatering news at my office doorstep every single day like a loyal feline.

Granted, knowing my father, I was positive he had more tricks up his sleeve to try to shit all over my progress at LBC.

When I got back home, I scheduled a cab for Judith. Normally, I didn't liaise with people, but I couldn't exactly ask my PA to send my reporter back to my building. I still had time to burn, so I went down to the building's gym, punched a bag, sat in the steam room, and then had a shower. I slid into a pair of dark jeans and a white V-neck shirt and decided I didn't want Jude to be hungry, cranky, or distracted when I defiled her face and ass, so I figured it would be in my interest to feed her before I had my way.

That was my line of thought as I poured out onto my well-lit street.

Chinese? Didn't feel like GMO breath all over my cock and sheets. *Indian?* Potential nut allergies. *Greek?* You could never go wrong with Mediterranean food, but Lily used to complain that the place took a fucking year to deliver. I briefly entertained the idea of texting Jude and asking, but ruled that out immediately. Last thing I needed was for her to think it was a date.

Instead, I walked the extra ten minutes to the nearest Italian place and ordered every pasta dish on the menu. I'd seen her eating it last night, in what certainly wasn't one of my finer moments, so she must *not* be one of those no-gluten, no-flour, no-carbs, no-joy type of girls. Never mind that I was privy to this information because, apparently, I could add stalking to my list of traits.

By the way, picking food for Lily was akin to performing heart surgery on a jellyfish.

When I rounded to my street carrying the bags of food, Judith was already standing at the building's entrance, tapping her foot and nodding to whatever she was listening to on her phone.

What are you listening to, Chucks?

I wiggled my wrist and glanced at my Rolex. Thirty minutes. It had taken me thirty fucking minutes to get food, during which time she'd been waiting outside the building door. I didn't have to wonder why she hadn't called. My phone was set to silent. Newspeople check their phones once a minute, so tolerating the added *ping* of every message and email was pure masochism.

The minute Judith spotted me, she shook her head and turned the other direction, walking away from me. "You're a pig."

Then I hope you like bacon, because I'm on the menu tonight, Chucks.

I didn't bother defending myself. I was many things, but not a liar. Besides, she was even more gorgeous when she was mad—with her swollen pink lips and dark blond eyelashes and compact everything. She was halfway down my block when she turned around and waltzed back to me, like she'd remembered something. Her frown melted into a look of astonishment.

I stopped in front of her, my palms facing out, the white plastic bags hanging from my fingers dripping olive oil.

"What's in the boxes?" She jutted her chin to the takeout.

"Body parts."

"Always a charmer."

"Can you ask that again, but dramatically, a la Brad Pitt in *Seven*?"

I expected her to roll her eyes at me like Lily did every time I teased her for being overdramatic. Instead, Jude turned around, giving me her back, then spun theatrically.

"What's in the boxes!" She pretended to point a gun at me, and for the first time in years—yes, *years*—I actually laughed. Full-blown fucking cackled. It felt weird on my face, in my chest, in my *lungs*.

"Italian."

"*Blech*. Anticlimactic." But her smile didn't waver.

She really wanted to be pussy-slapped with all this sass.

I put down one of the bags to punch in the security code. She picked it up like it was the most natural thing in the world. Lily would've died in the hands of sadists before helping me carry leaky takeout home.

Speaking of Lily, as we walked toward the elevators, I considered that my ex might be here, dropping by for another unwanted visit. She knew I was seeing other people, but I never went as far as bringing anyone to my apartment.

Judith, however, wasn't just a fuck. She was *the* fuck. I could keep her for years, if it wasn't for the fact that girls like Jude would never settle. This was a lapse in her judgment. She would come on my dick, and then around, and then realize she deserved so much better.

Upstairs we tore into the bags and ate pasta and pizza in front of the news, exchanging thoughts and opinions. After she ate her weight in carbs, Jude asked where the bathroom was. I pointed to the end of the hallway, then gathered all the empty containers and bags, throwing them in the trash. I stared down at my hands. They were still shaking from the taxi incident this morning. I knocked back a shot of vodka, chasing it with an Advil. Then I realized the shower in the main bathroom had been turned on.

What the fuck?

I padded barefoot down the hallway, knocking on the door.

"Everything good?"

"Yes!" she shrieked. "Fine. Great. Splendid. I'll think of more synonyms in a second."

"Are you taking a shower?" It was out of character for Jude to do anything without permission. She was straight as a ruler, which was why bending her over was my favorite pastime.

"Actually..."

"I'll join you." There had been a lot of eating and talking and not enough fucking this evening, and I think she'd had her quota of wining and dining. I'd been fantasizing about shoving my cock between her legs every minute during our workday. Waiting longer was pointless.

"I'd rather you not." She cleared her throat.

A slow grin spread on my face.

"Chucks, are you...?"

"No!" she screeched, knocking something over. A shampoo, maybe. "Of course not. Jesus Christ. I would never..."

"Take a shit? Yes, you would. Otherwise you'd die of constipation. Tell me why you can't open the door or I'll kick it down."

She turned off the water, and I heard her shuffling in the room before she opened the door. Her dress was bunched up around her waist, and she was gloriously panty-less. She stared at me with strawberry-red face, her Cupid's bow lips pressed into a scowl I shouldn't have found so goddamn adorable.

"Need your diaper changed?" I leaned a shoulder against the doorframe. She was somewhat younger than me, but not enough for me to give a fuck.

Her fingers looped together, and she stared down at them. "I just wanted to make sure I'd freshened up down there before you..."

It was my second time to laugh today, and that must've been some sort of record. My body was rejecting the laugh, though, I swear, because I actually coughed. "Carry on. Finish the sentence."

"Well, in case you wanted to...I don't know, perform oral. It's been a long day. I didn't want to smell bad."

I took a step inside and cupped both her cheeks, angling her face up to look at me. Her eyes were a wild shade of hazel, green, and suddenly sterling gray. Like the universe had wrapped around her pupils—lizard-like, really. She bit her lower lip and stared up at my mouth.

"I called you here because I want to eat your pussy and fuck your brains out. And I want your pussy to smell and taste like a pussy, not like soap."

Her tongue swiped over her lower lip, pink chasing more and more of her skin as her blush deepened.

"You talk dirty."

"I fuck dirtier, kid. Now, if you want to take a shower, you're welcome to. But first, I need my dessert." I cupped her bare pussy, my palm pressed against her mound, my fingers already grazing her entrance. My other hand wrapped around her waist and jerked her to my erect cock. She quivered against my body as the rough pads of my fingers dragged along her slit, dripping like honey.

"Soaked," I hissed into her mouth, pinching her clit, then plunging three fingers deep inside her and curling them to hit her G-spot. "And *delicious*."

"Jesu…" she started, then clamped her mouth shut.

I lifted an eyebrow in question. She laughed, biting down on that lip again.

One day I will bite it off for you, Chucks.

"I promised Jesus I'd stop using his name in vain when you and I are together."

"You're one weird girl, Judith Humphry."

"But a good Christian." She winked.

She wasn't going to stick around for long, and I knew it. Some asshole who was available, handsome, and not fucking engaged was going to whisk her away. And I wouldn't be able to say shit about it, because I was promised to another. I plunged my fingers into her pussy again and brought them to my lips, tasting her. "In the shower," I growled.

She climbed up the elegant, gray stone steps to the glass shower door and opened it. The floor was made of real pebbles, and she wiggled her toes at the weird texture, a snicker escaping her lips. I lived in a three-bedroom apartment in the most expensive part of the city, while she was struggling to make ends meet and pay the bills on her shitty, old shoebox in an up-and-coming neighborhood. Yet this was the first time she'd reacted to any of the fancy shit in my place.

She stared at me expectantly, wondering if I'd join her. I tucked one hand into my jeans and leaned against the sink.

"Take off your dress."

She did. She wore a simple, cotton bra underneath it. Her first mistake.

I squeezed my cock through my briefs lazily. "I said no bra. That's your first pussy spank. Turn the shower on."

She did, with quivering fingers. She disconnected the sprayer from its hub and pressed it against her tits and stomach, closing her eyes and enjoying the warm streams of water.

"Lower," I commanded.

She lowered the sprayer to her navel.

"I wouldn't test me, Chucks."

She groaned, sliding it down and pressing it against her sweet, tight pussy, which was mostly shaved, just a landing strip of fair, blond hair leading to my final destination.

My dick throbbed, aching with primal need, and now I was full-blown stroking myself, fascinated by how different she was in the office than when we fucked.

"Inside."

The sprayer was less than the size of an iPod because I had eight of them in this shower pointing from different directions. She could easily fit it into her cunt and even take a few of my fingers in, too.

She stared at me defiantly, her nipples puckering into little pebbles. "No," she moaned.

"That's your second pussy slap."

Jude smirked. I knew she'd be into it, but I'd expected her to be more sheepish about it. At any rate, this playlist-building, dirty-headlines-finding girl was going to get screwed extra hard tonight.

"Put it in now, or you'll be getting more surprises I'm not entirely sure you're ready for," I said, squeezing my cock until it pushed back into my hand involuntarily, begging for release.

Working on it, junior.

Jude slipped the sprayer into her pussy and shuddered at the invasion.

"Now fuck yourself with it, and beg me to be the one doing this to you."

She moved the sprayer in and out, trembling at the pleasure of the fast stream coating her walls, and I was just about ready to die here against the sink and let her inherit all of my shit. The girl was a lioness at work and a lamb in bed, the perfect combination for a predator like me. I wanted to fight her when we were in the office and fuck her when we were anywhere else. But it was the in-between part that worried me. Because I wanted to monopolize every second of her life, even when we weren't doing either.

"Oh, God," she moaned.

"*Célian*," I corrected. "Call me by my name. Tell me what you want me to do."

"I want you to screw me." She whimpered into her own shoulder, squeezing her eyes shut, her orgasm brewing, making her legs shake. I wished I wasn't such a bastard in this moment.

"Stop." *But I was.*

"W-what?" she stuttered, still masturbating with the sprayer.

I was so hard now I could barely think clearly. All my blood had rushed to my dick, and if you'd asked me for my own name I'd have had trouble answering.

"Stop right now." A raspy growl slithered between my lips.

She opened her eyes, confused, but slowly removed the sprayer from her pussy.

"Turn it off, and get to my bedroom. Don't dry yourself off." I turned around and walked away.

I perched on the edge of my bed, pushing my sleeves up and tapping my thigh. She appeared at my door seconds later, dripping water all over my floor, her hair wet and her eyes wide as she scanned my black and gray accented bedroom and gold silk comforter. Maman had brought it over from her last trip to Paris. Her friend Isabelle had gifted it to me, and my mother had been about to faint she'd been so proud of her wonderful son, who'd left such a great impression on her friend all those years ago when she'd visited us in Nantucket.

I'd spared my mother the fact that Isabelle was so fond of me because she'd popped my cherry when I was fourteen—while they were both drunk and Maman had stumbled off to make sure Mathias wasn't fucking any more of the staff. Such was my life. A great, colossal mess.

"In my lap." I slapped my hard thigh. She began to walk over to me, but I shook my head gravely before she got too far.

"Crawl."

She stopped, hesitated, and flashed me a feral look I'd never seen on her face before. It was somehow both rebellious and submissive. She knew she should say no, but her body was more than ready to comply.

"It will mean nothing outside this bedroom. I'm still your equal, Célian."

"I never said you weren't."

"I want to make sure you don't think that, either. Just because I like being bossed around in bed—"

"By me," I stopped her. "You like to be bossed around *by me*. Not by just any fucker on the street. On your knees, *Judith*."

And there it was, the most beautiful sight known to man: a lethally attractive, insanely intelligent woman begging to be fucked. She lowered herself, advancing toward me on her knees, her tits dangling between her arms. She stopped, her face level with my cock. I patted my thigh again.

"Up. With your mouth wrapped around my cock and your ass high in the air."

I lowered my jeans and briefs and watched as her lips wrapped around my veiny cock, barely taking my girth. I slapped her bare ass without warning. It was playful, but still did the trick. A few drops of cum escaped just from the intense pleasure of having her there, catering to my every whim, wanting everything I gave her, including the painful shit I would never share with anyone else, much less a one-night stand.

"*Hmmph*," she whimpered quietly, her mouth full of my erection.

Just to make sure she liked it, I slid my fingers into her pussy and found it dripping all over her inner thighs.

Yes. Pussy-slapping and Jude were a match made in my kinky brain's heaven.

"When I tell you to get rid of your bra before you get here, you get rid of your bra."

The next slap wasn't so playful anymore, but still nowhere near the hardcore shit. She was just getting used to moving her lips along my shaft and clutching the base. She moaned into my cock, and again I sneaked my hand down and borrowed some of the wetness dripping along her leg and over the golden comforter, rubbing it over her ass cheek to soothe the pain away.

"And this is for uttering the word *no* during foreplay. What else? I'm sure we can find reasons to punish you if we try."

She unlatched her mouth from my cock and looked up, grinning at me with her mouth so swollen and red, I couldn't help but sneak in a dirty kiss.

"One day, when you made Brianna cry, I hid your laptop in the conference room."

That had been her? I'd looked for that thing for three hours. My open palm landed on her ass cheek again. She whimpered, her knees quivering with lust, and the smell of sex was so heavy in the air, we both got drunk on it.

She looked back up. I stole another kiss, my dick throbbing between her tits.

"Sometimes when I get off by myself, I think about Noah from IT."

I had no idea who Noah from IT was; I just knew he was newly unemployed. I slapped her ass again, and this time bit her earlobe—not gently—for good measure.

"Give me his full name," I growled.

She laughed, throwing her head back. "There's no Noah in IT. I mean, maybe there is. But I don't know him."

"Tell me more." I began to gather the wetness in her pussy and play with her asshole. This time, I added some extra pressure and slid my index finger in and out every once in a while, keeping her engaged the whole time.

"I did give a guy my number the other day. At a diner, when I went to get coffee for Gray and Ava."

My jaw twitched, and I slapped her ass again. "Not funny."

"It wasn't supposed to be."

I knew there was nothing I could do about that information, not unless I was willing to make some major changes in my life. I slipped two fingers into her asshole, and she tensed around them. I could already feel how perfect she'd be once my fat cock was buried deep in her backside.

"You're wasting your time. No one can beat this, and you know it."

"I'm willing to try," she moaned, pushing her ass toward my hand, begging for more. More fingers. More pressure. More *us*.

I stood up and let her fall on my bed, headfirst. I slapped the side of her ass and pushed my knee between her hamstrings, signaling her to lift it up in the air. She complied, biting my sheets, her eyes squeezed shut. I pushed my cock between her ass cheeks and looped her long, wavy locks around my fist, pulling her head up so I could whisper in her ear, "You're going to change your number when we're done here."

She laughed erotically, her neck extended, long and delicate. I let go of her hair to squeeze it just a little, fingering her anus again to make sure it was lubricated enough with her juices.

"I think I'm going to give him a chance, actually. He seems like a nice guy. Available, too."

I thrust into her all at once, knowing it was wrong. Knowing it was a punishment, not a reward—a mixture of pleasure, agony, and guilt making my abs tighten against the mound of her ass. She was *Mine.* With a capital M.

It wasn't a request, a plea, or a hope, but a simple fact. Her eyes confirmed it, her body sang it, and if she thought I was in the business of sharing, she obviously needed a sore reminder that I wasn't.

She lurched forward from my thrust, standing on all fours, and purred as I pounded into her tight asshole, so impossibly snug I could feel it milking the orgasm out of me with a vise-like grip. I slipped my hand down her stomach to find her swollen clit. She quivered under my arm.

"Fuck." I bit the tip of her ear. "Fuck, Judith, fuck."

She groaned, her ass meeting my hipbones again and again, challenging me thrust for thrust, push for push, touch for touch. Just another day in the newsroom. Me pushing. Her pulling. Both of us chasing the feeling only the other person could give.

Fuck the guy who'd gotten her phone number. Fuck him and all the other men in New York.

"I need to quit you," she mumbled to herself.

I need to own you.

Her body convulsed under me, cresting and tipping deeper into oblivion with every plunge, and I couldn't help it, I had to do it, I bit the back of her neck like an animal—a savage, a delinquent—and plastered a palm over her throat, bringing her up so we were both standing on our knees as I shot my load inside her perfect, milky-white ass. She let out a scream that echoed inside my mostly empty bedroom as we both climaxed.

A few seconds later, she collapsed on my bed, spineless and thoroughly fucked. I fell next to her, facing the opposite wall. My default strategy was to pussy-block pillow talk and avoid eye contact. It wasn't personal. I'd done that to Lily, too, back when we were together.

I planked, just turning around to look at her face, when the words left her mouth.

"I should go."

"I'll call a cab." My ego was fucking me harder than I'd fucked her, and that said a lot about its stamina.

"It's okay. I…"

"I'll drive you." I changed my mind.

She hated me spending money on her, but giving her a ride didn't cost shit. Of course, it did require me to move my car from the garage for the first time in a fucking decade.

She nodded, her face solemn. I'd never really entertained the idea of having a woman stay over. The one and only time I'd done some actual sleeping with a woman in the past year was, oddly, with Jude, at the hotel suite. That time was different, because I knew she didn't want to go back to wherever she was supposed to be and didn't take it personally.

Besides, we'd hardly cuddled and whispered sweet nothings in each other's ears. I'd just crashed, and by the time I woke up with a raging hard-on and a mission in mind to fuck her into a coma, she was already gone.

"You know, I caught my boyfriend cheating on me, too. It made me feel like the world was ending."

I clasped a lock of her hair and fingered it. Pure gold. I went through the same shit, maybe even ten times worse, seeing as the guy who was fucking my girl was very familiar to me. "Did it?"

She chuckled. "I'm still here, aren't I?"

"Doesn't necessarily mean shit. Have you talked to him since?"

"No. Not since that call. I have zero tolerance toward cheaters. Unlike some people I know."

I deserved that.

"You can stay over." I ignored her jab. "The daily trip to Brooklyn is bullshit. I can give you the spare key."

Am I fucking high? What was in that pasta? I only had one shot. Still, I couldn't find it in myself to take any of those words back.

Judith tucked her yellow hair behind her ears and ran her pearly whites over her lower lip. She seemed to consider it.

It was a relief not to get shut down immediately, since the suggestion in itself was ludicrous.

"That's not a good idea." She paused, flipping on her cellphone and checking the time. It was well after eleven. "I will take that ride back home, though, if it's still on the table."

"It is."

"Let me get my dress and wash my face." She hopped out of the bed, all business, like we were back at work. I watched her perky white ass jiggling in my hallway.

I closed my eyes. A gust of air with the scent of her shampoo and body lotion caressed my nose, and I took a deep, greedy breath.

Not good. Not good. Not good.

Her phone was between the sheets, beeping with new text messages.

Brianna: Thanks for helping me with the filing today! xoxo

Grayson: If I were a Victoria's Secret model, which one would I be?

Ava: Going to get my nipple pierced this weekend. Wish me luck. Did that cute guy call you yet?

I grabbed it, took out the SIM and split it in half before inserting it back into her phone and smashing the whole thing against the floor.

If that guy wanted Judith, he'd have to look for her the old-fashioned way, among the eight million residents of New York.

Break a leg, buddy.

Jude

One day I noticed Dad's face was no longer the same pale shade as the bathroom wall.

He was going through something called adoptive cell transfer therapy. The treatments were invasive and uncomfortable, but every time he came back home, he smiled bigger than the last time. He was still weak. He was still gray. But he no longer spoke like he was ready to die but too ashamed to let go of life because he knew how much I needed him, and that made my heart soar.

We spent more and more time out of the house—short trips around the block, arm in arm, admiring the festival of colors as New York burst into full-blown summer. Green leaves rustled above our heads and barefoot children ran around the neighborhood pointing hoses at each other and spreading wild laughter like confetti. Flowers unfurled in their sleepy beds on the edges of our neighborhood's sidewalks.

I still hadn't told Dad I knew about Célian, and I intended to keep it that way. Even though we were cautiously optimistic, there was a good chance the treatment wouldn't work. In which case, I would forever blame myself for confronting him about lying to me and trying to save both of us when really, I should've been cherishing every moment with him. So I chose to do that instead of picking a fight.

"Are you going to the library today?" Dad asked.

"Yeah, I need to catch up on some reading material for work. Why?"

"Oh, we got an invitation from Mrs. Hawthorne to come watch that new Jack Nicholson movie. She's making Irish stew. But of course, you don't have to come."

"I'll take a pass. I think you'll have a good time by yourselves, anyway." I knocked my shoulder against his, smiling brightly.

"It's not what you think."

"You don't know what I think."

Dad had never dated after Mom died, and not for my lack of trying to fix him up with people. I'd spent the majority of my college years trying to get him to sign up on dating sites—before he got sick. I was desperate for him to be happy, and never wanted him to think he shouldn't be on my account.

"It's really just a movie and dinner."

"Dinner? I thought it was a lunch thing."

We stopped by the grocery store on the corner of our street, and he blushed. Actually blushed. I was almost giddy with excitement. Such a natural human reaction, but on his pale, ill skin, it looked like a glorious sunrise.

"Don't worry, I have other plans for the afternoon. How's Milton?" He scratched his head.

Right. Milton. It'd been several weeks since I'd mentioned him to Dad. Then again, he'd very rarely dragged his butt to Brooklyn even when we were dating. Dad wasn't too suspicious, because I worked insane hours—it still felt like I was barely at home to spend time with him. I didn't want to explicitly lie to him, but this lie had gotten so big, it felt almost criminal to come clean at this point. Especially on this beautiful, sunny day, when we were both happy and smiling.

"He's good, Dad." I pulled him into a hug. "Taking names and kicking ass at *The Thinking Man*." Not technically a lie. Our mutual so-called friends had been happy to break the news that Milton had recently been promoted to junior editor. For them, it was more reason for me to get down from the ego tree I'd climbed up and take him back. For me, it was yet more proof of the fact that he was still sleeping with his boss.

Of course, I wasn't a big enough a hypocrite to point that out.

"My cell is broken at the moment, so I'm going to call you when I get to the library from the public phone. I'll try you here, and at Mrs. Hawthorne's, so please be available."

Two hours later, I was walking to the subway on my way to the library. I'd dressed down, embracing the fact that it wasn't a workday. I felt juvenile and reckless in skull-themed Chucks. The world felt lighter when you wore flannel shirts, ripped jeans, and a messenger bag. I adjusted the strap over my shoulder, about to enter the station when someone honked their horn behind me.

Rolling my eyes, I proceeded.

"Judith." The commanding tone found its way straight to my core, making my stomach swirl with delicious heat. Jesus Christ, what was he doing here?

Jesus: "Didn't you say something a while back about hitting Sunday Mass sometime in the next decade? Maybe you could take your foul-mouthed, engaged boss with you."

I turned around slowly, feigning annoyance, because the alternative was showing him how much I cared, how much it affected me to see him here. In Brooklyn. On a Sunday. *Take that, Milton.*

Célian sat in his silver Mercedes-Benz in a navy, short-sleeved sport shirt, his Ray-Bans tipped down to examine me.

"What are you doing here?" I narrowed my eyes. I hadn't spoken to him since the phone incident. We'd talked business in the office, but every time he'd tried to pretend like that night hadn't happened—like he hadn't broken my phone just because I'd exchanged numbers with some random guy at a diner—I turned around and walked away.

"You can't keep ignoring me."

"Pretty sure I can. Exhibit A: this conversation."

"I'm your boss."

"Precisely, and you crossed a lot of lines."

"You could have made a great lawyer."

"Not satisfied with my performance as a reporter?"

"Quite the contrary. As a booty call, however, you do a lousy job."

"Good. Consider this my official resignation."

He lifted his hand, waving a brand new cellphone. It was the new model that had just come out a hot minute ago and was already out of stock.

"With twelve cases in different colors to suit your mood." He shot me his devastatingly charming smirk. "Truce?"

"Never. But I do need a phone."

This was a gift I was willing to accept solely because he was responsible for the untimely death of my previous phone. It'd been a rough few days without one, but I wasn't exactly swimming in money to buy a replacement. I'd had to arrive at work even earlier and leave slightly later to make sure I wasn't needed or MIA, and at home, I checked my email every half hour.

He clutched the new device to his chest, and mine tightened in response.

"Come get it, Chucks."

He was blocking the traffic, and someone honked behind him. Three, long beeps.

"You want to get her number, park like a goddamn man and let us through!" someone yelled behind him.

Célian ignored the guy completely, ruthlessly entitled to the bone.

"No, thanks," I resumed my walk to the subway.

He began to drive slowly beside me. Not unlike a creeper. I rolled my eyes, but couldn't help but feel a little satisfaction at the way he'd been chasing me the last few days. He'd even come down to the fifth floor to fetch me from lunch with Ava and Grayson, muttering an excuse about an urgent meeting, when really, all he'd wanted was to ask if we could see each other that night.

The answer, by the way, had been a big, fat *no*.

"I want to show you something." His car was blocking a long line of vehicles now.

"You already showed me plenty," I muttered, secretly liking that people were still honking at him, and that for the first time in our relationship, he was the one out of sorts.

"Get your mind out of the gutter. I mean geographically."

"Would you like to dazzle me with your rich-boy Hamptons house? Show me another glitzy hotel you own?" I made grand, hoity-toity gestures with my hands as I walked.

Four. You're acting like a four year old. That wasn't Jesus speaking. Just me.

"In the fucking car, Chucks."

"Say the magic word."

"My cock."

I made a gagging sound.

"I agree. It is abnormally big, but I haven't heard any complaints."

"The magic word," I repeated.

"*Please.*" The word rolled off his tongue like it was in a foreign language.

"Whoops. Still a no."

My determined stroll slowed when his catcalling stopped. Had he given up on me? I took a few more steps before a hand grabbed my wrist. I looked up. He was smirking darkly, his thick eyebrows drawn together.

"Grayson was right. This *is* kidnapping..." I said as Célian yanked me toward his car.

He'd parked in the middle of the street, blocking approximately thirteen cars now, all of them honking. Some had tried to reverse and slip out of the road. To say Célian didn't give a crap wouldn't be a stretch. I got into his car and buckled up, mainly because I didn't want anyone to put a bullet in his head for his behavior. He started driving and strapped in as he did, not wasting any time.

"Where are we going?" I asked.

"You'll see."

"You never apologized for the phone."

"I do. I am. It wasn't my finest moment. I would say I didn't mean it, but lying on top of breaking your shit would really be rude. You shouldn't have exchanged numbers with another man. I've been dutifully faithful to you from the moment my tongue touched your crack."

I threw my hands in the air. "You're engaged, psycho!"

"It's not real."

"It is to me."

"Bullshit. You wouldn't touch a taken man, and we both know it. We aren't cheaters."

"Does that mean we're in some sort of a relationship in your weird mind?"

"Not a relationship, but an arrangement. Yes. Do you think you can handle that?"

I laughed bitterly. "I can't fall in love, Célian. I'm broken."

"Good. Let's be broken together, then."

He threw the phone into my hands. It was fully charged and ready to be used. It should have made me happy, but it didn't. I enjoyed having sex with him, and butting heads with him in the newsroom, but what was the point of all this? Love might not be in the cards for me, but I was getting more attached, setting myself up to get hurt more than I already was.

"Open the glove compartment," he said, still staring at the busy road ahead.

And yet again, I had the feeling he knew exactly what I was thinking. I opened the glove compartment. "What am I looking for?"

"Morrissey."

I patted the mostly empty space, my hand coming to rest on the familiar shape of my iPod. I yanked it out and squeaked. My precious iPod, with the thousands of songs I'd collected over the years, was back in my hand, and it felt glorious.

"Did someone find it at the hotel?" I turned to him.

"Yes. I did. The night you bailed on me."

I frowned. "Why did you never give it back?"

He shot me a look I couldn't decode—maybe bewildered verging on annoyed. "You stole something from me, so I stole something from you."

Huh. I sat back, considering this. He rubbed his jaw.

"Who's Kipling?"

Kipling was my notebook. But of course, I didn't miss an opportunity to mess with him.

"A friend."

"A good friend?"

I nodded. "Very."

"How long have you known him?"

I grinned at this. I didn't know if Célian was aware he was jealous, but I saw it from the outside. "Long enough."

We drove into Manhattan and parked at his building. He rounded the car, took a duffel bag from the trunk, and we went up to the ground floor and out to the street.

"Where are we going?" I asked as he flung the duffel bag over his shoulder, looking royally pissed and completely disturbed by what we were doing.

"On a date." He sighed, like I was forcing him to hang out with me at gunpoint.

"Huh?" I laughed. I'd ignored him for just over four days, and he was taking me on a date now? Imagine what would happen if I actually went through with what my brain told me I should do on a daily basis and cut things off with him completely.

"I'm taking you on a date. What's not to understand?"

"What's with the duffel bag? Is that in case you're bad at romancing and have to kill me before I tell anyone?"

We rounded the corner to Central Park West and headed straight to the meadow. He scoffed. "I can charm the panties off of a nun."

"Charming your way into underwear and into hearts are two different skills."

"I'm a good multitasker."

"Not to mention I haven't agreed to date you. You never even asked," I pointed out.

"I thought it was a given."

"Why?"

"You gave me backdoor access—a woman's version of expensive jewelry."

"Anyone ever told you you're a delusional piece of work?"

He smirked. "Is that an actual question? I can count on one hand the number of people I know who *haven't* called me that."

"Just because I like it when you boss me in bed doesn't mean I want to be with you." I blushed, fighting the urge to look down and break eye contact. He stopped at the John Lennon memorial, where the word *Imagine* looked back up at us.

Imagine that Mom is wrong. That I am capable of falling in love. That I am heading into a collision of feelings. That lust and heartache are going to crash together soon, and tragedy will explode.

He laced his fingers in mine, turned me around to face him, and tapped my nose, his lips tilted up arrogantly. "You have skulls on your shoes."

"You have skulls in your eyes."

"Are we feeling morbid today, Chucks?"

"No. Just deadly."

The park was swarming with people. Clusters of tourists, couples, cyclists, parents, and children. Even though Célian wasn't clad in his usual expensive suit, we still looked so different. For one thing, he was ten inches taller, ten years older, and reeked of a privileged air I lacked in every way. I had dressed like a teenager. He'd dressed like a millionaire. And the way he stood, tall and proud, made people stop and stare.

He put his mouth on mine and kissed me in front of everyone—soft and slow and seductive. Kissed me like no one was around, like we were alone in this city, this park, this planet. He pressed a possessive hand over the small of my back and jerked me to his body.

Then he caressed my cheek. His lips dragged from my lips to my ear and he whispered, "This is where I went every time my parents fought—every time Mathias blamed me for being the little snitch who'd killed his marriage. This is where I went when we started fighting physically. And this is where I went when I knew he would have his staff driving around looking for me. They never came into Central Park. This was my place."

My heart fluttered inside my ribcage and I saw Célian not only as the man he wanted people to see, but also as the person he really was. Not completely broken, but definitely cracked enough for pain to spill through the fissures.

We unpacked the duffel bag under a huge tree. Célian was surprisingly organized for our picnic. We spread a blanket, and he took out grapes, cheese, crackers, wine, and fancy chocolate. I told him there was no way he'd done this himself, and he admitted he'd given his housekeeper pot in exchange for these goodies. I laughed, and he threw a grape at my face. It made me laugh harder.

The sun was glorious, and I laid on the blanket and stared back at the sky, munching on almond chocolate that melted between my fingers. He sat next to me, staring at me intently, like he expected me to get up and run away any second, like I could evaporate into thin air, like sharing this place with me meant something to him.

"How was your relationship with Camille?" I asked.

I'd always wanted a sibling. Unfortunately, my mom got sick shortly after I was born. She won the first round of breast cancer. The second one, too. By the third, her body was too exhausted to fight, but I knew my parents had always wanted more kids.

He smirked at the blue sky like the clouds had cleared up especially for us.

"We were a team. Maybe because Maman was busy running around with her lovers and Mathias made a point of sticking his dick into everything with a pulse, we figured out early on that we had to have each other's backs to survive."

I nodded. "You must miss her very much."

"Losing someone close defines you. I trust you know that by now. I'm sorry about your mother," he said. And he meant it. I appreciated him not extending his condolences to my dad. Some people did when they heard about the cancer.

I looked down and stared at a chocolate cube slowly melting in my hand, gluing my forefinger and thumb together. "I think I wanted to marry Milton just so I'd have someone to catch me in case I fall. You know?"

He stuck his hand in my hair and leaned down to kiss my forehead. "I do. But falling into the wrong hands is just as bad as crashing into nothing."

His phone, sitting between us, buzzed, and I looked down at it. The name Lily Davis flashed, making my heart sink. He hit ignore and tossed the phone to the other side of the blanket.

"You can answer it if you need to." *Don't cry.*

"I don't need to."

"I will never understand your relationship with her."

"That makes the two of us."

So end it! I wanted to scream. His phone started dancing on the blanket again. I rose on my forearms, as he sent the call to voicemail once again.

"I want to go home."

"Chucks…"

His phone began to vibrate for the third time. Célian muttered, "Jesus Christ" and shoved it in the duffel bag, zipping it shut and throwing it against the tree.

He sucked his bottom lip into his mouth. "Hey, hey…"

I stood and began to clean everything up. He didn't say anything else until we'd arrived at his building. I continued toward the train station, and he groaned, easily catching up with my steps.

"Let me get your ass home."

"Leave me alone, Célian." I stopped. Hot anger bubbled and sizzled behind my ribcage. "Huh? How about that? How about stop doing this thing where you treat me like I mean something, only to go and marry someone else? Because it doesn't matter that you don't love her, or touch her. If anything, it is much, much worse. You're not giving up on us—whatever *we* are—for some great love. You're canceling it for some sick need to get back at your father. And yes, falling into Milton's arms would have been wrong, but wrapping your arms around Lily is nothing short of disastrous. So don't you dare lecture me."

"The asshole fucked my fi—"

"Yes. I heard. Many, many times. So what if he did?" I cut him off, balling my hands into fists. "Him doing something wrong doesn't give you the right to do something even worse." I pushed his chest. Jesus Christ—what was I doing?

Jesus, filing his nails: "Using my name to excuse yourself of bad behavior, as per usual."

"*He* was the one who sent Phoenix to Syria. He was the one who insisted we keep it from her and keep them apart. But somehow her death is my fault?" he yelled in my face, as if I was the one accusing him. "Fuck. That."

"Stop the blame game, Célian. Every relationship you touch wilts. Every connection you make perishes. I don't want to burn. I want to flourish. I *deserve* to bloom."

I turned around again, heading for the station. This time he grabbed my wrist so hard I thought he was going to yank my arm off. I think he realized it, too, by the way he withdrew his hand quickly and gathered me into a hug—a hug I wanted to reject but chose to drown in, a hug I knew would catch me the right way if I ever fell, from a man who'd made no promises to be there when I needed him.

I wrapped my arms around his body, he buried his face in my hair, and for a few long seconds, we didn't say anything. Every bad feeling was crushed between our pressing chests.

"Weren't you the one who said you can't fall in love?" he sneered after a few beats, cocking his head sideways. "What happened to that?"

"Doesn't mean I don't care."

"I *care*." He took a step back, slapping his fist over his chest. "I should have been spending time with your father today. Instead, I took you on a goddamn *date*," he spat the word out like it was poisonous.

I couldn't even deal with the idea of him hanging out with my dad on a regular basis. When did that start happening?

"Know when the last time I took someone on a date was? Sixteen. Pretty sure I did that for a hand job. Since then, I don't have to try. I've never tried."

I snorted, too aware of the fact that an audience had gathered around us. "Should I feel special right now?"

His jaw locked, and his eyes darkened, like he'd remembered who he was. Who *I* was. "At least have the decency to be honest with yourself, Chucks. You don't want me to care. You want me, period."

I turned around and gave him the one thing he did not unrightfully yet claim.

My back.

"All I'm saying is he's like a half-priced facelift in an unregistered clinic in Eastern Europe. I would still do it, even knowing it's deadly." Grayson tossed a piece of Romaine lettuce into his mouth and chewed loudly.

We were sitting at Le Coq Tail on our lunch break—me, him, Ava, and Phoenix. It had been a few days since my failed date—or whatever that was—with Célian, and in a moment of weakness I'd decided to confide in my close friends about the affair. Although, suffice it to say, they'd already had a pretty good idea.

"Trust me, girl, we can all see Célian's appeal." Ava sucked hard on the straw swimming in her glass of Diet Coke. "But consider it your official intervention. After we got a first-row seat to the shitshow called your relationship, I can honestly say you need to put a lid on that thing before your crazy starts to simmer."

I bumped my fists together twice, Friends-style. "I'm not crazy."

I was seventy-percent sure of that statement.

Ava clucked her tongue. "Neither was Lily. I think it's something about the Laurent dick. They make their women unbalanced. I heard Célian's mother is not the sanest, either."

"We're casual." I tried another tactic.

Gray pouted and rolled his eyes. "Is that why he *casually* claimed your ass a la Khal Drogo saving his princess from an army of savages when you had lunch on our floor last week? Admit it. You got your boss pussy-spelled."

"That's not a word," Phoenix pointed out, pointing his sandwich at Grayson. "But it damn straight should be."

"What do you think?" I turned to Phoenix.

I knew Célian had paid him a visit the other day, and I knew he'd ordered him to stay away from me, beyond platonically. A part of me was furious with Célian, and another hoped what I thought he couldn't admit to himself: that I wasn't the only person falling around here, and he, too, didn't have a parachute to save him from the plunge.

It's just sex.

It's just a distraction.

You can't fall in love.

You've never fallen in love.

Phoenix bit the inside of his cheek.

"Are you high?" Ava asked. "Phoenix and Célian hate each other."

But Phoenix looked up and told me point blank, "I think you're his atonement. He wants to save you, but you're the one who needs to save him."

I did a double take, placing my roast beef sandwich on my plate.

He looked serious. "I've known Célian for a few years now—since before I started working at LBC. I've seen him and Lily together—even when they were *really* together." He lifted his chin, his voice cracking. "Célian looks at you the way I looked at Camille, like he would burn the world for you. Just because he doesn't want to recognize it doesn't make it any less true. If the rumors surrounding him and his family are correct…" He averted his gaze to Ava and Gray, and that's when I knew *he* knew about Lily and Célian's father, probably through James Townley, who had his hand and ears everywhere in the LBC building. "Then Célian's trust in people is nonexistent, and rightly so. He is calloused, distrustful, and hardened, but he is also screwed, and he knows it."

"He's never going to leave Lily, is he?" I rubbed my forehead, feeling a looming headache pushing at the back of my nose.

"He might." "No." "Yes." The three of them spoke in unison.

And that's when I chose to laugh, instead of cry.

That day I made sure I avoided Célian in the newsroom. He was business as usual, taking Elijah and a few other men to lunch and then disappearing in and out of the sixtieth floor for meetings all day. When I got back home, I threw some chicken nuggets in the oven and took a box of mac and cheese out of the cupboard. I was in no mood to fix myself something fresh. Dad, however, had been eating a lot healthier since the experimental program had begun. They sent him special meals to complement his treatment. I untied my rain jacket and threw it on the couch after I started hot water on the stovetop, kicking my shoes into the hallway.

"Dad?" I called.

I checked the living room, bathroom, and then his bedroom. He wasn't there. Groaning in frustration, I texted him: **Where R U? When will you learn to give a girl a heads up when you're gone? I'm worried.**

And selfish, I inwardly bit out. Having Dad around was convenient. I could coddle him all I liked, essentially forgetting about Célian and his looming wedding. My phone flashed with a text message immediately.

Dad: Sorry! At Mrs. Hawthorne's. Please feel free to come upstairs. She made cherry pie.

I shook my head, laughing to myself. Could my father be falling in love at the same time I was falling apart?

Could his sick body experience something my healthy one couldn't feel?

Have fun, and send her my love.

Dad: Will do, sweetie. Maybe she can make some more pie this weekend and we can invite Milton?

I decided that there was enough heartbreak to go around between all of us, so I kept the lie alive, though it nearly killed me.

I'd like that, Dad. A lot.

Chapter Fourteen

Célian

As far as I was concerned, crazy had a smell.

It was flowery body lotion and Chanel No. 5. And it diminished my appetite the minute it crawled into my nostrils through the open door of my office.

The day had been shitty to begin with. Judith was working hard on giving me the best fucking leads to land on my desk in the past year, while simultaneously avoiding me.

I wanted to marry Lily slightly less than I wanted to fuck a cactus on live television. I knew it would bring a lot of joy to my father to know I'd given up on world domination and Newsflash Corp, and that Maman would be terribly disappointed—not because she wanted grandchildren, but because she'd have loved for me to become the next Richard Branson. Regardless, I *did* deserve the media mogul throne. But even I had limits.

And they were currently being tested. The unbearably sweet scent was followed by a loud thump.

"*Where is sheeeee?*" a manic screech pierced the silence of the entire floor.

I looked up from my laptop and found my fiancée standing atop a desk in the newsroom, clad in one of her horrendously expensive wrap mini dresses and Louboutin heels. *Always red. Always black.* Lily didn't have moods; she had obsessions with looking rich.

She grabbed a monitor and crashed it on the floor, sending Jessica and Elijah jumping backward with a shriek. Kate stood from her seat and galloped in Lily's direction. I stood and made my way to the newsroom, looking for Jude. She wasn't anywhere to be seen. *Good.* Lily wasn't above starting a cat fight, but if I had to put my money on a winner, it would be Judith.

"Lily," Kate said with calm authority, "if you want to leave this place without a security escort and handcuffs, I'd strongly suggest you remove yourself from the desk and stop breaking things."

"Shut up, bitch. For all I know it's you he's having an affair with." Lily sniffed, pointing her long fake nail at Kate.

I marched into the room and stopped at the desk she stood on. The rest of my newsroom stared up at Lily like she was Moses delivering the Ten Commandments, but she didn't seem to notice me, perhaps because she was more occupied with having a public meltdown.

"So you think Célian is having an affair?" Kate tapped her lips, musing.

"I know he is! Someone has been coming to his building. I have eyes and ears everywhere."

"Oh, Lordy," Kate chirped.

Coincidentally or not, the desk Lily stood on belonged to Judith. I didn't know how Jude would react if she found out her monitor had been smashed by this chick, but I was going to guess Lily wouldn't be the only one screaming in this room.

"Lily, you're embarrassing yourself, but more importantly, you're an embarrassment to me. Get down immediately," I commanded, snapping my fingers at her.

But as I said it, I realized that it wasn't true. Lily did not embarrass me. In fact, she'd stopped triggering any type of emotion in me, and world domination just wasn't quite enough to suffer her presence, even if only on paper.

We were a match made in Manhattan royalty heaven, but in the end, we'd put each other through hell. And in this very moment, I was done. If that meant that I was going to be a little less rich and a little less ruthless, I was willing to make that sacrifice to get rid of this pest.

Because even Lily's dear family wasn't enough anymore.

They weren't mine. They'd never be mine.

"Who is she, Célian?" She stomped her foot on Judith's notebook, denting the pages and creating a hole right in the middle.

My teeth slammed together, locking my jaw so a curse wouldn't come out.

"Do you love her? Do you?" she whined.

I took my phone out, done with her games.

"You'd call security on your fiancée?" She raised her arms in wonder and her lack of panties showed. She was naked underneath the dress, no doubt for me.

"On the fucking pope, if he interfered with my staff's work. Last chance before you spend the next few hours in jail," I said dryly.

People behind me chuckled and whispered. I hated that we were a spectacle, but I liked that she'd played right into my hands. She'd just provided me with a golden opportunity to dump her ass with little to no social consequences, and Judith wouldn't think it was about her.

Because it wasn't.

Judith was just a fuck.

A brilliant fuck, but nonetheless a disposable one.

Lily lowered herself with a groan, sliding her ass to the desk and scooting down. She landed on her heels with a whimper and ran toward me, throwing her arms over my neck and weeping into my shirt.

"Why, Célian? I thought we were getting better, and now I have to hear that my fiancé is taking a new girl places? That she visits his building?"

I should have been disturbed by the amount of information Lily was privy to, but after all, her entire life consisted of sitting around in coffee shops and gossiping. For all I knew, she had socialite friends living in my building.

I retrieved Jude's notebook and pocketed it. "Apologize to Kate and get into my office."

Kate stood behind Lily and shook her head, telling me I shouldn't let her get away with it.

"But she hates me." Lily stomped her feet, whining.

"Can't deny that." Kate lifted her hands in surrender, and everyone laughed.

I looked around the human circle that had formed around us and realized everyone in it looked at Kate with love and Lily with sheer disgust.

As far as they were concerned, she was a spoiled little bitch. And as far as they were concerned, I endorsed that kind of behavior. I would berate someone for days for making a grammatical error in a news report, yet I was choosing to marry someone who thought *yass* was a word?

"Inside my office, right now," I murmured through gritted teeth.

We turned and made our way to the hallway, and that's when I saw Judith standing at the entrance of the newsroom, still clutching her phone to her ear. She was on a call, probably something Syria related. We were running a primetime special about it this weekend, and she'd been working extra hard to get all the numbers and statistics.

Her eyes ping-ponged between me and Lily for about ten seconds before she took a step aside and let us through.

Lily scowled at her, then barked, "What the hell are you looking at? You're the prime suspect, bitch."

"Huh?" Judith's eyebrows shot up. She ended her call and tucked her phone into her pocket. "What is she talking about?"

"I'm talking about the woman who's been keeping my fiancé up all nigh—"

But she never got to finish that sentence, because I pulled her into an embrace like she was an animal in captivity, slapping my hand over her mouth and dragging her into my office.

Judith turned a nice shade of tomato red, her eyes widening in alarm.

"Back to work, Humphry," I barked.

"Yes, sir," she said, but her voice flatlined, delivering the news that I was in even deeper shit than I'd previously thought.

In my office, Lily threw her body over the couch and began to sob.

"It's the blond girl, isn't it? She looks like a homewrecker. All sweet and pretty with her please-save-me cheap outfit. And Converse. Who wears fucking Converse with a dress?"

Judith Humphry does, and it makes me so hard I'm pretty sure the rest my body turns anemic.

"Shut up," I ordered, bracing myself against my desk and staring her down.

I swear the teenaged version of her I'd dated over a decade ago had been sane. Shallow, but sane. Then again, when you're a teenager, you're not looking for a great intellectual opponent. Her ass and agreeable nature had been enough to keep me satiated for the first decade of our relationship.

"You know I can find out with little to no effort, right?" She perked up on the black leather couch, sniffing again. Her mascara ran down her cheeks in thick streaks, and it made her look like Alice Cooper, not to mention that her dress was more appropriate for a Vegas strip club than a newsroom. She unwrapped said dress, flashing me her tits and pink pussy.

"That won't be necessary, and neither will strip teasing," I deadpanned.

Her eyes brightened. "Does that mean you're getting rid of her?"

"Not her. You," I said simply.

We stared at each other for a few seconds while she digested this information, her face transforming from agonized to amused. Did she not understand English? Why was she so smug?

"You can't break up with me. What about Newsflash Corp?"

"I'll live without it. Getting rid of you is top priority. Put some clothes on."

She stood up and shoved my chest, not moving me an inch—partly because I was braced against the desk, but also because I was quite literally twice her size. I wondered if she realized the right-hand wall of my office was made of glass, then remembered that she gave very little shit about who saw her naked.

"You're a bastard. We grew up together. We're childhood sweethearts."

"If that's your only defense, it's lacking. Because I can crush it to pieces by bringing up something you did a little over a year ago." I chuckled darkly. "Keep the ring, cancel everything else. There will not be a wedding in August, Lily. It's over."

And as I said that, I realized there was not even an ounce of me that was remorseful—not even for letting her keep my family's ring (it was tainted once she'd worn it anyway) or the missed opportunity for so-called world domination Kate was always teasing me about.

"I'm going to make your life a living hell, Célian." Lily wiggled her finger in my face. I took her finger and lowered it, wrapping her dress back around her waist for her.

"I dare you, sweetheart. It's been too long since I showed you who I really am. I cannot wait for you to get reacquainted with the asshole version everyone else has been privy to for the past year, partly because of you." I couldn't dump all the blame on Lily, though. My father had taken the Worst Dad of the Century trophy, leaving others to eat dust.

"You're insane!" she yelled in my face.

"That's rich, coming from a half-naked woman who just broke a monitor and accused a gay, middle-aged woman of having an affair with her fake fiancé."

"You're weird. And a smartass. I don't even like you anymore." She walked over to the door, made a U-turn, stared at me helplessly, and shook her head. "Tell me how to make it right, and I will." Her voice cracked around her plea.

"Get out."

The door slammed in my face, and my eyes immediately traveled to the newsroom through the glass walls. Judith was staring at me, like she wanted my eyes to bleed out the truth of what had happened in my office. But I couldn't invite her in. Not so soon after kicking Lily out. That would be transparent, downright risky.

I dialed Brianna's extension and asked her to summon Judith for a one on one rundown meeting in three hours. I asked her to do the same for Kate, Elijah, and James. I had nothing to say to the last three. I just didn't want it to look suspicious.

I fell into my seat and closed my eyes. A text message dinged on my phone, and I flipped it over to see who it was.

Dan: Your father is at a meeting right now, selling ad space to a Vegas-based marketing company that specializes in condoms, tobacco, gambling equipment, and sex toys. I'm sitting in the same restaurant. They're talking seven figures.

This deal would be suicide for the LBC brand, and my father knew it. This was a prime example of how far he'd go to sabotage things for me.

Record everything please, I ordered.

It was time to take this matter to the board and bury what was left of my relationship with the man who hated me just a little less than I hated him.

Three meaningless conversations later (Kate was happy to know I'd called the engagement off with Lily; Elijah and I talked baseball; and James tried to give me some fatherly advice about women and relationships, only to be sent out with his tail between his legs.), Judith entered my office.

The minute she walked in, the urge to push her against the door, spread her legs, and fuck her relentlessly burned through my veins, but I settled for an easy smirk.

"Humphry."

"Sir."

I was seated behind my desk—something my erection was very grateful for—and I motioned for her to take a seat across from me. She did so obediently, her back straight. I handed her the notebook I'd managed to retrieve from Lily. It was wrinkled as fuck. Jude took it in shaky hands.

"Thank you," she said quietly.

"I'll buy you another one."

"I don't want another one. I like this one."

Fuck. Why did that make me even harder?

She shook her head, sighing. "You wanted to see me?"

"There are a few matters we need to discuss as a result of the unexpected appearance of Miss Davis at the newsroom." I loosened my tie.

Jude smiled her sweet, innocent smile. "That's a lovely way of describing a batshit crazy woman who broke a monitor and ruined my notebook, if I ever heard one."

I smirked. Sat back. Knotted my fingers together. "I sent Brianna to the third floor to get one of James' stylists to iron Kipling back into shape."

Her eyes widened, her lower lip poking out. "How did you…?"

"Figured it out." I waved her off.

Not quite. The mystery had occupied my mind for many long nights. So much so that I'd pieced together every encounter in which she'd mentioned Kipling. She'd had the notebook clutched in her palm in all of them.

Jude looked touched, and I needed her not to be, so I continued. "At any rate, Miss Davis will be in no position to further damage property or harass LBC employees anymore, especially seeing as I terminated our engagement."

Which was really a nice way of saying we could go back to fucking peacefully without Judith giving me the third degree, just not in so many words.

"Is that why I'm here?" she asked, jutting her chin out. "Because you think I'll jump back into your bed?"

"And couch. And office door. And fucking public toilet, if I say so." I shrugged, sitting back and smirking at her.

"You're wrong, Célian. When I told you I don't do love, I meant it. But I don't do casual, either. I need it to mean something. I was with Milton because I'm capable of having a relationship. I'm capable of giving."

I really didn't want to hear about that douche, Milton. At the same time, my growing need to fuck Judith might very well make my balls explode. I decided I would compromise my truth—if not bend it just a little—to accommodate her needs.

"I can do a discreet arrangement."

"I don't want an *arrangement*. I want a *relationship*."

"Whatever you want to call it, Chucks. As long as you realize there is nothing at the end of that tunnel—no marriage, no wedding, no kids, and no cozy evenings watching Jeopardy with your dad—you can have it. Now pack a bag. We're going to Miami for the weekend."

I thought about all I'd said and decided to amend one thing. "Actually maybe Jeopardy is okay sometimes. Your pussy will need an occasional rest."

"Miami?" Her eyes widened like I'd suggested Afghanistan. She recovered quickly, clearing her throat and adding, "We haven't finished working on the Syria piece."

Right. *Fuck*. Of course we still needed to wrap it up.

"We'll work into the night."

"I promised Dad I would watch the Yankees game with him." She reddened.

I hated that I liked that about her—her fierce loyalty to her family. No matter how late she stayed at work, she somehow always made time for her pops.

But maybe Jude wasn't anything special. Maybe I just had no idea how a normal family worked and was giving her extra credit.

"You may have the night off," I said curtly. "I'll send a cab to take you to the airport. Anything else?"

She stared at me for a few seconds, still blinking in disbelief. I guess I'd expected her to be happier about the news, but I didn't exactly deliver it with flowers and sugary promises.

"You're single?" she confirmed.

I raked my eyes over her. "Seems that way."

"You broke it off with her?" She rubbed her forehead, looking around the room. Why? Was she expecting this to be a big prank? Clearly, she thought very little of me in the morals department.

"Do you need this in writing, Humphry?"

"That would be great, actually."

I smirked. "Get your smart ass out of my office before I spank it."

"You're awful," she said, getting up from her seat and walking back to the door.

I watched her every movement, wondering why I found her so fascinating, and inwardly asking myself what the fuck I was doing, taking this random chick to see my mother—*Maman*—who was still blissfully ignorant of the collapse of my engagement.

"You like awful," I retorted.

She stopped by the door, bowed her head and shook it, laughing. When she left, the smell of hope crawled into my nostrils, the smell of her vanilla shampoo and gingery, spicy perfume.

And I had to admit, I liked it a whole a lot better.

Jude

J*ust smile and act normal.*

Dad sat at my side, wearing an S. Carter jersey and a Yankees ball cap and drinking soda, which was definitely *not* on his current menu. I let it slide because he looked completely enchanted with the game. I, myself, wore a huge American flag hat and a Frank Sinatra shirt. Close enough, if you ask me.

I broached the subject when I got back from refilling our bowl of popcorn in the kitchen—another thing Dad shouldn't be eating, but a little couldn't hurt.

"Would you…would you mind if I took off this weekend?" I tried to sound casual through the lump of guilt forming in my throat.

My palms were so sweaty the popcorn bowl nearly slipped between them. I was going to lie to Dad yet again, and for what? Why did I keep the truth from my father, the closest person to me? I wasn't doing anything wrong. Then again, he was still so fragile and was only now getting back on his feet, literally and figuratively. He was feeling physically better, and between spending time with Mrs. Hawthorne and seeing me thrive at my new job, he was emotionally better too.

But I still didn't want him to know I'd broken up with Milton. That could set Dad back, and if his health took a wrong turn, I'd never forgive myself.

"Honey." He patted my knee as I sat down, his hand immediately sliding to the bowl of popcorn. "I think it's a great idea. You deserve some time off. Mil taking you anywhere fancy?" He smiled.

"You're going to hell for this," Jesus said inside my head. *"And if you think I'll claim your ass when you get there, you obviously weren't paying attention in bible class."*

I decided I would, in fact, tell my father I'd broken up with Milton after I got back from Florida. I could even tell him about Célian, as the two seemed to be in contact. I wasn't sure how much they had in common, but part of the reason I didn't despise Célian—though it was tempting—was because I knew he had a soft side. I'd seen it when he helped my father. I saw it when he tried to save *me.*

"I don't know..." I dodged the question. "We'll see. You know I'll be available on my phone, right?"

"Yes." He laughed, shuttling more popcorn to his mouth. "You've mentioned so, one or two or a million times before. Plus, if I need anything, Mrs. Hawthorne is just upstairs."

I eyed him curiously, smiling. "When do I finally get to meet her in the capacity of being her boyfriend's daughter?"

My father looked down and wiggled his toes inside his slippers.

That's the first time I'd noticed he was wearing a new pair. Actually, his whole ensemble was new—still the same gray sweatpants and white T-shirt, but they were ironed and looked good on him. He'd also shaved whatever was left of his hair to create a more unified look. I didn't know why I found it so heartbreakingly joyful to see him happy about another woman. Maybe I shouldn't have. But he did look kind of good, like a brow-less Bruce Willis.

"Does he make your heart sing, JoJo?"

"What?" I pretended to laugh. And failed. Oh, God.

"Does Milton make your heart sing? Music is such an important part of your life, and when you're happy, I can see it. Your steps have a rhythm. When you talk, you swing. Are you in love with him? Because if you're not, it's not worth it."

I looked the other way, pretending to clean invisible lint off of a decorative pillow on the couch. "I can't fall in love, Dad. I tried."

"That's a load of bull."

"It's true. Mom told me so. She said my heart was a lonely hunter—that it would never find someone else to beat next to. And she was right. It didn't."

I didn't tell him the whole truth—that I believed her, that I guarded my heart like it wasn't for the taking. That I probably could have moved in with Milton if I'd wanted to, but I'd never really wanted to. I didn't want to tell Dad that this one simple sentence had changed my world more than I was willing to accept, and that I was terrified my heart was losing its claws, its weapons, its hunger for blood, in the battle against Célian.

Dad's eyes crinkled, and I was so focused on the confusion and awe in them, it didn't even register that he was laughing. Not just laughing—hooting. Holding his stomach and everything.

"No, JoJo, no. She didn't mean *your* heart is a lonely hunter. She meant the book, *The Heart is a Lonely Hunter* by Carson McCullers. It was her favorite. The author was twenty-three when she wrote it. Your age." He looked at me pointedly, like this, too, added meaning. "Mick Kelly was your mother's favorite heroine. She was a tomboy who was really fond of music. You should read it. We have it somewhere here."

He rose to his feet with a groan and made his way to his room. I sat dumbfounded, feeling irrationally furious at both him and my mother for allowing me to look at life through the thick, dirty lens of a person who'd never believed she could experience love.

The game was still playing, with the Yankees dominating the Astros, and that's how I knew Dad really was serious about me reading this book. He came back, blowing the dust off the cover, and handed it to me.

"If you travel at all on your way to this little vacation, make sure you read it. Your mother believed in love. Very much so. She believed in fate, too. That's why you grew up to be the heroine she always admired."

I smiled and thanked him, and I didn't wait for tomorrow.

I devoured the whole thing in one night.

Every single page. A to Z.

Then I read bits of it again as I packed my summer clothes and dragged my suitcase down our narrow stairway in the morning, waiting for the cab.

My heart was not lonely.

It was desperate and beating and alive.

It frightened and delighted me at the same time, knowing that I could, and I would, and I *should* fall in love—whether it was with my boss or otherwise.

And when the alarm started singing, I slid into the right Chucks and wiggled my toes inside them, knowing he was going to notice. They were yellow.

Hope.

I'd only been on a plane two times prior to my trip to Florida with Célian.

One had taken us to California when I was six—Mom's sister got married, but she had since decided to divorce, then migrate to Australia. She sent a postcard when Mom died, but didn't bother to keep in touch. The second time was for a spontaneous vacation in New Orleans. That had happened when I was fourteen. Dad had been trying his best to act like everything was fine after Mom died. He dyed his hair at home to forget he had any silver strands, took cooking classes, and decided we should live in the moment. New Orleans was great. Us living off mac and cheese for two consecutive months afterward because we'd spent too much was not.

I'd assumed I was likely to get on a plane again sometime soon. I'd imagined Milton would plan something nice for our honeymoon, if we ever got married.

Business class, however, was something I'd never imagined.

Yet here I was, clutching my tattered copy of *The Heart is a Lonely Hunter* with a glass of champagne by my side, wondering where on Earth Célian was. We had five more minutes before the plane took off.

He stumbled through the door right before they locked it, wearing the same clothes as yesterday and nursing a cup of Starbucks. His leather Armani duffel bag hung lazily from the tips of his fingers, and the minute he saw me, his tired face cracked into a dangerous smile. I licked my lips, looking down and pressing my thighs together.

What the hell was wrong with me? Ever since I'd learned the truth about what Mom had told me, thinking of Célian was weird.

It felt like we were no longer rivals, like he had the upper hand. Which was ridiculous, because he always had. I'd simply refused to accept it.

Célian shoved his bag into the overhead bin and thanked the air hostess for hysterically offering to do so herself. He then slid into the seat next to me. He smelled of alcohol, coffee, and hope.

I wiggled my toes inside my yellow Chucks. "Came straight from work?"

Instead of answering my question, he cupped the back of my neck and erased the distance between us by sealing my mouth with a hot, demanding kiss. I groaned against his lips. When we disconnected, his eyes were half-lidded and drunk, and I assumed mine were too.

"That's...very relationship-y," I mumbled, staring at his lips. "Did I get all the information right?"

Célian plucked a red marker from the book sitting in my lap, uncapped it, and wrote A+ on the back of my hand. Then he kissed the inside of it, like Phoenix had done to me, and like I'd done to him. I swooned inside.

"Here's to many more revelations, and to saving the world, one item at a time." He took my glass from my side table, tipped it back, and then smashed his lips into mine again, this time letting me taste the alcohol in his mouth.

The plane had begun to take off when he looked more closely at the book in my lap. He grabbed it, examining it from all angles.

"Is it good?" he asked.

"The best," I said, resting my hand on the cover.

He put his hand on mine.

My heart smiled at that.

And all I could think was, *please don't hurt us.*

Chapter Sixteen

Célian

Shortly after takeoff, I sent Maman a heads-up of what was to come. Diplomatic it was not, but if she was looking for direct and honest, she certainly received it, and in spades.

Célian: Hopping on a plane to discuss Mathias with you, who, by the way, fucked my fiancée over a year ago. Consequently, I no longer have a fiancée. But I am bringing over a woman, so keep your claws tucked in.

P.S.

Brianna booked a conference call with the entire board later this afternoon, and that includes your philandering ex-husband. I sent you some recordings you need to listen to, so please do that in between auditioning new boy toys.

P.P.S.

I meant it about the claws. I am planning on keeping this one for a while.

After we landed, if Judith was surprised to find we were sharing a Mandarin Hotel suite, she didn't let it show. She dove headfirst onto the huge bed, making a snow angel on the sheets. I didn't know why that made me want to fuck her so hard I'd nail her to the mattress. I only knew that scraping her off of it was going to be a bitch, so I opted for jumping in the shower, seeing as I'd been working for thirty-six hours straight so we could take this trip and probably smelled like something had died inside of me, which wasn't far off.

We still hadn't discussed my engagement breakdown properly. I didn't think it was worth mentioning. We were both available now. I could fuck Judith raw against James Townley's green screen with zero consequences, other than having to replace the screen, which was something we were already planning on.

Everyone at work was already privy to the fact that Lily had gotten the boot after her little performance. Including, by definition, Ava and Gary-Graham-Grant. Whatever his name was.

When I left the bathroom, Jude was out on the balcony, her elbows on the white bannister overlooking the ocean. Her ass, clad in those ripped black jeans, swayed from side to side as she stood on one foot. I was still wrapped in a towel when I approached her, clasping her midriff from behind and grinding my erection into her ass.

"Spent some overtime to cover for your ass." I bit her earlobe, feeling her body break into chills beneath my touch.

"Looks like you're *still* covering my ass," she sassed, wiggling her round butt so my cock was now between her cheeks through her jeans and my towel. My hands slid down, undoing the button of her jeans and sliding the zipper down.

"Bend over and hold on to the bannister, Chucks. Gonna get a little rocky." I licked my lips, sliding down her jeans and underwear in one go and dropping the towel.

I wasn't much of an exhibitionist, which was why I'd also rented the rooms on either side of us. But of course I wasn't going to let her be privy to my level of crazy. What can I say? Having the option to fuck Judith Humphry everywhere in the room and outside of it took first priority, and I wasn't much of a hedonist, but booking an entire floor was a luxury I'd chosen to take this weekend.

I spread her ass cheeks and slapped her outer thigh lazily as I guided my cock into her already-dripping pussy. I wanted to go slow and steady this time. The last thing I needed was her tipping over the edge. Literally, not figuratively.

"Oh, Célian…" My name on her lips was a prayer.

"Yes?" I asked, thrusting a little harder, bending her down so her upper body was level with my cock and placing a hand over her lower back.

"I missed this," she whimpered.

I missed you. But of course, she couldn't milk those words out of me if my life depended on it. I slapped her ass instead.

"Didn't peg you for a filthy girl, Chucks. Yet here you are, fucking in front of him."

"In front of who?" A trace of panic touched her voice, and I laughed, gripping her head and fucking her a little harder.

"Kipling," I hissed, glancing at her notebook lying on the bed behind us, next to her book.

Yesterday, after Lily had unleashed her crazy in my newsroom, I'd caught Jude writing around the deep hole my ex had created in her notebook, and I'd suppressed the urge to rush out and bite down on her lower lip in front of everyone. Jude's loyalty, even to objects, mesmerized me.

"Jesus," she moaned as I thrust deeper into her. "You're such a jerk."

"So I've been told a million times. Half of them by you."

I dipped my hand between her legs and rubbed her slit, licking her neck and jaw and the inside of her ear. I didn't want to admit that fucking Judith felt different, that I was doing things with her I didn't usually do with my one-night stands. I wasn't a thoughtful lover. I wasn't necessarily against eating pussy if it looked delicious, but putting my mouth on a crack meant I was really crazy for a girl. And licking and sucking her every body part while fucking her? That was a first. I didn't even remember prepping Lily like that.

I felt Judith tighten and spasm around me, and then she came all over my cock, her ass shuddering against my groin. I wanted to come as hard as she had, so I grabbed her by the hair and turned her around, plastering her against the glass of the balcony door.

"Safety first," I groaned as I drove mercilessly into her. My balls tightened and I pulled out, milking my cum all over her lower back. That was more like it—a fuck, not lovemaking. I gave her ass one last slap and walked into the room, leaving the towel on the floor.

"I'm ordering room service. Clean up and let me know what you want, because your pussy is about to be my starter."

We never ate the lobster I ordered.

Jude said eating a room-serviced lunch was clinical and sad, that vacation meals equaled dodgy street food from questionable trucks and 7-11 candy bars you didn't know existed.

She was begging for food poisoning, but I couldn't deny her. And that was a problem I was beginning to recognize. There was something free and unhinged in the way she viewed life. Her lack of materialistic greed both stunned and ate at me.

So we went for a walk on the beach and ate Cuban sandwiches and drank iced tea on the promenade. The food was greasier than Elijah's hair, yet oddly satisfying.

Judith then asked if I knew how to skip stones across the water. I told her there were not many things I couldn't do, and meant it. I *didn't* mention that our servant had taught me how to do that during summer vacations at our chateau in St-Jean-Cap-De-Ferrat. I wasn't normally ashamed of my elite upbringing, but for reasons unknown, decided to keep this to myself.

She asked me to teach her. I did.

"Flat, round stones are best. And you want to go fast." I wrapped her fingers around a little stone I'd found.

She held it in her hand with a smile similar to the one Lily had flashed me when I gave her the engagement ring. Both were stones.

Only one was worth more than a fleet of Bentleys. Yet Jude only cared about the important stuff, which reminded me to look down at her feet.

"Yellow?" I asked.

She grinned impishly. "Figure it out."

We took a walk, and I didn't hold her hand, and I didn't kiss her, and I didn't fucking breathe, because I didn't trust myself not to do any of those things if I looked her way. I was torn between liking how it felt to spend time with her and hating how she made me want things I'd never cared about.

"How's your relationship with your mom?" she asked.

We're officially in family territory. Fun-fucking-tastic.

"It's okay. Why?"

"I sometimes wonder what it feels like. To have a mother."

I raised an eyebrow. I loved Maman, but I couldn't commit to saying we had a great relationship. For one thing, we were business partners, and I knew she'd run me over for the right price. Still, she was better than my father, not that it said a whole lot.

"Depends on the mother. I have a feeling your father is better than both of my parents combined, so I wouldn't worry," I mumbled.

"My *ill* father," she added.

"Not for long. The secondary growths are shrinking, and he's responding very well to the treatments."

"And how do you know that?" She stopped walking, her entire body pointing at me, like an arrow.

I shrugged. "I visit him every Sunday when you go to the library."

It wasn't a big deal. We were both Yankee fans, and it wasn't like I had anything else to do. My career was my life, which meant that on Sundays, I had no life. My soft spot for Robert had nothing to do with Judith, and I certainly didn't want her to think I was expecting anything in return. Plus, I didn't want her to get the wrong idea about a relationship. Rob was still certain she was with Milton, so my money was on her not really counting on our fuck-buddies status to last past this season.

"I can't believe you didn't tell me." She smiled, but she didn't look surprised.

I always arrived a few minutes early. I tried to tell myself it was because I didn't want Jude to bump into me on her way to the train, but in practice, I liked to stop at the Polish deli and watch her through the window as she walked to the station with her headphones deep in her ears. I always wondered what she was listening to.

"Yeah. Well." I resumed our walk.

She followed, jogging behind me. "You can't just walk away from this conversation. You've been visiting my dad and taking care of him and you haven't even told me," she panted.

I liked her little pants. I wanted them against my palm as I fucked her somewhere public, where no one could hear.

"Watch me do exactly that. Walk away from this conversation."

"Célian, why?"

"Why am I walking? Because I can. Because I have legs. Why am I walking away from this conversation? Because it's pointless, and it doesn't mean what you think it means." I stopped again, this time in front of an old record store with signs in Spanish covering its display window. I wasn't even sure if it was open, but I wanted us to stop talking, because I wasn't ready.

Calling it a relationship was one thing.

Acting like we were a couple was another.

I pushed the door. I walked in, and she slipped in after me. The place was dark, with only vinyl records in sight. A man who looked like Meatloaf (the singer, not the dish), was snoring behind the counter, dribbling into a copy of *NME*. Judith immediately shut up and started browsing.

Nice save, asshole.

Getting her into a record shop was like giving a baby a pacifier. Only hotter, because I still remembered her playlist and had imagined fucking her to it countless times while we were close to killing each other in the office.

"Did you know Barry Manilow didn't write his song 'I Write the

Songs'?" She slid said singer's record out of a batch, grinning at me.

I didn't. I liked that I didn't. My general knowledge was usually superior to everyone else in my vicinity—came with the territory of making news and having to know everything about anything. But Jude was just as hungry for information as I was, which made her even more attractive. Not to mention lethal.

"Did you know 'Jingle Bells' was originally written for Thanksgiving?" I countered.

"Impossible." She made a shocked face, her jaw slacking. I laughed. She poked me with the tip of the record she held. "The British Navy uses Britney Spears' songs to scare off Somali pirates. I shit you not."

We were playing like this now?

"The piano Freddie Mercury plays in 'Bohemian Rhapsody' is the same one Paul McCartney plays in 'Hey, Jude,'" I countered, leaning into her face and flicking her little nose. "*Hey, Jude.*"

Was I flirting? I was. But why? It didn't make any sense. She was already mine in all the ways that mattered. She was in my bed. I'd shoved my fingers in every single hole in her body. Why was I doing this?

She walked across the aisle, her shoulder brushing my arm, and dropped the record back in its place, picking another one instead. I didn't see what it was and decided I didn't care.

"Queen and Jimi Hendrix never won a Grammy. Justin Bieber did," she whispered, her grin signaling that she had won the battle.

"I didn't give you your iPod back because I wanted to keep a piece of you with me," I admitted.

And won.

And lost.

And what the *fuck*?

"What?" Her smile wiped off so quickly, you'd think I'd told her I'd been giving her father placebo drugs for the past few weeks.

I picked up the record she was holding and walked over to the register to pay for it.

Judith Humphry didn't want me to buy her nice things. But that didn't stop *me* from wanting to. Because the truth was, I'd never been taught how to show affection. I was taught how to buy it.

The salesman didn't even wake up as I slid a note across his counter, plucked a plastic bag, and put the record inside.

Pet Sounds by the Beach Boys. Underrated. Romantic. Different.

Jude.

I'd never introduced a woman to my parents.

Lily Davis had attended the same country club, same schools, and had a summer house right next to ours in Nantucket. They'd known her since she was a baby. Maman's best friend was her godmother, and we were both expected by our families to make it work, since they could see the potential revenue of such a union.

Fuck helicopter parents. Mathias and Iris Laurent were private-jet parents. They'd wanted me to marry Newsflash Corp's princess, Lily Davis, before I'd found out my dick was good for more than pissing.

I wasn't nervous. There was nothing to be nervous about. As far as Judith was concerned, she wasn't going to be assessed or judged. I'd told her my mother was under the impression that she'd come here to assist me with my professional duties.

My mother lived in a penthouse, of course. Rich people loved putting distance between themselves and grounded people. Golden marbled and palm-treed, the skyscraper did nothing for Judith, who was busy taking a picture of a colorful reptile with her new phone. We were ushered in by an entourage of staff the minute we arrived at the lobby. Judith wore a modest black dress and plain black Chucks, with her hair tied back. I was in my slacks and a casual shirt.

Maman would rather see me in a strap-on and ball gag than casualwear. Which, naturally, added a dash of sadistic pleasure to my state of underdress.

In the elevator—why did everything happen in the fucking

elevator?—Jude turned to me and said, "If she starts talking to you about Lily, I'm leaving the room."

"Hate to interrupt your guilt-fest, but you weren't the reason I called off my engagement."

"I know. But still."

Still, you have more morals in your pinky than Lily has in her entire body.

Maman was sitting on her throne—a cream-upholstered David Michael sofa, still adorned with the dangling 10k price tag—atop her Persian carpet. The lingering tag was a horrendous mistake, I assumed, but not one I wanted to correct, seeing as she deserved the embarrassment of having her friends judge her for it silently.

My mother was beautiful in a superficial way. The same way I'd imagined Lily would be in about twenty years. Everything was too groomed and too tight, leathery skin on newly bleached hair.

I couldn't fault her for wanting to look younger. My father treated his women like he owned a car dealership. A newer, shinier model rolled in every few years. Maman's hair was blow-dried to perfection, and she wore a satin gown in silver.

"My beautiful son," she purred, not bothering to get up from the couch. I sauntered over to her, placing a kiss on each of her cheeks. Jude stood behind me and offered a little wave.

I gestured to my companion. "This is Judith Humphry."

There was no point in calling her my employee, because she was much more than that, or my girlfriend, because I wasn't sure if she was. Maman's lips curved into a secretive smile, and she hooked her forefinger in the air, motioning for Jude to come closer.

"I don't bite, my dear."

"But your son does..." I heard Judith mumbling under her breath as she made her way past me.

She shook my mother's hand. A few minutes later, the housekeeper presented us with pistachio shortbread cookies and coffee, and we all sat down. Instead of fucking around, I decided to broach the subject I'd come here for.

"Have you listened to the recordings, Maman?"

"I have. How did you get them?"

"Irrelevant. Point is, Mathias is trying to kill LBC by selling ad space to questionable parties and cutting my budget even though we're making clean profits. In other words, he is trying to weaken our product while injecting harmful commercial content into the channel."

"Sounds like something my ex-husband would do."

Iris Laurent was the sole heiress of LBC News Channel. An American-born royal with French roots, she fell in love with my father on the shore of St-Jean-Cap-De-Ferrat, France, under the swooshing trees and the influence of expensive champagne. He'd been a nobody trying to be somebody, a French punk with a thick accent and nothing but a bag of dreams and a lot of charm. A year later they were already married and pregnant with me. Mathias knew a thing or two about social climbing, but my mother still held most of the power in LBC—not enough to overthrow him, but enough to keep him on his toes.

I powered up my laptop, connecting it to the huge flat screen in front of us.

"Give me the skinny on things." Maman alternated between puffing on a cigarette and sucking on a shortbread cookie without eating it. God forbid.

"Ratings are still strong for our main show, but we're flailing in other time slots. The morning show is a trainwreck, and the political talk show is losing steam by the nanosecond, due to the fact that Mathias hired someone who cannot string two sentences without offending entire nations."

"Your father has five more years in him, if he's lucky." Maman's voice was sweet with satisfaction. "Can you not wait it out?"

"At this rate, the network will be dead in five *months*."

"Well, it is quite unfortunate, then, that you broke off your engagement with Lily. The Davis family holds ten percent of the shares in LBC, and they and I would have made a majority. That's why I pushed you into dating her when you were kids. I predicted this would happen with your father."

"And I would have appreciated your endorsement of the Davis girl, had she not opened her legs to your ex-husband. Now, let's focus on getting the board to see how dangerous Mathias' game is." I hit the conference call button.

Jude sat beside us, away from the webcam, and stared at us curiously, Kipling in her lap.

My mother scowled, placing the thoroughly sucked cookie back in its plate.

The conference call was my idea of hell.

My father looked smug in a Hawaiian shirt, sitting on a yacht—hopefully somewhere with Sudanese pirates—his curly white chest hair peeking out of his collar, a cigar between his teeth, and a giggling woman in his lap. Maman kept her mouth pursed as he coughed out the details of the string of deals he wanted to sign, laying out all the millions the network was going to make.

The rest of the board ate it up the minute they heard the magic word *revenue*.

"LBC is a business like any other. It's not a nonprofit organization."—Bigwig 1

"And the fact that the main show is performing just as well despite the cut in staff means the extra employees weren't necessary."—Bigwig 2

"No, it means that my *remaining* employees are breaking their backs to maintain the level of accuracy and quality our viewers are used to so you can treat your third wives to a new set of tits," I stated matter-of-factly, pushing my hands into my pockets so I wouldn't punch the screen.

"My son is quite the romantic," my father snorted around his cigar. "He's a fine newsman, and a very bad businessman. Just look at his recent choices. Did you know he recently broke off his engagement to the beautiful Lily Davis, heiress to Newsflash Corp, because he fell in love with a junior reporter? From Brooklyn, no less."

Now I pierced through the fabric of my pockets and tore my slacks. Fuck if I knew how he'd gained this information, but my top guess was it had come from Lily herself. I didn't know where *she'd* gotten this information, but I was certain we had a mole, because the chances of Judith opening her mouth and talking about us to anyone who wasn't Ava and Gary were nonexistent.

A quick glance at her face confirmed she was Team #MaimMathias. She paled like the moon, standing up and excusing herself from the room.

My mother refocused her attention on the screen.

"You're being absurd, Mathias." Her red-lipsticked mouth puckered.

"Am I, my darling Iris? I married you and took half of what you have." He laughed evilly. "Clearly *absurd* is not the word you're looking for. May I suggest *harsh*?"

"If suggestions were your strong suit, you wouldn't be held by the balls by your son." I rolled up my sleeves, getting tired of his little charade.

Maman reddened quietly next to me.

"The last thing you want is for me to really go after you, Father Dearest. As for the deals—they're going to ruin our reputation and bulldoze over all the hard work we've done. We might as well publicly endorse kids drinking and teens catching STDs. By the time LBC dies, you won't be in charge anymore, and I'll be the one expected to provide the answers."

Mathias fingered an invisible goatee, pretending to mull over my last statement. "What do you say, fellas? You're the bigwigs. My son, on top of being a romantic, also hates money. Should we or should we not take the deals?"

My mother waved her manicured hand.

"I think we should pass on the deals and add more interns to the newsroom to maintain the current ratings."

"I'm with Mathias on this one, Iris. My apologies."—Bigwig 1

"Me too."—Bigwig 2

"Me three."—Bigwig 3

I slapped the laptop shut before my mother could answer, then threw it across the room. It crashed against the wall, fell to the floor, and broke in half. My mother sat back in her cushioned couch. Her chin wrinkled, like she was about to cry.

"Don't say anything," I warned.

"If you want to fix this, you need to talk to Lily."

Fuck you, Maman.

She reached for another cigarette, blowing the smoke to the side. I stood up and paced, running my fingers through my hair.

"Swallow your pride. Take her back. Judith is a nice girl, but there will be a lot of Judiths walking in and out of your life. There's only one Lily who can save you. Protect your mother's network."

"My *mother's* network?" I spat, laughing incredulously. "Where the fuck have you been for the last decade, Maman? Even before you moved to Florida, you didn't give two shits about LBC. You only attended board meetings, and even that was half-heartedly and solely for the chance of screwing Dad over somehow. You could have managed it yourself, but you chose to give it to some incompetent asshole because working is not your jam. I spend ten hours a day in the newsroom. I live it. I breathe it. I eat it. But when I make one decision that has nothing to do with it, it's suddenly an issue. This network is not yours more than it is mine. Just because Lily was born into the right family doesn't mean she's right for me. And that bullshit where you marry someone without standing up to their fucking face? I had a front-row seat to that scenario at home, and I'm sure I'm not spoiling it for you when I say it ended badly. One last thing—Judith is not, in fact, disposable," I noted. "But I know a few people who are."

Now it was my mother's turn to stand up and throw her hands in the air. "All we ever wanted is for you and your sister to be happy. Don't give me this holier-than-thou attitude. If I may recall, you're not innocent, either."

I kicked her precious sofa's frame. The price tag fell, and I took sick pleasure in how symbolic that felt. "Yeah, you made us very fucking happy. Especially the part where Dad sent Camille's boyfriend to a goddamn war zone to keep him away from her because his blood wasn't blue enough, then proceeded to fuck my girlfriend. All while you were standing on the sidelines doing what, exactly? Finding more hot, young ass my age? Really, you two should host a talk show on how to raise kids. Or, you know, on how to kill them."

She blinked at me, cupping her mouth with the hand that held the cigarette. "I thought you were the one who sent Phoenix away."

I turned around, glaring at her. "*Huh?*"

She rubbed the side of her forehead, looking around for an imaginary person to explain everything to her. Tears gathered in the corners of her eyes. Lost. She looked lost.

"When I asked Mathias what happened, he said you sent Phoenix to Syria, and that he would never forgive himself for letting you get away with it.

"I was mad, Célian, so mad. I divorced him solely for not standing his ground, but I couldn't divorce you. You're my baby. I tried so very hard not to hold it against you. I love you so much. I always will, but I didn't know why you needed to interfere with Camille's life like that. You and Camille…you were different. I called you Célian because you were like the moon to me. You shone bright in the darkest time of my life. I gave Camille her name because she was virginal, unblemished. She was always so different from us. A free spirit. She loved who she loved and didn't care about the consequences. That's what made her different."

No, I wanted to correct. *That's what made her good.*

Camille *had been* happier than the rest of us. Her smile had been contagious. I'd used to tug at her braids and call her sunshine, because her face was round and full of cheeks and always bright. Because I was the moon.

I shook my head. "He lied. He's always lied. Why would you ever believe him? Only reason I let him do that was because I figured if I could play house with Lily Davis, she could find another charming fuckboy to piss her daddy off. When I realized she was miserable and told her the truth, she ran into the street."

"I thought she was mad at *you*."

"No. She was mad at Mathias."

"Then why do you always think it was your fault?" She plopped on the sofa, holding her head in her hands.

"Because I should have told her somewhere else. Because I should have fought Mathias. Because I fucking failed her."

There was a coffee table and an ocean between us, and I realized I hadn't given Jude the entire truth when she'd asked about my relationship with my mother. In all honesty, I had no relationship to speak of with either of my parents. Truth was, I no longer had a sister, or a fiancée. I was no less lonely than she was.

"You never loved Lily," my mother's voice softened, and her eyes followed suit.

I shook my head. A year ago I'd cared for her—in some fucked-up way. But to say I didn't love her now was like saying I disliked eating shit-smeared rocks. A real under-fucking-statement.

Maman nodded. "Can you save LBC?"

"Not at the price of being unhappy for the rest of my life." I tilted my chin up. All the fucked-up mannerisms of a heartless prick had been picked up at home anyway, so she could hardly blame me for them.

Heart attacks at fifty.

Nameless girls in bikinis every weekend.

An ex-wife who would love to see me in a casket.

Yeah, no thank you. I didn't want my father's life. I'd take shitty pasta and a Yankee game in a two-bedroom Brooklyn apartment every day of the week over life in a lonely, sixteen-million-dollar penthouse.

However, watching my family's business die *was* going to make me unhappy. I was headed straight into misery no matter which path I chose.

Maman stood up, walked cautiously toward me, stood on her tiptoes, and kissed my cheek, her lips halting at my ear.

"You're nothing like Mathias," she whispered, "I promise you."

No shit.

Chapter Seventeen

Jude

I dragged my suitcase up the stairs to my apartment, letting out a feral groan. Why had I packed my entire room before I left for Florida? Oh, that's right. Because I'd wanted to dazzle my emotionally stunted boss by showing off my alluring wardrobe, consisting of eighty-year-old librarian's conservative dresses and an unhealthy amount of Chucks.

Célian had offered to help me with the suitcase, but I'd politely declined, and I guess he was relieved. He knew Dad still thought I was with Milton. As much as my dad liked him, he would punch both of us in our reproductive organs if he thought I was two-timing my long-term boyfriend.

Our Floridian getaway had taken a sour turn after we'd left his mother's place. The stone-skipping and record-shopping was replaced by the usual dark fuck-a-thon in which we were lost in a tornado of feelings and numbness. We'd walked the main street in heavy silence before Célian had dragged me into a Cuban dance club. We'd watched other people dance and grind into one another while we drank tequila.

"Your father seems to think you fell in love with me." I'd tried to laugh it off.

He'd pressed his thumb to my lower lip and pushed it down, licking the inside of it. "My father thinks women should stay in the kitchen and global warming is a hoax. Let's try not to take him too seriously."

"Célian…"

"I don't hate you, Judith," he'd said. "And that's more than I can say about the rest of the world right now."

We'd stumbled back to our hotel suite and had enough sex to repopulate an entire continent—if that was how sex worked. It was angry and sad and intimate. It felt like we'd risen together in the air and evaporated somewhere else safer, better. But in the back of my mind, I still remembered that I was an obstacle to Célian.

That all of his professional issues could disappear if I stepped out of the picture.

He could marry Lily. Or at least stay engaged forever.

He could save LBC.

He could have everything he'd worked for, for many, many years, and still be the detached bastard who picked up strangers at bars to satisfy his physical cravings.

Uncomplicated. Straightforward. *Simple.* Just the way he liked it.

That Sunday afternoon, I pushed the door to my apartment open and froze on the threshold, my heart dropping to the pit of my stomach. My suitcase fell to the floor with a thud. *No.*

My father was sitting at the dining table, having what appeared to be a pleasant conversation with Milton over my favorite Manhattan donuts and cups of coffee. My ex-boyfriend laughed wholeheartedly and pushed something over the table, and that's when I noticed they were playing Scrabble.

Fan-freaking-tastic.

"Oh, there you are!" Milton clapped and swiveled his body toward me in his chair, his face glowing with a genuine smile.

He looked handsome in a polo shirt and new haircut, but in a generic way. Not only did he not hold a candle to Célian, he didn't even hold a damp match. Not that beauty had anything to do with the fact that my room service breakfast was threatening to come up my throat for another puke-fest. The other thing Milton ate Célian's dust at was being faithful—even when we weren't technically together.

"Hello." I threw my keys into the ugly bowl Mrs. Hawthorne had given us by the front door, looking between them. Dad put his letters down and turned in his seat.

"JoJo! Milton told me all about your weekend in the Hamptons. You shouldn't have gone straight back to the office when you returned. You could have at least come back here and dropped the suitcase."

Milton grinned sadistically, arranging his letters on the board in front of him. "Deceiver. D-e-c-e-i-v-e-r," he spelled the word out loud. Goose pimples ran down my arms, making the little hairs stand on end.

"That's a good one." My father clapped. "Smart as a whip, son."

"Thank you, sir. Baby, can I offer you a heart with a hole?" He grabbed a heart-shaped donut from the open white box on the table, motioning for me to take it. He referred to me as *baby*, even though I'd spent the weekend doing very grown-up things with someone else, and he knew it. Milton had also known when to come here, which set off the alarms in all of my internal systems. My mouth dried up.

This is bad.

"It's okay. I really *stuffed* my mouth while I was on vacation."

The smile on my lips felt like clay. I hadn't been planning to tell Dad about Célian when I came back anymore. After the disastrous conference call, I'd felt like I was walking on a tight rope, about to fall from grace and into the arms of heartbreak.

I knew what would set my lover free of his father's claws. But it hurt like hell, the concept of letting him go so he could save the one thing he loved.

But wasn't that the essence of caring for someone else? Hurting so they wouldn't have to?

"Then how about a walk?" Milton perked up like a doting

grandmother. "The weather is nice. We haven't taken a stroll in your neighborhood in a while."

That's because you decided to screw your boss while I was busy running around Manhattan looking for a job.

Whatever. Getting him out of here wasn't a bad idea. I hitched a shoulder. "Sure. Let me get freshened up."

After a quick bathroom stop, during which I stared in the mirror and promised myself I wasn't, in fact, going to throttle my ex-boyfriend, I walked out and kissed my father goodbye.

"I'll be back in a few minutes," I assured him. *I*. Not *we*. The devil was in the details, and I hoped my own mini Satan overheard it while he waved goodbye to my father.

Milton and I stepped out of the building and took a right turn toward the main road, as we had many times before. I waited for him to talk, because I wasn't entirely sure of the extent of his knowledge about my love life.

"You're welcome for that save." He jerked his thumb behind his shoulder.

I pretended to wipe my forehead. "Thanks, Captain Save-a-Bitch. Would you like me to sew you a costume? What's your superpower, dicking your way up the company ladder?"

He knocked his shoulder against mine, smiling. "That's rich from a girl who was about to lose her house five minutes ago and miraculously found a man to pay her debt in exchange for sexual favors."

How the hell did he know? I choked on my saliva, coughing as he continued to saunter beside me.

"*The Heart is a Lonely Hunter*," he said, plucking a wad of leaves from the trees bowing over us.

I cringed. I hated when he did that. It was a big fuck-you to nature.

"Your dad told me all about the book. It makes sense now, Jude—that you thought it was your destiny, that you didn't let me in. You were the sweetest, warmest girlfriend I've ever had, but there was always something off about us. I always craved you a little more than you wanted me. And it always drove me crazy. Elise was...Elise. She made me feel like a big fucking deal, ya know? Smart, funny, young. All the things that didn't exactly impress you. Suddenly I was resentful that you weren't the person to tell me all those things."

"I'm sorry you felt that way, but this sounds a lot like an excuse, and cheating is not something you resort to. It's something you decide to do." I kicked a little stone on the sidewalk. Milton didn't look down to check the color of my Chucks. He didn't care.

"And that's why I'm here," he continued. "To tell you I get it. I made a mistake, and I'm sorry, Jude. So, so sorry. But it's time for us to move on. Look, I know how having an affair with Célian Laurent must make you feel invincible. I've been there with Elise, too. It's powerful, right? Makes you think you're on top of your game. You're desired by a force of nature, an authority, and you get all the affirmation you need. But it's not real, baby. What you and I have—that's real. We sewed our oats, and now it's time to come back. To us."

I stopped in my tracks. He stilled beside me, slanting his head sideways, half-smiling, half-squinting at the sun.

"Wait. Who told you this?" My voice was a too-full cup of coffee, held by a fragile hand, spilling at the edges.

"JoJo, it's not important."

"You lost the right to deem what's important to me the day you stuck your dick in someone else."

He frowned and took a step back, and when he blinked, his expression changed. It was like he saw for the first time who I really was, and he didn't like the view.

"Are you kidding me here? This is what you're focusing on? After you came back from a weekend of fucking with your boss—the director of news at LBC, no less—not only am I willing to take you back, but I also cover for your ass and play Scrabble with your goddamn father."

"First of all—" I raised my index finger. "He is not my *goddamn* father. Just my father. My sweet, caring dad, and playing Scrabble with him is hardly a burden. Second of all—" I pointed the same finger at him. "Nobody asked *you* to cover for me. I haven't committed a crime. I just wanted to spare my dad the worry of knowing I broke up with you. And thirdly—" I poked his chest, and he stumbled backward, his eyes widening in disbelief. "This conversation is over unless you tell me how you know about my alleged relationship with my boss."

"Between making dirty headlines, maybe Mr. Laurent should teach you that revealing sources is a big no-no in our industry." Milton recovered, smirking devilishly.

"We don't make dirty headlines." I scowled.

"You're about to." Milton's ears pinked, as they did when adrenaline ran through him.

Was he threatening me?

He scrubbed his jaw, turned around, and punched the red-brick fencepost behind him. "Motherfucker! Have you lost your mind, Jude? Célian Laurent is not your boyfriend. He's not even your friend. He is your well-heeled boss, and you, baby..." He shook his head, chuckling. "You're wearing Chucks. He'll marry the Davis girl, like the entire elite society of New York expects him to. I'm offering you security. I can make you an honest woman. I cheated. You cheated. Let's call it even and move on."

I cheated?

I cheated?

I bit my tongue so hard the metallic taste of blood rolled inside my mouth.

"Can I ask you for something, Milton?"

He leaned against the fence, his tense expression unknotting into a forgiving smile. "Baby, of course."

"Stay away from me. And I do mean for good. Even if you hadn't cheated on me—which you did, several times, I still wouldn't take you back. My relationship with Célian Laurent—if it even exists—is none of your business, never will be. But just for the record, everything I did or didn't do with other people was well after I caught you giving your boss an item that's above your paygrade. And before you even think of threatening me by telling my father the truth, don't worry—I will tell him myself. Right now, in fact. As for the rest of the world—I don't care. This is not goodbye. This is bad-bye. The bye that ends on a sour note, with us cutting ties completely."

I turned around and walked home, not bothering to look back and see his reaction. I walked in the door, and Dad was in the shower. The fact that he was feeling well enough to have one on his own without me in the house made butterflies stretch their wings inside my chest. I marched over to the Scrabble on the table—they were midgame when we'd left—and changed the letters from deceiver to *defiant* and smiled.

That's more like it.

Célian

Life is full of surprises.

There were good surprises, like finding out Jude's pussy tasted like honeydew and was tighter than my fist. There were also bad surprises, like finding my ex standing inside my apartment, my spare keys dangling from her fingers in triumph, completely naked.

Again.

I dropped my suitcase and cracked my neck, walking straight to the bar. Luckily, we'd broken things off before I'd had the chance to become a full-blown alcoholic. Lily certainly looked better behind the mist of hard liquor.

"Are you officially a nudist? I haven't seen you with clothes on in a while," I pondered, unbuttoning the first two buttons of my shirt.

"You're funny," she hissed in what I assumed was meant to be a seductive way.

"And you're naked. For a rich girl, you could sure use a new wardrobe. How did you get my keys?"

Part of me wanted to know, and the other dreaded killing the person who'd given them to her—not that there was a long list to choose from. But if it was someone from the management, they could kiss their job goodbye.

"Your father let me into your sister's apartment. She had a spare key, and when the concierge saw me with it, I told him we got back together."

Something dropped somewhere in the room, but fuck if I knew what it was. Maybe my heart. I heard the thud of it meeting the floor.

Camille was the only person I'd let into my apartment freely, and her place was still standing vacant, because none of us had the guts to touch it. Lily had been inside it. Moving things. *Taking* things. Breathing the same air Camille had. Anger bubbled beneath my skin, and I clutched the glass so hard I heard it cracking softly.

I stared down as small rivers of blood began paving their way inside my palm.

"What do you want?"

"I told your father about your affair with the little blond bitch. He's really happy for you."

"Bet he is, and she's not a bitch. If you need a point of reference about who is, just look in the mirror. I'll ask again, before I call security to escort your ass out of here, butt naked. Why. Are. You. Here?"

"I want us to get back together," she said after a beat of silence.

I didn't even have it in me to laugh. Whatever she was smoking, that shit was made solely of rat poison, laundry detergent, and laxatives.

"No. Anything else?"

"I have a case," she said. "Hear me out."

I turned around to face her. The first drip of blood from my cut palm hit my loafer. I ignored it. "A case? Do you even know how to spell the word?"

She took a step toward me. Funny, for all her nakedness, Lily never forgot to keep her red-soled heels on. I raised a hand, letting her know there was an invisible line between us, and it was not to be crossed. She leaned a hip against my TV stand, unfazed by my bloody palm.

"I had a long chat with your old man." She licked her upper lip.

Interesting choice of words from a woman who'd let him give her mouth-to-mouth with his dick. I raised an eyebrow.

"He was away this weekend, but he sent someone to open Camille's apartment for me. We ended up having quite the lengthy conversation, in which he made some interesting points. The first one being that you are exploiting your employee by sleeping with her. And before you say it's consensual, please try and think of how it would look in the eyes of every single competing network, that the person who pushed the #MeToo movement—that would be you, Célian—is not only sleeping with his reporter, but has actually…" She gasped theatrically, slapping a hand over her mouth. "Paid all of her debt off. And yes, I went through your trash to find your bank statements—for a man who advocates to save the environment, you should really go paperless—and it was *totally* worth it."

A satisfied grin graced her lips. "So what do we have here? A boss sleeping with his poor employee and paying her way out of trouble. To make matters worse, she's been promoted from the shitty beauty blog to the newsroom, and then promoted as a reporter. You actually *fired* someone to make room for her. Oopsie daisy—Steve is my mom's best friend's son. He told me all about how you looked at her when you had your meeting."

Should have known Steve had a few more fuckups in his disaster bag before he left my newsroom. He had a face begging to be punched, and I'd let him walk away with his nose intact. I had no one to blame but myself, really. I ran my red-tainted fingers over my jaw.

"I'm sure that's how people are going to see it." She clucked her tongue, stretching, and she was naked, too naked. I wanted to cover her up with something. A casket, maybe. Lily would look damn good in it.

"I don't care how people will see it. I employ Judith Humphry because she is a gifted, hard-working reporter, and I fuck her because she is an excellent lay. Those two have nothing to do with each another." I was downplaying my entire *arrangement* with Jude, but I didn't want Lily to pin this breakup on my employee. It wasn't fair to Judith, and it was far from being the truth.

"Is she worth everything you've ever worked for?" She pinched her lower lip between her fingers nervously.

Yes. Yes she is.

The thought struck me like lightning. Judith was worthy, and I hated that her value kept going *up* the more the people around me were letting me *down*. She was hardworking, funny, quirky, and sex on Chucks. She kept up with my sharp tongue, and gave it to me just as good. She brought donuts to work when she knew her colleagues were facing a long, challenging day, and sneaked mini Jack Daniels bottles to Brianna in times I was particularly shitty. When Jessica needed help with her workload, Jude always volunteered, but never made a fuss about it or made sure that I knew. She was so fucking graceful and unassuming, and I knew that even if I lost LBC tomorrow, got kicked out of my apartment, stripped out of my inheritance, and sued for every penny I'd ever earned, it still wouldn't change my value in her eyes. And *that* was invaluable.

"Leave," I snapped, picking up Lily's dress from my floor, deliberately using my bloody hand to stain her precious Prada number. "And this time, just so we're on the same page, if you come back here, I will make sure to slap a restraining order on your ass. It won't be pretty, seeing as you'll have to move away from Manhattan, and you can hardly find your way in fucking Bloomingdales. Am I clear?"

"I'll take this story to all the press. Too many people already know." She threw herself at me, her fists raining down on my chest. I pushed her away with my dripping palm, hoping to fuck her type of crazy wasn't contagious.

"You go do that, Lily. But put some clothes on first. You know, to make an impression."

"Why are you fighting us?"

"Why are you fighting to save us? *Us* ceased to exist a long time ago. You're going in circles. We haven't been together in over a year."

Her eyes darted down. "I thought it was going to change. I thought you'd calm down and realize we were compatible after the wedding."

Christ. That was her thought process? To think I'd almost married a genius.

"You thought wrong."

Two minutes later, I slammed the door in her face (after she put some clothes on, thank fuck) and fished my phone out of my pocket to text Judith.

Célian: Lily knows.

Jude: So does Milton. He was here when I came home. I'm telling my dad the truth about breaking up with him tonight. We need a game plan.

Célian: George Michael.

Jude: ?

Célian: George Michael is our plan. We're coming out.

Jude: Did you just make a Grayson joke?

Célian: Is that Gary's real name?

Jude: <sent a GIF of Ross from *Friends* bumping his fists>

Célian: At any rate, Lily is threatening to blackmail me by claiming I'm harassing you. Am I fucking you against your will, Miss Humphry?

Jude: No. But I don't want the stigma of being "that girl" at work.

Célian: What stigma is that? We're not getting married. We're fucking each other casually and consensually. No one is getting promoted anytime soon.

Jude: Right.

I wanted to diminish the weight she had in my world, knowing it could very well crush me if I wasn't careful.

I hated how the thought of coming clean and telling everyone we were together secretly appealed to me, even though it was about to kill my reputation and make Judith's life twenty times harder at work.

Most of all, I hated that I was going to hurt her.

Not because she deserved it, but because I didn't know how not to.

Jude

Guilt nibbled at my gut as Dad exclaimed how happy he was for me. For *us*.

Of course, I'd sugarcoated the situation to the point that it looked like a churro.

Instead of telling him I was now blissfully single and screwing my heartless boss, I painted a picture in soft pinks and vivid baby blues, in which Célian and I had fallen desperately in love with and decided to be together. He swallowed the entire thing and asked for seconds—came clean about the experimental treatment and said he loved Célian like a son. *Like. A. Son.*

Dad begged me to invite Célian for dinner in the capacity of a normal couple, and I caved, mostly because I knew Célian would not turn us down. Since he'd opted for not getting back with Lily, any united front we were going to offer would surely help our case. Plus, who the hell knew what we were?

Sometimes it felt like a relationship.

Oftentimes like a dirty secret.

Sometimes he ran cold.

Many times he burned hot.

On Monday morning, everyone walked into the first rundown meeting looking grim and overworked. I placed Kipling on the desk and slid into my usual seat, popping open a big white box of donuts.

"Habit's gonna get you broke, girl." Kate picked a chocolate-glazed one, greeting me by bumping her thigh against my shoulder.

"That's like threatening a nun with a crucifix. I already am." I licked the powdered sugar off a pastry as Jessica handed Kate and me some coffee.

"How was your weekend?" they both asked in unison, but Kate peppered the question with a knowing grin.

She and Célian were close, but he was still a vault, so I opted for vagueness.

"Relaxing?" Oh, sweet. I put a question mark there. That wasn't suspicious.

"That's one thing I *don't* believe."

The entire room raised a collective eyebrow as Célian breezed through the door. He looked both pissed and perfect in a pale gray suit, his frown was so deep I could barely make out his eyes. Brianna shadowed his steps, sliding his Starbucks and iPad in front of his seat.

"I would ask how everyone's weekend was, but that would imply that I give a fuck. And I don't, because we have bigger fish to fry. I'm talking whale-sized ocean creatures. This is the first and last time I will address this subject, so feel free to never ask me again."

He dumped his phone and some documents on the desk, shooing his PA away. "LBC just signed a clusterfuck of an ad deal with a marketing firm that specializes in alcohol, condoms, and gambling. You will hear about it in the media and in your local high-end bars and on goddamn Twitter. Do not engage. As far as we're concerned, we're making unbiased news. Period. Understood?"

Everyone nodded solemnly. Elijah raised his hand to ask something. Célian fell into his chair with a sigh. "Is it about the deal?"

"Yes."

"Don't wanna hear it. Let's get to business."

James Townley looked up from a newspaper he was holding. "Anything else you'd like to address?"

Célian shot him a look. "Are you referring to your fake tan problem? Because I can hold an intervention, but probably not until next week. Busy schedule and all."

"I'm talking about the elephant in the room." James frowned, concern etching his face. He slapped the newspaper with the back of his hand before boomeranging it toward his director. Célian picked it up, frowned at the little article circled with a yellow highlighter, and slid it my way silently. I picked it up, my heart pounding in my ears. There was no picture. Just text.

WHO'S THAT GIRL: New York media tycoon Célian Laurent is DUMPED by his fiancée, Miss Lily Davis, after the latter caught him in the act, cheating on her with an employee. The sordid affair is said to be at least a few weeks old. Both parties were unavailable for comment.

Célian sat back, lacing his fingers together. "Well."

Elijah's eyebrows jumped to his forehead. "You'll need to elaborate."

"It's true."

No, it's not! I wanted to jump up and yell, as gasps erupted all across the room. He hadn't cheated on Lily, and she hadn't caught us in the act. I stared at him, bewildered, feeling my pulse jackhammering against my eyelids. He tilted his chin up, his expression reeking defiance, ignoring me completely.

"Most of it, anyway. I am in a relationship with Judith Humphry. However, it is not sordid, hardly a secret, and we were never caught in any act. Judith didn't know about my relationship with Lily when we started dating, and is therefore not at fault. However, her position here has nothing to do with our relationship, which developed after she was appointed as a reporter." He was calm, cold, and smooth. Everybody's eyes ping-ponged between us, and my skin was on fire. I felt humiliated and helpless. And most of all, I felt furious at his random confession. When we'd agreed to tell the world, I thought it would be after discussing a strategy. *Together.*

"I think we can all agree that Miss Humphry has earned her place in this newsroom and did not need to sleep her way up the corporate ladder." Célian smoothed a hand along his crisp shirt.

"Agreed." Kate reached out, squeezing my hand. I was too stunned to react.

"I concur." Elijah raised his palms in surrender.

"She's the best." Jessica regarded me with a frown, probably for keeping mum about getting freaky with the boss.

I got why a lot of people felt cheated.

"Junior." James tossed me a toothy smile. "You're the real deal. We all know it."

But did they? There were at least eight more people in the room, and their silence spoke a thousand words. I knew, without a shadow of a doubt, that no one saw me in the same light anymore. To what degree was the real question.

"Thank you..." I managed, refusing to look back at Célian, who stared at me intently now, trying to read between the lines of my deep frown.

I didn't give him anything.

"With this out of the way..." Célian ran a hand over his square jaw. "Give me something good."

"Evidently, Jude already has..." someone coughed from my general direction, but I couldn't snap my head fast enough to see who it was.

I don't think Célian heard it. He wasn't one to miss an opportunity to berate a cheeky employee.

Kate began talking about the anti-drugs campaign failure, and Elijah butted in with a debt ceiling lead. Célian looked bored out of his mind, leaning back in his chair and staring into the air, his legs crossed over the desk.

"Humphry?"

At least he still called me that, like I was a genderless employee, like nothing had changed. Because nothing had. I was still a career woman. I was just a career woman who slept with her boss because we were both the same type of screwed up.

I flipped Kipling's pages, my tongue sticking out of the corner of my mouth.

"I was talking to this guy last night..." I started.

"Does Célian know? He always seemed like the possessive type to me," Elijah joked, tossing his head back and gulping down a bottle of water with a chuckle.

"Out of my newsroom, Elijah," Célian barked, looking back to me. "Continue, Judith."

I looked between them noiselessly. Elijah furrowed his brows, picked up his things, and shook his head.

"It was a joke," he whispered.

"Comedy Central is down the block. We make news here." Célian was still looking at me, but with a jaded expectation, not an ounce of sympathy or affection in his icy blues.

An unbearable tension squeezed the room from the moment Elijah realized he'd messed up to the second the door closed behind him.

"Anyway..." My face heated, and I kept my eyes on Kipling. "He's a Syrian journalist living in Germany. His name is Saiid. I found his Twitter account late last night."

"Or Tinder..." Bryce, one of the producers in the room, whispered under her breath.

Sitting at the head of the desk, Célian couldn't hear it. But I could. And I wanted to die. I deserved it. Even I could see why it would make my peers bitter. While they were chasing leads, I'd been chasing orgasms with the future president of the network. The *engaged* future president of the network.

I took a deep breath, borrowing Kate's iPad silently and entering a web address. "He uploaded this video, documenting Syrian refugees trying to smuggle their way back to Syria..."

"*Back* to Syria?" Jessica raised an eyebrow.

I nodded. "They find it difficult to integrate, and they miss their families. Hundreds of refugees come back into Syria every week, mostly through Greece. They enter their own country illegally, on foot, tracing back over the route they used to run away."

I clicked on the video and turned it around so everyone could see. Most of all, I was relieved to find people no longer looking at me like I was the root of all evil. Now they saw toddlers crying in their mothers' hands, their lives at great risk.

"Coverage?" Célian looked up at me after the video ended.

Shaking my head, I pointed at the screen. "This video has only been watched five hundred times or so, but I'm guessing more people will find it as time ticks by. This could be a great lead for the special we're airing next week."

"Good job."

Maybe his words would've been more believable if they hadn't felt like hail hitting my skin. I was growing tired of him being so callous. It's like his heart was wrapped in a thick layer of dead skin—the kind you have on the sole of your foot. A needle could pierce it, and you wouldn't feel a thing.

I bowed my head, not daring to look at the reaction his compliment had created.

People began to file out of the room, and so did Célian. He probably knew I was about ready to strangle him and didn't want a shouting match. I stayed inside, watching Kate pretend to collect her things at a snail's pace.

She looked down as she spoke to me. "Célian did the only thing he could to make sure both your asses were covered. He did it in his own fuck-you-very-much way, but he meant well. You're about to get a lot of heat for it, but remember—better to address it here than let *The Daily Gossip* give people their version of your story."

I looked up, through the glass wall, and watched the news spread like wildfire—people hunching down and whispering into their colleagues' ears, secretaries marching out with their cigarette packs so they could gossip downstairs, reporters passing the newspaper James had brought between them.

"I think he just killed my career." My head collapsed into my arms on the table.

"Killed? No." Kate tossed her things into her bag and stood up. "But he just made it a lot harder for both of you. So you better get out there and start proving to people what I already know: that you were born to be a journalist."

The next few days were a blur. Things somehow got both better and worse.

Better, because people had very little time to duck their heads down and whisper about us. Célian was running around the office, screaming his lungs out at them. We were severely short-staffed, and every calamity in the world had decided to land at our feet.

Worse, because ever since the new ads started rolling, Célian was in and out of meetings on the sixtieth floor, and every time he came back, he punched a wall to its untimely death. We were four holes in, with our ratings slipping each passing second and our competitors openly discussing our current situation as a network dying a slow, painful, and very public death.

Célian had not been kidding.

Mathias wanted to kill LBC before he left, and now that Célian was no longer engaged to Lily and in no position to overturn those decisions, he had to watch it crumble, eyes wide open, *Clockwork Orange* style.

Célian wasn't the only one trying to plug LBC into a life-support machine.

James Townley got into a screaming match with Mathias in the middle of the newsroom the day after the commercials started running and threatened to quit.

"You're ruining this business, and your son." He'd thrown a batch of documents in Mathias's face.

"If you're unhappy, James, you know exactly where the door is." Mathias had pointed at it for emphasis.

"Yes, Matt. You've showed it to me plenty. But I'll never leave here, and we *both* know why."

Célian had dragged his anchor to the conference room and had a heated conversation with him. They'd come out looking spent, just in time to see Mathias wink wickedly through the closing doors of the elevator.

If nothing else, Célian had found an ally in James, one person to cross off his Guinness records-worthy shit list.

The other downside of LBC's looming demise was that Célian and I hadn't had time to talk to each other since the news broke that we were together.

I was still mad at him, but it was difficult to confront him properly when he was running on coffee and energy shots, trying desperately to save his dying network. It was my educated guess that he hadn't slept more than ten hours combined this week.

So when Friday evening rolled in, I was surprised to see him walk to my desk, in front of everyone, and lean his hip against my file cabinet, his signature hands-tucked-in-pockets and devil-may-care smirk on full display.

"Chucks."

I looked up. He had dark circles around his eyes and a three-day stubble. I desperately wanted to give him a piece of my mind, but there was no point in kicking him while he was down.

"Jerk."

He arched an eyebrow, and I shrugged. "I thought we nicknamed each other the things that represented us."

He leaned down and placed a chaste kiss on my temple. Everybody stopped what they were doing and stared at us, and I felt myself turning crimson. The air stood still in the room. He was gasoline. I was a match.

"Dinner and an apology," he said—not offered—in front of everyone, so cocky and sure that I would jump into his arms.

"You should probably start with the latter to get the former." I sat back and looked at him blankly.

He hung his head and shook it, laughing. "I apologize for outing us in a less than diplomatic manner. But not for making sure everyone knows that you're fucking mine." He leaned down, his lips grazing my ear. "Hang on to this anger, Chucks. I'll be happy to work your crazy ass up in bed and fuck every doubt and complaint out of your tight pussy."

If I were an emoji, I would be drooling a little pool under my feet.

"I guess you could buy me dinner." I kept my expression schooled, and he tugged at my jacket draped over the back of my seat, helping me into it.

"Guessing is a gambling game. I'm definitely buying you dinner tonight."

"We're going to have a long talk," I said, feeling Jessica and Kate watching us with horror and fascination. I don't think they'd ever seen anyone talk back to their boss.

"And even longer makeup sex." He grinned.

Thirty minutes later, we were in a Chinese restaurant off Broadway. Célian was drinking bottled beer as I ordered every single thing on the menu.

"Sorry." I handed our waiter the velvet red tariff. "I can't eat when I'm stressed, and this is the first time we've spoken since Monday, so I'm making up for lost time."

Célian unfolded his napkin, frowning at it like it had accused him of something, considering my words.

"We're tanking," I told him. "Your father is on a suicide mission, and he's taken all of us as hostages. The only way to stop him is to overthrow his decision, which you can do by teaming up with the Davis family. Can you at least ask Lily's father? Go directly to him?"

Every word felt like a sword slicing through my mouth. I was sending him off to the last place I wanted him to be. With his ex.

He fingered the rim of his bottle. "They have their own shit to sort through, and the last thing they need is the motherfucker who cheated on their daughter showing up asking for solids."

"You haven't cheated on Lily, though." I rubbed my nose in frustration. "Why did you agree with that statement?"

If looks could slap you in the ass, I think his expression just did.

"I'm fond of her family," he said curtly.

"And?"

"And I'd hate to break it to them that their daughter is a piece of work."

"But...why?"

"They treated me like a son when I had no relatives to speak of but Camille."

"So you're content with being the bad guy?" I blinked, my mouth lax.

"Are we living on the same fucking planet? I *am* the bad guy."

He had a point, and I understood where he was coming from, even if it made me uncomfortable that he'd protected Lily.

"What about LBC?"

He clutched his beer so tightly I thought it was going to crack, ignoring the steaming dishes the waiter slid on to our table. I wasn't feeling so hungry myself anymore.

"I'm listening to offers from other networks."

"What?" I whisper-yelled. "LBC is yours."

"No. It's my father's, for the foreseeable future. Unlike ninety-nine percent of the general population, I'm both good at my job and I love it. I won't jeopardize my reputation. I'd rather work somewhere else."

"What about your staff!"

It was an accusation more than a question. No matter how much people feared Célian, they respected and were loyal to him, too. He couldn't just get up and leave. Not in theory, anyway. In practice, I knew better than anyone how he could be taciturn and detached.

"If it comes to that, I'll make a package deal to take Kate and Elijah with me."

He stretched in his seat, and I watched the muscles of his arms looping around his bones like ivy, every curve incredibly male. Then I thought about the muscle inside his chest. The one that pounded, but didn't get its recommended exercise.

His father was killing him slowly and enjoying doing so. His mother was mostly indifferent toward everything around her. Célian didn't have a shot, other than the Davis family, and we both knew it.

"And what about us?" I asked quietly. His eyes were cold, but his mouth was red and hot, alive.

"What about us?" His icy tenor glided like an ice cube along my spine. He waved his empty beer bottle at the waiter, signaling for another.

"Are you going to explain that little stint in the newsroom when James showed us the item?"

"Probably not. We agreed it was the best thing to come clean. So I did."

"Without consulting me."

"False. I consulted you the night before. I have the text messages to prove it."

"We agreed to it, but didn't talk strategy." I refused to back off.

"Strategy?" He scoffed. "We're not running for office, Judith. Just fucking in one."

He'd thrown our affair in everyone's face, and now he was acting like an asshole, because he didn't know how not to. But I was done—done eating it up every time he threw crumbs of attention my way.

I knew I had to stand up and leave before I cried.

We'd done everything backwards.

First the sex, then the feelings. We'd defied our workplace, and our colleagues, and our ethical codes. We'd ruined a perfectly dysfunctional engagement that had kept his company alive. But most of all, we'd also ruined ourselves.

My legs were up before I knew it, carrying me to the exit. No explanation. No apologies. I felt his grave steps thumping in my hollow chest as he followed me out. It was raining outside—the kind of dirty, humid rain to break the pulses of summer heat. It reminded me of the day we'd met, of the carnal desperation that ate at me back then, of the fact that I was still alone.

I felt his hand on my shoulder as he swiveled me around sharply. He jerked me into his arms.

I didn't want him to let go.

I didn't want him to keep me there, either.

"I wish I'd never met you." My fists pounded his chest, and he took it. Maybe because he knew he deserved it. His mouth pressed against my cheek felt like a rusty, hot blade. The world felt like it was ending, even though I knew it couldn't be.

The vane of his breath sliced through my ear. "I wish that, too."

That night, the sex was different.

Slow, intense, and angry. Every thrust was a punishment, each rake of my fingernails against his skin a reminder that I, too, could hurt him. We didn't talk about it. Not even when tears rolled down my cheeks and he kissed them, then licked them, then drank them thirstily, for they were his.

That night, we ended things differently, too.

He was sound asleep when I collected the few belongings I had and called a cab. It was going to cost a pretty penny, but I didn't want to be there when he woke up. We were miles away from Florida, literally and figuratively. And that, too, reminded me of the rainy night we'd met.

Later that night, I had a strange, somber epiphany.

Milton was right. I was a mortal playing with a deity, and now I was getting hurt, while he remained intact. There was nothing wrong with my heart. It was not lonely, and it was definitely not a hunter. It had been hunted. There was only one problem with the fact that my heart was so dreadfully, unexpectedly normal.

Somewhere along the way, it had stopped being mine.

Célian

There was nothing better than a fresh cup of coffee in the morning and getting Chucks's ex-boyfriend fired from his job.

I handed Brianna my planner. "Burn today's page. I have some shit to do." It was an exact, albeit unprofessional order.

Specifically, said *shit* was going to every bigwig who'd denied my request to cancel the new ad campaign and showing them the plummeting ratings chart I'd printed out as a last attempt to save this sinking ship.

I might have been a bit dramatic last Friday night when I'd spoken to Judith.

Quitting LBC was not in the cards for me any time soon, with or without the new ads, but I didn't want to lie to her, either. And I was listening to other offers, mainly so the bigwigs would get tipped by their moles and realize I was serious about leaving if we didn't get our ducks in a row.

Getting Milton fired by talking to my old friend Elise and telling her the fucker had tried to win my girlfriend back wasn't necessary, but it was definitely a nice bonus. Elise, who was a fellow Harvard graduate, wasn't impressed by her new boyfriend's antics. Also, Robert, Judith's father, was apparently on my team, because he'd chosen to share this piece of information with me in the first place.

As for Judith, I needed to get my head out of my ass, take her to lunch, and apologize for being my bastard self. *Again.* She'd taken a cab back in the middle of the night after we left things—though not orgasms—unfinished.

"Yes, sir. Oh, and sir, Miss Davis is here." Brianna jotted down my orders for the morning.

I took a sip of my coffee and gathered this week's statistics in a big, fat file. "Lily Davis?" I arched an eyebrow.

"No, sir, Geena Davis. She was wondering if you could be the Louise to her Thelma."

I looked up and caught her nibbling at her lower lip, biting on a huge smile. I smirked. Touché. She was beginning to fight, something she never would have done if it wasn't for Judith.

As for the matter at hand, Lily must have been quite drunk, because there was no way in hell and its neighboring sections she had the balls to come here. *Shit.* It was nine in the morning.

"Impossible. She knows she's one step away from a restraining order." Plus, I very much doubted Lily got up before noon. If hedonism was a job, the bitch would be Mark Zuckerberg.

"Well, she is, and she's in tears."

"I'm more interested to know if she's in *clothes.*" I slid the file into my leather briefcase.

Brianna blinked at me, cocking her head sideways. "Yes, sir, she's clothed."

I snapped my fingers toward the door. "Send her in."

A minute later, Lily stood in my office, still in her nightgown and a jacket. She sniffled, her tears coming down like a broken faucet. She wiped her cheeks and nose with the sleeve of her jacket, and looked like hell, but not in a way that concerned me.

"What's going on?"

"Grams died." She choked on a sob.

I stood, rushing to her. For all the shit she'd put me through, I hated to see anyone going through losing someone important to them. I cared about Madelyn deeply, and I hadn't gotten to say goodbye to her. She hadn't even known I was there.

I'd disappeared on the entire Davis family because I hated their daughter and was too busy licking my wounds.

I pulled Lily into a hug, and she buried her face in my chest and howled, the kind of yelp that ripped your chest open.

I cupped the back of her head. She swayed from side to side in my arms.

"Shit, I'm sorry," I whispered. I was. And it made me feel oddly human.

"I don't know what to do," she sniffed, rays of the old Lily—the one I'd actually liked—seeping through the cracks of her Botoxed exterior. "Will you come to the funeral?"

"Of course."

Her thigh nestled between mine, and I hated it, and I couldn't stop it, and I hated *that* even more. Because if it wasn't intentional, I would never forgive myself for pushing her away.

"Anything your family needs, I'm here."

"Will you come today? Talk to Dad? He's really beside himself. Mom, too. We feel like you were a part of us. Because for the longest time, you were. Grams loved you so much…"

"Not a good idea, everything considered."

She looked up and blinked at me.

"The item in the paper," I clipped. *That you leaked*, I refrained from adding. If I brought it up, I'd have to tell her what I thought about her version of our story, and now wasn't the place, and certainly not the time.

"Oh, I talked to them. They're willing to forgive you." She disconnected from me to wipe her tears quickly.

And the Botoxed bitch returns. "How kind of them." My sarcasm was pretty much dripping on the floor.

I glanced at my watch behind her back. I needed to get those reports out. At the same time, I couldn't go about my day, business as usual.

Maybe because I'd tried to do it when Camille died.

Went back to the office after the weekend of her funeral.

Buried myself in work.

Didn't talk about it with anyone.

Built a higher, stronger, thicker wall between me and the world, making sure no one could get through it.

Camille hadn't deserved it. Hell, Madelyn hadn't either. After all, she was the woman who'd given me the very best advice I'd never bother to take. It was after we'd exited *Phantom of the Opera*, arm in arm. We'd sauntered into our favorite Italian restaurant. She'd asked me if I thought I'd marry her granddaughter.

"Probably. It's what expected of me."

"But what do you want?"

"To make Lily happy." And my father, who might finally accept me for making the right decision. And my mother, who normally didn't particularly care.

"And yourself? Do you want to make yourself happy?"

"I don't think I can be." I hadn't. Not then, and not now.

Madelyn's face had fallen, and she'd squeezed my bicep between her fragile fingers. *"Then you need to keep looking, because my granddaughter isn't the one."*

"I'll come," I told Lily, taking a step back. Fuck the bigwigs and fuck the network. I needed to pay respects to the woman who'd put my happiness before her family's.

Lily's red claws sunk into my skin, and she pulled me into an octopus hug.

"Thank you."

Jude

On the way to work, Leonard Cohen told me in my earbuds that we're spending the treasure that love cannot afford, and I nodded, not only to the rhythm, but the sentiment. My Chucks were blood red, and I'd spent the train ride dying their laces black with a Sharpie.

I walked into the office not knowing what to expect. The professional side was going to be evidently extra depressing. But last night, Célian and I had showcased our hearts like they were on a window display when we touched—crawled into each other's mouths and seeped into each other's souls. Then I'd left, without a message or a phone call. Not my most mature moment, but I was sure he needed time to think, too.

I walked the hallway, ignoring the judgy looks and raised eyebrows people tried to pin me with. Jessica passed me and winced. She didn't say anything, but one look at her face told me I was in for an unpleasant surprise.

Uh-huh.

My phone beeped twice before I got to my station, and I dumped my backpack under my seat, swiping the touch screen.

Grayson: Girl. We love you. We're here for you. And just remember—he can take your joy (temporarily), but he can never take your good hair.

Ava: I heard his dick was too big, anyway. Jokes aside, those things only look good in porn.

What the hell is happening?

I decided to take it up with Célian, who was clearly the root of this weird behavior toward me. I stormed out of the newsroom and stopped when I got to his open door. His back was to me, and he was hugging Lily, who peeked behind his arm. She smiled at me, triumph glittering in her eyes, clutching the fabric of his shirt and nuzzling her nose against his arm.

He took her face in both his hands and leaned down, asking her something intimately.

She nodded, sniffed, and buried her head back in his chest.

His hands on her.

Her hands on him.

Red. My Chucks were red. My heart was black. My mind was white, thick fog.

I was a fool. An idiot. I was the other woman, who'd just gotten dumped very publicly, and as per usual—without notice.

I was able to hear them clearly through the open door.

"Can we go now? I don't want to wait another minute," she whined, smoothing his shirt with her palms. The act looked so natural on them. Like they'd done it a thousand times before.

They probably have, Jude.

"Yes," he said. "Of course."

I snuck into the room next to his office before he could see me. The last thing I wanted was a public showdown with a side of Korean-drama-worthy catfight. Already LBC was in deep trouble, and everybody looked at me like I'd screwed my way into the Laurents' royal family. No reason to give them even more ammo against me. Besides, maybe it wasn't as bad as it looked. I flipped up my phone and shot him a quick message.

Jude: Everything okay?

I went to my desk and switched on my monitor, ignoring the nausea that slammed into me out of nowhere. The room, which was spinning at the corners of my vision, was also eerily silent, and I knew why. If Célian was right about one thing, it was the fact that he'd never forced me into anything. I'd willingly slept with him. In my desperate, sad haze, I had even initiated this affair. I'd made my bed, and the fact that it now crawled with slimy creatures, eating at my reputation and feelings, was my fault and my fault only.

He answered at noon, long after he'd left the office.

Célian: Something came up.

Jude: Elaborate?

Célian: Family.

Of course. Lily was family.

And of course, I was the mistake he'd left behind.

Célian didn't come to work the next day, or the day after.

The rumor mill was in full swing, with Mathias poking his head down from the top floor and hanging out in the newsroom like it was his second house. He tapped Kate on the shoulder and made suggestions, walked up to Elijah and shot him orders, and tried to coax Jessica into having lunch with him. It was clear he was trying to screw with us as much as he could before Célian came back, which made me believe he knew something we didn't—maybe that his son had gotten back with his ex-fiancée.

It was a disaster in the making, and I had VIP tickets. On the flip side, he did ignore me the best he could, and I tried to disappear into my monitor and not lift my head from the keyboard until it was time to go home.

When I had a second to breathe, I ran to the fifth floor to Ava or Grayson's desk. Phoenix, who was a freelancer, didn't have to show up at work every day, but he did because I was in breakdown mode.

"You don't know what's happening yet," he tried to reason with me.

"What's to know? The Laurents do what they want to do."

"Exactly. And he doesn't want to do Lily. Hasn't for a while now."

"He wants his network, and that's what he'll get. I'll be a blip in his history. Nothing but a stain."

"Stain!" Grayson huffed, slapping his desk. "I hope you tarnished his whole life."

According to Gray, Célian had been seen going in and out of Lily's apartment building twice in the last forty-eight hours. At this point, I'd stopped trying to communicate with him and had gotten the general idea. The message had finally hit home.

I was disposable. Maybe not a one-night stand, but definitely a short-term one. I was past my expiration date, thrown aside for Lily to take over. He was patching things up with her family and spending time with her.

Phoenix, of all people, remained impartial.

"Célian Laurent is every bad thing under the sun, but he is not a pussy. If he wanted to get back with Lily, he would have given it to you straight."

Grayson filed his nails, rolling his eyes. "Then I guess he gave it to her gay when he kept mum on his engagement the night they met."

"He didn't think he'd see her again," Ava pointed out.

"But then he found out they were working together," Gray stressed, unwilling to give Célian any slack. I couldn't blame him. He'd been working here for four years, and Célian still didn't know his name. "Plenty of time to clear things up."

"It didn't make any difference. They weren't together, and he was trying to set boundaries with an employee, seeing as his father is a first-class douche with blurred lines when it comes to female coworkers," Phoenix shot back, picking at his takeout with a set of seriously short chopsticks.

"Why are you defending him?" I blinked. "He's been nothing but horrible to you."

Phoenix shrugged. "Because he's sorry."

"About what?" Ava asked.

"About everything. About what happened to Camille. About keeping us apart. The guilt practically pours from his face when he passes me in the corridor. He knows he screwed up, and he wasn't even the one doing the real damage. I don't like him—not even close—but then again…" He dropped his takeout box in the trash can, even though it was still half full. He shook his head, knotting his fingers behind his neck on a sigh. "Camille loved him. He protected her fiercely. He gave her the love and guidance their parents didn't. And I refuse to believe that's the same man who pulls shit like this."

"I haven't heard from him in almost three days." I cleared my throat, looking down at the takeout box in my lap. What the hell had I ordered, anyway? I'd thought it was orange chicken and noodles, but now that I looked, it was stir-fried seafood and rice. I'd eaten a quarter of it without even tasting it. Just how messed up was I?

My heart is not a lonely hunter.

My heart feels. It beats. It loves. It breaks.

It breaks. Oh, God. It is breaking right now, to pieces, and there is nothing I can do to patch it back together. I'm falling apart right along with it.

My phone pinged. I refused to look down and chance everyone seeing how my face twisted in agony and disappointment when I found out yet again that it wasn't Célian. I took a sip of my water.

Another ping.

Then another.

Then another.

Phoenix's phone started pinging, too, but he wasn't a coward. He pulled it out of his pocket and frowned. "Jude?"

"Yes?"

"It's Kate. There's an oil spill in the Gulf of Mexico. NOAA is freaking out, and there's an official statement coming in half a second. We need to go upstairs right now."

We both shot from our seats at the same time. Adrenaline pumped in my veins. Phoenix took my hand and tugged me into the elevator. He didn't let go, even once we were in inside. When our eyes met, he squeezed my palm.

"Want the truth?" he asked.

I grimaced. "Getting tired of the lies, that's for sure."

"That day, when I met you at the library, I wanted to hit on you. I thought, for the first time since Camille, that I'd found something good."

My eyelashes fluttered, my breath hitching. "Oh?"

"Then the next day, I saw you at your desk. Célian walked over to you. He looked down. You looked up. Your eyes met. He fought a smile. I had a déjà vu moment. Because the last time his face lit up like that was when Camille busted his balls for one thing or another. No one else ever made him smile. So I couldn't do it to him. Or to you. Or to me."

He let go when we arrived at the newsroom. Kate was ushering people to the conference room for an emergency meeting.

Célian wasn't there.

Mathias was.

Jude

Half my co-workers ended up spending the night in the newsroom to cover the oil spill. All evening people ran around asking where Célian was, but no one had an answer. I overheard stories from the same folks who'd so kindly made false assessments about my motives and personality when my boss had announced we were dating.

They said he had never missed an important item in his life, that he'd once shown up to work with a fever and lung infection to cover the Michael Flynn case with the Russians, that he was probably really eager to get back with his beautiful, albeit crazy, fiancée.

Kate sent me home when the clock hit eleven. She probably had mercy on me since I didn't live around the block. She also knew about Dad, and I wished she didn't, because I didn't want to be the token charity case.

"Jude, grab your things. I'll see you tomorrow morning."

"I can stay," I said, and I meant it. I didn't mind pulling an all-nighter. I hadn't slept much during my first year of college, between working two jobs and keeping my grades up.

Kate momentarily tore her gaze from the monitor she stared at. "No. You've already gathered all information I need. I want you to go home."

Arguing with her was just going to eat away her precious time, and besides, she wasn't wrong. I needed to check on Dad. I grabbed my bag and walked toward the elevator, a pang of guilt slicing my conscience as I watched everyone else still hard at work.

I'd called the elevator when a hand clasped my shoulder, swiveling me around. It was Kate. Her normally snowy cheeks were red, and she looked flustered and out of sorts.

"If I knew where he was, I'd tell you," she said, her breathing heavy from running.

"I know." I smiled softly. "But I wouldn't expect you to. Whatever Célian does with his life is none of my business, and it will not affect my performance here."

Kate pressed her forehead to the cool wall beside us, squeezing her eyes shut. She looked tired. I got it. She was sans Célian and short on staff. "He'll have some serious explaining to do once he finally gets back here."

The elevator slid open and I stepped inside, giving her a thumbs-up. For the very first time I thought, *and explain he might, but I will not be listening anymore.*

I was about to round the corner and turn onto my street when a limo pulled up at the curb and the passenger door flung open. My eyes widened, and I stopped in an instant. My dad was no Liam Neeson, and if I was going to get kidnapped, I very much doubted I could be saved. I turned around to look at the person getting out of the vehicle. It was Lily, dressed to impress in what looked like a cocktail gown. She seemed to be alone.

"Can I help you?" I cocked my head. I wanted to be strong, but I was tired, hungry, and annoyed. And pissed at myself—so pissed that I'd let myself get carried away with a man like Célian Laurent. I usually made smart choices. I was a salad girl, and he was a deep-fried cake.

"Me? No, though I'm sure you'll do it at some point once you get fired and have to become a waitress to support your slutty ways." She walked toward me on her high heels. The limo driver looked the other way, like he couldn't watch the scene. Her sentence hadn't even made any sense. I folded my arms across my chest.

"Why are you here?"

"To tell you to back off."

"If Célian doesn't want me, he's welcome to tell me himself."

I didn't agree with any part of that sentence. I was no longer sure I wanted him anyway, and at any rate, it wasn't entirely clear we were even together. But I'd be damned if I'd let her boss me around like that.

Lily kept coming until she was chest to chest with me. She was much taller and a little leaner. Most of all, she was meaner.

"You're ruining his life, Jade."

"Jude," I corrected. She'd seemed to love my unique name before she'd known her fake fiancé was sleeping with me.

She rolled her eyes, like I was an idiot for even pointing that out. "Whatever. You butting into his life means he's losing everything he cares about. He doesn't have any family of his own. We were his family—not to mention the network. You are toxic to him, and he's trying hard not to hurt your feelings, but whenever I call him, he comes back."

My face heated, but I said nothing. I didn't believe her—not completely, anyway. Yet her words got to me. I started walking toward my house, bypassing her on the sidewalk. I felt her turning around behind me.

"He's going to be back in my arms by the end of this week."

"Good luck," I shouted back, not turning around to face her.

"You've always been a fling! A meaningless one-night stand that got stretched into more because of the circumstances."

I smiled bitterly. Yes. That I believe.

At home, I made Dad his vegetable soup for tomorrow, following the recipe they'd given me through his program. I was cutting a carrot into depressingly small pieces when my dad hollered from the living room.

"Would you look at that? Your boyfriend is famous."

The first thing that popped into my head was that Milton had been arrested for killing a prostitute. He was so clean cut and morbidly middle class, it seemed like something he'd be capable of doing. I nicked my little finger when the thought of *Célian* sprung into my mind.

Was he in trouble? More importantly—was I supposed to care this much?

"How do you mean, Dad?" I tried to keep my voice light.

"He looks good in a tux, I'll give him that. Of course, if I was as tall as LeBron James, I would rock a designer suit like nobody's business. You have to see this, JoJo."

I placed the knife on the chopping board and wiped my hands on my jeans, walking over to the living room. I stood behind the sofa, so Dad couldn't see me. Good call, considering the horror I knew had plastered itself on my unsuspecting face as I realized what I was looking at.

It was a gossip show rerun from earlier in the day. Some New York socialite had celebrated her birthday and rented out half the left wing of some glitzy hotel. She'd ordered a cake the size of a house—literally, an actual house—and someone from the Guinness Book of World Records came in to measure it. As the camera spun around the horrendous excuse for a sponge cake ("*It took over five hundred sacks of sugar and six hundred pounds of flour to make the cake...*"), it caught some of the guests at the party. And there was my very own Waldo, who'd been missing in action for the past three days.

Lily's arm was looped around Célian's.

He smiled.

She clapped.

They looked *happy.*

Happy like record stores and stone skipping and stolen iPods could never make him. Happy like his fiancée had just helped him save his news channel.

"Who's the girl?" Dad scratched his bald head.

"His fiancée." Rocks. The admission felt like swallowing rocks.

Dad twisted his head, frowning. "JoJo?"

I nodded, squeezing my eyes shut so he wouldn't see the pain swirling inside them. I wanted to run to the cemetery down the block where my mother was buried and throw myself on her tombstone and tell her I wished she'd really cursed me—so my heart would be lonely and hungry, so it wouldn't be linked via an invisible string, like a balloon, to a man who was too good at sucking the air out of it.

"I thought you two were together." Dad brushed his fingers along my arm.

"I thought so, too, Dad. He decided to get back with her earlier this week."

"Idiot."

I knew he meant Célian, but the same could be said about me.

The whole world had warned me about him, and I'd chosen to stick my earbuds in and ignore them.

"Well, I'm pooped. I'll finish your soup tomorrow morning before I go to work." I dropped a kiss on his head, escaping to my room.

I checked the messages on my phone. There were none.

I set my alarm for six in the morning and buried myself under the covers.

Lily had spent the evening with him, then paid me a visit to warn me she was going to steal him back.

She could keep him.

Célian

I walked into my office with a fresh cup of coffee and another new suit that cost fuck-knows-how-much so Brianna wouldn't have to move her precious ass an inch. Kate was sitting behind my desk in my office, but I didn't have it in me to kick her all the way back to the newsroom with my Oxford still stuck between her ass cheeks.

She didn't look up from her laptop as I approached. "The dog house is all the way down, to your left, at the nearest Petco store."

She rubbed her eyes, causing a streak of black eyeliner to run down her cheeks. She looked like she'd been sucking dick for twenty years straight without taking a break—haggard, hair frizzy, with red blotches covering most of her skin. Her gray shirt had at least three different sets of unidentifiable stains.

"You look stunning, by the way." I slid her my cup of coffee.

"Well, you look like the asshole who's about to get dumped and fired on the same day, so I wouldn't go around offering sarcastic compliments." She shut her laptop, tucked it under her arm, and stood up.

I followed her with my eyes as she made her way to the door. If she thought she was walking away without explaining her behavior, she was gravely mistaken.

"Stop," I commanded. She did, her back to me.

"What the fuck are you talking about?" I leaned against my desk.

She didn't turn around. "I stayed here all night."

"Why?"

"Have you not checked the news in the last fifteen hours?"

Alarm trickled into my system. If the mayor had decided to go into cardiac arrest on the first day I decided to unplug, I was going to be ushered to a room right next to him.

"Get to the point," I bit out.

"Check your phone?" She spun on her heel slowly, arching a patronizing eyebrow.

I shook my head, regarding her through hooded eyes. "This game of yours might cost you your job, so I sure as hell hope you're enjoying it."

"Oh, I'm not. Trust me. Now, let's see." She made a show of turning to me fully, tapping her lip. "It started with the fact that the entire newsroom saw you leaving with your ex-fiancée a hot second after you'd declared that Jude is your girlfriend, which put her squarely in the position of being the official office joke—the building's leftover who's been dumped by the boss. Spoiler alert: she doesn't like it. Then, sometime last night, it was revealed that there's an oil spill threatening to kill thousands of mammals and birds. People stayed overnight. Jude didn't, because she had to take care of her father after working overtime. So don't worry, I'm sure she caught the *Gossip Road* rerun of you hanging out with Lily. Gosh..." She slapped a hand over her chest. "What a multitasker. Banging your ex and your life simultaneously."

I erased the space between us, jerking my chin up to look down at her. She hadn't told me anything I didn't already know—well, okay, except the oil spill—and I wasn't an idiot, so obviously, I had a good idea of what it all looked like. Keeping Jude guessing was the plan. Pushing her away—the goal.

But I didn't like what Kate had insinuated. "I didn't *fuck* Lily. Her grandmother died."

That was not something I could exactly shout from the rooftops. The Davis family was private. Her sisters were adamant about working regular jobs.

"Does Jude know?"

"She will." I was playing with fire, but the self-fulfilling prophecy wasn't uncalled for. I didn't really do girlfriends, and the shit with Chucks was getting to be a bit much.

"You're not listening, Célian. She's not going to hear your bullshit. How will you explain hanging at Lily's apartment building? Attending a birthday party with her? Disappearing on all of us?"

I shouldered past her, and she gasped, taking an evasive step. The impending calamity I'd inserted myself into with eyes wide open was going to come raining down on me. It wasn't pouring, but we were already at a steady trickle. *Shit.* I was in deep shit.

"I attended all those functions for her family," I told Kate, still unable to reach for my office door. "That included Lily's cousin's stupid birthday party. I went to her apartment, twice—*without* her—because I needed to get her fresh clothes and her toiletry shit. We were never in the same vicinity with our clothes off. She tried to hold my hand for half a fucking second at the party, and I bit her head off for it. We're over, but that doesn't mean I need to be an ass to her. I wanted to be there for the Davises, because when my life was crumbling and Camille died, they were there for me."

Lily had been a no-show during those terrible days, but I still remembered the flowers and pastry the family had sent every morning, her mother checking in on me, her grandmother calling me three times a day to make sure I ate and showered and *breathed.*

Kate turned around, reaching for the door handle. I kept my face blasé. "Good luck explaining it to everyone, Célian. Because let me tell you something—the moment Jude walked into the room, she changed you. It wasn't profound. It was even gradual, but it was there. In the way you started smiling, the way you softened toward your employees—just a little—and started doing the right thing by yourself and Lily. But standing here?" She shook her head. "I think that man just bailed on us, and it saddens me, because I was looking forward to working with, and befriending, the new Célian."

She closed the door behind her, and I looked to the glass wall, catching Jude unpacking her lunch and dumping her bag by her chair. She looked up to meet my gaze like I knew she would. We could sense each other from miles away. I arched a come-get-it eyebrow. Her face remained unaffected, like she didn't actually see me, and she began to roll her earbuds around her iPod, turning her computer on.

Stay calm.

Stay put.

Think it through. This is what you wanted.

Fuck it. I didn't need to think.

I pushed off my desk, blazing into the newsroom. Everybody was nose deep in work, because evidently we were on the verge of an environmental disaster and nobody had time to be impressed that I had, in fact, gotten my head out of my ass.

I knew now that for the last three days, I'd tried to deny my feelings toward Jude and make them go away.

I went directly to her table and slapped a hand over Kipling, which was open by her keyboard.

She looked up.

"Sir?" There was nothing in that voice. Nothing in her face. No fire crackling in the air between us. It was like she'd been turned off.

"Need you for a minute."

"I'm right here."

"Downstairs."

"Not happening," she said calmly, with everyone looking *now*, because that was the essence of Judith Humphry—a goddamn badass in colorful Chucks and a weird, too-grownup suit. "If you need something from me professionally, please say so right now, because I'm about to head into the conference room for an urgent call with NOAA's public affairs officer."

Only reason I didn't clench my jaw was because I knew that shit would snap and break from the force. If she'd been any other employee, I would've thrown her ass out of the building with the phone cord and receiver still clutched in her fist. But not Judith. Not after everything we'd been through.

Truth of the matter was, I couldn't verbally rip her limb from limb, even when she belittled me in public, because I didn't want to.

Because I cared about her.

I was in love with her.

Jesus fucking Christ. I was, wasn't I? First she got into my bed, then under my skin, then into my heart. There was no deeper tissue than that, so she stayed there, taking more and more space, until there was no room left inside me. If she cut me open, I would bleed her.

She reared her head back, like I was going to bite her face off. "Will that be all, Mr. Laurent?"

"Yes. Get on that NOAA call and report back." I took a step away, my head still spinning from the eternal revelation.

I loved Jude.

I'd pushed Jude away.

I could have told her what had been happening at any point during those three days, but I didn't.

I didn't want her to know.

I'd wanted her to assume the worst and to give up on me, like everyone else had. My mother was indifferent. My father actively hated me. And my ex-fiancée wanted me the same way you wanted a limited-edition Hermes bag—because I'd look damn good and pricey on her arm.

"Sure thing, sir."

"Stop calling me sir," I snapped. *My tongue has been inside your ass, for fuck's sake.*

"Yes, sir," she hissed, narrowing her eyes at me.

You came all over my face with my dick inside your mouth. "Appreciate it, Chucks."

In love. Fuck me.

With Judith Penelope Humphry from Brooklyn.

Who I'd met on a shitty rainy day after another fight with my father.

Who had stolen my wallet and my cash and my condoms and my heart.

Who'd sneaked into every fiber of my skin, one layer at a time, with her music and contagious laugh and daily moods and dirty Chucks.

I was in love, despite not wanting or agreeing to be.

So I'd pushed her away. If I disappeared, I didn't have to make a decision. It would be made for me.

A decision to take a chance on someone.

A decision to live again.

A decision to give up LBC, and everything I'd worked for, because power wasn't enough. Especially if you have no one to share it with.

That's how I found myself doing the whole flowers-and-chocolate routine when I came to her house that evening. Did people do that anymore? Every romantic idea I had—and granted, I didn't have many—was taken from stupid rom coms Camille made me watch when I was a teen. Lily had never bothered. She knew sitting me down in front of a Kate Hudson movie was a task akin to getting me to fuck a food grinder.

Maybe chocolate and flowers were a '90s thing. Judith was young. Perhaps to a point it made people feel uncomfortable. Ask me if I gave a fuck.

Célian, do you give a fuck?

Not even a half. Not even a quarter. Minus three fucks, and still counting.

I rang the doorbell several times, pacing back and forth. The door remained unanswered, much like my text messages. I'd tried to keep them curt and sane, but those were two traits I'd parted ways with for the past few hours, while dealing with an oil spill, a dying network, and a broken heart. I decided to shoot her one last message before I left.

Célian: We need to talk.

Célian: In a nutshell, I did not put my dick inside my ex-fiancée.

Célian: And she is still very much an ex.

Célian: Her grandmother died. We were close. I didn't want to lay out all the shit in a text message. Which is fucking ironic, because PICK UP THE DAMN PHONE.

Célian: Also—if you did catch the party, that was her cousin. The family was obligated to go. I left early.

Célian: And alone.

Célian: Why am I explaining myself to your message box? Let's make it awkward for both of us. I'm coming over.

Célian: Open the door.

Célian: I'll kick it down.

Célian: It's a dodgy neighborhood, Chucks. Going doorless for a night isn't ideal, but you asked for it.

I heard the click of the door opening a second after the last text. I looked up. Chucks had on a Sonic Youth hoodie and short shorts. She stared at me through a crack narrower than an ant's anus.

"Here," I said, thrusting the flowers—they looked about as wilted as me—and the red chocolate box with the pink cellophane in her direction. "For your stubborn ass, which I would very much like to eat again in the near future."

"Is this a joke?" She blinked slowly.

I looked around me. Was it? Because it felt serious on an existential level to me. "About the ass or the apology? Never mind. No, in both cases."

"Well, I don't accept your apology, and I will not grace the ass comment with a response. Anything else?" she asked, but she was already pushing her door closed.

I spotted her father shuffling behind her. He shook his head when he saw me through the slit in the door.

"*Célian*," he scolded. "You're lucky I'm too sick to kick your ass. Wait. I'd never be too sick to kick your ass."

"Sir, I'm trying to explain."

He walked off to the couch, not sparing me another look. I went back to staring at my girlfriend. Ex-girlfriend. Whatever she was. *Fuck*.

"There's a perfectly good explanation for everything that's happened in the last three days." I tried a different tactic.

For the record, my BA was in pre-law and my masters was in international relations. I was supposed to be good with words. In fact, I knew I was. That did not stop me from shitting all over this encounter.

"Yet there is zero way to explain why you went MIA and brushed me off when the entire world knew you were with your ex," she countered. "You know, Célian, Milton was wrong about a lot of things. One thing he was right about, though—royalty and plebeians don't mix. It's probably very nice to be sitting there on the throne, like you do."

Did it look like I was having a good fucking time? What gave it away, the fact that I felt like hell, or smelled like it? My teeth ground together.

She swung the door open all the way, parking a hand on her hip. "Actually, I do have something to say, so listen carefully. When my mother died, she said the heart was a lonely hunter. I thought she meant I was incapable of falling in love. Because I never did. I liked Milton, a lot, and some guys in high school, too..." She trailed off.

I was hoping she'd get to the point before I had to kill my way through half of New York. Especially Milton. That guy was so high on my shit list, I doubted it was safe for us to be in the same state.

"But then I found out that's not what she meant. It was right before we left for Florida. That day my father told me she was actually referring to a book. See, I'd never told him what Mom said. I didn't want to tarnish how perfect she was in his eyes. Because I *love* him, and when you love someone, you want to protect them, no matter the cost. And I can't afford to be with you, Célian, because I love you. But in order to learn how to love, you first need to learn how to *live*, and hating your parents, running around with your ex-fiancée, and playing power games is just not the way. I deserve more."

I would tell her I loved her right now if I thought she would believe me. But why would she? I'd acted like an ass for months. Fuck, I wouldn't believe me, either.

"Give me a chance."

She shook her head. "No can do."

"Judith..."

"Don't do this." Her eyes pleaded. I said nothing to that. "You will only prove what I just said—that it's all about you. If you care about me at all, let me go."

Fuck.

Fuck.

Fuck.

Hoping like hell it wasn't some test I was failing, I ran a hand through my hair, then slammed the chocolate and flowers against her corridor's wall. Pitted glossy cherries and chocolate smeared down the side of her door.

And they say the French are romantic.

"Okay," I said. "Okay."

I found the habit of repeating oneself unappealing. But that was because I was never out of sorts and clueless. I was now, and I didn't like it one bit.

"Should we revisit this subject next week? Next month? Next year?" Was I even going to survive that kind of time?

"No, Célian. I don't think we should."

The door closed in my face. Gently, but firmly, like everything else she did.

I hung my head and shook it, staring at the floor.

She had a *Game of Thrones* "Hold the Door" mat.

And I fucking let her go. Because she did deserve more.

Jude

The heart is a lonely hunter.

My heart was a lonely hunter.

Everything hurt.

I'd always thought I was doomed by not being able to fall in love, but once I did fall, I wished I hadn't. Now it hurt when I breathed, when I walked the hallways at work, and each time in between, when I caught sight of the person with a sharp suit and even sharper tongue moving past me, firing orders at Brianna or bantering with Elijah and Kate.

Eight weeks had passed. Four weeks after he'd shown up at my doorstep with flowers and chocolate, Célian had invited everyone into the conference room and announced that he'd taken a position at a competing network in Los Angeles and would only be staying for another month.

After he made that announcement, he'd shot me a look, searching my face. Whatever he found there made him ask me to stay after the meeting was over so we could talk about it.

I'd wanted to, badly, but I knew nothing had changed.

I wasn't going to move to Los Angeles, and we couldn't even make it work when we lived in the same city. So there was just no way we could pull it off if he lived across the country.

Besides, I still loved him more than he was capable of ever loving me back, and an unbalanced relationship was a doomed one.

"Sir, I have a lot of work. I'd really rather not." My fingers had twitched under the desk.

His bottom-of-the-iceberg blue eyes had run down my body to see my shoes. I'd worn generic black flats. I couldn't bring myself to show him how I felt every day. It felt too intimate, now that he knew what each color meant.

I'd also refused to unfold the little Post-it notes he'd started shoving into my desk drawer about a month after everything blew up. It wasn't every day, but whenever I found one, my mood would turn sour.

Even so, I knew he was not seeing Lily anymore, and that was official. The wedding venue had been canceled, Ava and Gray had reported to me excitedly one day, and after losing her beloved grandmother and her fiancé in the same month, Lily had decided to check into a Utah-based rehab center to treat her addiction to alcohol.

Ava and Grayson were obsessed with my post-Célian life. They seemed to know every single detail I wasn't privy to—like how Milton had been fired from *The Thinking Man* and was now working as a researcher at some local newspaper nobody had heard of. Or how Célian was packing his things and getting ready to move away. I couldn't bear the idea of not seeing Célian every day, but I also knew I didn't have it in me to be hurt by him again.

Nevertheless today, a Friday, when he served his last day at LBC and everyone stood in line to shake his hand and thank him for what many considered a national service, I did, too.

He squeezed my hand. "Judith."

"Si..." I started to call him sir, knowing he hated it, before sparing both of us more headache. "Célian." I shook my head, offering him a timid smile. "Thank you for everything."

"No need to thank me. It was only a fraction of what I was planning to give you, anyway," he said dryly, but his eyes were two pools of misery. It felt like I was drowning into their depths, unable to come up for air.

I shuffled a little to the side, making room for Jessica behind me. He squeezed my hand harder. "Read the notes, Judith."

"Safe travels." I ducked my head and went straight to the bathroom.

Brianna waited for me there with two open mini bottles of Jack Daniels.

The burn of the alcohol barely touched my throat. It slid straight to my chest. Standing there, in the unsanitary women's bathroom, made me realize what having good friends was all about. And I was darn glad I'd made a good friend in Brianna.

In the end, it was a Sunday afternoon when everything changed—when *I* changed. I realized it really didn't matter how Célian had treated me, because love was not a chess game. It was Twister. You got all wrapped up and stumbled over your own feet, but that was part of its charm.

I had holed up in the library, as per usual. I knew Célian had been spending time with Dad every Sunday, religiously, and how it was important to both of them. Dad had Mrs. Hawthorne and me every day of the week, but he missed the buddies he'd once had at work, and Célian was his dose of testosterone. I tried not to be bitter about how easily and quickly he'd forgiven Célian, but the sad truth was, even I couldn't hate him. Not really. Not all the way. Not the way I so desperately wanted to hate the man who'd quite ironically made me realize I could love.

Phoenix found me at the library. He was the one to sneak us in some candy this time. He looked perky and mischievous today, and better than he had the last few weeks.

He seemed like the guy I'd met the first time, when he'd approached me at this very library.

"What's with you? You look different." I stole a handful of Sour Patch Kids from his bag.

He chewed on his candy as he began to flip through the pages of *The Times*. "Different how?"

"Hmm…" I looked left and right, feeling uncomfortable. "Happy?"

"I *am* happy." He laughed. "It's not a foreign concept. You should try it, too."

"Maybe it's contagious and I'll catch it from you," I mused.

But that was wishful thinking, and I knew it. I was operating on autopilot, going through the motions, when really, all I could think about was the fact that Célian was probably in my apartment right now, and possibly for the last time, leaving his scent and testosterone and sexy air all over the place. Ugh.

"Actually, I'm also pretty happy because I have a lead to give you." Phoenix snapped the paper shut, his eyes zeroing in on mine. I closed my copy of *The New Yorker* and arched an eyebrow. He leaned across the table between us and squeezed my hand. "I think you're going to appreciate this one."

"Then why are you giving it to me?"

I'd been here for Phoenix since he'd gotten back from Syria. I'd refused to take Célian's side and choose between them, even though many women probably would have. But that still didn't warrant all the help he'd given me. I knew he was a freelancer, and he didn't particularly need the money, but I was beginning to feel uncomfortable at how much I owed him in leads and sources. Part of the reason I'd become appreciated and adored in the newsroom was because he'd handed me a lot of gems that should have been his.

"This one has your name all over it," he insisted.

"Why?" I asked.

No matter what Célian said, Phoenix was a good journalist. He had friends everywhere. He was charming and approachable. Since he'd gotten back to New York, he'd spent every evening hitting the trendy Manhattan bars where journalists swarmed and had made more contacts, even though he didn't drink a drop of alcohol. He knew everyone and everything—his father's son through and through. And James Townley? I was pretty certain he had a direct line to Jesus himself.

Jesus: "I was wondering when you were going to give me a comeback."

"Because," Phoenix said, snapping a purple Sour Patch in half between his teeth and flashing me a smirk, "it *literally* does have your name on it. Now, do you promise not to freak the hell out when I show you what my father found?"

"Your father?" My eyes widened. "James Townley did some actual journalistic work?" I didn't mean to be rude or anything, but I figured he didn't need to, seeing as he was a news god.

Phoenix waggled his brows. "Let's just say he had some open business with the person in question, so when he overheard this hot piece of gossip, he was eager to dig up the bone at the end of that hole. Turned out the bone was meaty."

"Okay." My teeth sank to my lower lip. "Tell me."

He did.

Everything.

Then he slid a file across the table.

I shoved it in my backpack and bolted to the train station.

I had to show it to Célian.

And I knew exactly where to find him.

...Or maybe I didn't.

Our apartment was empty when I got to it. I climbed up to Mrs. Hawthorne's place, but she said Célian and my dad had left in a cab a couple hours before. She asked if I wanted to come in for tea. I told her I did, but not right now, and I could see the disappointment in her face. I pulled the sleeve of her dress and hugged her on her threshold without warning. She yelped at the sudden gesture, but eased into the hug after a second. She patted my back.

"I would like to get to know you better, Jude. I see how well you take care of your father, and I admire that. A lot."

"We will," I promised, and I meant it, even though my mind was elsewhere—with the hot news I wanted to deliver. "I promise. I don't take all you do for Dad for granted, either. We will spend some time together. I know we will."

I then took the stairs three at a time, hitting the call button frantically. Célian's phone went straight to voicemail. I would've thought the worst if I didn't know he was with my dad.

Dad.

Oh, God, Dad.

I threw my backpack on the floor and started calling my father. He'd seemed okay before I left the house. He seemed okay in *general.* They said the tumor was shrinking, but how promising was it? It was an experimental treatment, and he was still weak. He never left the building. *Ever.* Now he was out with Célian, god-knows-where, and I was supposed to do...what, exactly? Sit around and wait for his safe return?

I started sending him and Célian messages simultaneously. For Dad, it was the usual call me back/I'm worried/you should have left a note/when are you coming back. With Célian, however, I allowed myself to be more creative. Maybe it was the pent-up anger I'd harbored for the past eight weeks that did it.

Jude: Where's my dad?

Jude: I'm going to kill you, Célian.

Jude: (Not literally, in case this message finds its way to the authorities)

Jude: I'm so worried. Please have him call me.

Jude: Where did you take him? Why? You know he never leaves the house.

I paced the apartment, back and forth. I didn't know what to do with myself, and that scared me to death. I went back to my backpack and pulled out the documents Phoenix had given me, examining them with shaky hands.

Kipling slipped from my bag and spilled open, spitting out business cards and the folded Post-it notes Célian had left me like confetti. I'd taken them out of the drawer before I'd left the office Friday because they were overflowing and I didn't have space for my own stuff.

Why didn't I just recycle them? Why did he send them?

I'd asked myself this question a million times. Why did Célian try to reach out to me with notes? He was the most verbal person I knew, and he seemed to have a magnetic power over me every time we were together. But maybe that was it.

He didn't want to have a magnetic power over me.

He wanted us to talk.

Or just to tell me how he felt.

Now, as I waited for him or my dad to answer me, I had no choice but to try to distract myself by finding out what the notes said. I sank to the floor, my back dragging along the wall, and unfolded the first yellow note.

The word "music" comes from the Muses, goddesses of the arts in Greek mythology.
I never said it before, because I thought it was tacky, but you're my goddess (especially your ass).—Célian

John Lennon started his music career as a choir boy.
I never said it before, because it terrified me to admit it, but you're my church (although I plan to be inside you way more than just on Sundays).—Célian

Your heart mimics the beat of the music you're listening to.
I didn't know I even had one before you came along, and now I do, and it hurts like a motherfucker (thanks for that).—Célian

I stole your iPod before you stole my wallet. It was tucked inside my jacket before I even removed your panties. I wanted to know what you were listening to. (And I was sorely disappointed there were no Britney Spears and Justin Timberlake songs in sight, because it made not falling for you so much fucking harder.)—Célian

I tried to tell myself I broke up with Lily because I was better than my father. Bullshit. I broke up with her because I couldn't not be with you (and I've spent a respectable amount of time denying that shit to myself).—Célian

The day I went to the Davises, I wanted you to find out. I wanted you to show me your ugly side. I wanted you to be ugly, for once in your life, so I could shake you off. (You weren't ugly that day. I was.)—Célian

The last one, which was actually many Post-it notes stuck together, had been tucked inside my drawer on Friday, and it read:

I'm in love with you, and I might not be able to tell you that in person, because you clearly don't want to hear it, and because I'll be gone soon. But I am, and I fucking hate it. Don't think for one minute I wanted to fall in love with you, Jude. But that makes my love for you so much stronger. So next time you wrongly assume you're the only person hurting in this, just remember the first rule of journalism. There are two sides to every story. (And if you're at all open to hearing mine, this is probably my last chance.)—Célian

The lock rattled in the door to the apartment. I quickly wiped the tears from my face, but there was very little point in doing that, I realized. My clothes were soaked with them. So were the Post-it notes. I gulped in a breath and turned around. Dad walked in wearing a

Yankees cap and waving a baseball in his hand.

"Guess what your old man caught?" His grin collapsed the minute he saw me sitting on the floor, surrounded by a sea of yellow papers. He rushed to my side.

"Is everything okay, JoJo?"

I stood up, not wanting to waste another minute.

"Where were you?"

"The Yankees game. Célian thought it'd be a nice way to say goodbye. Then we went for hot dogs. I figured I'd be home before you got back."

"I cut my library time short. Where's Célian?" I sniffed.

"Are you okay?" he asked again, rubbing my back.

Was I? A part of me was. A part of me was more than okay, knowing I was about to help a man who deserved my help more than anyone I knew, after everything he'd given me and my dad. Another part of me was gutted and torn—to give him a chance and to risk the full demolition of my heart or try to move on?

"I'm fine, Dad. Where's Célian?"

"He said he had to get something from the office..."

Of course.

I was out the door before I had the chance to hear what it was.

Célian

The cardboard boxes remained untouched and empty in the corner of my office. All I really needed to take was my laptop.

I rarely got attached to people, let alone possessions.

I had no pictures of my family and no bullshit funny mugs on my desk. Every award I'd received had been thrown in the trash the night it was given to me—I didn't make the news to get a pat on the back; I made the news because I wanted to change lives, and perspective, and the world, and to prove I was deserving of all I had been given. The only thing I had gotten attached to on this floor would like to see me castrated by a butcher, so there was really no need to prolong my departure. I'd insisted on not having a goodbye party, explaining there was nothing happy about my exit. I wasn't moving on to bigger, better things after a mutual understanding with the management. I was jumping out of a sinking ship, leaving my staff to drown.

It was like planning your own funeral.

I shut my laptop and shoved it into the trash with the heel of my Oxford, deciding I didn't want to take *anything* with me from this place. Fuck it.

CSP, a competing channel, was building a news division in Los Angeles, and it seemed like a good idea to put a few thousand miles between me and Mathias. But that wasn't why I'd quit my job.

I didn't want to see Judith's face every day, knowing I'd put the scowl there.

So I made way for her, because I would never fire her, and because really, she'd earned her place in my newsroom perhaps even more than I had.

There hadn't been a huge breakdown to compliment my heartbreak. It was quiet, yet somehow a thousand times worse than I'd ever experienced. Every day when she left the office, she took something with her.

Another piece of my fucking heart.

Another song on her playlist I'd never be able to listen to without thinking of her.

I'd had my phone off all day—I wanted to do this without interruption—and I finally turned it back on and shoved it in my pocket. I grabbed my jacket, throwing one last look at the place that had once been my kingdom, the place I thought I'd have my fucking retirement party, and shook my head.

I turned around, closed the door, and bumped into something small and hot.

Judith.

She shoved a file to my chest, pointing at me.

"First things first, next time you take my father out of the house, you let me know by text or a phone call. Agreed?"

I blinked rapidly. Was I imagining things now? Because that kind of shit needed to be checked and medicated. I arched an eyebrow.

"You do realize Los Angeles is not around the block, right? I won't be seeing much of him anytime soon."

Still an asshole. But hell if she didn't like it.

"There's a special place in hell for you." She shoved her delicate finger in my face.

Would it be too much if I bit the tip? Probably.

I smirked. "Not surprised. I have a rock star realtor. What are you doing here on a Sunday, Chucks?"

"Saving your ass." She unplastered the file from my chest and walked over to her station in the newsroom.

I followed. Her ass looked fantastic, as always, but that wasn't what made me smile until I'd almost cut my face in half.

She laid all the docs on her desk, yet wouldn't let me peek into the file. I eyed her curiously, not sure what her deal was, but intrigued nonetheless. More than anything, I liked that she was talking to me again, and wasn't planning on fucking it up.

"Prepare to have your mind blown," she said.

"Is this an invitation for a hookup? Because I find it hard to believe anything but your cunt can evoke such—or any—emotion in me."

I left the romantic stuff for the notes I'd written her. I still couldn't bring myself to say any of it out loud, but I wanted to. Badly.

She shook her head and smiled, sliding Polaroid pictures my way. Of my father dining at a restaurant with the channel's bigwigs.

I raised an eyebrow. "How did you get those?"

"James Townley."

"And how did *he* get those?"

"He hired Dan, who works here, to run an investigation on Mathias."

"So did I," I shot back. "So?"

She shrugged. "Townley paid double."

"That fucker Dan." I sucked in a breath.

Jude put her hand on mine and squeezed. "Not at all. He's brilliant. He took you both as clients because you had the same goal: bring Mathias down."

I leaned my hip against her desk and browsed through the images. There were more in her file, but this wouldn't cut it. "That's all nice and dandy, but what the fuck am I looking at? My father having lunch with the investors without me? I can use it for nothing, other than maybe research for making voodoo dolls."

Jude slid a bunch of documents from the file toward me. "Read the highlighted areas. There's a lot of fluff, profanity, and chauvinism to weed through, but in the end, you'll find the conversation quite interesting. Especially the revelations in this transcript of the original recording."

"This is all recorded?" I picked up the papers, eyeing her.

She nodded. "Yes."

"I still won't be able to use it in court."

I was testing her, treading carefully over my own secret—a secret I didn't want to make known yet so Judith wouldn't feel pressured into anything. My heart beat so fast I thought it was going to burn a hole in my chest.

She waved her hand in the documents' direction. "Just read it, Célian."

I started skimming through the text, hitting the highlighted parts:

M.L: "...ridiculously easy. I knew he was there, so I pulled out the CCTV footage and found the girl—Judith something. I made sure the right arrangements had been made and sure enough, the Judith girl got called for a job interview at LBC, although there was a mix-up and she somehow ended up in another department. I rectified the situation right away, though."

M.L: "...it was a long shot, but my son is not as calculating as I am. I figured it was worth a try. And it worked. He got attached so easily, and discarded his fiancée completely. Now, we need to decide what we're doing with LBC..."

M.L: "...I'm pulling out the ads slowly, though we will need to think of ways to terminate the contract completely. My lawyers are working on finding a legal loophole."

I set the papers down, sitting on the edge of her desk and lacing my fingers nonchalantly. So Mathias had planned it all along. My meeting Jude, my falling in love with her, giving up on the Davis family—every single thing. And I'd walked right into his trap. Well, *almost*.

I didn't make the mistake of asking Jude if she'd known about it. Of course she hadn't. Instead, I focused on how to deal with this shit.

"We've both been set up," I said.

She put a hand on my shoulder, and I resisted the urge to pull her into me and bury my face in her hair. Judith had this touch that made shit go away. Bad shit. She must have known I thought it—maybe I even said it out loud—because she took a few steps back and swallowed. It was the kind of swallow that said that there was something more, and I wasn't necessarily going to like it.

"I read the Post-it notes," she said.

"I thought you did a long time ago." It felt good, knowing she hadn't. Knowing she hadn't chosen to ignore me.

She shook her head. "It hurt too much."

"And now?"

"It still does, but a little less. Also I'm more concerned with your well-being than my own right now. James wants to talk to you."

I immediately wanted to say I wasn't interested, but I knew better than to fuck it all up. She was talking to me, after all. I needed to play nice if I wanted a nice girlfriend.

Fuck. Yes. That's what it was. I wanted Jude to be my girlfriend—not a fake one and not a temporary one.

"I'm pressed for time," I said instead, wondering if it were still true, now that she and I were on speaking terms again. "But I guess I could squeeze him in tonight if you come with."

"This is your family and personal business. I don't think I belong."

"I don't think I give a fuck. Wait, this just in..." I pretended to listen to something on an invisible headphone. "I *don't* give a fuck. Grab your shit, Chucks."

"This doesn't mean anything," she said as I tugged on her hand.

Like hell it didn't. She wanted to help me, and she'd come all the way to work on a Sunday afternoon to give me something she thought would be useful. It meant everything and more, and I was going to milk the hell out of it.

I made a stop in my office and took the laptop out of the trash can, putting it neatly back on the desk. Jude never asked what it had been doing there in the first place.

She knew.

I'd never been to James Townley's place, and I'd been content to think I never would. He lived in another penthouse, in another New York 'scraper, and it was amazing how one of the most dazzling architectural cities in the world had managed to be home to so many identical, clinical, and impersonal penthouses.

James opened the door in a robe (douchebag), and said he was glad to see me. When he spotted Jude next to me, he made a face like I'd pissed in his drink.

"Deal with it," I replied to his nonverbal annoyance, walking into his living room.

His twelve-year-old wife, who was 85% made of plastic, unglued herself from the couch, her heels click-clicking toward their hallway, and then I guessed their bedroom. James went to the kitchen to get us some drinks. I couldn't figure out why his wife would wear heels at home. I elbowed Judith lightly as we sat down on the same sofa the busty morning show host had vacated a second ago.

"Do you wear shoes indoors?"

Jude's eyes darted to me, and she frowned immediately. "I don't even wear underwear and a bra at home. Dad's lucky if my clothes cover my private parts. I'm a free spirit."

"I fucking love you," I blurted, and I nearly choked on the air inside my lungs.

Not that she didn't know by now, but still.

She grinned. "I think I'm beginning to believe you."

"Let the record show that I took another job just so you could keep yours at LBC," I told her before my throat closed. "Being away from you would feel like living without limbs. And I very much enjoy my limbs."

The look on her face was priceless. It was every fantastic Christmas gift a second after you unwrap it. I was about to dive down and go for the kiss, sealing this shit for good, when James sauntered back in with a tray and something alcoholic on it.

Fucker.

I couldn't pretend I didn't see him, so I straightened up on the couch and tried to think about sad things, like global warming and *The Big Bang Theory*, to take care of my inappropriately engorged cock. James dragged over a settee and sat directly in front of me, leaning forward. The silver tray with the drinks sat between us on the coffee table, but nobody touched it.

"Are you sure you'd like Junior to be here? What I'm about to tell you is very personal."

"Stop calling her Junior, and yes, she can be here. My life is her life."

They both stilled in their seats, but I didn't miss a heartbeat. I had a flight out of JFK to LAX in five hours, and I wasn't going to be on it. That made me feel eerily calm and happy. Judith was here. Everything was okay.

"Well..." James shook his head, running his hand through his hair.

He was so vain, I wondered if he shaved his balls completely or bleached them to match his fake hair color.

"There's no right way of saying this. Let me tell you, for the record, that I've been wanting to tell you for a while now, but Iris always stopped me. Never Mathias, though, son. I'm not scared of him."

"Stop calling me so—" I started, but he cut me off.

"But you are," he said, clearing his throat and blinking rapidly. "You're my son, Célian, and there's nothing and no one that can change that. Thirty-three years ago, I walked into the bar across from LBC after a bad job interview..."

No.

No.

Just, no.

I couldn't listen to this crap. I definitely couldn't bear hearing how similar it was to my story with Judith so far. I shook my head without even meaning to, and I felt myself standing up, legs on autopilot. I hated my father, but I refused to believe I'd been a fool for thirty-two years. A small, hot hand—a little sweaty, but in a good way—tugged me back down.

"Please," she whispered. "I know it's hard."

I found myself sitting again, even though every bone in my body screamed for me to do something different. This wasn't for this asshole. It was for Judith.

"Continue," I hissed.

James looked at me with eyes full of pity and regret, two feelings I despised—especially from a man I'd known as my employee for the past few years, no matter how much power he had in my newsroom.

"I wanted to become an actor," he said. "It was actually an audition, rather than a job interview, and I failed. Three drinks later, your mother and I were in bed. I didn't know she was a newlywed. But that's not the only thing she chose to omit from the equation. I would learn weeks later that this had been the day she first found out your father was cheating on her, which was why she had no ring on. She thought she'd never put it back on."

Fuck. My. Life.

The similarities were endless. Uncanny. And yet I couldn't help but pray to God that the outcome of our relationships would be very different. Because as far as my knowledge went, my mother and James spoke to each other once a year during the annual network Christmas party, and nothing more. Jude's hand reached for mine—not tentatively, no, this time she owned it—giving it a squeeze.

"You were married, too," I spat. Phoenix was only three years younger than me.

James shook his head. "No. I met my ex-wife the following fall."

Phoenix and I were half-brothers.

I wanted to throw up. My girlfriend rubbed my thigh now, trying to soothe me. James hurried to pour us all a drink—I think just to do something with his hands. The air wrapped around us in an awkward way, and maybe that's what having a heart attack felt like.

"After the one-night stand, I told her about my audition. She said there was a vacancy at LBC. They needed someone for their morning show—to host a daily ten-minute slot with the news. Nothing prime-time, but I knew it could pay the bills and—"

"Let me guess," I cut him off. "You needed the money because one of your family members was sick."

James's face twisted in shock, his entire expression opening up, unlocking like a safe. "My mother needed surgery on her hip. How did you know?"

Judith and I exchanged looks. *Atonement.* I was hers, and she was mine.

She thought she could never love.

I thought I didn't deserve love, and even if I did, I'd never find anyone half tolerable to spark this feeling in me.

"Just a wild guess." I rubbed my hand over my face.

Judith bit on her lower lip, and my dick jerked to attention again. *Really? Right now?*

James looked between the two of us. "I went in the next day and got the job. I couldn't believe my luck. I found out not long after that your mother was married, and she acted like I didn't even exist anymore, which in retrospect I don't exactly fault her for. She was in a very vulnerable state..."

I wasn't Mathias's son.

All this time, I'd thought I was inherently an asshole because of him, but really, I was more of a sociopath prick, like Maman.

The similarities were uncanny, much to my dismay.

"When did you find out about me?" I cut off his fluff-talk.

I hadn't come here to hear about his journey as a junior anchor at LBC.

James reached for his drink and gulped it in one go, shaking his head and slamming the glass against the silver tray. He wiped his mouth with the sleeve of his robe.

"Your mother came to me about ten weeks after. She knew it was mine because she and Mathias weren't..." He shook his head. "He'd cheated on her. She hadn't wanted to be with him."

I appreciated him not talking explicitly about anyone fucking Maman. That was one mental image I was happy to keep out of my brain.

"I told her I'd love to be a part of your life. I want you to know that not having you was never an option for either of us. But at the same time, your mother had decided to give her relationship with Mathias another shot, and she knew they could never explain such an arrangement to the press..."

"So Mathias knows?" I nearly laughed, though there was nothing funny about my situation. I was sitting in front of my biological father, a man I'd known all my life and hated for a decade, as I'd worked side by side with him for most of my adult years. He'd always called me *son*, and I'd always berated him for it. He'd tried to get close to me, but I'd repeatedly shut him down. He'd tried to talk to me, but I'd kept sending him on his way.

James bowed his head. "He knows. We were frank with him from the beginning. He was livid, of course—tried to get me fired. But by then, I had gained some momentum, and LBC was still working its way up. They needed me, and I needed them. But yes, Mathias knew about you. That's why he could never stomach your presence."

I smiled bitterly, though there was something liberating in knowing it wasn't personal. It wasn't specifically something I'd done. I'd grown up thinking I was so rotten, I'd become rotten. This changed everything. Mostly it changed how I looked at myself in the mirror.

Judith snuggled beside me, rubbing my arm.

"Mathias's approach to you has always been the center of my beef with him. Every Christmas, at our network party, I would beg your mother to tell you about me. And every single Christmas, the layer of security and fake-friends padding her and blocking my way grew thicker. I couldn't tell you this of my own accord. But I watched you grow from afar, and every night when I tucked Phoenix into bed, I prayed that one day I'd be able to make up for it with you."

I couldn't really articulate a response to that. I got why James hadn't been able to tell me he was my father. At the same time, I thought he was probably exaggerating the level of remorse he'd experienced. He was still newly married to a woman half his age and had dumped his previous wife because he'd wanted to go on a Celebrity Big Brother-like adventure. Still. James was self-absorbed and egotistical, but he wasn't a goddamn bastard like Mathias.

I blinked at him, checking my watch. "Safe to say it's too late for you to tuck me into bed. You realize I'm going straight to my mother with this, correct?"

My loyalty was to no one but Judith and myself at this point. And it didn't escape me that I'd just put Jude's name before my own.

James rubbed his face. "She can't hurt me more than the hidden truth did."

Tou-fucking-ché.

I jerked my chin toward him. "You hired Dan. Tell me everything about how this came to be."

James didn't spare one detail.

He said he'd had a feeling Mathias was beginning to shit on our quality in a bid to damage the network a second before he disappeared off the radar. He needed to tend to his health, and he seemed to know he didn't have much longer on the president throne. Hoping to counteract this, James had had the same feeling I did—that Dan was motivated by money and could be a good free agent. James also confessed that with Phoenix back in town and my engagement crumbling, he wanted to make sure I was protected against Mathias.

"Precisely," I said. "But all the shit Dan discovered still doesn't cover my ass against Mathias. You gave me nothing but hearsay."

James's eyes darkened, and he suddenly looked much older than his days. "We can let others do the job for us. Just send it to the different networks," he suggested. "Let the problem fix itself. He'll have to step down."

I appreciated it, him trying to help me out. But there was no need.

I shook my head. "LBC would take an even greater hit if we do that."

"But we can't just let Mathias get away with it." Jude squeezed my hand. A sweet gesture from my greatest sin.

I turned toward her, a smirk maneuvering its way across my face. "We won't."

Célian

Then I became homeless.

I'd terminated my lease effective Sunday, the day I was supposed to fly out to Los Angeles. Only it was technically Monday morning now, and I was nowhere near the west coast. That meant I had to spend the night somewhere, and fortunately that place was Judith's Brooklyn apartment.

To my cock's disappointment, I slept on the couch. But it was still better than sleeping in a million-star hotel or at the Laurent Towers, which I couldn't even look at after I'd learned what I had about Mathias not being my father.

I wasn't the one who'd cheated on him.

Yet I was the one who'd taken most of his wrath.

In the morning, Judith made her father a shake from what looked like sewer water, puke, and misery, and slid a bowl of cereal my way. It wasn't even a brand. It was poured right out of a six-pound industrial box with a Costco logo.

"Cavities and diabetes. Breakfast of champions," I muttered into the bowl as I took a spoonful.

"My apologies. Our room service doesn't work on Mondays." Jude took a seat next to her dad and patted his veiny hand.

I fucking loved this girl. What she lacked in funds she made up for with love.

"That's fine." I waved her off. "I can be in charge of breakfast when we move in together."

Utensils clattered on plates, and Rob's eyes ping-ponged between us. There was a lot of amusement in them.

Jude studied me, trying to gauge whether I was kidding or not.

I wasn't.

"I'm not a breakfast person," she said. "And yes, I know it's the most important meal of the day."

My eyes slid down her midriff and stopped where the table covered her. I smiled. "No, it isn't."

"You're awful." She hid her smile behind her coffee mug.

"And you're going to let me pick your Chucks today," I retorted.

Robert laughed. "Can you hear it?"

"Hear what?" Her cheeks were doing this hamster thing, where she stifled a laugh and looked too cute doing so.

It was sickening, really, how I felt about her. I would find the word *embarrassing* fitting if I didn't own up to that shit.

"Your chests humming. You're happy, kids." Rob took a sip of his shake, grimacing. "The happiest you've ever been."

A little while later we took the train to work, both staring at her dove white Chucks. My pick. I wanted a clean slate. A fresh start.

"You know, you can still take the job in Los Angeles." She flipped Kipling absentmindedly, staring at it as she spoke. "LBC is falling apart, and I don't expect these revelations to change your commitment to your new job."

"My only commitment is to the company I need to inherit, and to the only girl who's capable of calling me out on my bullshit. *Not* in that order."

She looked up. "And who would that be?"

I twisted the collar of her shirt into a ball and jerked her to me in a kiss, not giving a fuck that everybody was watching. Or that we were standing up, clasped between dozens of sweaty, exasperated people starting their Monday. Not caring about anything but her. Our lips touched, and my cock was a second away from shouting *Hallelujah*. Her mouth was soft and warm and *mine*, and her body melted against my own in a way that could only mean one thing.

It was back on. And this time, I wasn't going to let go.

"Célian?" Blu, AKA my so-called replacement as news director, scratched his curly, dandruff-ridden hair.

He was standing in my office, shuffling full boxes from side to side. I breezed right in, carrying my Starbucks and throwing two pieces of mint gum into my mouth. With all due respect—and let's admit it, I didn't have a whole lot of it for him, the guy was a former associate producer at a cable news channel in Nebraska—I didn't owe him more than a brief explanation.

"Sharp on a Monday morning. I like that, Blu. Now get the fuck out of my office." I dumped my leather briefcase under my desk and powered up my laptop.

Brianna came running from the hallway, panting out my name. "Sir! Célian! Sir! What are you doing here?"

Poor thing thought she'd gotten rid of me. I *tsked*. I decided to go easy on her, since I was going to have to be a little more tolerable for Jude's sake—especially after my so-called dumping of her so publicly.

"Brianna. Good morning. Feel free to drop my items at the usual dry cleaners'. You can use the wait time to chill." I hated that word, but it needed to be said. I also still hated doing my own dry cleaning, and I really did think Brianna could use a little down time. "But you can no longer drink on shift, unless you want your ass thrown into rehab."

"Rehab?" she wheezed. I motioned with my hand, drinking from an invisible small bottle of liquor. She nodded and bowed her head. "Yes, sir."

Blu and I were left alone in the room again. I crossed my ankles atop the desk, leaning back. "Well, Blu, there's good news and bad news. Which would you like me to break first?"

The middle-aged, beer-bellied man in front of me looked down at his shoes, his chest quivering with an uneven breath. "Bad news."

"The bad news is you will not be taking my position—not in the next few months, anyway—and the good news is that you still get a job, if you want it. And you know what the great news is?"

He looked up, and hell, the smile on his face told me he was on board. That finally, things were falling into place for me.

"What?" he asked.

"The news I am going to make in this newsroom today."

I'd expected Mathias to blaze onto the floor and make a spectacle out of the situation. The fact that he remained silent suggested he was strategizing about how to tackle the bane of his existence, AKA yours truly. I gave him his time because I actually had work to do.

The LA people were crushed to hear I wasn't joining them, but I invited them to send their staff to New York and promised to train their new employees. Judith ran from place to place around the newsroom, her cheeks flushed. Kate, Jessica, and Elijah seemed glad I hadn't left, and Brianna smiled guiltily and waved her hand every time I shifted my eyes to make sure she wasn't reaching for her top drawer to take a mini bottle out.

Five hours into our workday, while I was knee-deep in something in the newsroom, I got a phone call from the sixtieth floor.

"It's your father." Brianna came as close as she could, holding the corded phone in her hand.

No, it is not, and thank fuck for that.

He hadn't even called my cell. Instead he was making a whole fucking show about it, like I knew he would.

"He wants to speak to you," she said.

"He knows where to find me."

"He's asking if you can come up to his office."

"I can't. But he can come down. Or not. Giving a shit is not on my agenda today."

"He said he'll call security." Brianna's face was so red, for a moment I worried she might explode.

"Tell him that's a very good idea. I've been thinking about getting rid of his ass for a long time now." The room fell quiet, everybody staring at me. I nodded my chin to the phone.

"Tell him that, Brianna. You're just following my orders. Word for word, please."

She repeated my message to my father, wincing the entire time.

Jude appeared at my side, squeezing my biceps and looking up at me with a smile. I pulled her into a hug and kissed her forehead. I had a lot of damage control to do when it came to the way people perceived us as a couple in this place.

When Brianna ended the call, there was a pause, after which the entire newsroom erupted with a lengthy standing ovation. She laughed. I smirked.

When I turned around to walk back to my office, Mathias was standing at the door, waiting for me. Next to him stood my mother, fresh off of her private plane, judging by her casual clothes.

Her eyes were horrified.

I knew mine were dead.

Showtime.

"Can I offer you anything? Bourbon? Whiskey? Water? Perhaps a lie-detector?" I motioned to the mini bar in my office, my smile casual and charming—the way they'd taught me at the Swiss summer school my parents had dumped me in every year.

My mother seated herself on the couch in front of my desk, staring at her hands in her lap, and Mathias paced, pulling at his ear in a nervous tick. I was the only person in the room whose heart didn't seem to be beating a mile a minute, and that's because I knew something they didn't.

"I'm so mad at James for telling you," my mother muttered. "I was only trying to protect you, Célian. Think about the way it would have been perceived in our circle. In *any* circle, really. You'd have been a bastard. Your blood is blue. You are a Laurent."

"My blood is red, and being a bastard is better than being *his* son." I walked over to the front of my desk and leaned against it.

"Listen, Célian," Mathias raised a hand.

"Not even a word, Mathias," I warned, arching a brow. "Not. Even. One."

"I don't know what you think you have on me—"

"Oh, I think you do. That's why you're shitting your pants as we speak."

"You can't use it in court. Dan was not supposed to record those private conversations," Mathias stressed, his left eye ticking.

He had a point. After I'd left James's apartment last night, he'd emailed Iris and Mathias a file with the recording, along with a brief note about how he'd come clean to me.

Ignoring his words, I threw Mathias a pointed look. "You will drop the ads, terminate the dodgy contracts, and hire back every single person you have fired from my team by the end of the day. And if any of them are unavailable, you will find me a top-notch replacement. If I were you, I'd start working right now. Work is a foreign concept, so it will take you time to get the gist of it."

Mathias laughed. "What makes you think I will do *anything* for you? Nothing has changed, other than the fact that you now know why I couldn't stand your face from day one. You weren't mine. Your mother messed up. The only good things about my marriage to her were LBC and Camille. And you took them from me, too."

My mother darted up from the couch, walked over to him, and slapped his face, hard.

I watched them, emotionless. What a fucking mess. Surely I could dump some of the responsibility for me being a heartless prick on the fact that these two clowns had raised me.

Mathias stared at her, dumbfounded, and rubbed his red cheek. He narrowed his eyes. He was about to raise his hand to her, but thought better of it once I stepped between them and shook my head.

"I will fuck up your face so hard, you will have six new holes to sneeze from," I said dryly.

He took a step back, clearing his throat and fixing his gaze back on her. "You always loved him more than Camille."

"You always treated him like he was garbage," she countered. "And what happened to Camille was your fault, not his. You lied to me because you wanted to isolate him from his family."

"And you were the ignorant little thing who was too busy chasing fitness trainers to go to your son and ask him yourself." Mathias smirked, cocking his head with a devilish glint in his eyes.

He was right, and she knew it. I had visited my mother many times after what happened to Camille, but we'd never shared an actual meal, let alone a conversation. I'd tried, and every Sunday night, as I'd made my way back from JFK to my apartment, I'd wondered why I'd done that to myself in the first place.

"Now he's buried with the Brooklyn girl, and he has to wait until I drop dead before he takes over." Mathias waved a hand in my direction.

"Thanks for bringing her here, by the way," I interjected, clucking my tongue in approval. "She was the answer, and the solution."

"Huh?" He spun on his heel, staring me down.

I took sick pleasure in slowly pouring myself a glass of something I was never going to drink, whistling and thinking about white Chucks—of all fucking things in the world—and how damn good they were going to look with a white wedding gown, or better yet, without anything else at-fucking-all.

"Everything turned out for the best," I explained. "I met Judith, and we've found something you two miserable assholes will never have."

I swirled the liquid in my glass, looking up and saluting my parents. My mother looked on the verge of fainting, and despite everything, I still had sympathy for her.

"And I get to keep LBC," I added.

"How so?" Mathias parked his hands on his waist, scowling.

A vein in his neck began to pump visibly. I traced my finger over the rim of the glass, staring at it intently as I answered him. I was worried I was going to get a hard-on simply from seeing him crumble if I looked up.

"Life works in mysterious ways. When Lily came here a couple months ago and told me Madelyn had died, I was crushed. I rushed to the Davises' house and spent time with them. You probably weren't aware, but I had a very close relationship with Madelyn. I craved human contact, something I didn't have in spades at home." I rubbed my jaw. "So imagine my surprise when they called me a few weeks after her passing to confirm that she had left her granddaughters with millions and millions of dollars and the estate, and little ole me with her ten percent of LBC."

I didn't tell them about the letter Madelyn had also left me. It was more of a note, really. But it brought my situation with Judith into a sharp relief.

With business out of the way, it's time to listen to your heart.

Don't lock my granddaughter in a loveless marriage.

Don't lock my favorite boy inside one, either. It's a miserable place to be. I've been there with Lily's grandfather, and I never want my loved ones to pay this place a visit.

Make me proud.

Love,

Madelyn

I watched in my periphery as their eyes widened and reality set in.

My mother was guilt-stricken and on my side with fifty-five percent of the shares of LBC. I had ten additional ones. I could now throw any decision Mathias had made, easily.

"No," Mathias said, stumbling backward and collapsing onto the sofa.

"Yup," I confirmed, popping the "p" for good measure. "You've gotten everything you ever wanted by walking over people and making a fucking mess, Mathias, while I managed to save my company by forming a genuine relationship with an elderly, somewhat lonely woman who just needed someone to be there for her. Karma is a bitch, and I do believe she just justified her reputation by shoving a ten-foot pole up your ass."

My mother galloped in my direction, throwing her arms around my neck. I let her. Not because I wasn't mad at her. Not because I wasn't livid, and not because I thought her behavior was remotely acceptable.

No. I let her because if my little Chucks could forgive me for being an inglorious bastard, maybe I could forgive Maman for lying to me in order to protect me, even though it was the truth that ended up setting me free.

Maybe I could break the cycle of hate.

Maybe I wouldn't have any more misunderstandings that resulted in the unnecessary deaths of people I loved and cared about.

Maybe I could live. With Judith by my side.

With good music and bad exes.

And with so much sex, she couldn't fucking see straight.

Making headlines dirty between the sheets.

Jude

"I need you to turn my maybe into a definitely." Célian crawled into my bed at the end of that grueling Monday in the office.

I didn't kick him out, even though a small, vindictive part of me wanted to. Life was too short to deprive yourself of spending time with those you love, something I'd learned the hard way.

His body seemed to mold into my small mattress. Somehow, he fit. If there was one thing I'd realized this year, it's that sometimes we belong in the last place we thought we'd ever be.

"How can I do that?" I put my thriller in my lap and let his arm loop around my waist, dragging me into the crook of his shoulder. His lips fluttered along my neck.

"Stay at LBC, no matter how this shit turns out. I can't make it without you."

"Make what?" I laughed. "News?"

He sounded drunk, but he looked sober, almost grim. My arms wrapped around him involuntarily. We sank into the hug and didn't come up for air for long minutes.

"Sense," he said after a while—a minute or three, or maybe more. "Very little makes sense when Chucks is not around. This is the part where I should say something romantic and profound—that you're my beginning, middle, and end. But I don't even know what that shit means. All I know is the very idea of moving to the other side of the country was enough to make me want to kidnap your ass, and not in the sweet, joking way. You're brave, sexy, and beautiful, and there's not one woman on this earth who can push my buttons like you."

"Please say you're offering me the remote to make this super corny." I bit down on my smile.

He rolled his eyes, thrusting his groin into my stomach. "Only if you agree on flipping channels. So, what do you say we make it official?"

"This sounds a lot like a proposal," I snort-laughed.

"It is."

"Then no," I answered seriously.

"No?" He blinked, as if I clearly didn't understand the meaning of the word.

"Jesus, of course not. I want you on one knee, humbled and ringed."

Jesus: "First time you're calling me for the good stuff, and you're going to refuse his proposal?"

He rolled out of the bed, walked over to his duffel bag, and threw something into my hands. A new iPod box. I laughed, opening it. But instead of finding an iPod, I found a ring—a multicolored gemstone ring with yellow and blue, pink and silver, red and purple. It looked like a crown, and nothing like an engagement ring.

Célian went down on one knee beside the bed, bowing his head. "Make me a happy bastard, Judith. You're the only one who can."

Not a question, but an order.

And just like that, for the first time since we'd met, it wasn't difficult to be obedient.

Célian

Six months later...

"You look delicious."

Jude and I just got married in the art room of the Laurent Towers Hotel, in a ceremony that took us approximately four days to arrange.

After the private proposal in Jude's bedroom, I went down on one knee in front of everyone in the newsroom—on the day Mathias stepped down from his position as the president of LBC—and gave her the real ring, the one that cost enough to buy two apartments like the one she'd lived in.

That was twenty-four hours after the showdown with my parents in my office. The reason we didn't bother planning a wedding until this week was because we didn't care.

We are together.

Out in the open.

The world can fuck itself and jizz all over my new suit. I don't give a damn.

"You don't look too bad yourself," Judith counters.

My bride has on my favorite white Chucks under her affordable, fuck-knows-where-she-got-it gown.

For the past two hours, the DJ has played The Smiths and The Strokes and The Shins, and almost nobody has danced, other than Grayson, Ava, Phoenix, Kate and Delilah, Elijah, Jessica, Brianna, and us.

When Phoenix said he was happy for me earlier today, I actually believed him. All his facial features are still untouched and untarnished, so that tells you all you need to know about our relationship these days.

And earlier this week when Elijah, Phoenix, and James (yeah, no way in hell I'm going to call him the D word, unless I'm referring to the thing inside my pants) insisted I have a bachelor party, I almost didn't scowl the entire way through it.

Judith said she was proud of me for making an effort and being a good sport. I told her I needed to work on my cardio tonight, so she'd better fucking be a team player.

"You think I don't look bad?" I cock an eyebrow at her.

"Definitely handsome. But you can look even better."

I angled my head to the side, knowing where this is going. "Do tell."

She nods. "Naked. With your head between my thighs."

We didn't sign a pre-nup. My mother and Mathias did, and look how they ended up. There's something profoundly telling about committing to someone, but covering your ass in case shit fails. Jude Humphry is the only person I want to see every morning and kiss goodnight before I go to sleep, and admitting defeat when it comes to our marriage before it starts is not in the cards for me.

The guest of honor, our Lab pup, Charles "Chuck" Humphry-Laurent, is running between everyone's feet, barking and pulling at dresses.

The Warrior watched us earlier as we exchanged vows, and now we're on to cutting the cake. Our wedding cake is a giant red notebook, like Kipling, adorned with the words *Congratulations to Mr. Timberlake and Ms. Spears.*

Grayson's idea, naturally.

I feed my bride a slice of cake the size of her entire face, and she giggles into the frosting. I take the opportunity to lean down and hiss, "Deep throat it, baby," so only she can hear, and her face turns scarlet, even under the layers of professional makeup.

My mother sneaks up behind us and hugs us into a three-way embrace. Hardly the right time, seeing as I'm sporting some serious wood behind this giant Sour Patch Kids-flavored cake, but what-fucking-ever.

"Thank you for inviting me," Maman gushes. Her ice water eyes glitter in different shades of blue.

Before we know it, Rob sheepishly joins us in front of the cake, rubbing his daughter's arm, his smile so dazzlingly happy he looks like a dream. Mrs. Hawthorne stands behind him, looking down and worrying her lip.

Jude turns around and motions for her to get closer. "Anne, get your butt over here and join the hug."

I want to marry Chucks all over again for that huge heart of hers. Lonely, my ass. She lets everyone in.

"Of course we invited you, Maman," I finally reply. "You are family." And I guess, when it boils down to what matters, she is.

After the revelation that James Townley is my father came out, Maman surprised me by announcing that she was staying in New York for the unforeseeable future to try to save what was left of her family. Namely, her son. She cut ties with her regular booty call in Florida and focused on reconstructing the board of LBC.

We made some of the investors who were eager to kiss Mathias's butt step down and give up their shares by threatening to come out with all the bullshit they'd done along the way, and I finally got my staff back. These days, you can find ads for health care programs and gadgets on LBC. Not a condom or casino in sight.

For the past six months, Jude and I have been doing the whole family dinner thing with Maman, Robert, Mrs. Hawthorne, James Townley and his plastic wife, Phoenix, and Ava—who, by the way, has started dating Phoenix—and Grayson. We take turns, a la *Come Dine with Me*. So far we agree that none of us knows how to cook, and when it comes to smack-talking about people's culinary abilities, I take the cake. And eat it.

Saying it's weird to be a part of a family would be the understatement of the century, but we're trying to make it work.

Especially now, when Robert is doing so well. His tumor is barely a few centimeters long, and doctors are predicting a full recovery. He recently moved in with Mrs. Hawthorne upstairs, so Jude and I took over his apartment. We're refurbishing it, one meltdown at a time.

Next month, we're going to Syria for a few weeks. Jude wants to help cover what's happening there. And I want to be with Jude.

If you'd told me a year ago that I'd live in Brooklyn, I would have laughed.

But if you'd told me a year ago I'd be desperately in love to a point of madness, I would've admitted you to the nearest mental health facility and thrown the key in the ocean.

Yet both of those things have happened, and strangely enough, they didn't ruin my life. They saved it.

James appears behind me and claps a hand over my shoulder, whispering into my ear, "Proud of you, son. Junior is one hell of a catch."

I smirk, my eyes still focused on my bride, who is wearing the most ridiculous wedding gown. The hem of the dress is painted pale yellow, which makes it look like it was dipped in Chuck's piss. Jude says it reminds her of my Post-it notes—the ones I keep on writing to her now so she'll never forget how I feel about her, even when I suck at saying the words out loud.

"Call me your son one more time..." I hiss at James, as I always do. "And I'll move you to the marketing department and have you cold-call small businesses to convince them to place plumbing ads on LBC."

He laughs. "Call us from the honeymoon."

"Only if you promise not to pick up," I banter. He squeezes my shoulder.

Why does the gesture feel more real than any moment I ever shared with Mathias?

I look across the buzzing room, scanning for something to dampen the moment. I keep expecting to see him, even though he wasn't invited. But Mathias hasn't been in the States for over four months, if the rumors are true. I never bother checking. Giving a fuck and worrying about people who are malicious robs you of your power and purpose—otherwise they wouldn't want to harm you.

Coast is clear.

I pick up my bride and carry her to the elevator, honeymoon style, essentially bailing on everyone else. Her arms are looped around my neck and she purrs as she says, "I heard there are CCTV cameras everywhere in this place, so don't do anything stupid."

I lift my hand and give one camera the middle finger, still holding her, then kiss her so deeply and darkly she doesn't come up for air until the next morning.

In the South of France.

In my bed.

"I believe you just brought sexy back, Mr. Timberlake."

One Year Later…

Jude

"Pink Chucks, huh?" Célian smirks as he coils his arm in mine and we stride toward the elevators. He is on the sixtieth floor—the new president of LBC—and I'm on the sixth, an associate producer next to

Blu. Kate is the director of news now, a role she earned the hard way and fully deserves.

Every evening, my husband picks me up from the newsroom, seals my grinning mouth with a hot kiss for everyone to see, and whisks me to the elevators, where we share all our thoughts and secrets, because since day one, the elevator is where everything happens between us.

Why break the habit now?

The doors slide open, and we get in. As soon as they slide shut, I wiggle my toes inside my Chucks.

"Let's make a Le Coq Tail stop before we go home," Célian suggests, already advancing toward me across the tiny space.

"Sure, I could go for a roast beef sandwich," I say as he corners me against the wall and hoists me up by my ass, wrapping my legs over his waist.

"And a drink to go with your long day." He bites down on my lower lip and tugs it inside his mouth.

I groan into our kiss, grinding against him shamelessly. I've been needy lately. "I'll stick to the food."

"Good idea. I like you sober when I fuck you."

"And when I'm pregnant," I add.

"And when you're..." He continues the sentence, dipping his hand between my legs and shoving my panties to the side under my skirt.

He stops and frowns. "Come again?"

"Pink Chucks." I bite down on a smile, my eyes traveling to my stomach.

His do the same. They flare a little, and then he squeezes my ass, seemingly for affirmation that he's still breathing.

Good. We only talked about kids one time, just days after he proposed to me.

"*I don't think I'm much of a father figure, but if you want kids, we'll have kids,*" he'd told me. "*Hell, if you want rabies, we'll catch it together. Make a day of it.*"

I wanted to wait a bit longer before we became parents, and took my pill every day. But then I made a basic mistake this past winter and went on antibiotics to treat my sinus infection without using further protection. I'd been so busy with work and Célian and Dad, I didn't even realize I'd missed three periods.

When I finally bought the test—Ava made sure to hit me in the head with it before we opened it in the restroom of the fifth floor—it came back positive. I went to the OB-GYN the same day. That day was yesterday.

My husband is looking at me now, with a look I've never seen on his face. A look of redemption, and awe, and hope. The fact that I put it there makes me want to break into a dance, sing at the top of my lungs—even though nobody in this zip code deserves such punishment.

"I'm having a daughter?" He blinks.

"Technically, I'm having one. But I can settle for we. How would you feel about naming her Camille?"

He throws his head back and laughs, and it's the most beautiful thing I've ever seen. His blues are twinkling like stars in the dark, and he lowers me down, wraps his arms around me, and chuckles into my ear, sending hot, sweet air into it and making me shiver in pleasure.

I can get used to this.

I think I just did.

"I love you, Judith Penelope Humphry wallet-thief, Smiths fan."

"I love you too, Célian James Laurent one-night-stander, cold-hearted bastard."

In case you were wondering, we've already crossed off every item on the bucket list I'd made with Milton.

Visit Africa.

Get assigned to the Middle East.

Watch the sunset in Key West.

Eat one perfect macaron in Paris.

My heart is not lonely.

It's full and happy and whole.

Most of all, it is Célian's.

If you loved Dirty Headlines and would like to know when my next book comes out, sign up for my newsletter.
eepurl.com/dgo6x5

SIGN UP NOW

Newsletter: eepurl.com/dgo6x5

Official author page: www.facebook.com/authorljshen

Website: www.authorljshen.com

Reading group: goo.gl/QZJ0NC

Instagram: www.instagram.com/authorljshen

BookBub: www.bookbub.com/authors/l-j-shen

Goodreads: goo.gl/zQtBb8

Amazon: goo.gl/Y2iqY5

Book and Main: bookandmainbites.com/ljshen

Books by L. J. Shen

Tyed

Sparrow

Blood to Dust

Defy

Vicious

Ruckus

Scandalous

Midnight Blue

The End Zone

Bane

Coming Soon

Pretty Reckless (All Saints High)

First and foremost, I'd like to thank my readers for following me on this journey, as I continue to evolve as a writer and an artist. It means the world to me that you trust my words. I have so many crazy, exciting, new ideas, and I cannot wait for you to meet all the characters and worlds that I am building.

Huge thanks to my beta readers: Amy Halter, Lana Kart, Charleigh Rose, Helena Hunting, Melissa Panio-Petersen and Yamina Kirky. Each and every one of you brought something fresh and fundamental to this story. Special thanks to the person who has read this book approximately five-hundred times, Tijuana Turner. You can't ever, ever leave me. Just saying.

To my editors, Angela Marshall Smith, Jessica Royer Ocken and Tamara Mataya. Thank you so much for helping me get this book to where I wanted it to be. You have an amazing eye for detail, you challenge me with every turn, and make me a more skilled writer.

To my designer, Letitia Hasser at RBA Designs, and my formatter, Stacey Blake of Champagne Formatting. Thank you for making my product pretty from the inside and out.

To my superstar agent, who is so much more than an agent, Kimberly Brower, Thank you so much for your incredible input and all the hard work.

And, of course, Jennifer, Brooke and Sarah from Social Butterfly for the amazing work and devotion.

To my street team, I love you so, so much. You work so hard day in and day out: Lin Tahel Cohen, Sher Mason, Kristina Lindsey, Brittainy Danielle Christina, Summer Connell, Sarah Grim Sentz, Nina Delfs, Amanda Soderlund, Luciana Grisola, Vanessa Serrano, Leeann Van Rensburg, Becca Zsurkan, Sophie Broughton, Jacquie Czech Martin, Betty Lankovits, Tanaka Kangara, Yamina Kirky, Hayfaah Sumtally, Avivit Egev, Aurora Hale, Paige Jennifer, Erica Panfile, Ariadna Basulto, Vickie Leaf, Julia Lis, Sheena Taylor, Tricia Daniels, Lisa Morgan, Vanessa Villegas, and Samantha Blundell.

To the Sassy Sparrows—love your faces! Thank you so much for making my days brighter.

Finally, to my husband, son, my extended family and friends. Thank you so much for putting up with my weird hours and moods ever since I started this whole writing gig. You are, and always will be, the real MVP's.

Much love,

L.J. Shen

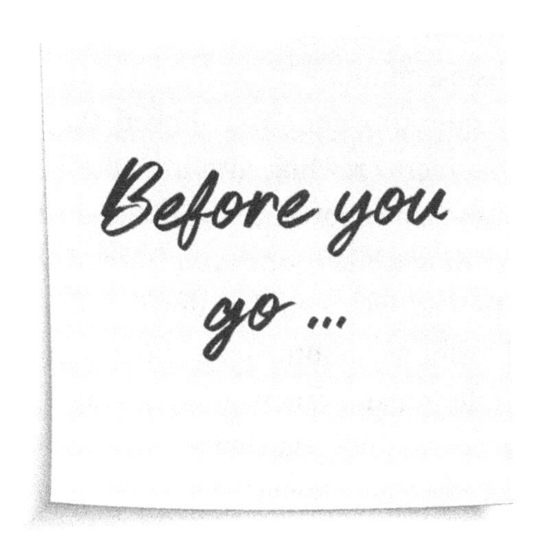

PROLOGUE

Troy

Trinity Chapel
South Boston, Massachusetts

Silence. The most loaded sound in human history.

The only sound audible was the *click, click* of my Derby shoes against the mosaic floor. I closed my eyes, playing the game I relished as a kid one last time. I knew the way to the confession booth by heart. Been a parishioner in this church since the day I was born. I was christened here. Attended Sunday Mass here every week. Had my first sloppy kiss in the bathroom, right fucking here. I would probably have my impending funeral here, though with the legacy of men in my family, it wouldn't be an open-casket event.

Three, four, five steps past the holy water font, I took a sharp right turn, counting.

Six, seven, eight, nine. My eyes fluttered open. *Still got it.*

It was there, the wooden box where all of my secrets were once buried. The confession booth.

I opened the squeaking door and blinked, the smell of mold and the sour sweat of sinners crawling into my nose. I hadn't set foot in reconciliation in two years. Not since my father died. But I guess confessions were like riding a bike—once you learned, you never forgot.

Though this time, things would go down differently.

It was an old-fashioned booth, in an old-fashioned church, no living-room bullshit design and fancy, modern crap. Classic dark wood covered every corner, an old grid divided the priest and the confessors, and a crucifix hung over the grille.

I settled in my seat on the wooden bench, my ass hitting the rough pew with a bang. At 6'4", I looked like a giant trying to fit into a Barbie dreamhouse. Memories of sitting here as a boy, my legs dangling mid-air as I told Father McGregor about my small, meaningless sins raced through my mind, tangling into a messy ball of nostalgia. The thought of how big my sins were turning out to be would make McGregor sick to his stomach. But my rage toward him was stronger than my morals.

I folded my suit coat on the bench beside me. *Sorry, old man. Today you'll meet the maker you've been preaching about all these years.*

I heard him sliding his side of the screen open with a screech, clearing his throat. I did the sign of the cross, reciting, "In the name of the Father, and the Son, and the Holy Spirit."

The creak of his chair, when his body stiffened at the sound of my voice, filled the air. He recognized me. *Good.* I relished the thought of his death, and I guess that'd make me, in your book, a psychopath.

But it was true.

I was fucking thrilled. I was a monster, out for blood. I was vengeance and hate, fury and wrath.

"Son..." His voice trembled, but he stuck to the usual script. "How long has it been since your last confession?"

"Cut the bullshit. You know." I smiled, staring at nothing in particular. Everything in the place was so goddamn wooden. Not that I expected an interior designer's touch, but this shit was ridiculous. It looked like the inside of a coffin. Certainly felt like one.

"Can we move on?" I cracked my neck and rolled up my sleeves. "Time is money."

"It's also a healer."

I clenched my jaw, balling and releasing my fists.

"Nice try." I paused, checking my Rolex. His time was running out. Mine, too.

Tick tock, tick tock.

"Bless me, Father, for I have sinned. Two years ago, I killed a man. His name was Billy Crupti. He shot a bullet straight into my father's forehead and blew out his brains, causing my family pain and devastation. I killed him with my bare hands."

I let the weight of my confession sink in and continued. "I cut his arms and legs, just enough so he wouldn't bleed to death, tied him up and had him watching as a pack of fighting dogs fought over his parts." My voice was eerily calm. "When everything was done and dealt with, I tied a weight to his waist and threw him from a commercial pier on the bay, still twitching, to die a slow, painful suffocating death. Now tell me, Father, how many Hail Marys for a murder?"

I knew he wasn't the type to bring a cell phone into the booth. McGregor was too old and cocky for modern technology. Even though he went rogue on my father, he never imagined he'd be caught. Least of all by me.

But now, as I confessed my sin, he knew I was going to wait at the other end of the booth and claim his life, too. He had no way out.

He was mostly silent, calculating his next move. I heard him swallow hard, his fingernail scraping at the wooden chair he sat on.

I crossed one leg over the other and cupped one of my knees, amused. "Now your turn. How 'bout we hear about them sins, Father?"

He released a breath he'd been holding in a sharp sigh. "That's not how confessions work."

"Don't I fucking know it," I snorted. "This one's a little different, though. So…" I brushed the screen dividing us with my gloves and watched as he flinched on the other side. "I'm all ears."

I heard something drop from his hand and the creak of his chair when he kneeled down to pick it up.

"I'm a man of God," he tried to reason with me.

I seethed with resentment. He was also a man who spilled secrets from the confessional.

"Not a soul on earth knew about the whereabouts of my father every Tuesday at ten p.m. Not a soul other than him and his mistress. And *you,*" I drawled. "Billy 'Baby Face' Crupti tracked down my father, unprotected and unarmed, because of *you*."

He opened his mouth, intending to argue, but clapped it shut, thinking the better of it at the last minute. Somewhere in the distance a dog was barking and a woman was yelling at her husband in their backyard. Classic Southie reminders of the people I used to know before I moved to a skyscraper and reinvented myself.

McGregor gulped, stalling. "Troy, my son…"

I stood up, pushing my sleeves farther up my arms. "Enough. Out you go."

He didn't move for a few seconds, which prompted me to take out my knife and slice the grid open with a ripping sound. I shoved my hand into his booth, grabbing him by his white collar and pulling his head through the hole so I could take a good look at him. His gray hair stood out in all directions, damp with sweat. The horror in his eyes lightened my mood. His narrow, thin mouth hung open like a hooked fish.

"Please, please. Troy. Please. I beg you, son. Do not repeat the sins of your father," he chanted, crying out in pain as I jerked him closer to my face.

"Open. The fucking. Booth." I extended every word like it was a sentence of its own.

I heard a sleek *click* as he fumbled for the door. I released his hair out of my fist, and we both stepped out.

McGregor stood before me, several inches shorter. A chubby,

sweaty, corrupted man pretending to be God's messenger. A tasteless joke.

"You're really going to kill your priest," he pointed out sadly.

I shrugged. I wasn't a hitman. I drew a thick red line somewhere near homicide, but this was personal. It was about my father. The man who raised me while my mom was too drunk on Pottery Barn sales and Sunday brunch cocktails. She was so absent from my childhood, not to mention adulthood, that I was practically half orphaned. If nothing else, my father deserved closure.

"You're just like them. I thought you were different. Better," McGregor accused.

I pressed my lips into a thin line. My job had nothing to do with Irish mobsters. I didn't need the Feds crawling up my ass every time someone farted in my direction and certainly didn't take a shine to the framework of gang leaders and soldiers. I was a lone wolf, who hired a few people to help him out when help was needed. I had no buffer between me and my clients, colleagues and enemies. And most importantly, I sailed smoothly under the radar. Didn't need to hide behind a dozen soldiers. When I needed someone gone, I handled them myself.

And Father McGregor had to pay for his sins. He was already supposed to be dead—collateral damage. But he hadn't shown up where he was supposed to when I took out the guy he'd ratted my dad out to. Billy Crupti. The asshole.

So now I had to do this in a fucking church.

"Be quick," he requested.

I nodded grimly.

"You were always his child. Had the Irish mob gene, the ruthlessness in your blood. You had no fear. Still don't." He sighed, extending his hand to me.

I stared at it like it was a ticking bomb, finally shaking it. His palm felt clammy and cold, his handshake weak. I pulled him into my body for an embrace, and clasped the back of his neck with one hand.

"And I'm so sorry," he continued, sniffing into my shoulder, his whole body quivering as he struggled to hold back the tears. "Lapse of judgment on my end. I knew that he'd kill them, both of them. But at the time, thought I'd be doing everyone a favor."

"It was money, wasn't it?" I whispered into his ear as we clasped each other, me pulling a knife from a sheath at my waist. "Billy paid you?"

He nodded, still sobbing, unaware of the knife. Someone had to pay him off, and pay him good to spill the beans about my dad. Someone who wasn't Crupti who couldn't even afford a fucking filter coffee at his local diner.

"Not just for the money, Troy. I wanted Cillian out of this neighborhood, out of Boston. This place had suffered enough under the realm of your father. Our people deserve some peace."

"*Our* people are not your fucking subjects." I dragged the knife along his neck until I found his throbbing carotid artery and slashed deep, immediately shoving his body back into the booth so that the spray of blood wouldn't meet my newly tailored suit. "You should have minded your own business."

He gagged and jerked on the confession floor like a fish out of water, losing buckets of blood. The scent—sour, tinny and thrilling—fogged the air and I knew it would linger in my nose for days to come.

When his spasm died down, I got down on one knee, staring back at his brown irises, still open, still filled with horror and regret. I pulled out his tongue and cut it from his mouth.

This was gang-member code for a snitch. Let the police try and figure out what the fuck Father McGregor did to deserve it and which of the hundred Boston gangs killed him. There were too many of them to count and hell knows they were intertwined with one another more often than not. Gangs took over the streets a decade ago, when my father was dethroned from his seat as the Boss of Boston.

Ironically, in trying to give them peace, Father McGregor had sentenced his parishioners to a life of panic and fear.

The streets were still chaotic—some would say more than ever—with the crime rate picking up at an alarming speed. Keeping an eye on the Irish Mob, I assumed, was far simpler than trying to tame dozens of gangs running the streets.

I knew the police would never get anywhere near me with this murder case.

And I also knew where I'd bury father McGregor's tongue. In his own backyard.

I casually wiped my knife clean on his pants leg and pulled off the leather gloves I was wearing, shoving them in my pocket. I took out a toothpick and put it in my mouth. Then I rolled down my sleeves and retrieved my suit coat. When I got out the door, I glanced around for potential witnesses, just in case.

The neighborhood was deader than the man I had just dealt with. Going for a stroll wasn't really our thing in South Boston, especially not around noon. You either worked hard, took care of the little ones at home or nursed a fucking hangover. The only witness to my visit to the church was a bird, sitting on an ugly power line up above, eyeing me suspiciously from the corner of its eye. It was a bland looking sparrow.

I crossed the road and got into my car, slamming the door behind me. Taking out a Sharpie from the glove compartment, I crossed another name off my list.

1 - Billy Crupti
2 -Father McGregor
3- The asshole who hired Billy?

I sighed as I looked at number three, shoving the crumpled paper back into my pocket.

I'll find out who you are, motherfucker.

I looked out the window. The sparrow didn't move, not even when a gust of wind sent the power line dancing and the bird lost its balance. The irony wasn't lost on me. Fucking sparrow, of all birds.

I fought the urge to throw something at it, revved up the engine and spat the toothpick in my mouth into the ashtray after it was thoroughly chewed.

I thought I saw the stupid bird still following my car with its tiny eyes as I stopped at a red light and looked out my side mirror. Averting my gaze down, I checked for blood traces. There weren't any.

McGregor was dead, but the void in my stomach didn't shrink an inch.

It was alarming, because in order to keep my promise to my dad, I had one more name to tick off my list.

But this was a person I wasn't supposed to kill. This was a person I was supposed to resurrect.

I, of all people, needed to be her savior.

Other people—normal people, I guess—would have never agreed to sacrifice this part of their lives for their father. But other people didn't live under Cillian Brennan's shadow, didn't feel the urge to constantly step up their game to be equal to their late legendary sire. No, I'd follow his wishes. And I'd even make it work.

All I knew when I drove away from my childhood church were two things:

My father had sinned.

But I was to be punished.

CPSIA information can be obtained
at www.ICGtesting.com
Printed in the USA
BVHW091512220520
579925BV00014B/442

9 781732 62470